CANIS THE WARRIOR

Also by James Sinclair

WARRIOR QUEEN

CANIS THE WARRIOR

James Sinclair

St. Martin's Press,
New York

First published in the United States of America in 197

Library of Congress Cataloging in Publication Data

Canis the warrior.

1. Great Britain—History—Roman period, 55 B.C.—
449 A.D.—Fiction. I. Title.
PZ4.S7935Can 1979 [PR6069.T296] 823′.9′14 78-19413
ISBN 0-312-11839-2

To Kate

PLACE NAMES

Aquae Sulis	—	Bath
Calcaria	—	Tadcaster
Calleva Atrebatum	—	Silchester
Cambodunum	—	Slack
Camboritum	—	Cambridge
Camritum	—	Extinct
Camulodunum	—	Colchester
Deva	—	Chester
Durolipons	—	Godmanchester
Durvulavum	—	Extinct
Eburacum	—	York
Lindum	—	Lincoln
Londinium	—	London
Legiolium	—	Castleford
Mancunium	—	Manchester
Mona	—	Anglesey
Parridium	—	Extinct
Venonae	—	High Cross
Venta Icenorum	—	Caister St. Edmunds
Verulamium	—	St. Albans
Viroconium	—	Wroxeter

CANIS THE WARRIOR

AUTHOR'S NOTE

Canis (Kay-nuss) the Briton, also known as the Wolfhead, was general to the confederated Iceni and Trinovante armies of Queen Boadicea during her rebellion against Rome.

After the defeat and death of his Queen, Canis followed his destiny, which was to lead the surviving Iceni and Trinovantes into the mountains of Wales and there to re-establish the house of Boadicea for her daughter, Princess Cea, by founding a new kingdom.

Facts tell little of what befell the Iceni and Trinovantes following their unsuccessful revolt, although it is known that those who survived were constantly harassed by Suetonius Paullinus, Imperial Governor of Roman Britain. Paullinus, not content with defeating Boadicea, was determined to destroy all who had supported her. History has concluded that the Iceni and Trinovantes became extinct. Perhaps they did as far as their identity in East Anglia is concerned, but almost certainly the hardiest of them escaped Paullinus by migrating from the east to the west of Ancient Britain.

This story is about that migration, which took place under the leadership of Canis, whom Cerdwa the forest maid—sometimes called a wood-witch—declared indestructible. During the hazardous journey Canis defeated Romans, cheated Paullinus, confounded Queen Cartimandua of Brigantia and put upon her daughter, Princess Venturia, the certainty that he was mysteriously identifiable with Cyantillus (also known as Camulos), the lusty and philandering Celtic god of war.

The story is also about Princess Cea and Lydia, the Roman woman, who gave up her house and riches to follow Canis.

1

Grey was the dawn and desolate the land. The mists wreathed and eddied like formless wraiths, and although summer's warm kiss had caressed yesterday's moist grass the new day was breaking chill and damp. Through the forests the foxes ran with noses pointing towards the havens of their burrows, and over the wild heathlands the grey wolves moved like glistening, silver ghosts, muzzles close to the ground and red eyes aglow. Their night was over, their torn prey filling their bellies, and they loped homeward silently and contentedly.

In a forest not far from the western boundary of the land of the Iceni, where the mist curled wetly around every tree and deadened the whisper of every leaf, a young boar predatory with hunger forsook the cover of a thicket to lumber on thick short legs into the shrouded half-light of a clearing. There it froze into rigid immobility, snout raised, hackles stiff and little eyes peering. Here the mist spiralled and drifted. Here stood two-legged man.

He was tall, and as immobile at this moment as the boar. The swirling vapours disembodied him. The point of his raised javelin was dulled by the clinging wetness of the bleak dawn, and seen through the mist his eyes were like melting agates of grey. For a suspended second of time, rigid boar and disembodied man communed in fateful recognition. Then the boar rumbled, squealed and burst into movement, head lowered and tusk pointing. The bruising rush of heavy body sundered the fragile mist, but an arm jerked, a hand leapt and the javelin flew. The piercing impact of sharp deadly iron communicated itself in twanging vibration to the slender shaft, the boar plunged, staggered, rolled over and snapped viciously at that which was cruelly foreign in its body. Bravely the animal struggled to its feet, but its eyes turned inward, it coughed, buckled and died.

The tall man came to wrest the javelin free of the quivering body and to speak in softly ironic sympathy.

"I waited a long, uncomfortable time for you, little fat one, and alas for your bright hopes this day, in the end you came in such noisy hunger that your grunts ran ahead of your caution."

And Canis the Briton shouldered the dead boar and began to make his way back to those who were restlessly and anxiously awaiting him.

Death runs like an eternal shadow at the heels of all forest creatures, even on a morning when old wolves move as invisibly as silver ghosts.

*   *   *

Some distance from where he made his kill, in a place of gaunt, grey-barked trees, the rising sun was dispersing the mist and welcome was the pale warmth. It began to take the worst of the chill from Lydia's body. The place was one ill-conceived of nature, without loveliness and without game; but safe enough from Romans, simply because fugitives could not long survive there. Lydia drew her woollen cloak more tightly around herself; for though she was not as cold as she had been, the fear within still brought its own chill. She paced uneasily over thin, spiky grass. Around a cooking pot, men and women squatted patiently, voices low but cheerful, hands quick to tend the fire and ensure it did not smoke. Romans hunting at first light looked for smoke. There were fifteen men and women, Iceni and Trinovantes. All had been brought by devious means to this place, and soon the hairy ones would come to lead them deep into the heart of a trackless forest. There they would join the main force of Princess Cea, only surviving daughter of Queen Boadicea. They would swear her fealty, and go with her and Canis the Briton wherever fortune and circumstance took them. They could not negotiate the mighty forest without the help of its natural denizens, the hairy ones.

There was also a girl child of nine, with golden hair and a shy way of peeping a smile. She was hungry, she sniffed at the cooking pot, then went to Lydia, the Roman woman, who belonged, so it was said, to Canis, although everyone knew Canis was betrothed to Princess Cea. The child looked pinched in her threadbare tunic.

"Brynilla," said Lydia, her green eyes soft, "where is your cloak?"

"I'm not cold," said the child, "only a little hungry. There is not much in the pot for so many of us. I looked into it and saw scarcely anything."

"No matter," said Lydia gently, "Canis will not be long now. He will bring us enough to tide us over until our forest friends come." She hoped he would. Hunger was the persistent companion to all Britons who, in the pillaged and wasted lands of the Iceni and Trinovantes, would not collaborate with Rome. Terror and death, in the guise of the Roman soldiers of Suetonius Paullinus, the Imperial Governor, stalked every encampment and every known way. So men, women and children who still wished to serve the house of Boadicea rather than Caesar's came to Cea and Canis by every desperate means possible. There were always innocent-eyed ones who whispered the way to them. Those who arrived at a rendezvous, such as this one, were invariably thin and peaked with hunger.

But it was not the common hunger that made Lydia fret. It was the fact that Canis had still not returned after slipping away in search of game well before dawn. She did not know how far he had had to go, but the whole area was one in which the Romans were on the prowl from dawn to dusk.

"Perhaps Ebbyd and Twycel will soon come back with food," said the child Brynilla.

"Perhaps they will," said Lydia. With her raven-black hair and vivid beauty, she was a joy in the eyes of all men. But all men to Lydia meant only one man—Canis. There were no

12

others. As to Ebbyd and Twycel, she had her further worries. They too had gone a while ago to look for game. They had come to Lydia. Twycel, a Trinovante warrior, ragged and bony, had shown her the sharpness of his bronze-headed spear in the misty light.

" My spear is as hungry as I am," he said. " There is a little food for the women and the child, but not for the men. So Ebbyd and I will go and find enough for all of us."

" Canis has said no one must move from here," said Lydia, " so you must wait until he returns. He will bring all that we need."

" He has been gone long enough already," said Ebbyd, whose youth as an Iceni had been spent joyously under the banner of Boadicea. He now looked old before his time.

" You must wait," insisted Lydia, " there is no game here. That is why this place is safer than others. We will eat when Canis returns, never fear."

Twycel regarded her with quiet obstinacy. His face was gaunt, his frame starved. He knew, as did many others, that Lydia Osirus was the Roman woman who had left her house and her wealth to follow Canis and serve his people. Twycel did not trust any Roman, man or woman; but the business of Canis was not his business. He had only come to serve in his own way as a warrior. His hunger gnawed at him, and he knew the other fugitives, especially the women, suffered likewise.

He insisted that he and Ebbyd would go.

" I know what it is to be as hungry as you are," said Lydia, " but Canis will not like it if you go. You are more likely to nose out Romans than game, and you will be courting ill-fortune on two counts. Not only will you have disobeyed Canis, but you are also liable to encounter a Roman patrol. And you will not like the effects of either."

" We must go," said Ebbyd, " for the women and the child are starving."

So they went, despite all Lydia's sharp protests.

Lydia was the daughter of Marcus Osirus, a high-born Roman official of Calleva Atrebatum, who had been slain

13

during the rebellion of Queen Boadicea. Lydia in the beginning hated Canis, the Queen's renowned general, for he had mocked and humiliated her on the day she first met him. She pursued vengeance so obsessively that when Boadicca was defeated and dead she made the captured general her slave. But vengeance became as nothing when she conceived a love far greater than hate, a love that consumed her, tortured her. So she gave him his freedom. He returned to his defeated and oppressed people. And Lydia went with him.

Not since the fierce, singing warriors of Boadicea had spread fire and slaughter over the land had Lydia known such desperate days as those she experienced in company with Canis, Cea, Grud and others so closely associated with the cause of the dead Queen. Countless times they escaped capture by the merest good fortune. Lydia died a hundred times. A fearless but highly-strung woman, she had not become less fearless; she suffered not because of what her countrymen might do to her as a renegade, but because of what they would surely do to Canis. They would nail him to a wooden cross before the ruined temple of Claudius at Camulodunum, for he himself had commanded the host which sacked that city and razed the temple to the ground.

During these months since she had given up her wealth and comfort to help the stricken Iceni, she had been in constant fear for him, though sometimes there was strange exhilaration too. In the darkness of night, they would lie with others in what was no more than a fold in the ground, whilst the Romans rode by so near that she would smell the sweating leather of their equipment and the pungent odour of the horses. Exhilaration born of the taut embrace of fear would rise above the fear.

Once she had loved Rome fiercely. Now she loved her enduring Briton far more. If Paullinus ever took him and crucified him, Lydia felt she would deliver herself up to die with him. Even her gods she had forsaken for Canis, saving only Diana. Great Diana, protector and cherisher of all women, would not deal unforgivingly with one as faithful as Lydia. Only Diana

14

could give Canis wholly to her in the end, though how this might come about she did not know, for Canis was already foresworn to wed Princess Cea. But Diana would resolve the problem. Here Lydia was sometimes worried about how Diana regarded the Briton, who was not averse to mocking every god, even the Great Huntress herself. He had even said that any woman, goddess or not, who had a man torn to pieces for admiring her shape, could hardly be called endearing.

But how she loved him, had wanted him! She had lain in his arms only once, and the longing to do so again was often a pain. But now she was carrying his child—yet had not dared to tell him, for Princess Cea would have to know too. And Princess Cea would surely deal furiously with Canis and demand that she, Lydia, be bundled back to her Roman friends.

To her relief Ebbyd and Twycel returned. They were exhausted and brought with them no more than two snared ground birds, which they had plucked on their way back and which would taste coarse and unsweet for going into the pot so soon after death.

" We saw no Romans," said Twycel, " and no game save for these stringy ground warblers."

" You were foolish," said Lydia abruptly. The men had prevailed on the women and the child to eat what was in the pot, but Lydia had touched nothing herself. She was now consumed by fear. Canis was long overdue. As always, she had wanted to go with him; but he had enjoined her to stay, to give comfort to the women and the child. Lydia had a vitality and a courage which he admired. She tried to close her mind to the unendurable thought that at last he had been taken, but the thought was feverishly persistent. She shivered. At that moment, one of the men abruptly lifted his head. Instinctively his hand closed on the hilt of the old Roman sword he wore. The company of Britons froze. The pale sunlight of this inhospitable place, favoured more by wolves than men, became suddenly cold as they heard the muffled yet distinct sound of horses and armour.

15

"Romans!" Ebbyd was white, Twycel stricken. They had, then, caught more than stringy birds. Even in this lonely area there were ears which listened, and not all of them listened on behalf of Britons. The Romans had their spies, and paid them with food as well as gold. Ebbyd and Twycel sensed they had been heard, seen, betrayed, tracked and found.

The sounds became a clatter. The Britons leapt to their feet. The gaunt woodlands burst into life, there was the glitter of armour, a single shout of command and a patrol of Roman cavalry rode in on the fugitives. A centurion, curbing his mount, watched expressionlessly as his men quickly surrounded and contained the Britons. Ebbyd, anguished beyond life to have been the cause of bringing the enemy, ran in savage fury to seize the bridle of a horse and strike at the rider. Next moment, Ebbyd was swung, kicking with his feet, as the horse flung up its head. Lydia, standing apart with the child Brynilla clinging to her in terror, watched horrified as the Roman trooper smashed in Ebbyd's skull with a violent blow of his sword. Ebbyd dropped lifeless, and the Romans tightened their circle.

An Iceni spear caught the light, the sun danced dully on a rusting sword. All the Britons had weapons of some kind, the women drawing daggers from the girdles of their tunics. The men and women stood, all of them, shoulder to shoulder, in their own circle, facing outwards. They knew what would follow. They would sell themselves dearly, for to be taken alive meant a savage death for the men, and a fate unendurable for the women.

The Romans, on a quiet command from their centurion, steadied their mounts and formed an inescapable barrier. Only Lydia and the child stood outside this. The officer rode up to them. His face was pale and fleshy, his mouth strangely soft like a woman's, but his cold eyes were soulless. He gave Lydia and the girl a brief glance, then spoke clearly to the trapped Britons.

"Lay down your weapons, one by one. Then you will all be taken quietly and without a scratch to Camulodunum, where you may argue such case as you may have for gathering together in this prohibited area and for bearing forbidden arms."

An Iceni woman spat. A Trinovante warrior spoke.

" Aye," he said, " and perhaps we may also argue our case for drawing breath. Take us, Roman, and in the final count measure your own scratches."

The centurion smiled as softly as a woman.

" Who is mother to this brat?" he asked, reaching out a foot to prod the terrified Brynilla. It was Lydia who answered as she pressed the golden head into the comfort of her cloak.

" She has no mother. She has no father. Both were taken a month ago, and both are dead."

The centurion looked down. His pitiless eyes had a marbled protuberance.

" Who are you to speak not with the accent of the barbarians?" he asked.

A thousand years ago, for so far away did her indolent life as a capricious Roman woman seem to her now, Lydia would have told him bitingly that she was sister to Julian Osirus of Calleva Atrebatum, a man esteemed by the Imperial Governor himself. But to declare herself now would be to betray the nearness of Canis, since all Romans in this territory knew that Lydia Osirus had deserted Rome to stand with Canis and his people.

" I am of these people," she said, and did not show him the fear she felt.

" Say you so?" said the centurion thoughtfully. He rubbed his fleshy chin. " Where," he asked her, " is the one we seek?"

" You seek a thousand and a thousand more Britons," said Lydia, " which one is this?"

He smiled again. Lydia felt the child trembling violently against her. The centurion spoke a second time to the encircled fugitives.

" I will give freedom not to one but all," he said, " if any of you will say where I may find a rebel dog called Canis the Wolfhead."

The Iceni woman spat again, this time on the blade of her

long dagger. The officer sighed, his men watched the Britons and the Britons looked inward, for they knew their day was done.

" I say to you again," said the centurion, " advise me for your own good where I may find your leader, who is a dog of all dogs and is called Canis."

The coldness and fear within Lydia froze her. She pressed the child closer. But no one answered the Roman, and her heart breathed again. Tears for the loyalty of the Britons to their leader pricked her lids. Suddenly the centurion leaned from his saddle, and with a quick dexterity that robbed Lydia of the time and ability to frustrate him, he seized Brynilla by her hair and wrenched her free of Lydia's protective embrace. The child screamed. The centurion backed his horse, pulled the child off her feet, and using her hair like a golden rope, he swung her. With incredible strength he pitched her. Lydia, eyes wide with horror, saw the outstretched body fly through the air, crash against the cooking pot and scatter fire, pottery and kindling. The broken child lay still amongst the shards, embers from the fire smoking around the golden hair.

" Now, where is Canis?" The centurion's voice was as soft as his mouth, but as clear as a footfall in a house of the dead.

" He is far beyond your vile hand," cried Lydia, " as you are beyond the mercy of the most forgiving god." She made to run to the senseless child but a hand reached, a hand of brass. It plucked her back, it ripped her cloak and tunic like rotten reeds. She staggered. The hand came again to buffet her so violently that she was knocked to the ground, where she lay stunned and anguished. The sky was above her, as was a soft, pale face. She was aware of eyes like cold, petrified emeralds.

" I will attend more fully to you in a moment," he said. He brought his horse round and rode to the unconscious, shattered child. To the fierce-eyed Britons burning to avenge Brynilla, he said, " For the last time, is there one among you who will lead me to the man called Canis? Failing any answer I will finish this spawn of an Iceni whore—"

The Britons sprang outwards, men and women all, so that

their bunched compactness opened like a bursting plant. A horse screamed as an Iceni woman ran under a darting sword and thrust her dagger into the animal's body. The horse splayed and collapsed, toppling its rider. The woman drove her dagger into his neck. His comrade smote her instantly. She coughed from the deep bite of the sword, and fell dying.

The fugitives fought with savage desperation, gouging horses and men, the melee bloody and without quarter. The Britons died, overwhelmed on all sides, but took six or seven Romans with them, much to the cold-eyed fury of the centurion. Only a young Iceni woman, blood staining her shoulder, managed to break out of the ring. Courageously she snatched up the now moaning girl child and ran sobbing and panting to where the gaunt woodland was thickest, the child clasped to her breast. The centurion caught up with her. He rode her down, broke her under the iron feet of his horse, leaned from his saddle with drawn sword and with it slew the writhing, injured child.

Lydia, sick and dizzy on her knees, her head a cavern of roaring darkness, her eyes horrified and incredulous, saw what she could not believe. She vomited. She was only dimly conscious as they took her, bound her wrists and threw her across a horse. Then the sickness was so unbearable that as they rode away with her she was drawn mind and body into the roaring pit.

*　　*　　*

Canis knew before he reached the place of assembly that the Romans had been there. He had been too often in company with danger and death not to be able to smell one or the other from a distance. It pricked at his senses, the instinctive warning, while he was still some way off. He halted the enduring horse he rode, his body still, his head bent, the carcase of the slain pig cold now in its lashed embrace with his mount. The iron blade of the axe in his belt ran with reflected light, but he was as still as an animal scenting the hunter.

Then he lifted his head and rode on.

One forest dweller was at the place of death, a short and

vastly hairy man, who bore in his grieving arms the body of a cruelly slain young girl.

" All dead, lord," he said to Canis, " even this innocent."

Canis looked down on the bloody and broken body of the child. It was sweet Brynilla. He had known overmuch of bitter and tragic events, and the memories were often bleakly visible in his eyes, as now. He saw the bodies of the men and women. Through grey harshness he spoke quietly.

" Aye," he said, " even innocents. The Romans ever remind us, Agra, of their own slain children."

" Which happened in the heat of bloodiest war and battle," said Agra. " This is not war, lord, but foulest murder."

Canis slipped from his horse. So many dead, so many. All would have served Princess Cea, all were now lost to her. Seventeen men and one child were very many.

" Where is Lydia, the Roman woman?" he asked the hairy one.

" Gone, lord, gone with the dogs of Rome," said Agra, looking up into the hard face of the tall, grey-eyed Briton.

" Gone or taken?"

" Taken. From her they will wring every secret, from her they will discover how many have reached Princess Cea, and where you all dwell. From her they will pull the confession that the Princess has survived. Then Paullinus will burn the forest he cannot penetrate. He will burn it tree by tree until he reaches you."

Canis, the sun fingering the coppery tints of his thick brown hair, held out his arms.

" Give me the child. And go you, Agra, bring me as many of your friends who are near enough and willing enough. I care not if you bring me a full score, or no more than five, as long as you return with them before the scent of Romans has grown cold. There is a child to avenge, and Lydia to deliver."

Agra put the dead child into the arms of Canis and, quick of eye and speedy of leg, vanished into the trees. Canis laid the cold body gently on the sun-warmed ground.

" I will give you not to blind, deaf gods, Brynilla, but to

the Queen, who will receive you with love and will cherish you." He marked out the grave, cut back the turf and shaped a deep hollow. He placed her therein. He put a posy of wild flowers into her still hands, covered her with earth and replaced the turf. " Agra and his comrades will presently see to these others, your brave friends. Dream sweetly, little lonely one, and go in your dreams to Boadicea, for she was your true Queen and loved all her people."

Agra brought his comrades, half a score of shaggy men, and in addition two who would attend to the simple burial of the dead Iceni and Trinovantes. These two stayed, while Agra and the other wild men of the forest went with Canis in a grim, silent pursuit of the Roman cavalry detachment. Canis went to avenge an innocent and to do what he could for Lydia.

* * *

When the redness of the evening sun had died and the last light of day was in purple mourning for all that had gone beyond recall, the Roman centurion, Sulla Petonius, came to tickle his captive with his foot. Lydia lay in his tent, her clothing dirty and torn. Her hands were bound behind her, her left ankle chained to a short stake driven into hard ground. Her black hair lay wild about her head and face, her green eyes stared up at him through the dark curtain of the disordered strands, her expression of hate and defiance betraying nothing of her anguish. She knew that to save herself she must identify herself, but then Paullinus himself would take her, treat her as a renegade and extract from her by the cruellest means all that he could of Canis. Or, in a more sadistic way, this centurion with a soft voice and eyes of cold marble, the blood of a child on his hands, would use her as bait to lure her Briton into an inescapable trap. But in his own hardness, in his dedication to the surviving and suffering people of Boadicea, Canis could not and would not take the bait. She was lost to him. She would never see him again. The best that could happen to her was that Paullinus might send her to Rome, where Nero, because she loved the Briton who had been Boadicea's general, might or might not regard her as a traitor. The worst, she knew, would be if she remained in the hands of this soulless centurion. She closed her eyes to hide her anguish and pain.

Sulla, sword in hand, leaned over her. With the point of the double-edged sword he flicked at her torn robe and disturbed her sundered tunic. Lydia wore not the robe and shift of a Roman woman, but the tunic of an Iceni woman. The fattish face of the Roman creased in his strange smile as he uncovered her firm, curving breast. Her eyes opened, and for a moment her teeth showed in a grimace of disgust and contempt.

"Ah," he said. She would have spat but did not. "Come," he went on, "though you are shabby enough and dusty enough, you speak with the accent of Rome and own a fine Roman shape. And I dare swear that if what you show now is any true guide, then you show even finer under the rest of your poor rags. Will you not put aside this dumbness, which is quite out of character in any woman, and converse in agreeable and informative fashion? I am not here to slice your tongue, but to hear it wag. So come, wag it and tell me of Canis, for you know him, do you not?"

Since the moment they had taken her and bound her, Lydia had not spoken. She did so at last.

"I have seen many evil men," she said in a fierce whisper, "and all have been as pure as new-born babes compared with you."

"Woman," he said, "if that is the sum total of your agreeableness, I will come to like your dumbness better, after all. You have seen nothing I have done that has not been done for Rome."

"If Rome can smile upon the murder of helpless children in her name," said Lydia just as fiercely, "then Rome too is evil and an affront to all her gods."

Deliberately Sulla put the point of his sword to her naked breast. She felt it prick her flesh. A tiny bead of blood welled up. A shudder ran through her. His smile was softer, his eyes more protuberant. Increasing anguish tore at her.

22

"Do you think to provoke me?" he said. "Save your breath. Attend me, for your fate is governed on the one hand by your foolishness, on the other by your good sense. I would advise good sense. Foolishness will bring you to slow death. So, my soft dove, will you not twitter agreeably?"

The sword flickered and set aside more of her sundered clothing. Her flesh gleamed, but despite her tremors she did not deviate from hate and defiance.

"I will never speak except to say you are using Rome to outrage Rome," she whispered, "and that true Rome will cast you in the end into the foulest pit, where you will dwell with all the other fiends of darkness. I saw you murder a broken, bleeding child—and for that alone you are accursed. All your soft talk is no more than the frightened babble of a man who knows the gods will monstrously destroy him."

His laughter was light and hissing. It put a great coldness upon her. He threw down his sword. He took off his helmet. His dark hair was short-cropped, showing round skull. Un-helmeted, he had an even softer paleness to his face, and was to Lydia like something which had dwelt long in the dark. He dropped to one knee beside her, and put his hands on her shoulders. She knew the strength of those hands, inordinate in one so pale. He was of a kind the sun could not touch, whether he campaigned under the brassy sky of Africa, or through the misty golden summers of Britain.

"You will speak," he said, "for I will rid you of your childishness and make a woman of you. I will release your bonds, and so make your subjugation more violent. Aye, you may scratch and claw. Are you sure you will not tell me of Canis and where to find him?"

Lydia writhed, loathing his hands upon her. Her body sensed the pain and degradation of violation, her mind the agony of the unspeakable.

"I am with child," she gasped between anguished lips.

His smile became one of pleasure.

"If true, then it is a better circumstance than I thought," he said, "for if that will not make you babble of Canis in your

distraction, what could? First, then, I will cut your bonds."
He turned to take up his sword. A foot, sandalled in strong,
worn leather, was there before him, planting itself on the
weapon. Sulla did not spring to his feet, for he was cautious
and subtle in the face of the unexpected. He merely let his
glance travel upwards. He looked into the bitter, worldly eyes
of Canis, into a face as hard and brown as his own was soft and
pale. There was a bright axe in the Briton's belt, but it was his
drawn dagger that was only inches from the Roman's throat.

"You may speak," said Canis softly, "but no louder than
a squeaking mouse. Who broke the body of the girl child and
then slew her?"

Sulla came slowly to his feet. He found himself a head
shorter than the Briton, whose dagger now teased his groin
beneath his armoured kirtle.

"Who asks the question?" asked Sulla.

"One who will have the truth," replied Canis.

"How came you so unobserved?"

"I tread as lightly as a nymph," said Canis. "Who slew
the child?"

Lydia lay there, still shackled and bound. She was shivering,
her green eyes suffused, her tremors born of beautiful, incredulous bliss. He had come for her. He belonged to Cea,
daughter of Boadicea, but he had come for her, Lydia.

And for this Roman centurion too.

Canis' eyes, as bleak as frozen winter, told her that.

"I slew a barbarian chit, and so saved her from the offen-
siveness of barbarian life," owned Sulla calmly. "I do not ask
for gratitude in being so merciful. I would rather be remembered for my discrimination. Put your dagger away, man, it will
not save you now you are here. If you have come to exchange
your life for the woman's, I accept. For you are evidently the
man called Canis, whom I seek on behalf of Paullinus. The
woman is free, therefore, and may go. I will unbind her."

He turned without haste to Lydia, then caught the hand
that held the dagger. Lydia, remembering the cruel strength of
the Roman's grip, opened her mouth in a silent scream. Sulla

24

smiled as he wrenched the Briton's arm upwards, then astonishment seized him as a hand of iron took him by the throat. His instinctive effort to shout for his men was squeezed to a gurgle. A thunderbolt struck him. Canis caught him as he fell and lowered him soundlessly to the ground. He stooped to Lydia.

" Canis—oh, I thought—"

" Softly for the moment," he whispered. He slashed with his dagger and her bonds dropped from her aching wrists. He looked at her chained foot, placed both hands around the stake and it dragged at the earth as he pulled it from its hard bed. She stared at him, her tears welling hugely, then caught his hand and pressed it to her bare breast. " Lydia," he whispered gently, " you are among Romans, among countrymen, and because the way has been so difficult for you of late, declare yourself to them if you wish to remain with them. You may talk as freely as you wish when they take you to Paullinus. I cannot put more of our burdens on you, for you are Roman and it is much harder for you than for us."

" It is not," she whispered, almost angrily, " and I should be out of all my senses to remain with men like these. You have come for me and must take me, and do not dare to think you can do otherwise."

" I will take you, Lydia. In a moment."

He turned to the stunned centurion. Sulla, stirring, rolled dazed and numbed, then opened bemused eyes—only to find a gag of linen being thrust into his mouth. His hands and feet were quickly bound. Returning consciousness brought livid awareness, and because he was a man who could not stomach reverses of any kind, red fury crammed his eyeballs. Canis moved to the far side of the tent, taking up an oil lamp. He lifted the leather fabric a fraction, showed the light once, twice, then put the lamp aside.

" Canis," whispered Lydia, in frantic fear for him, " the Romans will have seen that light."

" Those who saw it will be those who were looking for it," said Canis. " The Romans will be quiet enough while they think your unwanted lover is at his work." He smiled at the

25

sound of a sudden shout. This was followed by a man's throaty scream. Then came a confusion of noises and the rushing of feet. Sulla, prone, twisted his head round, the red fury in his eyes. "Merely a diversion, Roman, to draw off your thickheads," said Canis, going to the door of the tent. Outside confusion turned into clamour. A man called for Sulla, as somewhere on the fringe of the small, tented camp a braying melee developed, and the sound of frightened horses added to the uproar. A man came running, the tent flap was thrust aside and he burst in, unhelmeted, to arouse his centurion. A bright axe flashed and the soldier fell, smitten cleanly to death.

"That was for sweet Cerdwa," murmured Canis, "she is entitled to one occasionally." Cerdwa, Lydia knew, had been the Briton's own bright warrior maid who had died in Boadicea's last battle. It was her axe he carried always in his belt.

The tumult was louder, the earth drumming as horses stampeded. Lydia was pale and tense. "Now," smiled Canis, "now we will have you safe under the night sky as easily as a bird rises from a blind fox. Come, but stay close to me." Lydia caught up the stake that held the chain fastened around her ankle, and moved quickly, if awkwardly, to the opening. Canis picked up a lamp and tossed it against the side of the tent nearest the bound, helpless Sulla. The oil spilled and flared, the flame darted and ran like a yellow snake along the fabric. Sulla gurgled around his gag, his eyes starting from his head, his body a writhing madness. "Burn, Roman," said Canis, "and as you burn remember the girl child."

He slipped from the tent, Lydia with him, she quaking in case her chain should rattle and betray her. They heard men rushing around on the camp perimeter, they saw flaring torches and glimpsed quick-moving shadows. Because of her impediment, Canis swung her up into his arms and bore her through the darkness with such sure instinct that she let sweet, blessed relief take limitless hold of her. Joy in her deliverance enraptured her. Her arms clung tightly. How swiftly he went, as if she were no burden at all. The noises of the disturbed camp dwindled, the lights died at their backs, and she was carried into a night so black that it swallowed them.

She did not speak, neither did he. He brought her in a while to his horse, tethered in a shallow wood. She could see a little better now. He mounted, Lydia up behind him, her arms ecstatically encompassing his waist, and they rode through the wood, the horse sure-footed even in this darkness. Behind them a blazing tent had collapsed and fallen upon the writhing body of a helpless, maddened centurion, while scorched soldiers frantically endeavoured to pull him clear.

Canis rode steadily through the night, his horse making light of its double burden. Lydia's tenseness and fear were gone, she was close to the warm, hard strength of Boadicea's greatest warrior, still an elusive thorn in Roman flesh. She pressed her mouth to his sweat-stained tunic, her body moving with his as they rode on their dark, winding way. Eventually he eased the horse to a walk, and a little farther on pulled up. He dismounted, reached up for her and brought her lightly down, she making no fuss about the chain and stake.

" Here, then, is your night sky," he said.

In the darkness he was like a tall, protective shadow. She felt an intense yearning to be held, cherished and loved. But he belonged to Princess Cea.

" Here is more than my sky," she said, " here is my life."

" But we lost seventeen others, and the girl child also," he said sombrely.

The horror of the massacre returned to her, together with an unhappy thought that he perhaps felt she was in some way to blame.

" Canis, you did not return. We waited so long and Ebbyd and Twycel were desperate for food. So they went to find what they could, and brought Romans upon us. I urged them not to go, indeed I did—"

" Do you think I blame you?" He shook his head. " It was their lack of food. Empty bellies father incautious heads. I

27

could not get back sooner than I did because of early Roman patrols. But it is hard to have lost so many."

Lydia's day had been long and anguished. Hot tears spilled.

" Oh, I am in such sadness for them," she whispered, " they died so bravely, yet so cruelly. And that sweet child—he took her from life so brutally."

She wept. He put his arms around her and said gently, " Did I not say it was harder for you than for us?"

She forced back her tears.

" However hard each day is," she said, " not one is without some sweetness. You are my joy, you know that. What are the worst and most fearful moments, when set against the one on which I saw you with your foot on that man's sword? Oh, to know that you had come for me—you do cherish me a little, do you not?"

" Lydia, you are a brave and sweet comrade, and one I would not be without."

She was emotionally disposed to kiss him at that. But always Cea stood between them.

" Surely Diana has made you the guardian of my life," she said, " you have saved me more than once from death."

" Ah, Diana," he said caustically, at which Lydia put a fearful hand over his mouth.

" Canis, you must not," she breathed, " she will hear you one day, and know that you mock her. Why do we stay here? We are still too close to those soldiers and I am not at all weary. Let us go on."

" They will be busy enough digging out their smouldering centurion. We will wait here until our friends come. They know this is where we are. And I think they will bring horses." He saw her torn robe. " Were you hurt, Lydia?"

" Only for the innocent child, oh so much for her," she whispered.

" Perhaps," he said sombrely, " they cannot forget they lost so many of their own innocents during Boadicea's campaign."

" There is cruelty in any war," said Lydia, " but it is not the same as cold, sadistic murder. Canis, I weep for Rome, but I cannot return to her, I cannot. Oh, despite Cea, never send me away, never let Rome claim me."

"Did I not say you were one I would not be without?"

"As was Cerdwa," she said, remembering the wild beauty of the forest maid who died for him, and whose axe he carried in his belt.

"As was Cerdwa," he agreed.

"Who also loved you."

"Who was a sweet comrade and died on the field of our only defeat."

"There are songs your people sing of Canis and Cerdwa," she said, "and I have also heard them sing many times of Canis and Boadicea."

He was silent then, as withdrawn as the night sky. She knew why. She knew which woman it was for whom Canis had an imperishable and bitter love. Boadicea. It was not because of what he himself said, for he never spoke intimately of his beautiful Queen, but of what others said. Every Iceni who had served under Boadicea knew that Canis had loved her, knew that she had loved him more than life itself. Lydia was aware of who was in his thoughts when sometimes his eyes were full of the shadows of that which had gone. She was also aware that he loved Princess Cea, because she was Boadicea's daughter and her mother's reflection. Such love, thought Lydia hopefully, must lack substance. Her own love for him was as inextinguishable as his for Boadicea. The gods, it seemed, took perverse pleasure in making life much more difficult for people than people did themselves. They intertwined the destinies of individuals in the most tortuous way.

Soon Canis would have to know that she carried his child.

It was no physical problem. She was healthier than she had ever been, even though far hungrier at times. Her body was as supple and active as any of the warrior maids who had come to serve Princess Cea and Canis. Her worry was of another kind. How would he receive the news? And how would Cea?

She would tell him now. After such a tragic day as this, he would be tender with her.

"Do you hear them?" Canis said then. "Our friends are on their way."

She heard nothing. But she had not been listening as he had. How he knew they were the sounds of friends, and not of punitive Romans, she did not know. But they came, the band of wild, hairy ones, straight to them out of the darkness. They were all riding horses, though in the beginning they had followed Canis on foot. There was a chuckling triumph about them, like the whispers of a forest when the breeze is warm and merry. They had left the detachment of Roman cavalry horseless, for they had first attacked the small compound that held the animals, taken all the mounts they wanted, driven off the others and then skirmished on the fringe of the camp in noisy clamour. This provided the diversion necessary to allow Canis to bear safely away with Lydia.

"How many lost?" asked Canis.

"None, lord," said Agra, forest chieftain looking like a hairy humpback in the night, "though some of us took the odd prick from a weapon or two. See you, it was only a shouting and a dancing for the most part, except we slew four of them before it was over. And there was one who went up in fire and flame to make their confusion a burning discomfort."

"I love you all," said Canis. The hairy ones of the forest were his fiercest and craftiest allies.

"There is a horse for Lydia, lord," said Agra, and blushed in the darkness as Lydia joyfully and gratefully embraced him.

"Then take her," said Canis, "and I will join you later at the door to your domain. I have an appointment with Paullinus."

"No!" Lydia was frantic. "No!"

"Go with Agra," said Canis, and mounted his horse. "But wait for me where I have said." He turned his horse; and even while Lydia was still begging him to stay, he had disappeared.

She would suffer until he returned to her, but she went quietly through the night with Agra and his hairy ones, though not before Agra had sundered the chain around her ankle.

30

When she thanked him, he said, "By Pror, my own god, I would strangle wolves for a woman as brave as you, mistress." Lydia rode then with tears in her eyes, the tears because of many things.

2

Suetonius Paullinus, Imperial Governor of Roman Britain, most westerly province of Caesar's Empire, sat brooding on the problems posed by the continuing survival of Canis the Briton, erstwhile general to the confederated armies of the rebellious Boadicea. Paullinus, hero in the eyes of all Rome by virtue of his great victory over the Iceni Queen, was certain that despite the rejoicing in Rome he would not be rid of the problem of the Iceni and their chief allies, the Trinovantes, until he had crucified Canis and exterminated all others who had fought for Boadicea. There were many warriors who had escaped the slaughter of that last battle; and there were people who may not have borne arms against Rome, but had played their own part and were still doing so, even though Boadicea herself was dead. All such men and women he was determined to hunt down and destroy. If not, then they would rise again under Canis.

He had harried and hounded them, and all whom he caught he did destroy. It had been a year since he defeated Boadicea, but still he was not finished with her. The Britons, elusive and fierce, made the work difficult. They slew his soldiers in ambush, they murdered solitary sentinels and outposts. They even decapitated centurions, sending back only the ears to Paullinus—with the message, "Speak to them, Roman, for they have long been deaf to all but the voice of tyranny." If, in this way and other ways, they made his self-appointed task more bitter, he in turn made their survival grievously harder.

Julius Classicianus, the new Imperial Procurator, sent by Nero to replace the corrupt Catus Decianus, whose outrageous

32

behaviour had provoked the rebellion, was critical of the Governor's continuing harassment of the defeated Britons. He thought the time was overdue to offer the Iceni and Trinovantes a just and honourable peace.

Paullinus considered Classicianus a fool, and accordingly conducted his business as if the Imperial Procurator did not exist. He alone knew the formidable influence of Canis, and he also knew the Britons. Classicianus did not. A just peace they would construe as forgiveness, and an honourable peace they would make a mock of. They were barbarians, and lived by violence, not by treaties or civilised laws. Better to destroy them completely, these Iceni and the Trinovantes, and make their lands over to the soldiers of Caesar.

Some of Boadicea's warriors had surrendered to him in the belief he would pardon them. He had pardoned none. Their rebellion had been too insolent, too arrogant, their defeat of Roman armies unbearable, their slaughter of men, women and children too unforgivable.

Classicianus, a liberal and humanist, knew that it was the defeat of Roman armies that stuck in the Imperial Governor's gullet, that and the belief among Romans themselves that as a general Canis was superior to Paullinus. He felt that the harshness of the Governor towards what was left of the Iceni and Trinovante nations was inspired by personal spite. He had argued the case for the Britons earlier that day.

Paullinus, a spare and austere man, with bony nose, thin lips and cold blue eyes, listened unmoved as Classicianus sought in a quiet, civil way to convince him that his policy of attrition was at best unkind, and at worst shortsighted.

" I do not seek to quarrel with your purpose, Excellency—"

" Then let your discretion in what you do seek be matched by your discretion in what you say," said Paullinus.

" I well realise your purpose," said the Procurator, " is to bring the Iceni and Trinovantes into peaceful cohabitation with Rome once more. It is only our means of achieving this that I have doubts about."

" Peaceful cohabitation?" Paullinus was coldly sarcastic.

" What, do you speak of a love match between Rome and these dogs which the widow Boadicea has-left growling?"

It was common for Paullinus and certain other Romans to refer to Boadicea as ' the widow '. It was symptomatic of their refusal to accord her the rights and dignity of a queen. To have scourged a widow was of little account, to have scourged an acknowledged queen was a vastly different matter.

" I speak only of peaceful argument," said Classicianus, " which has a more agreeable persuasiveness than war."

" Aye, having howled for war and having lost what they howled for, the dogs now yelp like unloved pups for milk. I am not their mother. Are you?"

" Excellency," said Classicianus, " yours is the difficulty of restoring order in these unhappy lands. Mine is the lesser difficulty of achieving efficient administration, which is the special concern of my office."

" Your special concern," said Paullinus, " is to do with the names of men and the names of places, with what is destroyed and what is left, and how all may be construed as simple assets and liabilities. You are a keeper of books and scrolls. I am Caesar's keeper of a province. I am not to be questioned in what I do, except by Caesar himself. I do not intend to rest until I have so put down these rebellious Britons that never again will they defy Rome."

Classicianus rose from his seat. He could not stomach the ascetic obduracy of his superior. He paced the square, tiled room, his sandalled feet clicking. Paullinus viewed him with scarcely veiled contempt.

" This is the heart of the matter," said Classicianus, " for you seek to put them down, when by your great victory over Boadicea they are down as far as they can go. I doubt if they understand why you are still at war with them, for they have been decimated and can never be a threat to Rome again. They can only look for peace and hope for mercy."

" Ah, peace and mercy," said Paullinus coldly. " You cannot solve this problem with charitable words, or with the gift of liberal laws. Sweetmeats do not satisfy uncivilised dogs hungry

34

for blood. Aye, blood. For though you speak of them looking for peace, I only remark how they lie in wait for my soldiers at the going down of every sun."

This was too much for Classicianus.

"But your soldiers are hunting them," he said. "Do any men and women, brave or merely desperate, wait unresistingly for death? You yourself as a soldier must know their only hope is to strike first. Will you not consider an amnesty?"

"Amnesty?" Paullinus was icy. "For barbarian dogs who murdered our people here, while you were safely abed in Rome? For godless rogues who destroyed the sacred temple of Claudius in Camulodunum? Do you know of the man who contrived this, who led their armies, the man called Canis?"

"I have not met any man who does not know of him," said Classicianus, aiming a quiet but sharp dart.

"By all the gods," swore Paullinus, "there you have a rogue more cunning and more murderous than all of them. I was cheated of him, for after the battle he was claimed by the house of Osirus as slave to Lydia. In a moment of weakness, and because I was in some debt to the house, I conceded this claim. I gave up my right to crucify the dog, and so Lydia took him and later gave him his freedom. This I hold against the house of Osirus, for at the moment when Canis no longer belonged to Lydia, he belonged to me and to Rome's just vengeance. Both Lydia and her brother Julian knew this, though Julian professed ignorance. Aye, smiled at me he did, and spread his hands and purported to be quite distressed at the confusion of it all."

"I have heard that Lydia went with the Briton," said the Procurator.

"And he only a barbarian rebel," said Paullinus acidly. "Is there a man, high or low, who can understand the mind of a woman?"

"The gods have given all things to men except the understanding of any woman."

"I am not concerned with understanding Lydia Osirus," said Paullinus, "only with bringing her before a magistrate, or

35

despatching her to Caesar, as she will discover in time. As to Canis, he is somewhere within my reach, and in the end I will take him. Until I do, there will be none of this peace you dote on. Somewhere he is raising a new banner of rebellion, and enlisting all Iceni and Trinovantes who will support him. I will find him, take him and crucify him. This I have sworn to."

"Excellency, I agree, a rebellious general is not to be treated lightly, even though defeated. But for the rest, who is there to destroy except him? Boadicea is dead, and her surviving people in dire straits."

Paullinus grew harsher, bleaker.

"I am here to serve Rome," he said, "you are here to serve me. Serve me by marking your tablets. Leave me to deal with the rebels. I will bring justice to all of them in time, and all who are left will be like lambs. And you, in your concern for their well-being, shall be their tender shepherd."

"Excellency," said Classicianus, self-discipline hiding his anger, "Canis and his people cannot, and will not, treat with us when we offer only death. They will fight us."

"I will take Canis," said Paullinus, "I will discover him, take him and nail him to a cross."

*　　*　　*

The sun had long since taken its light from the sky, and the land was in darkness as Paullinus brooded on all that still irked him. Classicianus still irked him, but not more than Canis. Lugano, the Governor's secretary, came in with slaves to light more lamps. In their glow, Lugano remarked the thin-faced wintriness of the legate. He would have sought to lighten the moment for his illustrious master, but was abruptly dismissed. And Paullinus, sipping his meagre measure of wine, for he was an abstemious man, took up again his dissatisfying reflections.

He was a patient man but a vengeful one, and patience and vengeance were irksome companions. He would never forgive

36

the dead Boadicea for her revolt, nor Canis, her general, for all the destruction he had wrought. Nero had not liked it, and the fact that it had happened while he was the Governor would no doubt be weighed against him if he were ever out of favour, no matter that he had crushed Boadicea in the end. If it took him all his remaining time in office, he would execute the man Canis, and leave all surviving Iceni and Trinovantes prostrate under the iron heel of Rome.

Because of the gentle warmth of the evening, the quietness had a velvet quality which began to soothe the Governor's irritations. The villa was always quiet at this time each evening, unless there were urgencies thrust upon him, for this was the hour when he demanded quiet. Within his large, well-guarded villa the sounds of all servants were muted, his soldiers patrolled noiselessly and his sentinels stood silently. Therefore the faint slither of sound at the arched doorway to his plainly furnished retreat—he being a man who did not care for soft cushions—made Paullinus look up sharply and disapprovingly.

He expected to see Lugano, for only his secretary had the right of entry at this hour, and then only if the matter justified it. But it was not Lugano or any Roman. It was undeniably a Briton, a man in a fustian, kilted tunic. He stood in the doorway, inside the heavy, hanging curtains, a tall man with hair of thick, deep brown that was tied at the nape of his neck by a thin strip of leather. He was lean, his flesh close to the bone so that his face seemed carved from brown stone, and his mouth made a man think of humour bitter and mocking, and a woman of kisses to turn her faint. But it was his eyes that held Paullinus, wide eyes of deep grey, in which a perceptive beholder could discern a knowledge of men and a compassion for women. They were eyes of life, of death, of cruelty, wisdom and pity.

And Paullinus knew that the man was Canis, the erstwhile general of the tempestuous, majestic Boadicea, Queen of the Iceni, who had died in his arms on his bitterest day. Paullinus knew, although he had never seen him before.

37

" It is usual," said the Roman, not ostensibly out of countenance at the intrusion of the man he most wanted but least expected, " for my secretary to first bring me notice of those who wish to see me."

Canis smiled. It was as if wintry sun touched dark ice.

" What is usual is often dull," he said in his resonant Celtic voice, " and it is only the unusual which brings to a man an appreciation of the commonplace."

" On this occasion," said Paullinus acidly, " it has brought to me the uninvited. Yet you are welcome. I have long been looking for you, Briton."

" Aye," said Canis. He approached with a quietness that pleased Paullinus but did not deceive him. " I am here, Roman."

" I would have taken you eventually," said Paullinus, hands resting lightly on the table at which he sat, " and therefore it is of no consequence that you have delivered yourself up, although I would have preferred to have had you here by my own endeavours."

" One way or another, have no regrets," said Canis, looking down at Caesar's chief representative with a smile, " I am not here to deliver myself."

Paullinus regarded his man from beneath pale lids. In the bronze chain belt of the Briton's tunic was thrust a bright-bladed axe, and strapped to the belt was a sheathed dagger. A brown hand rested on the hilt of the dagger. Paullinus sighed.

" My words were wishful," he said, " for I knew this."

" Perhaps," said Canis, " I am here to bargain with you."

" Or to murder me? For how might you, a man who has nothing, bargain with one who has as much as I have?"

" By my command of axe and dagger," said Canis, " so do not call your servants, Roman, but let us discuss the gift of compromise I bring."

" Compromise?" Paullinus was bleak.

" Did I not say I might bargain?"

" This," said Paullinus disdainfully, " is arrogance, not compromise."

" This," said Canis equably, " is to offer you that which you least deserve. Your life. I hear you have sworn to destroy me. I long ago promised Boadicea to destroy you. However, if you will call off your dogs of war and leave my people in peace, I will forswear this promise."

The coldness of Paullinus was stony. But his nostrils twitched, and his hands, taking hold of the wine cup, gripped it so convulsively that his knuckles showed white. Inner heat began to burn him.

" Take heed, barbarian," he said harshly, " I will not suffer you overlong."

" Resign yourself," said Canis, " for your secretary is deaf at this moment, as is one sentry. Both are afflicted with blank minds and sleep blissfully unaware of your mortification. This is the hour you set aside for meditation, as is well-known, and accordingly no one will disturb us."

" They will come if I call."

" Call them, Roman, and when they come they will find you dying in agony."

" In which event," hissed Paullinus, " you will die in even greater agony. And death holds no terrors for me. I have looked on it too often to shrink from it now."

" Oh, brave and fearless legate," mocked Canis, " that such fine words should come with so green a face. By all the thunder of your hairy Mars, is that your true face? Gently, noble hangman, contain your bile. I only jest. In truth it is not your bravery I am concerned with, but your malice."

" Barbarian," said Paullinus lividly, " be concerned only for yourself. You have in some way slipped through my guards and into my house, but such advantage as you have is tenuous and insecure. Do not abuse it, or I will indeed call my servants, despite your axe and dagger. For while I can stomach arrogance, and even insolence, I cannot endure jesters or fools."

Unperturbed, Canis drew his dagger and placed it on the plain surface of the table, so that it lay between himself and the Roman.

" Aye, we will give up jests," he said. " There is my dagger in evidence that now we treat in earnest. It is no farther from your hand than mine. Over it let us bargain."

If the cold blue eyes hid the Roman's fury, Canis did not disguise the contempt he had for the Governor. He had not forgotten how Paullinus had threatened to give Boadicea to Roman soldiers for sport, and to consign her daughters to a house of harlots. Paullinus saw the contempt and felt it; and though outwardly he maintained his icy bleakness, the inner heat burned through every vein. He looked at the dagger, then at Canis.

" You are arrogant indeed," he said.

" Be not misled," said Canis.

In fury, Paullinus shot out a hand and snatched up the dagger. But another hand closed on his, and iron fingers squeezed. Paullinus saw the pitiless smile on the Briton's face as his own momentarily betrayed his pain.

" Be not misled," said Canis again. The dagger fell from tortured fingers and clattered as it dropped back onto the table. " Shall we bargain, aye or no, Roman?"

" If there is a Roman who would bargain with a murderous rebel dog such as you," said Paullinus, " I am not that one. I have sworn to nail you to a cross, and even if you were here with a hundred other dogs at your back, my oath would remain constant. I will make no bargains, give no pardons, grant no amnesties. I serve Rome, and Rome lays just vengeance on all men who affront her laws, her citizens, her soldiers and her property."

" Truly," mused Canis, " who can deny this? Rome boasts a multitude of laws and citizens, soldiers and property in every land. People are unavoidably tripping over one or the other on all sides, so that Rome is in a turmoil of affront and vengeance night and day. Indeed, it is said that there are cities in some Roman provinces where a man can offend Caesar merely by putting his nose out of the door."

" Briton," said Paullinus, " play no more comedy, for even in comedy cruel fate has a way of ousting fickle fortune. Go now while you may. I will not call my servants, since only a fool

40

would commit suicide, but one or more will surely interrupt us eventually, and then you will regret lingering to play the jester."

The Briton's smile was bitter, pitiless.

"I came to kill you, Roman. You deal in dishonourable oppression of my people. You deal dishonourably with queens. You are a soldier of malice, a statesman without principle. You would have put unspeakable shame on Boadicea and her innocent daughters. Because of this, Boadicea chose to die."

"I am not to be judged by any barbarian dog," said Paullinus.

"I came to kill you, not judge you. Did I not say so? Your soldiers hunt my people, and to satisfy your infamous spite put them to death. You are no true servant of Rome, Paullinus, you are only a hangman, and I am here to hang the hangman. For my own satisfaction I might, before I hang you, give you a little of the pain you have inflicted on others—but I will spare you this, and even the hanging, if you will call off your soldiers, every one, and have done with your vengeance."

There was silence, broken only by the soft sounds of night, before Paullinus spoke.

"I say again," he said, "I will not bargain with you, though you prick me to every bone with your dagger. And I also say—"

"Say it later, Roman," murmured Canis, "for we are no longer alone."

The muffling, hanging curtains parted, and there in the doorway stood a girl, dark and pleasing to the eye. She was Claudia, daughter of the tribune Perealix Justian, a kinsman to Paullinus. She wore a white robe, and as she looked upon the two men she was in a little embarrassment to find her uncle was not alone. Paullinus drew a sighing breath and Canis smiled.

"Why," said the girl, "I did not know—please forgive me."

"My guest is unspoken," said Paullinus calmly, seeing in Claudia his salvation and the apprehension of Canis. "Therefore he will not complain at being interrupted. Indeed, you are more welcome than you realise, Claudia." And he rose, his smile thin on his lips, to stand beside Canis and greet the hesitant girl.

" I am Claudia Justian," she said simply to the Briton, though she did not smile on him, for she thought him a collaborator or a spy for Romans. She had no liking for the Iceni, who were apparently still giving trouble to her august kinsman, and she had even less liking for renegades.

" I am Canis," said the Briton just as simply. His voice made her stare. It was strong and deep; and he was tall, with grey eyes that encompassed mysteries, and a mouth that would surely give a bitter, stinging sweetness to a kiss. She felt strangely affected. He was, after all, only a barbarian Briton in a worn tunic, with a glittering axe in his belt; so why her heart beat a little faster she did not know. He said with a smile, " It is not so much your person which Paullinus finds agreeable, Claudia Justian, as your timing." She thought that remark discourteous. She looked at him again, a little coldly. The smile was in his eyes, and she thought then of dark mountains in the heat of summer, and of cascading seas against shining rocks. It took her speech and filled her with uneasy wonder.

Paullinus, thinking to see a diversion, turned quickly and took up the dagger.

Canis laughed.

" How could you resist it?" he said to Paullinus. " But will you spill my blood in such sweet company as this?"

" What do you do?" asked Claudia of her uncle, paling to see how harsh was his look.

" Put an end to arrogance," said Paullinus. " Go, Claudia, call the guards. Our uninvited guest is going to stay longer than he intended."

Again the girl looked at Canis. He was still smiling. He shook his head. She felt bemused, agitated. She turned to her uncle.

" Surely, there is some mistake—is he not here as a friend?"

" Do as I bid you," said Paullinus sharply, putting himself and the dagger in a position to obstruct the Briton's exit.

" Where are your wits? Did you not hear him name himself in his conceit?"

Claudia was a maid wholly unspoiled. The decadent arts practised by the bored patricians of Rome had not yet touched her, and there was something in this situation which made her heart beat with the apprehension of the innocent.

" Canis?" she said, and as the name fell from her own lips her eyes widened and she stared at the Briton, this time in some fear. So this was Canis, this was the British general who had cruelly slaughtered a hundred thousand Romans and more. This was the man whom her kinsman had sworn to crucify. Suddenly she felt his presence chilling.

" If you bear Paullinus any affection," said Canis, " do not call any guards. Do not call anyone, unless you wish him to die very painfully."

" You would not kill him," she said in horror.

" I came here to do no less," said Canis, aware of Paullinus weighing the odds. The Governor was raising no alarm himself. He might be willing to bravely face death himself, but he was not willing for the girl to die too. He wished to get her out of the room. He might raise the alarm then, while using the dagger to defend himself against the axe. " Yes, I would kill him," said Canis, " I owe it to Boadicea and my people."

" Then you are as cruel as men say you are," said Claudia in a low voice.

" And as boastful as a cockerel in an eagle's nest," said Paullinus, " so do not stand there witless, girl, but go. Rouse the guards." He turned as if to hasten her on her way, then made an adroit sally to the doorway, pulling her with him. But Canis was there before him. Paullinus, not now to be cheated, thrust with the dagger and opened his mouth to shout. Canis slipped the thrust like a shadow, and at the same time smote the Roman senseless. Paullinus fell like a folding sack. Claudia strangled an involuntary cry. Canis recovered his dagger.

" Oh, monstrous barbarian," gasped the girl, " you have surely slain him!"

" What, do you say Paullinus is a man to die from a tap on

43

his neck? He has earned a harder and longer death than that, mistress." Canis shook his head as the girl knelt beside her unconscious uncle. "I have put him into a far pleasanter state than he deserves. He will tell you when he comes round that he has been listening to the songs of Circe."

"But you would have killed him," cried Claudia, in strange distress that the Briton could be so hard and mocking, "you would have killed me too, if I had raised my voice. I will defy your brutality, I will fetch the guards, after all."

"I might have set Circe singing in your own head," said Canis, "but it would have been no more than that."

"You are a hard man, with a vain tongue," said Claudia, "and I can believe now that you were the one who destroyed the temple of our beloved Claudius."

"An emperor beloved of Romans is not necessarily beloved of others, sweet child. Look to Paullinus, and when he wakes up tell him I will one day come again, and surely put him to death unless he has done with his spite."

Then he was gone, leaving her wondering and confused, her mind burdened by not knowing whether his cruelty made a mock of his compassion. She cushioned her uncle's head on her knees. She did not for the moment call the guards.

Outside in the darkness, avoiding all lamplit areas, Canis set up a quick, noisy commotion close to the wall. The guards rushed from within and without, converging on the spot, while Canis, quick and elusive, gained the wall elsewhere, climbed it and melted into the night.

3

Deep in the heart of the great forest, dwelt the refugee people of Cea and Canis. They were the Iceni and Trinovantes who had escaped the massacres after Boadicea's defeat, and latterly eluded the hunting soldiers of the Imperial Governor. The Trinovantes had been Boadicea's chief allies during the rebellion, and those who came to place themselves in service to her general also took the oath of fealty to her exiled daughter, Cea. Their own Prince was dead, their land waste, and they became Princess Cea's people. It was true that the Iceni and Trinovantes had their own cultures and customs; but they were all Celts, and to a stranger it was difficult to tell them apart. They did not have this difficulty themselves; and besides, as the Trinovantes pointed out, what Iceni man could grow a moustache as luxuriant as they could?

It was to this forest camp that Canis and his aides contrived to bring all the oppressed Britons who cared to come. His main aides were the hairy ones and their daughters, the wood-witches, all natural forest dwellers. They harboured the refugees, scouted for them and frequently fought for them. The forest was on the western boundary of the broken Iceni kingdom and the hairy ones conceded allegiance to the house of Boadicea. It had been said of Cerdwa of the axe, lieutenant and comrade to Canis throughout the rebellion, that she was born of the hairy ones and was accordingly a wood-witch. But Canis remembered her as a wild and beautiful forest maid who had no equal, for no one, he said, could match her in battle or in words. Her liquid tongue still pursued him, but only in his dreams.

The hairy ones knew the secret of every tree and bush, and could mark which was the hundredth acorn of the year to drop from an oak. It was the hundredth acorn which, when added to the cooking pot, gave a hairy one eternal life, just as an undisturbed oak was itself eternal. The hairy one did not die, he merely lapsed into unbreathing stillness at a time of weakness, and was taken at dusk and left on that edge of his forest which faced the rising sun. In the night the spirits of woodwitches raised him and bore him away, and he awoke at first light in a different forest. In this new domain, he lived until the time came for him to be transported in the same way to another. There were people who said this transportation was merely the removal of the body from the ground into the bellies of wolves, but there are always cynics who will deny the existence of their own navels, if by the sin of gluttony they are denied sight of them.

To reach the Britons' camp, a man had to travel through the densest ways, where some trees spread branches that shut out the sky, and others had such mighty girths that ten of them would have taken the light from the great fort of Lindum. Because of this, the forest in many parts was almost as dark by day as by night. It appeared quite trackless; and if a man lost his way, either the forest swallowed him and destroyed him, or the wood-witches took him, seduced him and made him bloodless.

Or so it was told, and who knows what these vast forest domains held for a man or a woman in the days when the Roman civilisation of Celtic Britain was in anguished birth?

It was because of the way news travelled among the hairy ones that Princess Cea knew Canis was returning before he arrived. When he did emerge into the natural clearing where the Britons had their camp, she ran to him, her rich auburn hair flying, her honey-brown face alight. She had loved Canis since she was a girl of ten. Now she was almost nineteen.

She called to him. He was leading a horse. He smiled at her and she threw herself into his arms, heedless of many eyes. She sometimes forgot she was a princess.

" We looked for you yesterday," she said breathlessly, " but there was only news of delay and trouble. Almost I died."

Lydia appeared, leading a Roman horse. It looked bemused,

46

it had never tracked its way through such a place as this forest. Lydia smiled to see Cea in the Briton's arms, but with pain in her eyes. She passed them by. The moment was for them alone. If Cea owned a hurting jealousy of Lydia, Lydia had a great envy of Cea.

Following Lydia were two men and one woman, and a number of hairy ones, all bringing Roman horses to the Britons.

" Canis, almost I died," breathed Cea again.

" Others did die," said Canis, looking into caressing brown eyes. " We lost seventeen and a sweet girl child. It was bitter. They had starved in reaching our meeting-place. The three you see now we plucked from under Roman noses on our way to the forest last night, and though we also gained eleven Roman horses I would rather have saved the one girl child and given up all else."

" Do not be so sad," said Cea, " for we must lose, even children. And see, since you went our friends have brought a score more to us. Canis, we have a full seven hundred under our banner. Seven hundred."

" So few?" he said, remembering the fifty thousand warriors of Boadicea.

" Seven hundred are better than seven score, and a miracle compared with none at all," said Cea.

" I will talk to the newcomers in a while," he said.

" I know you will," she said. Always he insisted on interrogating every person who came to join them. He was so cautious in some things, so reckless in others. She had fretted during this last absence of his. She had wanted to go with him, but he would not permit it. He had permitted Lydia. Ha, that hussy. She herself was never allowed to go with him, to help him snatch fleeing Britons from the hounds of Paullinus. She knew it was because he would give no Roman the chance of taking her. She was Boadicea's only surviving daughter, and if she fell into Roman hands they would surely execute her, and the house of Boadicea would no longer exist. He would have failed his beloved Queen.

All the same, he did not have to take Lydia with him so

often. Lydia always begged to go, because she wanted to do as much as she could to help the Iceni and Trinovantes; but to have Canis indulge her as frequently as he did put the young, imperious Princess out of temper at times.

The camp rang to the sounds of life. There was the song of cold iron beating hot iron, the music of women weaving, the laughter of children playing and the buzz of activity everywhere. There was also a sense of security from Romans. It was a tenuous security, but it was enough. They had built dwellings from timber, from branch, bush and earth, and would live in this place until Cea and Canis were ready to lead them westward to the mountains. There they would found a new kingdom, where Cea and Canis would wed, rule and provide. There was no princess they would rather have as their queen than Boadicea's daughter, no man they would fight better for than Canis.

Lydia, a little weary, was being greeted by a number of Britons. Many had come not only to accept the Roman woman, but to hold her in affection. She had a way of bringing laughter to their children, she had courage enough to defy her omnipotent countrymen, and sometimes a quick, spirited temper that nipped the ears of Canis himself. Also she was darkly, vividly beautiful.

Canis saw her amid the welcoming Britons and his face softened. Cea, perceiving this, felt the stabbing dart of jealousy.

"I see that Lydia was spared," she said in some sarcasm. It was not easy for her to crystallise her feelings towards the Roman woman, for despite everything, despite even the fact that Lydia at times was unable to hide her love for Canis, Cea liked her. Canis, knowing life now to be cruelly hard for the once spoilt and capricious Roman woman, sometimes seemed to Cea to be overly protective towards her. It made the Princess want to scratch both their faces. She was her mother's daughter, which Canis acknowledged with a smile, occasionally even with a laugh. To be laughed at when she was in rightful pride was not to be borne. She remembered how her mother in similar circumstances would say, " Oh, the dog, I will put his face where he will not find anything to laugh at for a month and a day."

" Did you hear me?" Cea demanded. " I said that Lydia was spared."

" But only by the resourcefulness of our hairy ones," said Canis and told her all that had happened. Cea went pale in the sunshine.

" Oh, to have risked yourself in this way! It is almost beyond forgiveness. Lydia herself would not have asked it of you."

" It was not done foolishly, sweet one, but with care and thought. And there was no risk once I had that Roman by the throat. Agra and his men did the harder work. The Romans danced and rattled and smote each other more than us. They are not as fond of night capers as the hairy ones. Cea, would you have let brave Lydia be broken and torn? You would not. And I could not."

" And did not," said Cea jealously. " It would not be so bad if she were bent of nose and crooked of back. But no, she must be beautiful, and I must endure the way she looks at you. Yet I confess I would not have wanted her cruelly tortured, for she has been a comfort to many of our women and children, and not dealt falsely with me."

" Ah," said Canis obliquely, for there was an item to come to Cea's ear which might make the sensitive Princess change her mind.

" However," said Cea firmly, " if I ever see you kiss her, I will burn your stomach with one of Grud's viler poisons, and her I will make hideous by having her nose cut off."

" You are the tenderest of princess," said Canis, " and will be sweet to her."

" I will if I will," said Cea, " but I will not be commanded."

He looked at her. She was becoming tall, willowy and striking, as her mother had been. But for all her imperiousness she was still an endearing maid.

" Be sweet to her," he said again.

Cea's brown eyes darkened at this insistence.

49

"Am I not sweeter to her than her own sister, all things considered?"

"Be sweeter yet, Princess. She is with child."

She gazed at him in shock, seeing from his look all that those words meant.

"Villain!" Anger and mortification came hard on the heels of shock. She took his hand and bit it with sharp, furious teeth. "You have betrayed me at the outset!"

"Not so," he said with a rueful smile, "it happened before you returned to me, on a night when Lydia and I were travelling together after she had given me my freedom. As the only Roman among so many Britons, life is hard for her here. She needs to be loved. So deal tenderly with her, Cea."

"Tenderly! I shall have her thrown from the tallest tree," stormed Cea, "and you shall hang by your wrists from a branch until you slip from your bones."

She was at times the true daughter of her tempestuous mother. Canis acknowledged it with a smile.

"She bites her tongue on her secret," he said, "and thinks no one is aware of it. But ask Grud, he will tell you she carries a child."

"Villain," cried Cea again in angry torment, "I wonder how you can stand and speak so calmly on so outrageous a matter, especially to me! To dare tell me you have lain with the hussy, and with the same breath that I must be sweet to her, is not to be endured!"

"You are a proud princess," said Canis soothingly, "and I love you well. It is not expected that you should be pleased about it, but then again it was not at the time intended to displease you. It was a moment of warmth on a desolate night in a grieving land. Lydia is not to be blamed, so I know you will be kind to her. She has striven well and bravely for us against her own people."

"She has striven only for you," said Cea. There was pain in her heart, and hurt in her eyes. She had loved him for as long as she could remember, and could love no other. For all her proud heritage she could not put aside her dependence on his

50

strength and protection. "Oh, you are a fox and she is a hussy!"

"And you are our sweet cause," he said. He put his arm around her and Cea's stiffness yielded, although she knew she would suffer anger and unhappiness for many days because it was his child Lydia was carrying.

They went to join many of their people who had not intruded on them yet, but who now greeted with delight the safe return of the Wolfhead, as Canis was often called. They could not forget he was the man who had welded the confederated armies of Boadicea into one mighty host, giving his majestic Queen her hammer of vengeance. With it she had broken and crushed Roman legions.

"Wolfhead," called a warrior maid, bright in her newly-dyed tunic, "do you not bring us one Roman head?"

"Are you still hungry?" asked Canis.

"It is not to pleasure my stomach, lord, but my eyes," she said. And she laughed. Among the seven hundred refugees here were a hundred or so warrior maids, all survivors of Boadicea's last tragic battle. Once the Queen had commanded thousands of them. The greatest had been Cerdwa, who now lay buried beside Boadicea in a place where a forest whispered to the wind.

One hundred warrior maids out of all those thousands. Canis sighed for those who had gone. But there might be others still alive, others waiting to slip the Romans and join the growing band of refugees. Because of Paullinus, the best Cea and Canis could offer their people was a migration to the west, where in the safety of the mountains they need not interfere with Romans or Romans with them. The Princess would commence the hazardous journey, however, only when she and Canis had gathered under her banner as many Iceni and Trinovantes as was humanly possible.

The seven hundred ate. Their provender was of the forest, and they took their meal undisturbed. Not even the best-trimmed cohort of Romans could squeeze through this forest without arousing the hairy ones and their witches. With a multitude of sharp ears acting for them, the Britons felt relatively safe, although they knew that if Paullinus were apprised of their exact location he would not be unwilling to burn his way through to them.

As it was, they sat around their fires and ate and talked, and when they had done with that they sang for a while. They were as addicted to song as to talk. They were motley of dress, but this was nothing. The women weaved to provide the short tunics favoured by the long-legged, supple warrior maids and robes for modest mothers-to-be. All of them, men and women, boys and girls, would serve Cea and Canis fearlessly and without counting the cost. Such was their revived spirit at this time that although a man might cheat his neighbour of a priceless iron spearhead, or a woman smile falsely on the wife of a lover, yet they would not cheat Boadicea's general or give Cea anything but fierce loyalty, unless they were of the kind conceived in an unwilling womb.

After the meal the newly-arrived refugees were brought before Canis. Cea was with him, and also Grud, ageless mystic who had served the father of Canis and Queen Boadicea herself. In addition there were Andudo, a veteran Iceni captain, and Hywel, a good-humoured Trinovante officer with a handsome blond moustache. The new arrivals were made up of five women, ten men, three girls and two boys. All were thin and ill-clad, except two of the men, these being quiet of demeanour, frank of countenance, but neither thin nor ill-clad.

Canis asked each of the ten men in turn, "Why do you come to us?"

To which each replied, more or less, "To follow you, lord, wherever you will take us." Except the two of the quiet demeanour. The first of these replied, clearly and firmly, "You are of the Iceni, lord, as I am. You are our nominated Prince and are against Rome, as I am. Your purpose is to kill Romans, as mine is. You have an ambition to destroy Paullinus, which is my ambition also. I offer you my hand and my spear in these endeavours, for Romans breed a fire in my belly and Paullinus a redness in my blood."

And the second answered, just as clearly, " I come because I wish to fight the evil which is Rome, and I come to you because you give greater inspiration than all other men. I have no spear, but if you will give me one I will be your man against Rome, come what may."

Of the women, four were widows who had lost their husbands to Paullinus and his vengeance; and in answer to the question from Canis, they each said, more or less, " To whom else should we come, lord?"

The fifth was a young woman, a forest maid, with long hair the colour of ripe corn and the untamed beauty of her kind. She had eyes of tawny-brown like those of a deer, and wore the short, untrammelling tunic of forest maids, her slim legs and strong, smooth thighs gleaming below the kilt. Within a strap of leather above her right knee was thrust a dagger of bright, polished bronze. Her long hair was about her face, she flung it back as she looked at Canis with a smile that had more guile than honey to it. Canis returned her look, his eyes pensive and his expression ironic with the knowledge that her smile was not a smile.

" Why do you come to us?" he asked.

" Because you are Canis the Wolfhead, and I have sought you for a long time."

" So might a Roman answer," said Canis.

" I am no Roman. I am a forest maid."

" Not of this forest, unless you were born of the hairy ones."

" Of another, many leagues from this," she said, her eyes softly flirting with his.

" Why have you sought me?"

" My kin died in battle against the army of Paullinus," she said, " on a day when Queen Boadicea died also. I would avenge my kin and also the Queen. How might I do this save under your guidance?"

" You may find Romans easily enough without guidance from any man. What is your name?"

" I am called Wanda."

The grey eyes of life held her own.

" Why must I find Romans for you, Wanda?"

" I would avenge my kin, as I said, and it is written that I will not achieve this save within your shadow, lord," she said. " Send me away if you will. I will follow in your shadow for all that, since now that I have at last found you I will not relinquish my advantage."

She advanced, sinuously graceful, and went down on one knee before him. She inclined her head, and so hid her eyes from him. Canis smiled, yet it was not a smile, any more than hers had been.

" Cea," he said, " what do you have to say about one who would avenge her kin within my shadow?"

" I say," said Cea, " that she sounds as if she will creep about you and be under your feet. Also, she uses her tongue artfully, so that I am not sure if she is for us or against us."

Wanda rose and went to Cea, kneeling to her as she had to Canis. She took the hand of the Princess and touched it to her forehead in fealty.

" I am Wanda of the forests and will serve you both, Princess, so do not let Canis deny me," she said.

" You will serve us in your own way, I do not doubt," said Canis. Wanda swept him a look that was full of laughter. He gave her no heed, but called for the two men of earnestness to stand before him again. Curiosity was sharp on the faces of the gathered Britons as the men came forward, cheerfully expectant; and the second of them said, " You will give me a spear, lord?"

Canis shook his head.

" You were wise," he said, " to come openly to us, to have our forest friends help you find the way. But you were less than wise to come with full bellies and too much flesh on your bones. And you are far more eager to go against the might of Rome than any of us here are."

" And you are too suspicious," said the first man reprovingly. " But because your circumstances have been desperate since the widow of King Prasutagus lost her last battle, I understand

54

such suspicions and take no offence at what you say, only offer you my hand and my spear once more."

"Friend," said Canis, "do you not know that only Romans and friends of Romans name Boadicea widow?"

"I speak of Boadicea as I hear others speak of her," said the man with candour. "Perhaps they name her Queen, perhaps they name her widow, but who names her so, one or the other, I take little notice of, for indeed she was both Queen and widow."

"None of our people name her widow," said Canis.

"Then perhaps it is Romans who have come to my ear more often than other people, but since they are all about us and loud of voice, this is natural."

"Where," said Canis, "is the true Iceni or Trinovante who would come to us with a full belly and name Queen Boadicea widow after Roman fashion? Show me such a one, and I will tell you he is not true to his nation or to Boadicea, but is a collaborator who eats by favour of Romans and does their errands for them."

"In our desire to serve you," said the second man, "we came to you with honest hearts. But I perceive you only wish to quarrel with us."

"I say again," said the first man, "I understand your lack of trust. However, I am a proud man, as is my friend also, so we will speak no more about serving you but go on our way."

"Aye," said the second man, "we will go."

"By all means," said Canis.

The two men went. Britons drew silently apart to make way for them, and watched just as silently as the men disappeared into the forest. Bow-legged Grud, round of eye, lifted his head and pierced the quiet with a clear whistle. The sound was like that of a blackbird calling in recognition of life's sweetness.

"They will make plump dog's meat," said Hywel.

Indeed, in less time than it takes a dog to strip a bone, the hairy ones took and chopped to pieces the two Roman spies as they hastened into the green and brown depths of the forest.

Several days later, some of the hairy ones emerged from their branch-tangled kingdom to talk to Canis. They were short men, but immensely broad of shoulder and fleet of foot. Shaggy of hair and bearded of chin, they worshipped only the forest gods and paid homage to none save Cea and Canis.

"Lord," said Agra, foremost of the hairy ones, whose daughters were wood-witches, "in a certain matter there is nothing we can do that you cannot do far better."

"What matter is this, Agra?" asked Canis. Cea stood by with Lydia and Grud, Lydia a little disturbed by Cea's aloofness these days. She was unaware that Cea knew of her condition, although when the breeze bound her robe close to her body, any discerning eye could mark its thickening. Cea had been unable to speak of that which troubled her as much as it troubled Lydia.

"Today," said Agra, "there came to the forest a youth looking for any man who would carry his story to you, lord. Having told his story he would not stay, but returned at once to his dwelling in Durvulavum, which is a poor place since Paullinus put a garrison into it. It seems, lord, that when the Romans are not pricking the people of Durvulavum from their sleep, they are probing beneath their resting places for signs that all is not as it should be. Lord, they looked beneath the resting place of the comeliest widow there. As you may know, there are a multitude of widows today, and this one is quite the comeliest in Durvulavum and so the Romans are always disturbing her and having her from her bed. Yesterday beneath her bed they found, alas, a dagger, which they said had not been there when they searched before. Though rusted and useless, it bore the crested haft of a warrior of Boadicea. And because of this they swore it was a sign you had lain with the widow, and received shelter as well as comfort from her."

"Ah," said Canis, while Princess Cea ground her teeth.

"So the Romans have taken the widow, lord," continued

Agra, whom some said was a hundred and fifty years old, " and also her small son and even smaller daughter. They have said that unless she speaks of where they may find you, they will at the end of seven days bind her to a tree with her feet clear of the ground. In this way the night wolves will have sport in leaping to tear her down mouthful by mouthful. Her children they will sell as slaves."

" I know Durvulavum," said Canis, " but I do not know the comeliest widow there, nor she me."

" That is some blessing," said Cea in his ear, " if not to her or to you, certainly to me."

" Perhaps the Romans care little whether you and she are acquainted or not," said Agra, " and are but using the widow to make sport. It is great sport to bind any widow in this fashion and offer her as a delicacy to wolves."

" Am I to snatch her from the Romans?" said Canis. " Is this what I may do better, Agra?"

" Her children also, lord," said Agra, " they are Iceni and belong to you."

" If I do this, Agra, if I rob the Romans of three hostages, do you know what they will do in return?"

" We all know," grumbled Grud, " they will take three more hostages and all their families and put them to death."

" Is the widow a woman who would not mind this once she and her children were safe?" asked Canis.

" Lord," said Agra, " how might I answer this without looking into her mind?"

" Come," said Grud to Canis, " you are tormenting Agra with questions to which he has no better answers than any of us. Make your decision."

Lydia felt apprehensive. It was not uncommon for Canis to take a band of warriors and lift suffering Iceni from punitive Romans, and she herself had been with him more than once on such sorties. But she was always fearful that he himself might be taken. Canis did not seem to be apprehensive himself, only thoughtful. He knew Durvulavum. Once it had been a strong encampment, mustering a thousand inhabitants. Now there were only two hundred, and all under the eyes of the Roman garrison there.

"They are weeping for the widow and her children," said Agra, scratching his single garment of sewn skins.

"A man may weep a lifetime of tears in a single night," said Canis, "yet win himself only a wet pallet. Or he might strike only one sound blow and win a lifetime of freedom."

"It is hard to strike at all," said Grud, "when a man and his family are close to starvation and can only eat what Romans throw them."

Canis asked for details of the garrison. Agra screwed up his eyes and his forehead, thought about what the messenger had told him, then said the Romans of Durvulavum numbered nine score and ten, all horsed. Resident there, and in command of all Roman troops in the region, was a tribune, Marcellus Mercurius. Canis thought about the widow, the wolves, the garrison and the risks. One risk he could not afford was that attendant on a direct assault. It would cost the lives of too many of his men and his warrior maids. It must be done another way.

"We must play the fool," he said.

"With a capering jester?" asked Grud.

"With our matchless Roman," said Canis, looking at Lydia. Cea bit her lip and regarded him darkly. He could be the slyest of villains, as the Queen her mother had so often said. "Lydia," he smiled, "will you put your foot into the Roman trap and so help us spring one of our own? For the widow is more of a trap for us than sport for them, make no mistake."

Lydia drew a deep breath. His grey eyes held her, compelled her. He commanded her life, her love, her being. Was there a woman who could say no to him? She could not.

"For you," she said, though inwardly the apprehension reached into her stomach, "and for Princess Cea and her people, I will. But oh, Canis, you will not ask me to betray my own people to death, you will only ask me to fool them, will you not?"

"I will," said Canis, his smile hiding that which he did not want her to see. He knew, if Lydia did not, that in fooling Romans it was not possible to immunise each and every one of them against death. If a man wished to tickle the eagle, he must also be ready to smite it. " Grud shall go with you to keep you from harm, and I will tell you what it is I wish you to do."

All this despite the smouldering jealousy in the brown eyes of Princess Cea.

*　　*　　*

They rode a single horse, Grud and the Roman woman, the animal plodding under its double burden on the upward ascent to the gates of Durvulavum. The encampment seemed quiet, the only movement to catch the eye being the flutter of the Roman banner above the tents on the west side. The Roman sentry watched the approach of horse and riders, his eyes curious but alert. They did not look like the usual kind of scavenging Britons.

" Who are you?" he asked, as Grud dismounted to lead the horse. The woman looked calmly down at the sentry. Her expression was almost supercilious, her green eyes dwelling on his shining armour as if it was tarnished, which it was not. She flung back long glossy hair the colour of a raven's wing, and the soldier's flickering eyes acknowledged she was no ordinary-looking woman. " Who are you?" he repeated.

" I am Lydia, daughter of Marcus Osirus and sister to Julian, deputy fiscal procurator at Calleva Atrebatum," she said imperiously. " Who commands the garrison here?"

" No less illustrious a tribune than Marcellus Mercurius."

" I have not heard of the illustrious one, but no matter, take me to him."

" Not so fast," said the suspicious sentry, " not when the ignorance is no doubt mutual."

" Be assured that although he does not know me, he has heard of me," said Lydia. " Take me to him."

" You speak like a Roman and name yourself a high-born

59

one," said the sentry, "but you come like a Briton and in company with one."

"I am nothing," said Grud, looking at the sky, "do not concern yourself with my unimportance."

"I will bear with your dull wits," said Lydia to the sentry, "but your tribune will not if you persist."

The sentry shrugged and summoned the guard, to let them shoulder the responsibility. They took her, attended by Grud, to the tribune. Marcellus Mercurius received her in his leather-walled, pavilion-style tent pitched in the centre of the Roman camp that overlooked the dwellings of the Durvulavum Britons. Flanked by two centurions and cloaked in magnificence, as befitted his rank and command, he eyed the Roman woman curiously but coldly. Marcellus had heard of Lydia Osirus, a renegade citizen of Rome who had forsaken her own people to follow Canis. And what was Canis but a barbarian upstart and presumptuous dog, a man who, while he lived, was an offence to Rome? Marcellus would give much to lay his hands on the Briton. It would win him the commendation of Paullinus himself. For that matter, the Imperial Governor would not be less than pleased to have Lydia Osirus delivered to him.

She must know that Paullinus would not deal gently with her. Yet she showed a calmness and a rich beauty entirely admirable. He was not to know it was not complacence that made her look so tranquil, but immeasurable courage, for he had no idea of the true character of this woman. He was, however, disdainfully aware of her shabby cloak and patched sandals.

"So," he said, "you are Lydia Osirus, a woman I have been looking for."

"Tribune," said Lydia, "I did not know you were in any need of me."

"Do not mock me, madam." He was bare of head and stern of eye. He sat while she stood. "I have not half the need of you that noble Paullinus has." He would not condemn her, however, strip her of her facade of pride, for though he was haughtily intemperate with lesser people, it was not in him to

60

shame a high-born woman too cruelly, renegade though this one was. "Why have you given yourself up to me?"

"I am here not to give you myself, but to help you take a man called Canis," said Lydia.

"Canis?" His sternness was coupled with suspicion.

"I am not, after all, a Briton myself," said Lydia, "I am a Roman. If I made a mistake, then I would ask Caesar not to make too much of it, for mistakes are common to all of us."

"Not your kind of mistake," said Marcellus coldly.

"Alas, no," sighed Lydia.

Because of her poise and her vivid beauty, Marcellus could not help being impressed. He thought he understood why she was here. Such a woman must have begun to yearn for that which only Rome could bestow. Graciousness, culture, luxury, pleasure.

"So you are wearied of your barbarian, are you, madam? And wish to throw yourself on the mercy of the Governor. Yet if this man beside you is Canis, he is remarkably unlike even the vaguest description I have had of him."

Lydia looked at Grud. Marcellus looked at Grud. Grud looked at Marcellus. Grud was bland, round-eyed, innocent and ageless. He stood quietly inoffensive on his sturdy bow legs, and few would have believed he had been the physician and counsellor of Queen Boadicea. Fewer still would have believed he had ridden with the Queen in her chariot of war, bearing her shield and her standard against the legions of Rome.

"I did not say I had brought Canis," said Lydia, "but that I would help you take him."

Grud spoke.

"I am Grud, and I am all that is left of loyalty to mistress Lydia. I do not question her whims or her reasons, for there is no woman who can give a man logical answers to such questions. Nor is there any woman who acts as a man acts, who thinks as a man thinks, or who reasons as he does. Therefore, I am loyal to mistress Lydia—not for what she does or thinks, but for what she is and for what I am myself. And what I am

61

myself is next to nothing in the eyes of most men, and nothing at all in the eyes of a tribune."

Marcellus, held by the round, innocent orbs of light, felt as if warm seas were enclosing him. He shook his head and made a gesture of impatience.

"I mark you more for a windy, confusing fool," he said, "who babbles to divert me from what I am most concerned with. Namely, a barbarian rebel called Canis. Hear me, Lydia Osirus. This man has slipped great Paullinus himself many times. I question whether he will fall into the pit you are about to dig for him."

"You are a discerning tribune," said Grud, "which is what I have already implied."

"Take care, fool, in me you beard not a pup but a lion," said Marcellus, not given to falsifying his importance. "Stay your tongue, or I will have it slit. Madam," he said to Lydia, "you have betrayed Rome in the past, and now it seems you intend to betray the dog whose kennel you have shared."

"Marcellus Mercurius," said Lydia calmly, "I am here. That is unarguable. I am in your hands. That is also unarguable. You will deliver me to Paullinus—"

"That too is unarguable," said Marcellus sarcastically.

"I cannot go to Paullinus with empty hands," said Lydia, "for if I do he will, as you know, not deal gently with me. But who is to say he will not wholly pardon me, if by my endeavours Canis is delivered to him?"

"I myself would be more than generous," admitted Marcellus. He chewed on his lip. To take Canis, to hand him over to the Imperial Governor. Lydia Osirus looked and spoke as if confident she had the means. Marcellus, reflecting, found himself gazing again into the eyes of the man Grud. Innocence and integrity shone there. "Speak on," he said to Lydia.

"You hold a woman here, a widow, and her children," said Lydia. "By her you think to come at Canis or have him come at you. I am able to tell you, tribune, that Canis will attack Durvulavum an hour before dawn tomorrow."

Marcellus permitted a gleam to brighten his eye.

62

"That is no great news, madam," he said. "I have been expecting the dog for days now. I will take him without your help."

"You will not," said Lydia. "You have dug a pit far more obvious than mine. Canis has scented the trap. Yet he is hot to take the widow and her children from you. But he himself will not lead his warriors. However, if you will generously commend my actions to Paullinus, I will lead you to a place where Canis musters three score warriors in readiness for tomorrow."

"Three score?" Marcellus let his bold Roman nose twitch, such was the measure of his scornful amusement. "Is he so much the braggart he thinks he can take Durvulavum with three score, all with weapons rustier than an earthed iron plough?"

"By no means," said Lydia, hiding the thumping of her heart, "for he will draw far greater numbers from the men of the forests. They are to rendezvous with him tonight. But if you are brave enough to rendezvous with him first, you will take his three score warriors and Canis also. Is that a handsome enough offer, tribune?"

"By Jupiter," said Marcellus, "it is so handsome I mistrust it more than I can say. I also have a nose for a trap. Where is your warranty of good faith?"

"Tribune?" said Lydia, as if in question of his intelligence.

"Where, madam?"

"Where but in myself?" she said. "You hold me as securely as if I were bound and under your feet. You can put me to death at the first sign of falseness." Suddenly she hung her head. "I will take you to Canis," she said in a low voice, "this is a desolate land and I wish to return to Rome."

Here Marcellus remarked the fall in her voice, the glitter of tears in her eyes. He pondered.

"I am impressed," he said, "but I am not convinced."

Grud interposed.

"I am here because she is here," he said, "so I do not think you will hold against me the fact that I too have followed Canis. In the event that you decide my mistress is lying, which

63

she is not, I ask you not to deal unsympathetically with me, for I have unexampled skill in preparing the finest tonics from the humblest ingredients, and an unequalled talent for burnishing armour. I am, therefore, a man worth saving, not hanging." The tongue was confusing, irrelevant.

" Old one or young one, whichever you are," said Marcellus, before his mind could be dulled the more by the bow-legged villain's round eyes and murmurous words, " you afflict my ears like a buzzing. Clamp your teeth on your tongue, I say, and wag it no more." He turned again to Lydia. " Consider this, madam. You have left that rebel dog, you have deserted him; and if he has only half as much sense as arrogance, he will know you seek to return to Rome and will likely betray him. Or, if between the two of you, you seek to betray me at the cost of your life, perhaps your life you have willingly pledged. I am told there is something about the dog which is sinisterly compulsive."

" Tribune," said Lydia in affected weariness, " Canis thinks that Grud and I are on our way to the men of the forest, to bring them to the rendezvous tonight. I asked to undertake the journey with Grud." To Marcellus, her faint smile seemed cynical. " There are no two people Canis trusts more. If you doubt me, then sit here and do nothing, and lose your chance. If you believe me, then come with me. I will take you to Canis, I swear." She hesitated, and her voice was low again as she went on. " There is one reason alone why I must return to Rome in fair favour, and why I do not want to lose my life. I am with child."

" Ah." The doubts of the tribune were blunted. She was, after all, still a Roman and a high-born one. He saw now what she desired. The forgiveness of Rome because of her child. The blessing and fortunes of Rome on the child. But it would be the issue of a barbarian rebel. " You have been unfaithful to Rome in all ways," he said in disgust, " if what you now say is true."

" If there is a physician here he will know I speak true," said Lydia. " I wish for the child to be born in Rome. And because

64

the child is his, for that reason alone Canis will think that I cannot betray him. Tribune, I am a little weary. Give me leave to rest. Then, if you will, let me lead you to Canis. You will take him, I swear."

" Swear not so easily, but on the god you hold dearest," said Marcellus, the anticipation of triumph hot now in his head.

" By Venus, fairest goddess of all," said Lydia evenly, " I swear that all I have said is true, and that I will bring you to where Canis hides with his warriors. It is a three-hour march. Do you have enough men to take him?"

Venus meant nothing to Lydia. She was faithful only to Diana.

" I have men enough," said Marcellus confidently. She had convinced him. Yet not completely. If, despite all, there was some deceit in her, if she hoped he would leave Durvulavum defenceless, she would be disappointed. He would ride out with six score men, and leave almost eighty men. In addition, he would despatch an escorted galloper to bring reinforcements from the garrison quartered at Camritum. Such reinforcements would reach Durvulavum inside four hours. It was midday now. If Canis essayed an attack during the afternoon, the defenders could hold out until the reinforcements arrived. All that Canis could command was a pack of ragged, indifferent, ill-armed Britons. It made sense that Lydia and the man Grud had been sent to call on men of the forests for help.

Marcellus had been in Gaul at the time of Boadicea's rebellion, and had only vague ideas of how Canis used whatever kind of warriors he commanded. None of these ideas coincided with fact.

While the tribune gave his orders and made his dispositions, Lydia took a short rest. Two centurions selected the men who were to ride out, and those who were to stay. One centurion was to stay to conduct any necessary defence, the other was to accompany Marcellus.

In this way had Canis, through the courage of Lydia and the confusing innocence of Grud, contrived the splitting of the forces of Marcellus. And Marcellus, having made his decision and given his orders, wondered how the august Governor would receive the news that Canis had been taken at last. It made for pleasant reflections.

* * *

Agra, the hairy one, concealed within the thick leaf of high branches, watched the Roman cavalry detachment ride out through the gates of Durvulavum, headed by Marcellus himself, red-cloaked and brightly helmeted. Riding with him was Lydia, and behind Lydia rode Grud. Agra counted the horsemen. Six score, according to the number of times he closed his fingers. That left less than four score in Durvulavum, sufficient to contain two hundred dispirited Britons there, but by no means enough, thought Agra, to hold off three hundred warriors trained by the Wolfhead. There was a great chieftain for you, a man to command all Britain. Agra chuckled within his bushy hair, then his narrow eyes sharpened. Through the gates rode three more Romans, taking a southern route that skirted the wood in which Agra was perched. He whistled softly and sweetly. There was movement below him. He pointed. There was an acknowledging whistle, a birdlike piping, and a scurry of legs.

He stayed hidden until the last glitter of armour faded from his eyes, then descended as nimbly as a squirrel. The last of August's sun was at its zenith, pouring heat over forests and heaths. Durvulavum was an encampment built on a gentle hill, and the surrounding country was deeply wooded in parts, wild with heathland elsewhere. Agra sped westwards until he reached a wood mighty with spreading oaks. Lying secure therein were Andudo and Hywel, in command of three hundred Britons. Cea was also there. Fierce because Lydia was so much a part of the plan, the Princess had refused to stay and sit counting her fingers this time. She wore the bright tunic of a warrior maid, and she carried both a spear and a shield.

" In one hour," said Agra, " you may take the place, for the gaudy cockerel has gone with his chickens, six score of them.

66

With him went your brave Roman woman and your man called Grud."

" In one hour, then, we will," said Cea.

Andudo, an iron-grey veteran of craft and strength, who had lost a wife and a daughter to Romans, said, " You are an observant bird in your tall tree, Agra."

" Be you as competent as I am observant," said Agra and went to eat amid the silent ranks of the warrior men and women. Then he remembered the three gallopers, and told Andudo and Cea that although he did not know what their purpose had been, he had not liked their faces. So he had whistled up his fellows. " They will take their heads and their horses," he said, " their heads being for us, their horses for you."

So it was that when the Roman messenger and his two escorts were out of sight of Durvulavum and skirting deep woods to come to the road, whirling thongs of leather weighted with stones came singing through the air to bring down each horse. The whirling thongs wrapped around forelegs and hindlegs. There was no harm to the animals, but the Romans were quickly dead under the daggers of chuckling hairy ones, who carried off their heads and took their horses also.

4

The Romans of Marcellus rode steadily for two hours over country wild and lush. At the end of that time, they reached the edge of a thickly wooded area. It was no great forest, but it was deep enough for the soldiers not to like it. The most compact and disciplined body of troops could not fight an organised battle in an environment where every bush and tree was on the side of the enemy. Marcellus debated whether he was altogether happy. The woods and the forests of Britain were the natural habitat of the darkest barbarians, and there were no barbarians anywhere in this land who could be called spreaders of joy and light.

Lydia assured the tribune, however, that there were no hairy men in these woods. The place was not dark enough for them.

" Canis and his warriors lie north of this point," she said. She was pale, strained. " They are in the valley of the deer stream, and to come to them you must first strike north-west into the woods and then turn east. You will emerge at the head of the valley. If you go any other way it may be easier, but they will mark your coming and slip you." In truth, Lydia did not know any other way, only the track by which she had come. " Your eyes are clouded, tribune, your face dark. Are you beginning to think I am deceiving you?"

" What is upon me is for me to solve," said Marcellus, " and what is upon you is the fact that I have you close and will not easily let you part from me. Cestor! "

The centurion Cestor rode forward. Marcellus directed him to link his mount to Lydia's. The centurion did this by using a rope made of plaited strips of leather. Lydia smiled and put her weariness from her.

68

"Marcellus," she said, "is our going to be a jingle and a clatter? Will you come at Canis as you come at city gates, in mounted panoply? He will hear you while you are still far from him."

"Ride," said Marcellus grimly, "this is no place to leave the horses."

So the detachment rode into the woods, Lydia tethered to the centurion so that the way was awkward for both of them. All others rode in single files. Marcellus called a halt when they were safe from all eyes outside. They dismounted, and Lydia was roped to Cestor. Marcellus left the mounts in the care of ten men, and with the rest of his force thrust forward on foot. Lydia led them silently, through ways that seemed only lightly used, and over tracks that were squeezed by bush and tree. Grud was close to her. Marcellus and Cestor watched both of them intently. The sound of the foraging advance was of breaking twigs, of rustling leaves and of a man's hissing curse as his equipment fouled a branch. Here and there birds twittered and rose in startled flight, or a tiny creature flashed in bright brownness and was gone.

It might not be dark enough for the strange hairy men to dwell in, thought Marcellus grimly, but by every god of darkness it was not a place of sweet light, either.

Each man marched with sword drawn. Each man turned his eyes as often to his left and right as his front. If this was not a forest, what else was it? Whatever it was, it drew them deep into its wild embrace, until those at the rear could not see those in the van. No one spoke. Their feet turned the leaves and the world was an oppressive hush. At intervals they were halted, straining their ears for hostile sound, but heard only Lydia whispering to Marcellus. Constantly she claimed knowledge of the way, constantly she urged on him the necessity for silence, a silence that became a turgid effort on the part of all, so that it startled a man if he heard himself catch his own breath.

And Grud looked at the leaves and marvelled at the performance of the Roman woman.

69

The troops were more than uneasy. They thought themselves locked within an unbreachable barrier of trees. Lydia could have shown them a vaster, thicker prison, that of the great forest north-west of this place. She knew the way through this pleasant if profuse wood. Every other tree bore its guiding mark, every mark the work of Canis and his Britons.

For what seemed an unendurable length of time, the Romans followed Lydia, and because of the strain and oppressiveness the sweat filled their eyes. The soldiers thought Marcellus a fool. Here was no place to fight Britons, here was only a place for ambush and murder. The light itself was eerie. It was not like the clear, bright light of the Seven Hills of Rome. A man did not mind sweating in the open air, but sweating in a forest was like being clothed in hot, wet sacks. Every sword hand grew limp and clammy.

Lydia stopped. Marcellus flung up a hand. The long line of perspiring men halted with no more sound than a heavy sigh. Marcellus drew closer to Lydia, his sword ready to deal with any sign of treachery.

"At fifty paces from here," she whispered, "you will break from this cover and look down into the valley and see the stream. There you will also see Canis and his three score. I have brought you to him. Your work is your own from now on."

Marcellus looked at Cestor. The centurion nodded and put the point of his sword to Lydia's breast, while the tribune went silently and stealthily forward for fifty nerve-racking paces. He looked down through trees and what he saw was what Lydia had said he would.

There was a small valley, its banks clear and green save for a few bushes. It was a bright green after so much wild and confusing colour. There was a tiny stream, summer low, and on the left bank above the sparkling water lolled a number of Britons. Aye, and scurvy enough in truth to belong to none other than the scurviest of upstarts, he thought. There were short-kilted warrior women among them, and these made his mouth tighten in distaste. Then he smiled. He permitted himself this, though it didn't go beyond a smile of stern satisfaction.

There lay the Britons' weapons, piled untidily to one side of a smouldering fire, and in charge of them were two men who whistled softly as they burnished each one clean of rust. The other Britons lazed in idle, oblivious talk, or even in oblivious sleep. There was only one man on his feet. Marcellus remarked him a taller man than usual, a strongly lean man, who stood near the fire talking to a laughing warrior woman with long hair the colour of ripe corn. The tall man turned from her at that moment and stirred the embers of the fire with his foot.

Marcellus, tightly concealed, began a quick count. Lydia Osirus had been right. There were no more than sixty Britons, give or take a rogue or two, and all of them as unsoldierly as only barbarians could be. Warriors, were they? Marcellus permitted himself another smile. This rabble could not have lifted a stone from a crumbling city wall, much less successfully invest Durvulavum. Yet, knowing their slippery ways, he would not have put it beyond them to accomplish something by cunning.

As for the women, young ones at that, they were parodies. Marcellus, like all Romans, was disdainful of the Iceni custom of turning women into warriors. Paullinus had been so incensed by the shameless presence of Boadicea's warrior maids in battle that he had been merciless in his defeat of the Queen. By the example of Paullinus he, Marcellus Mercurius, would sternly deny these motley warrior women all rights as true women.

"By fiery Mars," he told himself, "if I do not take every rogue and harlot here, I will break my own sword and carry it no more. Instead I will wear in my belt any pretty thing common to a tittering female. Canis, rebel dog, if you are there among your rogues, then bedevilled you are by complacency, indulgence and your trust in a woman faithless to both you and Rome."

He made his way back. He met Lydia's eyes, greenly brooding now. He smiled. Lydia shivered and hid her face within her curtain of hair. Marcellus whispered orders and his men filed forward, some to the left, some to the right, to

71

enfilade the valley. They moved as silently as they could. Marcellus, with ten men, advanced again to the point that gave such a clear view of the stream. Cestor brought Lydia and Grud on the heels of the tribune. Marcellus waited with his nerves sharp, Lydia in pale apprehension and Grud imperturbably. To Grud all things were either pre-determined or inevitable. Neither man's anxiety, nor his hope, influenced the course of life or events.

With Marcellus and his ten men holding the head of the valley, and with the rest of the Romans taking up positions on each side of it, it seemed that the Britons must smell the creeping advance in the flanking woodlands, even if they could not see. But in their indolent sense of security they appeared to have neither eyes nor noses. As for their ears, these were full of the sounds of their lazy voices, of the running stream and the clatter of weapons as the burnishers rummaged for the rustier ones in the untidy pile.

Lydia could not look, but did. She had eyes then only for the taller man, observing his lack of concern, his unawareness. He spoke to one of the burnishers and stirred the fire again.

Lydia felt play-acting such as that was not to be borne.

The centurion Cestor, after one sweeping glance down the valley, kept his eyes on her. She would pay dearly if anything went amiss. Shackled to him by the leather rope she was the Romans' surety against trickery. Her hands closed into white-knuckled fists, her nails gouged into her damp palms and desperately, silently, she prayed to Diana.

Grud sood in bow-legged contemplation, his mind apparently blank.

The signal came from down the valley, beyond the idling Britons, one sharp clear call. Instantly both sides of the defile were alive as the armoured Romans poured from cover. A hundred bright swords caught the filtered light and the light danced. From the head of the valley came Marcellus himself with his ten men, and while the Britons were still stunned and agog at the suddenness of it all, the Romans were plunging down on them and surrounding them. The Britons leapt to

72

their feet. They ran, they darted, they went all ways, but all ways were blocked by Romans. They turned in panic to rush for their weapons, but their weapons were kicked aside. Men and maids ran into the stream in an attempt to splash through the closing net. But the net drew tight and the Britons, for the most part unarmed and helpless, were squeezed and trapped.

Cestor came down the sloping bank with Lydia and Grud, and Lydia watched as short, heavy swords beat flat all Britons who sought to make a stand. Blood ran from cracked pates. One by one the motley band of warriors flung themselves down amid grass and pebbles in gestures of surrender. The tall man, seeing no escape, placed himself as inconspicuously as he could within a group of moody, cursing comrades. Marcellus, noting this, smiled.

It was over within minutes. He had taken all of them alive, and without a single one of his men showing a scratch. He entered the ring of soldiers to look more closely at his prisoners. The women hid their faces, the men showed theirs, eyeing the magnificence of the tribune without comment.

"Should any of you move, it will be the worse for him, or her," said Marcellus, and was gratified to remark the air of resigned humility this induced. "Speak now, which of you calls himself Canis and was once infamously associated with the widow Boadicea?" Despite their humility none of the Britons answered his question. Nor did anyone point a finger. Far from being disappointed, Marcellus dwelt on the more subtle pleasure of having Lydia Osirus name the wanted one. The wanted one was assuredly there. But that need not deprive anyone of the spectacle of betrayer and betrayed coming face-to-face. Marcellus called for Cestor. The centurion approached, Lydia perforce with him.

The Britons raised their eyes to stare at her. They saw how she was roped to the centurion, and how she bent her head and let her black hair fall over her face.

"Well, madam? Which of these brave warriors is Canis?" Marcellus was mocking in his sarcasm. The Britons twitched, Lydia winced and the Romans smiled.

73

But the denouement was not the drama Marcellus expected to savour. There was no emotive note, no sense of fine tragedy. Lydia merely pointed to the tall man and said, " He is Canis." And Canis did not even look at her. He sat with some of his men, and seemed concerned with nothing except his feet. However, in a briefly dramatic way a warrior maid spat. A Roman soldier cuffed her. Marcellus gestured, and two of his men laid hands on Canis, hauled him upright, and brought him before the finely-clad tribune. It would have accorded better with the tribune's pride in himself if he had not found himself a head shorter than the dog.

However, he had him.

So this was the man whose capture and death Paullinus obsessively desired.

The grey eyes drew his own, the strong brown face expressed rueful whimsy. Marcellus frowned. Where was the alarm at having been caught, the fury at having been betrayed? If there at all they were out of sight, hidden in those compelling grey eyes, which seemed only to ask: 'What now?' Within Marcellus an uneasiness stirred, a suspicion that this was not the end but the beginning. He shook it off, for whatever else might obtain he had Canis, and he also had Lydia Osirus. She had kept faith, for Marcellus knew without a doubt that this man was indeed Canis, whom some said rivalled Paullinus himself as a general. Perhaps that was what irked Paullinus so much.

" So you are Canis," said Marcellus.

The Briton's hard mouth broke into a friendly smile.

" I am. Who are you?"

" At this moment," said Marcellus, willing to exchange whimsy for whimsy, " I think our illustrious Governor would say I am the worthiest tribune under his command."

" Ah," said Canis.

" You have cost us dear in many ways, dog's meat, but be in no doubt that Rome will exact full and sufficient payment."

" I am in no doubt at all," said Canis, while Britons and Romans looked on—and Lydia, now that the issue had become

74

so nerve-rackingly dangerous, strove to hide her shivers. "Other nations might accept payment in gold," continued Canis, "but Rome, in the person of your illustrious Governor, will only accept blood."

"When Paullinus has had yours," said Marcellus, "both he and Rome will be content. Bind him."

They bound the wrists of Canis behind his back. Canis said, "Since I am so much in your hands, tribune, will you grant me one favour?"

Generosity sat magnanimously on Marcellus, as it does on any triumphant commander.

"Speak your favour, Briton, and I will give you aye or no according to its reasonableness."

"I ask that you keep the Roman woman from my sight, for in truth what I thought fair and sweet to look on has in fact the core of wormy fruit."

Marcellus smiled. So did Canis, in seemingly bitter acceptance of that which the tribune found amusing. And Lydia bit on a trembling lip; her green eyes glittered wetly, and she turned her face from Canis. Grud mused on the running stream.

"Blind fool," said Marcellus pleasantly, "do you not know you may have pleasure from certain women, but not fidelity? You are not the first to kiss the sweet face of falseness. I will grant this favour, in that when we go from here she shall ride with her back to you."

"It is not full dispensation, but it is enough," said Canis. He wore only his woven tunic, and was without weapons. Even Cerdwa's axe was not in his belt. He had given it into the safe keeping of Andudo, not wanting it to fall into Roman hands. When Cerdwa lay dying on the field of Boadicea's tragic defeat, he had promised his bright and beautiful warrior maid that he would take her axe and return it to her when he himself died. He did not, however, envisage dying today.

Marcellus issued crisp orders. His soldiers broke the weapons of the Britons and cast them into the stream. Others bound the captives' wrists, then roped them one to the other in a long line. At the head of the line was Canis. Wanda, new comrade to his warriors, contrived to be roped immediately behind him.

" We are taken, lord," she murmured, " and I confess I did not think, despite your strange orders, that you would let it happen without a little Roman blood being spilt, or allow them to bind us like slaves."

" When the odds are so heavy, Wanda, it is wiser to wait for lighter ones."

" All the same," she said, as the Romans made ready to march their captives away, " the tales I have been told of you did not paint a picture of your timidity, but your valour."

" Tales are woven around what the poets wish men to be, not what they are."

" Aye, lord, perhaps this is so," murmured Wanda, " and I have not wholly lost faith in you."

" My relief is beyond anything," said Canis.

He had not told Wanda, or any of his warriors here, all that he hoped would unfold. He had told them to surrender if Romans arrived, and thereafter to trust him.

Marcellus was intent on taking his prisoners to Durvulavum without delay. If all went well, they would arrive before sunset; Canis secure, the garrison intact, and the reinforcements there to command additional surety. It would not do for night to fall before Durvulavum was reached, for at night the barbarians and their uncivilised friends could be even more slippery than by day. There was no telling whether their friends were not already aware that a boldly venturesome tribune had taken Canis. A single disturbed leaf could tell all to the kind of friends the Britons had.

So Marcellus had his men and his captives quickly on the move. Lydia and Grud, under the purposeful persuasion of Cestor, led the return through the sprawling woods, this time without the necessity of making any tactical detour. Taking their bearings from the sun, they headed direct south to the place where they had left the horses. Lydia said they would

76

get lost. Marcellus said, "March on." Lydia said she did not know this way, and she did not. Marcellus said "March on, march south."

Grud said, "We are marching east." Marcellus shot him a stony look, but was disturbed all the same. The woods in the heat of the afternoon were more oppressive. "Let me lead," said Grud, "I have the nose." And he had, for he was a man of the forests before he went to Venta Icenorum to serve Boadicea. He took the worry from brave Lydia, and led the way.

It was an ordeal for all; one of harried nerves for the Romans, and one of endurance for the roped Britons, discouraged from lagging by blows and buffets. Lydia remained shackled to Cestor, and Grud now had a noose around his neck, the end of the noose wrapped around the wrist of the soldier who marched behind him. Not until they were inside the walls of Durvulavum, would Marcellus relax his watch on Lydia and her man Grud. His every instinct told him not to fully trust a woman who had forsaken Rome and then betrayed her lover.

Lydia moved like a sleepwalker, with only her courage to numb her fear.

Grud went unconcernedly and in a sure line.

Marcellus marched in magnificence, though this was clammily attacked by sweat. It was a perspiring effort for all, more especially for the armoured Romans, who found the wild, lush woodland like a humid oven. The heat that invaded it seemed unable to escape. It was with relief that Marcellus eventually realised the man Grud had kept faith on behalf of his mistress. They reached the tethered horses. Here the Romans mounted, Lydia and Grud also. As the column of prisoners became flanked on each side by horsed soldiers, Marcellus rode up to Canis.

"Because of the desperate battle you gave us," he said ironically, "it slipped my mind to speak of the Roman woman, Lydia Osirus, being with child."

Canis lifted his gaze to the leafy roof of the woods.

77

" It was not a grievous omission, tribune. What man wishes to be reminded of his foolishness in lying with so worthless a woman?"

" She is a high-born Roman," said Marcellus coldly, " and you but a barbarian dog. The child will be born in Rome and then strangled." And he leaned from his horse and struck Canis across the mouth. He turned, rode to the head of his detachment, and signalled the advance. As they broke out of the woods, the mounted Romans began to canter, and the roped Britons had to trot. Lydia again went linked to Cestor. It did not endear either him or Marcellus to her.

For lengthy stages they proceeded in this fashion. The sweat dribbled blindingly from the skin of the Britons, but they endured, for life under Canis in the forest was not the kind to make weaklings of any of them. Because their hands were bound behind them, the going was difficult and often cruel, running as they had to between the columns of cantering Romans. Blows delivered with flat swords quickly brought a stumbler upright again. At the end of each stage, Marcellus called a brief halt, whereupon the Britons were allowed to sink to the ground and rest. During one such rest Wanda, in some temerity, called the tribune. He came, his stern countenance imparting disdain as he took in the gleam of her bare thighs, below her shamelessly short tunic.

" Noble and most generous Roman," said Wanda, gold in her hair, " since you have Canis and he is to suffer slow death, will you not have his bonds eased? Their tightness is taking the blood from his hands."

Marcellus would have ordered a soldier to look into the complaint, but sharp with sudden suspicion he dismounted to inspect the bonds himself. This done he turned a cold eye on the forest maid.

" There is more in your mind than sympathy, harlot," he said. " His bonds would not even chafe the wrists of a child. Am I a fool? I am not." .

He had them all on their feet and trotting again. Wanda, panting a little, managed to reach the ear of Canis.

" I did but hope he might ease the leather, lord, and so help me to help you escape, for I am one who wishes to save you for a better day."

" Save your breath instead," said Canis.

Driven through areas thick with brushwood and briar, the way became brutally painful for the captives. Thorn reached and blood ran from scratched and torn flesh. In places where they were compelled by thicket to go at walking pace, the Romans hustled them. In the end, however, their health and strength prevailed, and they reached Durvulavum without loss or casualty. The land was wild with colour, the sun a radiance of burning gold. Marcellus was relieved to see the encampment nestling squatly peaceful against the gilded evening sky. It was still an hour before sunset. It had been no mean accomplishment. They rode up the winding, undulating ascent, reaching the road that led to the gates, the line of captives gleaming with sweat. Two helmeted sentries stood at the gates. Cestor, as conscious as his tribune that they were still vulnerable to ambush, roared for the gates to be opened. The sentries moved, the gates were opened, and the cavalcade of soldiers and prisoners almost flattened the men against the gates as they charged in. The sentries made no complaint, however. The manoeuvre was as expedient as they could have wished, and as soon as the cavalcade had passed through they closed and barred the gates.

And within the encampment Marcellus found only silence and a seeming emptiness. Of humble Iceni citizens there was none, of his garrison force there was no sign. The silence was as brooding as the emptiness.

" What is this?" he shouted. " Cestor! "

Cestor, Lydia still linked to him, rode up to the tribune. The centurion was as aware of the stillness as anyone. Marcellus turned a coldly rageful eye on Lydia.

" Woman," he said harshly, " I have Canis, aye. Who has Durvulavum?"

Exhaustion racked Lydia. Her thickening body swayed in the saddle and Grud, close to her, put out a helpful hand. Marcellus

79

fetched him a blow that toppled the young-old mystic from his horse.

"Truly," he murmured from the ground, "I will not hold the blow against you, tribune, for I understand why your mood is not as proudly cheerful as it was."

Fortunately, Marcellus did not hear this. He was listening to Lydia.

"Aye, you have Canis." Her voice was tired. "But as to Durvulavum, who has it or who has lost it, this is not my responsibility. Such responsibility as I did have, I have discharged."

"I smell treachery," hissed Marcellus, wheeling his horse this way, then that, and still seeing only emptiness. "By great Jupiter himself, madam, and by every god who condones the right of vegeance, you shall be the first to feel mine. Viper and harlot, where are the people of Durvulavum, where are my soldiers?"

"Tribune," said Lydia palely, "I have kept my word, I have done what I said I would do. And I am still your prisoner. Will even a harlot court death so foolishly?"

"Tribune," interposed Cestor, his expression harsh, "is the man we hold the one we want? Is he Canis? It is in my mind that we have been tricked on every count, that Canis has been here while we have wandered elsewhere."

Marcellus swore, but Lydia said quietly, "Be in no doubt, tribune, the man you hold is Canis."

"The sentries," said Cestor, "call the sentries! They will provide the answer to this mystery in one way or another."

But before Marcellus could bring his confused, angry mind to bear on this suggestion, the emptiness filled and the silence dissolved. From folded ground, from the Roman compound and square hutments leapt three hundred Britons and groups of their hairy friends, the hairy ones dancing like shaggy bears. Redly the sun flashed on spears and swords. The Romans, reacting quickly, wheeled all ways so that they formed an outward-facing circle of defence. A few mounts shied before planting all four legs in trained immobility.

Marcellus, the tables turned, was white with fury. He was surrounded by a sea of spears and captured Roman swords and javelins.

"Lord," whispered Wanda to Canis, "it was unkind to tell me so little and fool me so much."

"Some women are for comfort, not for telling," said Canis.

Marcellus drove his horse forward, leapt down and put his sword point to the Briton's throat. Lydia stiffened in her saddle, and rushed a hand to her mouth to stifle a frantic cry.

"Do not even blink," hissed Marcellus, "or I will drive in this blade until it reaches your backbone."

Canis, the point tickling his skin, regarded the enraged tribune with clear, frank eyes. Voices hummed, confusion and bitterness took the Romans and triumph showed on the faces of Britons.

Canis said, "You are bested, tribune. You would have spared this, if you had stayed to hold Durvulavum instead of taking me. With your full garrison, you could have held the place against us. I am of no more account than any man, except in the eyes of Paullinus. In your consideration of Paullinus, you have lost Durvulavum and must relinquish me."

"By no means," hissed Marcellus, "for I will not give up the joy of spitting you, barbarian dog!"

"Tribune!" A great voice roared. Marcellus did not move. A soldier dismounted to take hold of Canis, forcing him to his knees and pulling back his head so that his throat was mercilessly stretched to the sword. "Tribune!" roared the voice again. It belonged to Andudo. "Of your men here, thirty still live, but all these and those with you, and you also, tribune, will die most bloodily if you do not ground your sword. None will die swiftly. Do you hear me?"

"I hear you," shouted Marcellus, "as now you shall hear me! Lay down your arms, lay them down, I say, or I will slit your leader's throat. I have him here and I swear he will drown in his blood if you do not heed me. Come what may, I have the rogue and will keep him, sweetly dead or warmly breathing,

81

according to your discretion or your foolishness. Lay down your weapons."

For a moment there was silence. Then came a woman's voice, clear and musical and fearless.

"Open your ears, Roman." Lydia, frantic at the sight of Canis so close to death, recognised the voice as Cea's. It went on, its clarity marked by underlying vibrations of anger. "Put so much as the smallest wound on Canis and I swear your men will die in agony. And you, tribune, will be returned to Paullinus with your eyes put out and your tongue torn from your mouth and your fingers hacked from your hands to provide tidbits for the dogs. Thus you will be unable to speak or write of how ten score Romans died under your command here. Nor will you be able to see how Paullinus will regard you for your miserable incompetence."

Sweat stood suddenly cold on the brow of Marcellus. A shiver beset him, a shiver of rage, of fear, of impotence. Cestor growled. The shackled Britons looked upon Marcellus, and saw his cold sweat.

Diana, oh Diana, prayed Lydia, let him not use that sword.

"Give the word, tribune," spoke Cestor, "and we will scatter them to the walls, and break their backs against the stone."

"Fool!" Marcellus flung the word bitterly. "They will let the horses through and pull every man from his saddle." With an imprecation that was a savage denunciation of Mars for his indifference, he grounded his sword. Lydia breathed again, and Canis eased his head free. He rose to his feet.

"You are bested, tribune," he said again, "but you shall have your lives—though you swore Rome would deprive me of mine—if your men will give up their arms. We will then treat with you."

New fury showed on the tribune's livid face. His sword point was grounded, but his hand tightened around the hilt. Lydia's green eyes begged Canis not to provoke him so. But though provoked, Marcellus was not so much the fool as to give in to

82

the impulse of rage when his hands, his eyes and his tongue were at stake. In frustration he threw down his sword.

"Aye, I am bested," he said bitterly, "but as I granted you a favour, now grant me one. Let me keep that woman."

"Ask a different favour," said Canis, "for that woman must stay with me."

"If you will hang her from a tree and roast her feet with hot iron while she swings," said Marcellus, "that will be favour enough."

It was not enough for Cestor. He drew his sword.

"They may do what they like with me," he said to Lydia, "but I shall see you die first."

He drew back his arm to strike, but Agra came like a round shaggy ball catapulted from a giant sling, his leap taking him up to wind his long arms around the centurion. He pulled him from his horse, and they hit the ground together. Agra bounced, Cestor thudded. He lay still.

"Speak, tribune," called Cea.

"We will treat with you," shouted Marcellus in savage irritability. Cestor sat up. Marcellus pulled him to his feet, shook him to his senses and spoke to him. Cestor, incredulous but obedient, ordered the Romans to dismount and lay down their weapons. Marcellus in his pride would not give the order himself. Cursing, and vowing by Mars to repay the Britons one day, the troops obeyed the centurion. Canis glanced up at Lydia, still on her horse. She was white with strain and exhaustion, but returned his look with green eyes swimming. He smiled his admiration for her initiative and courage.

As the Romans flung down their weapons, Cea rode out from the circle of Britons. Marcellus, arms folded, his magnificence diminished by his mortification, looked up as she approached. He stared broodingly at her. She was lissom, shapely, beautiful, and sat on her horse in almost regal fashion, her chin high. Her flowing auburn hair was aflame in the evening sun. She wore a blue cloak, girdled to cover her tunic; and she looked as Boadicea her mother had looked, when she too was young.

The Britons were in pride of her. Except for Canis, whose expression was grim. Agra cut his bonds, he rubbed his wrists and stepped forward, eyeing Cea with anything but approval. He knew the folly of having her disclose her identity to Romans. They still thought her dead. If Paullinus suspected otherwise, he would send an army in search of her—for he would never permit the decimated Iceni nation to rise again under the banner of Boadicea's daughter. Cea had much of her mother's pride and temper, and might in an impulsive moment betray her identity by making a declaration of her rights. A Roman tribune was just such a man to provoke that impulse. Far better for her to remain dead in the minds of all Romans until they reached the western mountains.

"Tribune," said Canis, compelling the attention of all, "she who sits her horse so well is our chief warrior maid, and is called Cedra. Speak softly to her if you must speak, for she has a mettlesome spirit."

"Ah," said Cea with a sigh, and her brown eyes acknowledged his design. The look he gave her in return, however, made her seethe. It was one of grim rebuke.

"Suffer me to own a disapproval of all maids who inhabit fields of war," said Marcellus stiffly, while his Romans mulled and glowered.

"Well, Canis?" said Cea.

"It was a long day," he said brusquely.

"Is that all? No, it is not," she said, as her eyes travelled over the roped Britons. "They are bruised and bloody," she said. "Is that the work of the tribune here?"

"You may say so," said Canis, "and you may also say he has a tendency to smite a man for something which is not his concern."

"Unbind my warriors, tribune," said Cea, high on her horse.

"Am I myself to do this?" asked Marcellus incredulously.

"Roman," said Cea without sweetness, "if you can show me another man who was more responsible than you for binding our warriors and bringing them scratched and bloody

84

to Durvulavum, then I will command him to unbind them."

Marcellus sensed a consequence painful and degrading if he did not shoulder his lot. He turned. He saw the thorn-gashed, briar-scratched flesh of the roped Britons, but what the fuss was about he could not see. Andudo approached and handed him a dagger. Marcellus, in a fury of irritation and humiliation, took it. His silent men watched him as he began to cut the Britons loose. No one spoke, either Roman or Briton, as in the loneliness of his deflated pride, Marcellus moved down the line of his erstwhile captives until he had slashed the bonds of all. Lydia put out her arm. From her wrist trailed the tether by which Cestor had kept her close for so long. Marcellus, looking as if he would have preferred to cut her head off, cut the tether instead. Lydia sighed and drooped, the sun a red mist in her eyes. She began to topple from her saddle. Canis reached to take her, and as blackness descended she felt herself in the strong comfort of his arms. He called Hywel.

"Take her to the best women you can find in this place," he said, "they will know how to see to her. Tell them she deserves their sweetest charity, for this day she has been braver than any of us."

She was a Roman; but Hywel took her limp body from Canis as if the burden was precious. He carried her with a warm heart to the women of Durvulavum, who with the rest of the inhabitants lay concealed in their dwellings. They had been told by Hywel and Andudo to bury their heads and make no sound, on pain of having their noses cut off. Now, however, they were free to breathe again.

Under the red-gold light of the dipping sun, the warriors and the hairy ones still stood motionless, some of the Trinovantes chewing their moustaches and some of the warrior maids looking hungrily at the morose Romans. The freed captives were counting each other's scratches, and Wanda boxed the ears of a man who, taken with the golden look of her thighs, was counting scratches that weren't there.

Canis took Marcellus aside, the Roman soldiers turning

their faces from their discredited commander. Cea, Andudo and Grud listened as Canis spoke.

"There is no time to sit round a table with you, tribune," he said, "nor is there need to. Let us have brevity and no argument. Your lives have been spared, as promised. In return, you will allow us to carry away all weapons, all equipment and all food—save that which will feed you and your men for one day. We will also take all your horses and all the people who are not Romans."

"Ye gods," breathed Marcellus, thrusting his armoured chest from his red cloak, "you spare my life and my command, but take so much else that all you leave me with, even my life, is worth nothing."

"It is worth more than you have ever left any Briton with," said Cea burningly.

"Since Britons became rebels they have deserved less than nothing," said Marcellus, "which is reasonable except to rebels."

"Rebels?" Cea's brown eyes were hot. "Did you not scourge my—did you not scourge Queen Boadicea for claiming her rightful due? Was that reasonable? Did you not—" Cea broke off, feeling the admonishing grip of Canis's hand on her arm. She flushed a little, but did not quarrel with his warning. She went on, "Roman, do not speak to me of the infallibility of Rome and the undeserving nature of all other people, or I will sit you in a cauldron of boiling water and watch you steam."

She would never have done so; but being a princess and her mother's daughter she liked the sound of such proud words.

Marcellus, feeling that for a warrior maid, even the most finely robed one, she had more than enough to say for herself, said disdainfully, "Madam, I am hot enough already, I have been on fire from the moment I rode through the gates. Would that I had looked on the faces of those sentries, and not seen only their backs." To Canis he said, "I doubt if the people of this place will go with you. But I am unable to prevent you taking the town itself on your shoulders, if you feel you must. However, I am still curious about Lydia Osirus? I heard you praise her bravery. Was it myself she fooled? Or was it you? Or both of us?"

"Alas, tribune," said Canis frankly, "it was you. With her help and with the assistance of Grud, a man of confusing words, we contrived the splitting of your force. Lydia, once committed to her part, had to bring you to me and see me taken. Otherwise you would have slain her or delivered her to Paullinus. Remember, however, that you owe your lives not to our clemency but to Lydia's plea on your behalf. She did not wish death for any of you."

"But some are very dead," said Marcellus, "I heard a fellow with a loud voice say so."

"That was in fair battle for this place," said Canis, which reminded Marcellus that in the event of any battle he had placed reliance on reinforcements from Camritum. He had a feeling now that the Britons had taken care of that too.

"I am destroyed," he said gloomily, "for though I have my life, I would be better dead."

"We will leave you one weapon," said Canis agreeably, "and with it you can bring yourself to this better state."

Andudo muttered at the time-wasting niceties of it all, and Grud grumbled under his breath. Purple streaked the sky, and the armour of the dejected Romans glinted redly. Cea's auburn hair caught fire. She watched Canis as he gave Andudo instructions concerning all that had to be done. He was so enduring. He had been the love, the inspiration and also the torment of her tempestuous mother. Now he was her own love, her strength and joy. All the same, he sometimes gave himself airs which made her grind her teeth and stamp her foot.

She had waited anxiously and feverishly with Andudo and her warriors, after they had swarmed over the walls of Durvulavum and captured it with a small loss. Canis had taught them how to attack a depleted enemy. Never frontally, but from all sides. And the encampment of Durvulavum was

87

no high-walled fortress. She had thought of so many ways in which the rest of their plans could go wrong, and had been passionately opposed to the fearful risk of Canis allowing Marcellus to take him. She had wondered if once Lydia was in Roman hands herself, she might not be genuinely tempted to betray Canis. Providing Canis had still slipped the net, the Princess would not have been too sorry, for it would have meant the end of Lydia in his eyes; and she, Cea, could have put aside her jealousy of the Roman woman. But no, Lydia had succeeded in doing all that Canis had asked of her.

Cea sighed. For all the fact that Lydia was a mote in her eye, she felt a generous love for her in the way she had so valiantly played her part.

Now they must be gone from Durvulavum. But first Canis must explain why he had been so grimly disapproving of her, when she first showed herself to Marcellus. Dismounted, the Princess drew him aside. He was overseeing the activity. But that was not as important to Cea as her complaint.

" Why, when the day had gone so well for us," she said, " did you look pleasantly upon others, but sourly upon me?"

" Cea," he said, " you appeared before Marcellus looking like a princess, and speaking like one. I will allow you to be impulsive, but not foolish."

" You will allow me?" She was so hotly incensed that she could not draw breath for a moment. " Oh, my ears! They ring. You are not King yet!"

" Nor will you ever be Queen, if you give Romans reasons to suspect your true identity." She had rarely had him so stern with her. " Did I not say you were not to show yourself?"

" I am not to be commanded by any man," she breathed, her brown eyes furious that he could speak so grimly to her. " I am the Queen's daughter, and I will not have you scold me, I will not!"

She was Boadicea's sweetly proud daughter, and Canis loved her for her temper.

" Sweet Cea, have I put salt on your tongue? I am sorry,"

he said. He saw her lip quiver. He smiled and said gently,
" Princess, do not put your tender life at greater risk than it is
already, by making Romans look twice at you. Be to them
only another warrior maid. We lost our majestic Queen. We
do not wish to lose her daughter also."

Her pride was no match for this. Mist rushed into her eyes.
" Oh, do you not see?" she whispered. " I only want you
to love me, to be sweet to me."

" Who else is in my eyes but you?" he said.

Grud came to grumble a few minutes later.

" Time," he said, " is not something that stands about for
people."

" What is time to you, old goat?" said Canis. " Go and sit
with Lydia, for you and she share this day."

" I counted for nothing," said Grud, " and it is you who
should sit with her, if you wish to please her. When you go
to her, remember her courage. What is to be done with the
people of Durvulavum? They still sit in their dwellings."

" They would rather you let them sit," said Marcellus,
appearing at Grud's shoulder. Canis, saying nothing, watched
his warriors divesting the encampment and the garrison of all
they intended to carry off. " You must know, even if the
people here do not," said Marcellus in bitter malice, " that if
you take the widow and her children with you, Paullinus will
claim other hostages—aye, treble the number of Romans you
have slain here—and put them all to death to show you that
your trickery cannot outlast his vengeance."

" His vengeance," said Canis, " will one day make him put
out his own eyes for seeing rain when he ordered sun." He
called Hywel. " Hywel, have the people show themselves.
Have them assemble away from all Romans here. The
business between them and us is not for Roman ears."

Marcellus was taken back to his own lines. His men turned
their backs on him. A ring of armed Britons squeezed them
tightly. Hywel began to assemble the inhabitants. They
emerged slowly from their dwellings. They were anxious,
worried. They knew how Durvulavum had been taken, the

widow and her two children delivered, but they did not seem overjoyed. They were thin and hungry people, and among them were many widows and many children.

Canis addressed them, his resonant voice carrying to every ear.

" I have been told," he said, " that yours is a community given to weeping. I do not suffer tears unless they are for lost child or dead mother. From this day on, none shall weep without fair cause. All will contrive to live, if not with a smile, then with brave endurance. Your kin fought fiercely for Queen Boadicea, and I have never heard that any of them wept unduly, not even on our most tragic day. So I tell you, from now on you will lead braver lives, for you will serve Princess Cea, daughter of Queen Boadicea—your ruler by right and heritage."

They saw Princess Cea. Canis did not point her out, but they knew her. In her blue robe and natural pride, she stood out among the warrior maids there. They would not betray to Romans the fact that they had seen her, but they did not acclaim her, either. If Romans came to know that she had been here, and that they had acclaimed her, then the consequences would be miserable. And what they wanted was not more misery than they already had, not different privations under the refugee Princess, but more bread, and more bread they could only have by behaving themselves.

" Who among you is eager to come with us?" asked Canis.

They looked at him, tall, lean and cruelly hard. They shifted their feet, they coughed. But one woman stepped forward, a comely woman with two children by her side. She was the widow. She did not know how to thank Canis, and could only say quietly, " Lord, we will go with you, and gladly."

No others moved or spoke. Canis waited. Some of the people did not like the look on his face. It held nothing of pity or kindness. In the end, a man coughed himself into speech.

" Canis, lord," he said, " if many of us do not show cheer at

90

your victory today, it is because we have come to a sorry state here. In truth, we do not know one day whether we will be alive the next. Such an existence makes most people dull. So, though the day is great for you, we beg you not to make any issue of it with us, but to go on your way and leave us in peace."

"Someone," said Canis bitingly, "must tell this man of dullness what will happen to him if we leave him in peace." He sent Hywel to bring Marcellus. With a sweet smile, Cea withdrew, placing herself amid the warrior maids. Durvulavum was glowingly luminous under the dying glory of the red sun. Marcellus came, empurpled by the light. "Speak to these people, Roman," said Canis, "and tell them what will happen if they do not go with us."

Marcellus was only too willing to vent some of his spleen on people whose ordinary existence constituted one of the most irritating causes of his most humiliating day.

"By reason of what has happened this day," he said to them, "the Imperial Governor will charge me to take from among you hostages which will more than equate his loss of the widow and our slain soldiers. And all such hostages will be put to death. Only in one way can you escape this, and that is by using courage and ingenuity to render this man Canis helpless, imprison his warriors and free my troops." He saw the consternation on the people's faces and went on, not only to mock them, but to mock himself. "Come, then. If you wish to have illustrious Paullinus regard you benignly, seize Canis, smite his warriors and return to my men their weapons."

"We are mocked and laughed at," cried a youth, seeing the derision on the faces of the warrior maids.

"Aye, so you are," said Canis, "but if you love the joy of weeping above all other joys, then return to your dwellings and wait for Paullinus to put upon you an ocean of tears. And since we shall carry away most of what food is in the Roman storehouse, you can abandon yourselves most rapturously to woe." With that, he turned away from them and sent Marcellus back to his Romans under escort.

There were murmurs, cries, arguments, despair. But in the end the elder of the people stepped forward.

" We will go with you, lord—for we have lived too long with self-pity, and need to be uplifted. But how may we go with brave hearts?"

Canis answered, " By remembering you were the people of Queen Boadicea, and are now the people of Princess Cea. By remembering that the house of Boadicea is indestructible, as are her people. And by remembering you were once proud and fearless, and can be so again."

" And by not forgetting," murmured Grud to the sky, now in purple retreat from the day, " that we shall have the food."

The decision made, the people of Durvulavum laughed and wept and ran about, imparting to each other the infectious courage that lay on excited tongues. The warriors began to prepare for imminent departure, and Andudo hustled the people into making similar preparations.

Grud said to Canis, " You have wagged your tongue at everyone—at us, at the Romans and at the people here. All except Lydia. Is she alone to be ignored, given no thanks for her bravery?"

" I have not forgotten her," said Canis. " Nor you, old goat." He clapped Grud on the shoulder and went to see Lydia. She lay pale and wan within the dwelling of some widows, but her eyes brightened to see him.

" I am better now," she said, " my weakness was foolishness. When the blade was at your throat, I thought you had taken one risk too many."

He went down on one knee beside the pile on which she lay. She put out a hand. He took it. He smiled into her swimming green eyes.

" My risk was small beside yours," he said, " and what man could have put his trust in a braver woman? We owe you much, Lydia."

" Is it enough for me to command a small part of your love?" she asked.

92

"More than enough," he smiled, "you are an endearing Roman."

Because of his tenderness and the strain of the day, she turned her face from him to let hot tears flow. Outside, there was the noise of warriors and people hurrying to and fro, fetching and carrying.

"So many of my days are anguish and joy," she whispered.

"Lydia," he said, "I will not have you shed tears, when you have achieved so much for us. Or is it because of the child?"

Her hand gripped his tightly. She looked at him, desperately seeking to discover whether he was pleased or otherwise. When she saw his smile her heart leapt.

"Canis, I have carried it since the night it was conceived, and this too has given me both anguish and joy. Only say you are pleased, for it is yours, you know this."

"Even though it will not make Cea too happy," he said, "how could any man not be pleased? Its mother is brave and beautiful." And he laid his mouth on hers. Sweet fire rushed through her, for though the kiss might only have been given in gratitude and concern, it meant so much more to her. He loved Cea because she was the daughter of Boadicea, and Lydia would not have been the woman she was if at that moment she had not reflected on ways and means to divorce him from his shadowy love. But as if he knew what had come to her mind, he said: "The child is a complicated issue in itself, Lydia. And tell me, why did you let Marcellus know about it?"

"Because there was a moment when I did not think he would take the bait," she said, "and that only this would convince him I truly wished to return to Rome."

"Lydia," he said, smiling, "you are blessed with more than a fair face. We are leaving this place soon, and Andudo will contrive a litter for you. You have endured enough discomfort for the moment."

"I am not yet an old woman," she said spiritedly.

93

"You will go in comfort," he said. He arose. She sought to keep him with her a little longer.

"If I give you a daughter instead of a son, will you be less pleased?"

"Lydia," he said, "a man has pride in his sons, but his daughters are the light in his eye. Son or daughter, you yourself will be cherished, do not doubt."

"Oh," she said wistfully, "if only you had cherished me just a little when we first met, instead of treating me so ill."

"Had I done that," he said with a reminiscent smile, "you would have called me a presumptuous barbarian, instead of a low one, and taken your dagger in earnest to me."

"I would not, I would not," she cried.

"You would," he said, "for you were deplorably arrogant in those days, even for a Roman chit."

"Oh, you are monstrously cruel to speak to me so!"

He tweaked her hair in consoling affection, and left her with her green eyes hot and suffused. She hated beyond anything to be reminded of the days when she had so abominated him that she was possessed by blind vindictiveness. Now her whole being was devoted to him and his people.

Somewhat stiffly she rose, drawn by the sounds outside. When she emerged from the dwelling, the light cast by the purple-rimmed sun momentarily confused her sight. A man took her by the arm. It was the veteran Andudo.

"Come, mistress," he said in gruff affection, "I am to see you are made comfortable."

"Andudo, I do not wish to be cossetted," she said. "I do not need to be." But she went with him.

Within the ring of Britons watching and guarding the Romans, Marcellus took Cestor aside.

"There is still hope, centurion," he said.

Cestor made no comment. His face was expressionless. He could never forgive the tribune for surrendering his men and his honour. He listened unmoved, as Marcellus whispered of the reinforcements he had sent for—which might yet arrive in time. The centurion could not credit that Marcellus, having been made to look a fool, should now begin to think like one.

"Tribune," he said, without troubling to whisper, "think you the Britons, who must have been ready to attack soon after we left, would have allowed our three gallopers the convenience of unhindered passage? Think you they would not have guessed why the men were going and where?"

"That has been in my mind too," said Marcellus sagely, "but there is always hope. If not, then Mars has suffered us to endure our most unendurable day."

"Yours at least, tribune," said Cestor coldly.

The Britons were finishing their work. They had already broken open the Roman storehouse and taken most of the food. They had already lifted every weapon and much armour. Every Roman horse was now theirs, and they were now loading the animals with their booty, the flour, the meat, the wine and all else. Aware of the coldness of Cestor and his men, Marcellus prevailed upon two Britons to take him to Canis. The company of the hated barbarian would be no worse than that of his Romans, who thought he had shorn them of honour. Unlike him, they had not been able to recognise that in the face of such odds surrender had a practical purpose. Now, they would be able to fight the Britons on a more opportune day. The present sat too gloomily on them. They looked as if they thought he had done what he had done only in order to save his eyes, his tongue and his fingers. So, with the two Britons, Marcellus went in search of Canis, to settle the score of his honour with him.

It was now that the people of Durvulavum realised they were not only to leave their homes for good this night, but that Canis was giving them no time even to pack their humble belongings properly. Indeed, laughing warriors were tossing all kinds of appurtenances aside—telling them to rid themselves of all toys and trinkets, and take only what could be eaten or worn. Their woe was more than considerable, but Canis was deaf to it, so much so that Cea stamped her foot.

95

" I will not have my people made miserable for the sake of saving a small hour," she said.

" As Grud will tell you, time puts its impatient hand on all ordinary people," said Canis. " He alone is ageless. Am I so hard?"

" Aye, cruelly so," she said. And he knew she was not referring only to her people.

Hywel came, shaking his head.

" They are a joyless lot again, these people," he said, " they have indeed lived too long under Romans."

" You shall give them back their spirit, Hywel," said Canis, " and help rebuild their sinew too. Princess Cea will give them back their pride. A month from now, they will not remember their woes of today. We will take them with us, joyless or no. In five years time, their young sons will be young warriors. Tell them we depart when the sun has bedded. Tell them that old and young, mothers, widows and children, all will march through the night with us, and any who wish to sleep will do so on their feet."

" More woe," said Hywel merrily, and went to acquaint the people of their forthcoming travail. At which a distracted mother rushed upon Canis, who was at this moment encumbered by the arrival of Marcellus. He ignored the tribune, and listened to the woman.

" Who will take up my children?" she cried wildly. " They cannot walk through a whole night."

" Your husband will take them up."

" Husband? Husband? How many of us have had husbands since our queen Boadicea took them to fight for her and lost them in battle? Husband, say you?" And she laughed and wept, distractedly and alternately.

" Shed no tears," said Canis, " but go and smile brightly on one of my warriors. He will take up your children for you. Do not say I said so, but have him take them because of your smile."

The woman, who was not without handsomeness, was suddenly less distressed, and said: " There is one I have seen

96

with white teeth and a kind eye for my children. Will I say I have come to him by your command, before I smile on him?"

"Say only that you like his strong arm and tender heart."

The woman went, biting on her lips to make them red, and smoothing her fair hair.

"Briton," said Marcellus, "by my honour I would liefer you took me with you as hostage, than left me here."

Canis, not concerned with the problems of the tribune, said: "Hostages are like splinters in a man's flesh. We take none. If you feel your men are little surly with you, roast their feet with hot iron. Use the iron you were saving for the widow."

"Romans do not use hot irons on other Romans," said Marcellus. "I granted you a favour—though it was a false favour, and one more piece of trickery—but nevertheless I granted it. I asked in return for favour which you could not grant, so you owe me favour yet."

"Ask it," said Canis briefly, watching loaded horses being led to the assembly point.

"You are a dog for besting me in so unsoldierly a fashion," said Marcellus candidly, "but a brave one even so. I ask, therefore, that you return my sword to me—so that in the sight of all men here, and while there is still light, we may fight until one of us lies dead. This will restore my honour and do no harm to your own. How say you?"

Canis regarded the tribune with hard grey eyes, seeing in him the man who had struck him, the man who would have delivered his warriors to slow death and who had talked about Lydia's child being strangled at birth. He called Andudo. The brawny veteran came. Canis told him to return the tribune's sword, to give him a Roman shield, and to bring a sword and a shield for himself.

When Cea heard about it, she knew what it meant, and arrived in hot anger. Canis was already weighing a sword.

"Oh, you are in insufferable conceit," she cried, "and it is not to be borne. You are yielding out of conceit to this cunning Roman. Oh, my mother said so many times you were ungovernable—and you are so, in very truth! I will not have this. Do you hear? I will not!"

"Not so loud, sweet one, or you will come to the ears of cunning," said Canis. "And stand ten paces off, then you will not be trampled. Marcellus needs to be pricked a little. But do not laugh as it happens, for his honour is already much beset by other things."

"Oh, arrogance! Oh, conceit!" Cea stamped her foot. "Oh, I say to you that if you let him so much as scratch you, I will roast all your intemperate ways out of you!"

Princess Cea was taking upon her spirited self all the tempers of her mother. It delighted Canis.

The fiery sun was on the edge of the world as intrigued Britons and brooding Romans watched Marcellus Mercurius come in martial magnificence against Canis. But first the tribune removed his helmet, for Canis wore none, and Marcellus disdained to be at too much advantage.

The Roman was proud, grim and purposeful, Canis wily, agile and sly. Each bore a short Roman sword. Marcellus used a square Roman shield with spiked boss, Canis a round British shield of lighter weight. But the way of the engagement was simple enough—Marcellus swivelling with front foot stamping, and Canis lightly circling. Canis's shield was a ploy more than a defence, for while Marcellus watched the shield and made his thrusts as it moved, Canis slipped each one by his art of wily evasion. Again and again, the Roman's sword flashed and darted; but each time the Briton was not there. Marcellus, who understood the psychology of the resolute eye, fixed his gaze sternly on the Briton's face. He stamped and thrust, his sword running with red light. Canis slipped aside. He had made no thrusts of his own so far, his ploy was to tease Marcellus with evasiveness. His deadliest art was in the counterstroke at the right time. Marcellus refused to be diverted from classical Roman offence, and continued with his stamping and his thrusting. It wore an opponent down in time and unnerved him.

Lydia, having heard what was afoot, came hastening to Cea. "What is this?" she demanded. "Cea, what is Canis about?"

"He is indulging his fine conceit," breathed Cea, "and when it is over, I will not speak sweetly to him for seven days. But a moment ago, he would not let the people here have time to collect their belongings—but see how he himself now dallies. And dances too! Oh, reckless. Lydia, it is not to be borne, I tell you."

"Perhaps it is an unnecessary indulgence, but it is not reckless," said Lydia, seeing how adroitly Canis moved, while Marcellus began to breathe noisily. "Canis is a man, Cea. Marcellus an infant. Do not be angry with Canis, when you should only feel sorry for Marcellus."

Marcellus was still purposeful, but a sense of inadequacy came to torment him. Lunge as he did, and often, his sword pierced emptiness. In sudden temper, he smote the Briton's shield.

"Stay your twice-damned feet," he shouted, "how may I let your blood else?"

"This way," said Canis, and as the Roman's sword darted angrily, his own weapon slid glitteringly to prick the tribune's thigh below his armoured kirtle. Blood sprang, and Marcellus leapt back. "Be in no alarm," smiled Canis, "it was no more than the bite of a thorn."

"Dog! Arrogant dog!" shouted Marcellus, and ran at the Briton with blood in his eyes. Canis swayed to the left, just at the moment when the Roman thought he had the blown-up jester for very dog's meat. But he pitched into that damned emptiness, the flat of a sword struck the back of his neck, and he fell into the dust. Canis kicked the sword from the tribune's hand; and as the Roman turned onto his back, the point of the Briton's weapon tickled his throat.

"You are cursedly detestable in the way you best a proud man," panted Marcellus, "but for the favour of your own gods strike swift and clean."

"That is a very heroic request," said Canis, "but must

99

stay in the melting pot. This day we have each struck a blow. I am content with mine."

From the dejected Romans came a groan, from the Britons a sigh. They had hoped Canis would take off the tribune's head. It would have made a fine trophy mounted on a spear.

"Ah, well," said Andudo, "it does not do to be greedy."

"And there is Lydia," said Canis, "who endured so much because of our promise to give no Roman unnecessary death."

"Still, with a tribune," said Andudo, "a promise can be bent a little."

Grud appeared like a murmurous shadow.

"What other sport do you contemplate?" he muttered at Canis. "Darkness is almost upon us, yet you stay to tickle Romans. The people, as you commanded, are ready. Our warriors are ready. All are ready, except you. Shall we go on our way and leave you to playfully wrestle a Roman or two? It need not concern you that our Princess is in a high fret over your dalliance, for I will muffle her and bundle her over a horse—and you will not even hear a whisper from her as we go on our way."

"Stop your grumbles, old Grud," said Canis, "for I am ready. Andudo, see to it that some of our warriors lie dispersed from the foot of the hills onwards, to mark that no Romans follow us. They do not like the night, but in their present temper they may be tempted to scout in our rear. If any do—"

"Aye, if any do so?" said Andudo.

"Tell our warriors to take them and feed them to the wood-witches,' said Canis. "For a promise cannot be drawn out for ever."

They filed from Durvulavum in the gloom of the darkness, leaving the Romans confined behind the barred doors of their own storehouse. It would not take them long to break out, but it would give the Britons enough time to be well on their way. The columns marched through the gates like black shadows, the warriors escorting the lines of civilians, among whom the young assisted the old. On the shoulders of some warriors small children perched. One warrior with a kind heart and a strong arm carried a small girl on his shoulders, and held her brother by the hand; and with him walked the mother of the children, not now so distressed by her plight. The widow whose plight had been the cause of the whole fracas walked in warm thankfulness with her children, near the head of the column. She was comely indeed; so much so that although the night hid her shape, her robe was so enchanted by the body it covered that it whispered against every curve, and caressed them all.

"By the Great Father," Andudo said to himself, "I will never believe the Romans would have fed her to the wolves."

The loaded horses were led. They were cavalry animals, and resentful of being used like donkeys. But the Britons cajoled them and fussed them, and proud heads stopped tossing.

Lydia, protesting, was carried in a comfortable litter by four men. Andudo brought her some bread and wine, for they had made no meal at Durvulavum. They ate modestly as they marched.

"Andudo, speak to Canis," she said. "Tell him I can walk as well as any, or at least sit a horse."

"Eat, mistress," said Andudo, "and go in comfort. Canis will slit my belly if I let you put so much as a toe to the ground. By my gods, you have earned more than this bread and wine. I know not how you came to be born Roman, for you make a truly sweet Briton."

Then he was gone in the darkness, leaving Lydia warm with pleasure. Though Andudo was a man of hardy cheer, he was not given to flattery. What he said he meant.

Cea rode mounted, and so also did some of the crochety old women; and all travelled at the pace of the marchers. Warriors scouted ahead to make sure there was only night and black, rolling land before them. Canis walked by the side of Cea; and as they went, the night closed more darkly around them. Cea would not speak; she intended to run the light of her life clean out of conceit, and would not address him in any way until her haughty silence had diminished him somewhat. Oh, the temper he had put her in! It was enough to make her want to bite him.

Canis understood her sweetly high nose. It was all one to him, since he knew she would lower it eventually. She would make a spirited young queen, when they made their new kingdom in the west and the crown was put into her hands.

Up and down the columns of people, watchful warriors went, bringing what encouragement they could to the wights of Durvulavum, who thought longingly of their beds and the homes they would see no more. It was hard to come under the protection of Canis, who thought so little of making them travel through the night. A man in a long shabby cloak strode the length of a column, until he reached the head of it, and found Canis.

"Briton," he said, "I come as voluntary hostage."

"How came you here at all?" asked Canis.

"By not being thrown into the storehouse, by wrapping myself in this poor cloak and bending myself like an old man," said Marcellus. "I have been deserted by Mars himself, and at some time must have offended the rest of the gods. I can no longer consort with my countrymen, and will not do so until I have redeemed myself. Aye, go with you I must—or my men will take me to proud Paullinus, and make his ears buzz with mockery of me."

"Go to Paullinus yourself," said Canis. Cea had her nose higher in the air.

"He will bid me fall on my sword," replied Marcellus.

"By which you will redeem yourself."

"By which," said Marcellus, "I would be a greater fool than I already am. If every man tricked by a woman fell on his sword, the world would be empty of us."

"It is better for a man to die a fool, than linger on as one."

"Aye," said Marcellus, tramping moodily, "such advice comes easily from a man triumphant. If it is in your mind to have one of your barbarians slit my throat as I sleep, ask him to do it with civilised neatness."

"Tribune," said Canis, "return to Durvulavum—for I

cannot promise what my warriors might not do to you asleep or awake. We do not travel with Romans."

" Lydia Osirus is Roman," said Marcellus spitefully.

" Oh, go buzz in her ear, then," said Cea crossly.

Canis called two warriors, and put Marcellus into their charge.

" Lydia is to sleep, tribune," he said, " so let her be. Go instead with these two men. Find ⟨the oldest man who is walking, and take upon yourself the task of carrying his bundle."

" I dislike your manners, as much as I dislike your trickery," said Marcellus, but went with the men and vanished in the darkness.

" Cea, your nose will be nipped if you lift it any higher," said Canis.

She forgot her vow of silence and said, " You are not to concern yourself with my nose, if you cannot first consider my feelings."

So he did not concern himself, but walked with a smile on his face. This provoked her into more words.

" Did you not hear me?" she said.

" Ah, you were sweetly haughty," he said.

" At our first stop," she said, " I shall scratch you."

" At our first stop," said Canis, " I shall kiss you."

Cea did not respond to this for a while. Then she said, " Canis, when do we stop?"

He laughed; she reached down, and he took her hand. In the darkness, he was misty in her sight; but she felt her hand turned upwards, and the pressure of his mouth against her warm palm. She melted.

" Oh, Canis, I know why the Queen my mother loved you so."

" She is with us," he said, " and you are her daughter."

They went on then in a silence that was tender, leading the cavalcade in the wake of the scouts—the night full of murmurs, of creaking leather, the snuffle of horses and the sighing of people. They would not reach the forest until morning, because of the compulsive slowness of their march, but they would reach it.

The night was without moon.

Within its black embrace, Canis did not walk with the spirits of darkness, nor even at times with Cea. He walked with Boadicea, drawing her image out of the night: proud, tall and radiant, for this was how she always came to him in his dreams and his silences. There was nothing about her he would ever forget, and in spirit she was his undying Queen.

Blue are your eyes that once were my life,
As soft as the mist of a forest at dawn,
The mirror of skies that kissed the bright hills,
The first fragrant moment of every sweet dream.

Lydia also dreamed.

5

Julian Osirus, brother to Lydia, had fought and lived through the frightening violence of Boadicea's rebellion. It had given him an intolerance of fools and villains, the kind of people who brought such things about. He had witnessed the scourging of Boadicea, and that was something he could neither forget nor forgive. At the time he would gladly have put to the sword all those responsible. Julian was no less a Roman than any of his countrymen; but he was more liberal, in that he did not unconditionally dismiss all other people as inferior. He knew there were Romans whose actions discredited Rome, and he did not hesitate to say so.

He was the deputy fiscal procurator in his late father's municipality, of which Calleva Atrebatum was the chief town. He did not need the post for its financial reward, such as it was, nor was it a post a high-born Roman usually took. But like his father, he cared for administrative work which offered contact with the British subjects of Rome. He also cared for the Britons. And his concern for the surviving Iceni, who were not of his municipality, was because of the high regard he had felt for Queen Boadicea.

He was visiting Julius Classicianus, who had replaced the corrupt Catus Decianus as Imperial Procurator of Roman Britain. And he was out of temper.

"Is Paullinus gone quite mad?" he demanded. "What, is the whole of our province here to be torn asunder; and the pieces gobbled up by wild Britons from the north, who have the appetite for such tidbits? Aye, in his insane quest for personal vengeance, our rancorous Governor will achieve no less than that in the end. Boadicea is dead, the Iceni put down, the Trinovantes scattered. My sister lives like a bar-

105

barian in some wild forest, hunted by the Governor's soldiers because she works to comfort Iceni who are in desperate need. She dare not show her face, and she a higher-born Roman than ever Paullinus is, I swear. I cannot send word to her, nor she to me, and I am forever threatened by Paullinus, who cannot put from his mind that which should have long been forgotten. I say to you, my friend, I will beard our illustrious avenger one day, and warm his icy nose for him."

" Be content with bearding me," said Classicianus, " for at the sight of either you or your sister, Paullinus will bring on the lions. And his ice is about to burst into flame in any event, for this Briton called Canis has not only defeated our garrison at Durvulavum, but has also carried away all its people. Also, he seems to have taken the tribune Marcellus Mercurius as hostage."

" No, I cannot believe that," said Julian, who knew Canis well, " he disposes of Romans, in one way or another, but he takes no hostages. By Jupiter, he is a brave, belligerent prince —though a thorn as well—and there is no man I like more."

" Is he a prince?" asked Classicianus.

" A prince in the eyes of his warriors. And a king, they say, in the eyes of Queen Boadicea. May the gods cherish her proud spirit." Julian would not deny his admiration of the dead Queen to any man. " And to Lydia he is everything. Give her Apollo, and she would still choose Canis. Never did I know a woman more hopelessly infatuated than my sweet, wayward sister."

" It is waywardness that makes a woman sweet," said Classicianus. " As to Paullinus and his vengeance, I have argued with him on behalf of the Iceni and Trinovantes, but he is immovable. Come, let your temper mellow, here is wine to help the mellowing."

A girl had entered, a maid with hair the colour of honey and with eyes like the blue-grey seas of Britain. She wore a white, loose-flowing robe. She carried a beaten silver tray, containing goblets and an earthenware flask of wine. Julian, full of that which irked him, in especial the Governor's inhumanity, was unseeing of her as she poured the wine. She brought him a goblet. He took it silently; and she flushed very faintly, because he neither acknowledged her, nor thanked her. Julian, raising his eyes above the swimming goblet, was suddenly aware that he had been unpardonably discourteous. He smiled wryly at her, and at himself.

"I am growing into a surly fellow," he said, "please forgive me."

She smiled at that. He looked into the eyes in which the seas swam, and her flush deepened at his regard. She dropped her eyes. Julian, dark and handsomely Roman in his toga, saw how her honeyed crown shone. Classicianus coughed gently. She was in some guilt then, and said swiftly, "Oh, I beg you, good Procurator, I had not forgot you. I merely thought I saw a spot on your floor, and wondered how the servants had overlooked it."

Classicianus looked at his floor, at the bright tiles.

"Is there a spot, Cyella?" he asked gravely.

"No, I was mistaken," she said, and she took his own goblet of wine to him. Julian was now taken with her willowy grace and colouring. He glanced at Classicianus. The Imperial Procurator smiled and nodded.

"What is your name?" Julian asked the girl.

"Cyella, as my protector said."

"Good Classicianus is your protector?" Julian was intrigued by the way she carried herself. "You are Belgic?"

"I am not." She drew herself up in indignation.

"Cyella was brought to me and is under my protection," said Classicianus. Which was to tell Julian the girl was free, and not a slave.

"I must put myself in a better light," said Julian, "so let me name your proud race, Cyella." He regarded her thoughtfully. It made her a little shy. "I name you Iceni," he said.

He saw the pride and pleasure she showed at that.

"Which is not Belgic," she said.

"And what of your family?" asked Julian.

She was sad then.

"My mother is dead, slain by soldiers. My father was once a chieftain, and his name is Andudo. Now he is outlawed and is with Canis, lord of the Iceni, but where I do not know. The life of Canis is forfeit, because he destroyed your armies and cities and temples."

"That was in war," said Julian, "so why forfeit?"

"According to Paullinus, it was a rebellion," said Classicianus, "so must be forfeit."

Cyella wished to argue, but would not because Classicianus was kind and Julian a guest. She asked for leave to withdraw, and Classicianus nodded. Julian watched her go. She was a sweet creature, and sensitive. He sighed.

"We might have achieved much in our northern provinces," he said, "if we had encouraged Britons to build with us here. But the foundation stone has been wantonly cracked, and it will take many years to seal it. By Lydia's own august Diana, if Paullinus continues with vindictiveness, I will go to Rome and petition Caesar himself. I will not have my sister hunted like a dog."

"For the moment," said Classicianus, "you had better lie lower than a winged bird, for it was your sister whom Canis used to fool Marcellus Mercurius. Aye, she fooled him and tricked him out of Durvulavum in the space of half a day. His centurion Cestor tells the story with strange laughter, as if his mirth is strangling him."

"Oh, Lydia, you are wayward still, and a joy in my heart," said Julian in rich amusement. "To fool the wordy Marcellus, to trick one so full of self-esteem, that was something to bring laughter to Olympus."

"Paullinus speaks not of trickery, but betrayal," said Classicianus soberly.

"He would," said Julian. "Aye, he would. But I know my sister's spirit. She might trick us to help the Iceni, yet she would not betray us. But it is all one to Paullinus. He can only cry betrayal."

"Be patient, my friend," said Classicianus, "for I do not

think Caesar holds Paullinus in quite such favour as he did. I have not neglected to advise Nero of what I think he should know. I am not in office here to help exterminate Britons, but to bring them back into peaceful accord with Rome."

" So I have heard," said Julian, in a slightly better temper. " May I walk in your garden for a while?"

Classicianus had not missed the sight which had caught Julian's eye outside—the whisk of a white robe.

" I must tell you," he said, " Cyella does not suffer Romans too gladly. Her mother was cruelly slain after Boadicea's defeat, and despite my protection she is, like most Iceni, under constant threat from Paullinus, who trusts none of them. Also, she is sometimes apt to speak too loudly about the virtues of Canis, and too frankly about the vanity of Paullinus."

" My sister would love her, then," said Julian. He went from the villa into the bright garden, tinted by the sun of early autumn. He found Cyella. " Might we speak together?" he asked.

" If you wish," she said.

They sat on a stone seat facing an ornamental pond, in which vivid fish darted. She did not as a subject Briton seem any less proud than the patrician Julian. He began to speak not of Rome but of Britain, and in a way to encourage frank and friendly response, to discover, perhaps, some of her likes and dislikes. But Cyella was not to be wholly drawn. At the end of a great deal about Britain, she committed herself only in respect of the Belgic tribes, saying that they were apt to consider themselves far better than they were.

But when Julian turned the conversation on Canis, her eyes grew warm.

" One day, when I find a man brave enough to defy the odds, and knowledgeable enough to guide me, I will ask him to take me to Canis," she said.

" You know Canis well?" asked Julian.

" I have never seen him."

" But you love him?" said Julian curiously.

"He is a great warrior and an uncrowned king. Who could not love him?"

"Ah, who indeed?" Julian did not smile. Maids like Cyella were given to hero-worship and it was not kind to tease them.

"Do you not know he has slain a thousand?" asked Cyella. "But no, you are in courtesy with me, I should not speak of what Canis has done to your people."

"It will not upset me too much," said Julian, with an amiable wryness that pleased her, "for the actions of idiots provoke me far more than the deeds of Canis."

"Yet does it not put you out to know he has slain a thousand Romans with his bare hands?" asked Cyella.

"A thousand?" Julian was awesomely impressed. "I have heard of no warrior greater than this. I have heard of fearsome Hercules and mighty Achilles, and I have also heard of gods who have not performed indifferently. But a thousand Romans, all with his bare hands. Aye, that is the stuff of truly gigantic heroes."

Cyella had met other sceptics. She was not discomposed.

"Of course," she said, "one must allow for a little exaggeration."

"A little here and there," said Julian. "All the same, I accept Canis is a great warrior. I know him and would rather have him friend than enemy."

"You know him?" Cyella's sea-green eyes opened wide. "You have seen him, spoken with him, perhaps even been in battle against him?"

"Aye, all this," smiled Julian, "and can whisper to you that fire does not issue from his mouth, or smoke from his nostrils. I have heard there is no woman who would not leave her own bed and go to his, if he so desired."

"He would not so desire," she said hotly. "He is faithful to Princess Cea, whom he is to wed. I would go to him and serve him, but I would not go to his bed."

Julian was suddenly serious.

"What is this about Princess Cea?" he said. "She is dead, like her sister Dilwys. They died on the day of Boadicea's defeat, as is well known. It may suit some Iceni to protest that Princess Cea is alive, to perpetuate a myth, but she is dead, Cyella."

" She is not, she—"

" Cyella, hush." Julian was in concern. " If what you say is true, say it no more. Paullinus thinks Queen Boadicea and both her daughters are dead. If he thought Cea was alive, he would become even more hostile than he is already. He would lay waste every encampment and every forest to get at her. Do you understand?"

Cyella bent her shining head.

" You are truly kind," she said emotionally, " I understand what you have said—and you have been gentle with my indiscretion. I will not let my tongue betray my sense again. I am glad there are Romans—that is, there is good Classicianus and now you—I mean—" But she was suddenly confused, and when Julian sought to lift her chin and find the cause, if he could, she rose in further confusion and hastened away. Her swift flight through the garden was like the flow of white through a profusion of colour.

*   *   *

Julian stayed longer than he had planned. Classicianus and his gracious wife found him intelligent and amusing, and as liberal in outlook as they themselves. And Cyella was a paradox of shy modesty and eager curiosity, for Julian was a Roman of the kind new to her. In her curiosity, she was constantly appearing; in her shyness, quickly retreating.

His presence at the villa of Classicianus became news for the ear of Paullinus, and Julian received a summons to attend on the Imperial Governor. He went in cool temper. Paullinus received him with cold eyes. Julian's greeting was as formally courteous as he could devise, the Governor's response brusque, and that done with, Paullinus came icily to the point.

" Bring me your sister Lydia," he demanded.

" If I could, I might," said Julian. " But I cannot."

" If you could you would," said Paullinus.

" But I cannot."

". Cannot means will not. Will not means defiance."

" Excellency, cannot means cannot," said Julian. " If she is out of your reach, then she is farther out of mine. Or am I to succeed where you have failed?"

Flame licked at the ice.

" Take care, Osirus. You are brother to renegade sister. Therefore, find her and bring her to me. If you do not, or will not, then the consequences will be displeasing to me, and intolerable to you."

Julian stood silent for a moment, noting the harsh lines that had cut deep into the Governor's face. Then slowly he shook his head.

" I am, as you know, Excellency, a true servant of Rome," he said, " but what my sister is, what she has done or not done, has come about in her pursuance of what she considers right."

" Right for whom?" Paullinus was thinly sarcastic.

" I am no more in her mind than you are," said Julian, " and even if she were standing here now, I could not say how she construes rights and wrongs. Each of us has his own concepts of truth and behaviour, and perhaps your own and my own are only peculiar to ourselves."

" Concern yourself only with concepts of loyalty and obedience," said Paullinus. " You are not here to parade insolence, but to attend on my commands. You are an officer of the reserve. Hear me. I am beset not only by rebellious barbarians but by incompetent commanders, and witless tribunes. I believe you to be neither incompetent nor witless. So from this moment on, your term of office as deputy fiscal procurator in Calleva Atrebatum is ended, and you will take up command of a force that will smoke Canis and his rogues out of whatever doghole they lie in. Aye, it is my decree that you find them and destroy them, one way or another. Except that you will bring me Canis alive, and also the daughter of the widow Boadicea, who styles herself Princess Cea."

Caution quietened the hostility in Julian's eye.

" Excellency, I did not think that a rumour flying high would make your feet leave the ground."

" This is more than a rumour," said the Governor. " The centurion Cestor is sure she was with Canis at Durvulavum, and that Canis took the people of that place to serve under her banner. You will treat rumour as fact until it is proved otherwise. Hear me on. With Canis and the daughter of the dead widow, you will also bring me your sister Lydia. When you have done this—then and only then—will I pardon Lydia." He was thinly sarcastic again, as he added: " Are you in my mind, Osirus?"

Julian regarded the Governor grimly.

" Aye," he said, " I am commanded to achieve what others have failed to achieve, and to bring to you a man no others could. Also, a Princess who is only a ghost."

" Contain this insolence," barked Paullinus, " or it will go harder for you than any, despite your house. Hear me further. Since Canis took Durvulavum and its people, people elsewhere have begun to swarm to him. They have destroyed my outposts on the way to him. Formerly the dogs only crept to him by ones and twos, like hyenas in the night. Now they are running to join him, and in scores. So, it will not be long before he will feel strong enough to break out of his burrow and march west. That is his intent—to place himself out of my reach in the mountains. Your commission is to frustrate him, to manoeuvre him into battle, and to crush him. And to bring him, his self-styled Princess and Lydia to me. Come closer, tribune—for tribune you are, from now on."

Julian, seething, joined Paullinus, and the Governor spread a crackling, parchment map.

" Here is his territory," said Paullinus. He indicated an area bounded by Lindum in the north, Verulamium in the south, Camboritum in the east and Venonae in the west. " Somewhere in one of the greater forests within this region, he lies secure—building his new army. As soon as he is ready, he will attempt to break out and move westward. Discover where he lies. Your immediate concern is not time, but method—for it is not days but weeks he needs. You will begin your campaign in five days, when I will have assembled for you a force of two thousand five hundred men, cavalry and foot. For needed reinforcements, should you deem the balance too critical, you may call on Quintus Cerialis at Lindum."

" Quintus is poorly supplied, Excellency." Julian trapped by compulsive obedience, had accepted his commission—but he rejected meek compliance.

" True, since he lost his Legion to Boadicea there has been some difficulty in re-garrisoning him. Yet he has enough men to give you some help, if you consider it necessary."

Julian said quietly, " I am to wage war against my own sister?"

" Fool! " Paullinus smote the map with an angry hand. " Does she not wage war against us, her own people?"

" Her heart is such that she claims the Britons as her own."

" It is her head that contrives treachery, not her heart. If you wish to save her head, tribune, if you wish peace to come to this province, can you not see we must make an end of Canis? He is the fount of rebellion, this Princess its inspiration. Find them and bring them to me. If not, if you force me to command a more obedient tribune to do this work, your sister will not receive the smallest mercy."

" I am commanded, Excellency, and will be your most obedient servant," said Julian bitterly.

For the next few days he attended on Paullinus, his attitude polite and correct. Together with the Governor and certain appointed centurions, he planned this minor campaign, which had as its purpose the destruction of the last warrior force the Iceni and Trinovantes were capable of organising. It was Julian's opinion that if Canis did make his break for the west, it would not necessarily be made at the most suitable point. He would not look for the direct and obvious route; he would be much more likely to march through country affording him the greatest cover, even if it added considerably to the journey.

114

Julian further contended that the Briton would tack his way across the length and breadth of Middle Britain if necessary, leading any Roman force so exhausting a dance that it would be hard put to contain him, even if it caught up with him.

Paullinus did not attempt to break down these arguments. A shrewd general, he did not press his own views too dogmatically on any commander whom he thought intelligent. He merely said that all eventualities were possible, but that he did not think Julian the man to dance a Roman army senselessly in the wake of barbarian Britons.

" Excellency," said Julian, " when I have discovered the forest in which they lie, I shall sit on their west side and wait. I will establish a series of outposts north and south of our position, mount patrols and also encourage men with long noses and itchy palms to make themselves known to us. There are always some whose itch is stronger than their loyalty."

A centurion asked to speak. He was a man with a hideously scarred face and protuberant, marbled eyes, whom Julian did not care for. His name was Sulla, and he seemed in his malice towards Canis to be a man who was still burning. The livid, twisted scars were still fiery, not completely healed; but in his sworn intent to destroy Canis, he had prevailed upon Paullinus to give him a place in Julian's command.

" You will not find many Iceni or Trinovantes with such an itch," he said, " but there might be a willing Belgic man or two. The Belgic nose is longer than all others when it comes to smelling out men of other tribes." Because of his scarred mouth his speech had a strange slur to it, so that they had to listen keenly, as one does when listening to a man too full of wine.

" It is one way of acquiring information," said another centurion.

" It is not the only way, perhaps," said Julian, " but we will see."

However, later that day he said to Classicianus, " But if I know there may be men willing to betray knowledge of Canis, I will wager that Canis knows this also."

"This is a land full of tribal rivalries," said Classicianus, "and any one tribe thinks little of all others."

"Paullinus calls this endeavour a campaign," said Julian, "thus implying it has a beginning and an end. But you cannot campaign in and out of forests. He commands of me the impossible. Yet were it not for Canis, whom I admire, and my sister, whom I love, nothing would give me greater satisfaction than achieving the impossible—for our sour Governor would then have to swallow the bitter fact that I succeeded where he had failed."

"You must succeed," said Classicianus, "and so bring to an end the suffering and tragedy of sporadic war. Paullinus is right on one count. If you take Canis, the Iceni and Trinovantes will finally yield and fight no more. I would not crucify the Briton, but send him to Rome to be judged by Caesar—yet dispose of him in one way or another we must. It will preserve the lives of others. Better for them to lose Canis than to lose all."

A while later, Cyella requested to speak in private with Julian. He saw her in the room that overlooked the garden.

"It is true, then," she said, "that you are to command a Roman army against Canis."

"And my own sister," said Julian.

She was perturbed.

"You are not like other Romans," she said, "and I wish it could be some other man in your place. If you go against Canis and my Princess in this way, you are only pursuing the wrong already done to them. Why are my people not to be left in peace?"

"I have only been given command of soldiers, Cyella, I have not been given command of policies."

"Canis will destroy you," she said.

"It will be as the gods decide."

"Whose gods?" She was not challenging, she was sad. "Canis will win the battle, and leave you dead."

"Or I will win, and leave him dead." Julian was anything but joyful himself. "I would not deliver him to Paullinus, fair one."

A moistness came to her eyes.

"I know why it would be better to give Canis merciful death," she said, "and truly I do not know any Roman more understanding. Noble tribune, I have spoken to good Classicianus, and he has said I may speak to you on a matter important to me. In speaking I shall be asking."

Outside, the garden lay under clouds, its colours touched by hues soft and sombre. The clouds were in Julian's eyes, and they too were sombre.

"Ask of me only that which you know I can give, Cyella."

"Patrician," said Cyella, "you are strong enough to protect me, brave enough to defy the odds, and knowledgeable enough to guide me. So I ask you to take me with you. You go to find Canis—and where Canis is, there also is my father."

"I cannot take you, Cyella."

"How can a tribune, in command of an army, say he cannot?"

Julian did not find the argument easy.

"You are a flower here in the household of Classicianus, who gives you a guardianship many gentle Iceni maids would covet in these unhappy times. So stay here, Cyella. You were not born for strife and tragedy, but for sweetness."

"I scorn you," said Cyella quite fiercely, "I scorn you for such weak words. I do not mean I have no regard for my protector here, for indeed I have. But I am no fragile flower, I am daughter to a warrior chieftain. Ah, you are not really afraid of refusing me, only of offending Paullinus, who would not like you to take me. So you answer me like a weak woman, instead of courageous man. I scorn you."

"By Venus," said Julian in wry amusement, "you have the same art for scorning a man as my sister, and it sits as proudly on you as it does on her."

"That is quibbling," said Cyella. "Will you take me—an enemy, but an unspiteful one—to Canis and my father? Will you or not?"

"No."

"Oh, I thought you brave, not timid," she said, and tossed

her head very scornfully. He smiled. She was not to be taken seriously; and in any case, he would not put her in risk. She could not be more than eighteen, and had yet to find out her true mind concerning life. " Oh, now you smile," cried Cyella. " Confess, you refuse me because of Paullinus. Then I will smile myself. No, I will laugh."

" Cyella, there is nothing about this at which either of us should laugh," said Julian soberly. Cyella drew a deep breath and put out her hands, palms upward.

" Save only for the kindness of Classicianus, who clothes me and feeds me," she said, " I have nothing here. But in a different place I have my father. Tribune, will you not take me to him?"

He wondered how she regarded the fact that if she came with him, and he found her father and the other Britons— let alone deliver her to them—she might well witness their defeat and death.

He said, " I can refuse a foolish maid, but not one who is as determined as you. Come with us, then, Cyella—but precisely how I may deliver you to your Britons I do not know."

She thanked him breathlessly. He would have none of it, and left her. He disliked intensely the command Paullinus had forced on him, and the problem of Cyella was a small one compared with others. Twice during Boadicea's fiery rebellion Canis had given him his life, and spared Lydia also. Now he was to endeavour to destroy the Briton. If he succeeded, he knew he might also destroy his own sister. She would not want to live without Canis.

And if he failed, Paullinus would be merciless.

It was not going to be the most exhilarating of campaigns, however it ended. He wished the Iceni maid, Cyella, had not prevailed against his better judgement. If she came to harm or tragedy, he would be responsible.

*　　*　　*

It was Agra who brought news that Paullinus had despatched

a strong, well-equipped force to find the fugitive Britons and bring them to battle. And it was Agra or friends of his, who during the first months of winter brought reports concerning the progress of this force. The news travelled from forest to forest.

Julian's progress was slow. It was slow because it was exploratory. It was a search for the location of the Britons. The exact whereabouts of Canis and his people were known to men who were wanderers of those regions, but to few others. Julian was forced to comb the territory methodically. This was by no means simple, for one forest fingered and stretched into another, and great sheets of water ran into marshlands. But among the wanderers (who were people who believed men had not been born to root themselves) there were some whose palms itched just as much as those of rooted men. They were willing to sell a rumour or a fact for Roman gold. They began to appear not long after Julian had commenced his search.

Julian did not say, " Tell me where I can find the Iceni dog Canis, and all the other dogs, and I will give you gold—refuse me, and I will slit your belly." Instead he always said, " I am looking for Queen Boadicea's greatest warrior, a man called Canis. Can you help me, friend?"

Mostly, they always said they could. Some of them, having imparted information and taken the gold, disappeared like snakes in the undergrowth long before Julian discovered he had been cheated. His centurions could not understand why, whenever a patrol returned from one more fruitless reconnaissance, he was able to shake his head and smile at himself.

" It is because I know I should take every other long-nosed rogue and hang him," he told one centurion. " Every rogue who comes on the heels of the preceding one is a spy or an agent for Canis. Not only do I let them delay me and confuse me, I also pay them for it."

" Why, then, tribune, have you not hanged them?"

" Because I am never sure, and because I will conduct this campaign my way. We will follow both truth and lies. For in the end one truth will outweigh all lies and bring us to the right place. But perhaps I will yet hang one of the liars as a discouragement to all others."

Thus patiently and methodically, he led his force and paid the informers. He sifted rumours and facts by searching. Sometimes a wanderer would say, " Go that way for five hours, and then ask again." And Julian would go, or send a patrol— and another gold-seeker would sell information that was credible. Or contradictory. But Julian still refrained from hanging anyone. Instead, he began to shackle the informants, until he had decided whether they had sold him truth or lies. If it turned out to be lies, he withheld the gold and left it at that. It was his way of showing his disagreement with the harsh policies of Paullinus.

Slowly, very slowly, the line of his search brought him east of the Roman town of Durolipons, and just as slowly it developed north-west from there.

He would find Canis in the end. He had to.

*　　*　　*

Agra arrived to advise Canis that the Roman force was but four leagues away. The forest was chill and damp, winter was upon them, and the earth and timber hutments of the Britons dripped wetly on the outside. But they were hardy and they were cheerful. They now numbered sixteen hundred. Agra heard the sound of hot iron being beaten, of timber being hammered, and of voices raised in song. It was easier to work to the sound of song, the work made men and women warm, the song induced rhythm and dispelled melancholy. The people of Durvulavum now worked and sang. And everyone was better-clad. The women wore soft, shining coats of skin over their tunics, while children wore these skins alone, the skins of foxes being the most prized for their softness and warmth. The children played their ancient games of mock battle in laughing freedom. Their freedom was only of the forest, but it was joyful even so to scamper about without offending Romans.

Blue smoke rose from the fires, twisting in the moist air, and the smell of burning wood and leaves was pungently sharp. Canis received Agra's news with a glint in his eye.

"You are indispensable, old hairy one, in the way you stretch your ear into the eagle's nest," he said, " and favour us by keeping it stretched even until it aches. When we go from here, I cannot think how we shall manage without you and your friends."

Agra shuffled about, grinning embarrassedly in his beard.

"We will travel part of the way with you, lord," he said, " and when we finally leave you to return here, be assured you will remain in our hearts."

"Agra," said Canis, " though you have ten thousand hairs in your beard, we love every one."

Agra grinned even more embarrassedly. The smell of the fires was healthy to his nose. Outside one turf-rooted hut, a group of women whispered.

Lydia, the Roman woman, was in labour.

"As to what pertains to armoured men of Rome," said Agra, " I will bring you what words I can each day, lord."

"And bring also any iron that comes to hand, Agra," said Canis, " be it the smallest piece. Stay now for a cup of wine."

"Lord, it is not like you to offer wine to a man who only drinks mead."

"A single cup of mead, then," smiled Canis, " for I do not want you to swagger home and lose yourself on the way."

Agra grinned again. A hairy one who lost himself in his own forest, even when blind with drink, had yet to be born. And by the time Agra had finished his third cup of mead, there was occasion for a fourth. Lydia had been delivered of a dark-haired daughter. Though the old year had only recently turned into new, and the chill had increased, the infant was warmly swaddled and brought from the hut. It was presented to the earth and the sky, as a symbol of new-born hope. The faces of the women there were bright, for the infant was also a symbol of the fruitfulness of woman. Upon Canis, the father, the men pressed their gifts to ensure his continued virility. It was one thing among the Iceni to be a great warrior, it was another to be virile and have proof of it. The proof wailed faintly one moment, lustily the next, and this brought more joy to the women.

At the door of Lydia's dwelling, the women laid their offerings. She was Roman, but few of them now thought of her as one.

Cea stood far apart, her brown eyes tragic; and Canis, after touching the brow of his child, went to his unhappy Princess.

" Cea, sweet one, look not so sad," he said, " for the babe is sweet fruit, conceived at a time when I thought you lost to life."

After the defeat of Boadicea, Cea had indeed lived for many months with her mind blank and her eyes blind to life.

" I cannot be happy for you," she whispered brokenly, " I cannot. Oh, Canis, cruel you are if you wish me to smile, for you know my heart is in pain. She has borne your child. You have lain with her, and given her your body and your love, and I cannot endure its consequences, I cannot. Leave me, do not come near me, leave me and let me die."

" Die?" Canis spoke gently, compassionately. " Cea, you are full of life and sweetness. Tomorrow's light will chase away today's darkness—"

" No. I will die in the night," she cried, " and tomorrow will find me cold and still. Leave me, leave me."

She would not be comforted. He went to the women, took the babe and cradled it. He returned to Cea, carrying the infant.

" It is Lydia's child and mine, aye," he said, " but it is yours also, Cea, for it belongs to you and your house, as do all of us here." And he placed the child in her arms. Cea took it weepingly, and turned her back on him.

" Canis, return to the gods you have rejected, and ask them to forgive you. For you are cruel beyond anything to strike so unfairly at my heart with this babe. Oh, soft she is and small, and you are sly and devious. While this pain is on me, I will not let you speak to me. Oh, take the mite, she will perish from the cold." And Cea handed the babe back. It broke into a hungry yell. Only its tiny nose and mouth showed, for it was hugely swaddled—but it made noise enough for ten quite naked mites.

"It is a woman already," said Canis, "or at least almost a warrior maid."

"Oh, folly," cried Cea, "you are a miserably doting father already! It is not to be endured, and I hate you and will never forgive you!"

She ran from him.

"It is understandable," mused Canis, taking the infant back to the women.

Lydia lay spent and drawn, the perspiration on her slowly cooling brow glittering wetly. Above her arms was the warm, friendly face of a woman called Canuda. It was she, together with Grud, who had helped with the delivery of the babe, and now cossetted its mother into rest. Grud had been a boon, his knowledge and skill invaluable, and he had served her in muttering but comforting tenderness. She was still bemused from her labour, and from the wonder of bearing her child of love. But the labour was over; and the pain, because of Grud and his physician's art, had slipped away. Her racked body was assuming an almost ecstatic lightness. Through heavy lids, she looked to see whether Canis had yet come. Surely he would. Surely he would not give all his attention to the child and none to its mother.

He appeared at last. Canuda wiped Lydia's damp forehead with soft linen, and left Canis with her. His hard face was tender, his eyes full of compassion.

"Lydia," he said, "you have taken much hurt."

"None that I could not endure," she whispered, though she knew he did not mean the physical hurt alone. "And she is my gift to you," she added.

"She is the sweetest gift," said Canis.

"Then will you kiss me for her?" she asked.

He came down beside her bed of warm skins, and put his

123

mouth to her pale lips. It gave her dreamy pleasure. He looked into her green eyes, which seemed mistily huge, and he shook his head.

"Lydia, you left your house and people to be with us," he said, "and it has been even harder for you than either of us thought."

Lydia, stirred by his compassion, weakly shook her own head, her lustrous hair moving over piled skins.

"I would not give up one moment of all the days I have been with you," she said. "Sometimes, because of circumstances, you are hard and cruel, I know—but never to me or to your people. If Diana had truly favoured me," she went on feverishly, "if she had brought you to my eyes before you knew Cea, I would have had you, I would, and no one would have taken you from me."

"Lydia," he said, taking up the soft linen to wipe her flushed, damp forehead, "my people love you. Cea and I love you. The child is your joy and ours. No more now, for you must sleep. In your dreams remember you are beautiful, and that in time your benevolent Diana will bestow the bravest husband on you."

"Oh, Canis." She tried to laugh. "Will you so soon after I have given you a child of joy, thrust me into the arms of another man? You know there is no other man. You are my only love—and when you wed Cea, I do not know how I shall endure."

"Enough," he said softly, "or I will kiss you into sleep."

Her eyes begged for this, and her long lashes drooped in languorous content as his mouth gently caressed her lips again. Her exhausted body floated blissfully. Grud came in, bearing a battered silver cup containing a potion; and his young-old eyes were full of grumbles as he saw Canis lifting his mouth from Lydia's. Lydia opened her own eyes as she heard the mystic muttering.

"What," he was saying, "have you not already done enough to my sweet mistress? Do you now give her further pain with your worthless caresses?"

Since the day Grud had accompanied Lydia to Durvulavum, the ageless one had taken the Roman woman to his heart. It had been all so hard for Lydia at the beginning, for she had not been wanted by the Britons and only Canis had stood between her and impossible loneliness. But now she was accepted, trusted and loved, and Grud had taken it upon himself to serve her with as much muttering affection as he served Cea. Lydia knew she had been accepted when the Britons began to call her Ludicca, their Celtic name for her. She knew they had begun to trust and love her when they mentioned her in their songs. As there were songs about Boadicea and Canis, and about Canis and Cerdwa, so there began to be songs about Canis and Ludicca, which told how Marcellus Mercurius had been bested in a single hour. In verse and song a single hour sounded much more heroic than a full day.

Grud had taught her much of the ways of the Iceni, their customs, rites, superstitions and gods. Lydia knew that different people had different gods, and however much one felt that the Roman gods were cast in a finer and more awe-inspiring mould than others, nevertheless each people's deities represented that higher intelligence responsible for bringing the world from darkness to light and for fashioning its wonders. She could not understand why Canis bore such a charmed life, for he was more than indifferent to gods—he had rejected them all on the day Boadicea was scourged. He said things about great Diana which made her fear for what the goddess might do to him, and he was not very charitable about Andrasta, the Iceni goddess of victory.

She listened drowsily as Grud continued to grumble at him. She roused herself to speak.

" But, Grud," she said, " who should be the first to kiss me if not Canis? Have I not made him a proud father?"

" I know not why he should be proud," said Grud, " for he got you with child like a scurvy villain with no thought for a woman."

" It was not quite like that," said Lydia.

" Whatever it was like, it was not what he should have

done," said Grud, while Canis rubbed his mouth and hid his smile. " Queen Boadicea knew him better than any, and named him villain more often than most. Come, mistress, drink this and you shall have sound sleep until dawn tomorrow."

" But my babe," said Lydia in concern.

" Your babe," said Grud, " is now in warmth and content. It is at the breast of Feola, who has more than enough for ten the size of your mite. So you may sleep, mistress."

" You are full of fussing and cossetting, Grud," murmured Lydia.

" Aye, Queen Boadicea knew him better than any," said Canis humorously, " and named him old woman more than most." Canis smiled at Lydia, and went. Grud chuckled as he held the cup to her lips, lifting her to take the potion. She drank the stuff and made a face.

" It is vile," she said, " so why are you laughing, Grud?"

" He has a tongue that tickles me," said the bow-legged mystic.

" It does more than that to me," murmured Lydia. She lay back and closed her eyes. Then her heavy lips lifted for a moment. " I know much of you now, Grud. I know what you have done for me, and what you might do for me. But do not in your mysterious way contrive to ease me of my love for him, even though I am never closer to him than now. For if you take this love from me, I shall have less than nothing."

" Sweet dreams, mistress," said Grud and went quietly away, though he muttered a little outside.

*   *   *

The night was quiet save for the patter of cold raindrops. The leaves of evergreens dripped. Canis lay thoughtful in his hut. Around the perimeter of the camp, the warriors on night watch moved like black, glistening shadows. And in their forest caverns, the hairy ones laid sharp ears on their pillows of dried fern. From birth they were gifted with ears that could pick up every sound, even while they slept. Such a gift was a necessity, for at night every forest was full of creatures looking not for sleep but succulent prey. And hairy ones were very succulent.

Canis was thinking about the immediate future. He knew, as Paullinus knew, that sooner or later he had to break out and lead his people into the west. Paullinus, while he remained in office, would do everything to prevent this.

Who commanded the force which now lay within four leagues of this forest? Was it a man of guile, a man of dedication, or a man of martial unimagination?

Agra, perhaps, could find out.

A faint sound pricked at Canis's ears. He looked up from the fur-strewn pallet on which he lay, mind and body alert. Inside his door Cea appeared, the curtain of skins set aside by her hand. She wore only her tunic and looked cold and peaked. And her eyes were red.

" Cea?" He sat up.

" Canis, speak me sweetly," she whispered. She ran to him and went down on her knees. Her face was woeful and joyless. " I am in such hurt," she said, " I cannot sleep or contain my anguish. So speak me, am I your true love, am I dear to you?"

" You are your mother's daughter," he said tenderly, " and therefore my true love and dear to me in every way."

How deep his voice was, how compelling his grey eyes, in the light of the single oil lamp.

" How may I know this, how may I know you will not lie with her again?"

" Circumstances can confound any man's honest intent," he said. " It may happen that because of circumstances I will lie with a thousand women—if I had the strength of a thousand men—but none would be as dear to me as you."

She discerned, as her mother so often had, that he could couple tenderness with sly jesting—all too provokingly.

" Oh, slyboots," she cried, her breast heaving, her auburn hair spilling as she tossed her head. " Is that the answer of true love? No, it is the answer of a red fox. If you ever lie with

127

another woman, no matter what the circumstances, I will contempt you all my days—and never let you wed me." A thought struck sharply at her, through her woe and temper, and she came at him with it. " Aye, as to that—if I am your true love, why are we not wed already?"

" It was your wish, and your people's wish, that it should be a royal ritual when we reach our new kingdom in the mountains. Desire of my heart," he said, " you pummel me with angry words, as if we were very wed."

Cea at nineteen was no match for the fox. She saw herself trapped by her reproachful tongue. Her lips fell apart, and she looked almost desolately unhappy.

" Canis, oh, this is not sweet. You are calling me shrew. I am not, I swear. Oh, I could not endure myself if I were. I beg you, my love, do not put more woe upon me than I bear already."

Canis drew her to him, and put his eyes close to hers. She saw laughter in his, and trembled with hot desire to scratch him.

" Shrew? Sweet Princess," he murmured, " I know you as endearingly haughty at times, but I do not know you as a shrew. It is not shrewish to be your mother's daughter, or to box me with tender fire. It is only more endearing."

" Oh, you laugh at me," cried Cea, and put her face into his shoulder and bit his neck with fierce teeth. At which he wound his arms around her, and held her in forgiving warmth and love. She trembled. " Oh, be sweet," she whispered. At which his lips engaged hers so warmly that it was all of sweet, and more than that. Blood rushed to heat her body and colour her face. " Canis, do all men kiss as you kiss?"

" I am not all men, or even several."

Alarming were the sensations as he kissed her again, the blissful but confused Princess aware that under the coverings he was clad in nothing.

" Canis, oh, much as I love you—do not kiss me more, for it is not to be endured."

She was warm, soft and bemused in his arms; and he said

with gravity on his tongue, " Only a princess, I suppose, could love a man and find his kisses not to be endured."

" I did not mean it that way, you know I did not," she blushed. " Free me and let me depart."

He freed her and said, " I will take you to your door, Princess."

She thought little of compliance as ready as that, and said, " Well, perhaps you may kiss me once more."

He did so, warmly and lovingly, and she lay bemused again in his arms. Sweet weakness engulfed her. There had never been any other man for her. She had loved him even as a girl of ten. And what she felt now was love so alarming that she reached and put out the lamp. He was aware of the yielding softness of her shapely body, her hot confusion because of sweet desire, and her need for him to compensate her for her woe. She must be loved.

Tenderly he gave her love, and the moment came when her long sigh was like that of a maid expiring in rapture.

It was sweet beyond the telling.

*　　*　　*

He was up early, not long after dawn the next morning, and he took himself off to the deep pool fed by a tumbling waterfall. The mist lay thin over the water, the ground chill and damp. He saw a warrior, one who had been on sentry patrol during the hours before dawn. The warrior's brown, rugged face was sharp with the cold, and as he hailed Canis his breath was like puffs of steam.

" Wet and bitter it is here, lord—a morning to stay abed."

" Well, I am up and here," said Canis, " so go and warm your feet at a fire."

The warrior needed no urging. To stay and see Canis slip lean and naked into the water would only have made him feel colder. And Canis was a whimsical man, who might have commanded an onlooker to join him in the pool, which would not be less than icy.

Later, when the first food of the day was ready, Cea emerged from her dwelling and looked about her with new eyes. And her new eyes fell first on Canis, a sharp freshness and vigour about him. She stood rooted as he regarded her, sharing a sweet secret with her. Her face flamed, and she could not help herself—she fled burningly from him. She was, for all her growing imperiousness, a shy princess in the matter of such secrets as that. So she fled into the trees. There she confided her thoughts to a great, twisted yew of immense age. But the yew, for all its years, could make nothing of her confused admission that the night had been sweet, and her guilty admission that it had happened while she was still unwed. At any rate, it said nothing. And if it had, Cea would have fled in another direction.

When she finally composed herself, she returned to break bread with him; but she had mantled herself in her heaviest cloak, so that Canis was denied even a glimpse of an ankle or the light of her auburn hair. Within her hood, her eyes looked only at her food, and she spoke only to Grud. But the flushes came because she knew there was laughter in her lord's eyes, and because his thoughts must contain new knowledge of her. Oh, he was knowing enough already, without needing that to add to his store.

Princess Cea blushed, lifted her eyes, and saw that he did not look knowing but tender. Her blush sweetly deepened.

Canis finished his meal; and when he had given thanks— not to the gods of provender, but to the woman who had baked the bread and cooked the meat—he went to see Lydia. Fury swept all sweet emotions from Cea.

Oh, the philandering villain!

*   *   *

Marcellus Mercurius dwelt among the Britons, tolerated but scorned. It put him right out of temper to find that people who were only barbarians accounted him a lesser man than any of them. He did not want to return to Paullinus until he had redeemed himself in some way. It was demoralising, however,

130

to feel that the Governor was willing to leave it at that—as he was, apparently, if the Britons were to be believed. According to them, no promulgations had been issued by Paullinus concerning any Roman desire to ransom Marcellus. In any case, the Britons refused to regard him as a hostage—and indeed, Canis had told him he was free to go. Marcellus might, during one of his many moments of frustration, have taken the plunge and departed; but he knew he could not find his way through this primitive forest without an escort, which Canis refused to provide. And without this, Marcellus realised that he would perish at the hands of creatures as primitive as the forest. It was a pity, for if he could have survived the forest darkness, he could have carried word to Paullinus of the location and strength of the Britons here.

Further wounds were inflicted on his pride by his being forced to join the Britons in hunting game; but he had to eat, and to eat they made him work. One day he was speaking bitterly about the cursory way the Britons treated a captured Roman tribune. Lydia was the listener but not the comforter. They sat by the fire outside her hut. The day was cold, but crisp and bright, so that all the fires in the camp burned with crackling, popping cheerfulness. Lydia's babe gurgled contentedly at the breast of Feola nearby, Feola herself happy to suckle the infant daughter of Canis.

"It is not all a matter of pride," said Marcellus, "there is right and wrong to consider. As a hostage, I might demand for myself that which is right. But Canis is like so many barbarians, and does not subscribe to civilised codes. He will not concede that this is wrong."

"But you are not a hostage, nor were you captured," said Lydia. She was healthy, alive, and glad to be no longer unwieldy. In her time in the forest, she had acquired the vivid, animated look of all forest maids. Her limbs were supple, smooth and strong, her beauty more richly striking. Cea could not bear to look too often at this beauty, adorned as it now was with the lustre of a woman who had borne Canis a healthy, happy child.

"Nevertheless," said Marcellus, "it cannot be denied that since Canis is responsible for my fall from grace, he should, as a warrior, see to it that I am given courtesy and comfort."

"Ah, he is a warrior now, and not a barbarian?" said Lydia. "And do you cry for comfort as a tribune, Marcellus, or as a man?"

"Lydia," said Marcellus reprovingly, "I know you are out of sympathy with me, and have been since I called you hard names at Durvulavum. I confess I have come to know you better since then, and I realise that you are, after all, still a true, high-born Roman. It is my opinion that Canis has bound you to him by some uncivilised spell. Admit this is so, and that you desire to win free of the spell."

"I have no such desire, Marcellus, because I am under no such spell. I could tell you the true way of it, but I will not."

Marcellus could not believe that any Roman woman, except a harlot with no sense of culture or discrimination, would live with Britons—unless she was imprisoned by their witchcraft. So he said, "Be assured, Lydia, you and I will yet redeem ourselves and return in favour to Rome. I shall achieve this by coupling opportunity with courage, and you shall achieve it by assisting me."

"Do not look to me for help," said Lydia. "You may return to Rome when you will, but I shall remain here."

"Return? Ye gods," said Marcellus, "when the way is so hazardous? There are creatures akin to fiends in this forest. I have heard them howling at night."

"These are not fiends," said Lydia, hiding a smile, "only the dogs of the hairy men."

"Who has ever seen such dogs by day?" said Marcellus sceptically. "Not I, not you, not anyone. This is the wildest place, but there are rumours that Canis will soon be leaving it to march westward. When is this to be?"

"I cannot tell you," said Lydia, "for I do not know. Put your question to Canis. Have you campaigned much in Britain, Marcellus? If so, do you know what it is like in the land of the western mountains?"

"I only know what I have heard," said Marcellus, "that it is sharp in the winter, when the mountains never lose their snow."

She turned her eyes on him. They seemed full of dreams in which, he thought, he played no small part. He was not to know Lydia did not even see him, only mountains reaching whitely blue to the sky, mountains that would give Canis and his Britons security from Paullinus. There would be a region which Canis and Cea would make their own; and she, Lydia, would be with them. It would be hard for her; for she would be in torment if Canis in the end did take Cea to be his wife. But it was she who had his child. The little dark-haired bundle of joy bound him unbreakably to her. And one day Diana would surely give him to her, and not to Cea.

It was all in her eyes, but Marcellus construed it as mostly to do with himself. As to that, although he had made his mistakes at Durvulavum, no one could deny that as a tribune he was a man whom any true Roman woman might dream about. And Lydia, he confessed to himself, had a beauty that sometimes took his breath. True, it was hard to forgive her for bedding with that arrogant dog Canis, but she was still a prize for any proud Roman. And the child could be left with Canis.

"Lydia," he said, "not only have I come to know you better, but to hold you in affection. When I have bested Canis and won freedom for us both, as I will, we will return to Paullinus. Then we will both go to Rome, where I will make you my wife. Women are often in error, but I am a man who can forgive all the mistakes of one like you."

She looked at him, and observed his self-esteem. If such a man as this could be a tribune, she wondered to herself, then Canis should surely be nothing less than Caesar.

"Marcellus," she said in a way to make him frown, "there are your own mistakes to consider. Truly, your offer is generous—but how might I make a grateful wife to a man whose errors are born of elementary indiscretion, while mine were only born of my weakness as a woman? I am to be grateful, am I not, tribune?"

Marcellus regarded her coldly.

"Madam," he said, "you will regret so offensive a speech."

He strode away, leaving Lydia amused.

Agra loped into the camp, seeking Canis.

"Canis is away with warriors and some of your friends, looking for game," said Lydia, "and intending to lay in great store. Do you bring good news or bad, Agra?"

Agra grunted, and said, "He may choose to sit and eat it here in the end, for they are no more than a league from the western boundary of the forest, and are making a great camp."

"Who are?"

"Those I warned him about several days gone," said Agra. "An army of Romans."

He would say no more to the concerned Lydia, but sat to wait for Canis to return.

*   *   *

They were hunting deer. Venison which had hung in warm places for seven long days was sweet to the palate, or could be preserved in dried strips for days of need. Wanda was at the heels of Canis, with other warriors not far behind. She was at his heels frequently, making slightly bitter complaints that he had not brought too many Romans to her dagger.

They slew a fine buck, leaving it for others to take charge of. They slipped between trees touched by the first green leaves of spring, and went swiftly in the wake of plunging, fearful does. The warriors fanned out to encircle the game. There was the noise and tumult of a rush, and the crashing of startled animals through thick undergrowth. A doe leapt into the sight of Canis and Wanda, its eyes like saucers in its fear. It stood between them, poised, quivering, mesmerised. Wanda, excitement exhilarating her, cried, "Stay, lord, I will take it!"

Canis conceded. Wanda's arm flashed, her javelin sped, passing over the rump of the doe straight to the heart of Canis. He swayed his body with lightning reaction, the point of the javelin plucking at his tunic as it hissed by. The doe was gone, and Canis stood in thoughtful reflection, contemplating the fallen weapon.

"Lord," said Wanda in confusion and sorrow, "almost I gave you grievous hurt."

"Almost you did," said Canis.

"It was the heat of the chase," she said, "and never was excited aim so nearly a matter of sad reproach."

"Never," agreed Canis.

"Your warriors will not regard me happily, when you tell them how wild was my throw," she said, hanging her head.

"I hope some will regard you very happily when I tell them you missed," he said. "Pick up your javelin."

Wanda, full of humility, recovered her javelin. Not far away, there were shouts of triumph, the noise of bursting foliage and the sounds of trapped and dying deer.

"Lord, I am hot with mortification," began Wanda.

"Aye," said Canis evenly, "for you missed the doe as well. Perhaps you would have better luck with a different art, that which concerns cooking pots."

"Cooking pots! Lord, you would not shame me so!"

"Where is the shame in discovering you are better with cooking pots than with javelins?"

"I am not to bend over pots," she cried, "I am to seek vengeance."

"On whom?" he asked.

"Why, on Romans," she laughed, "as I have said."

"They try your vengeance on Marcellus, he is Roman."

"On Marcellus?"

"Aye," said Canis, "with your cooking. I predict it will make a sorry end of his stomach."

*   *   *

135

Agra was still there, muttering to Cea and Lydia, when Canis returned. Canis paused to tickle his infant daughter in her wooden cradle, and Feola, minding the child, blushed deliciously when he tickled her too. Then he listened to what Agra had to say. According to Agra, a compact army of Romans had encamped only a league away from the forest, on a high place that would give them a view of all the country around.

" Lord, had you marched before they arrived at this point, you might have escaped," said the hairy one.

" We cannot march until we are ready," said Canis, " and even when we are ready, we will not march until every tree and bush are in leaf. Winter is a time for keeping the women and the old ones warm, not for marching them. Do you know in what numbers the Romans sit on our flank?"

Agra began to count his fingers, then his whiskers. Grud arrived, Andudo and Hywel with him. Hywel was as much interested in the presence of Lydia as in Agra's counting of whiskers. He was a young, vigorous Trinovante warrior who sighed a little over Lydia.

" Lord," said Agra at length, " I have counted those I have seen, and those my brothers have seen, and they are so many I have lost them in my beard. Many are horsed, and such is their armour that its glitter is as bright as the sun. And their noise can deafen a man a league away."

" Did you discover who commands? Is it wintry Paullinus himself?"

" Not so," said Agra. " It is a tribune, one called Julian Osirus."

Lydia paled.

" Oh, the gods forgive Paullinus for giving my brother this command," she said in distress.

" Julian will make a shrewd commander, but an unhappy one," said Canis, " and I wish Paullinus had sent another."

" This is your brother?" said Cea to Lydia. " He who spoke out bravely in defence of the Queen my mother on the day they scourged her?"

"Aye," said Lydia. Her distress made Hywel lay a comforting hand on her arm.

"Canis will say, and I will say," said Hywel, "that if your brother brings us to battle we may defeat him but not destroy him."

"It is malicious of Paullinus," said Canis, "but not his most brilliant piece of work. Julian will not like this command. Cea, give me your hand." He took her right hand, and placed it palm upwards in the left hand of Lydia. "Lydia," he said, "you have been our bravest comrade, but because of what may now develop between Julian and us, you are to remember you owe no kiss of fealty to Princess Cea. You have endured much with us, so speak now not to please us, but in consideration of yourself and all you deserve. Will it give you comfort to return to Julian? If so, then you shall be taken to him under safe escort, and there will be no one who will not wish you well. It will take from Julian his worry in going against you as well as us."

Lydia paled in new distress.

"But are there none here who would have me stay?" she said in a wild voice. "Are there none here who love me?"

"There are few who do not love you," said Hywel stoutly. But it was Canis she looked to for the answer she wanted.

"No one wishes you to go, Lydia," he said.

"Then do not ask me to, for I cannot go and will not!" She looked at Cea and said, "Cea, do not send me away, I am no longer of Rome, I belong to your people." And she bent her dark head and put her lips to the palm of Cea's hand, kissing it in fealty.

"Lydia," said Cea, her eyes moist, "I cannot deny you. Despite all else that is between you and me, I cannot ask you to go when you do not want to. Stay with us, then."

"That is all I wish," said Lydia emotionally.

"But remember your kiss of fealty," said the Princess.

6

Julian surveyed the territory his army commanded by its might and disposition. He stood on the highest point of a rough plateau, in company with six of his centurions, among whom was Sulla of the hideously scarred face. To the east, stretched a forest so wide and deep it extended beyond their scan. On all other sides, the country lay rolling and broken, the undulations of gentle hills and wooded valleys softened by the thin, sun-speckled mists of spring. The farther limits were lost in the mists; but on a different kind of day, when the atmosphere might be sharp with the threat of rain, the eye could encompass leagues.

On this soft morning, Julian could see nothing which did not look quiet and peaceful. It was as if the desolation of hungry winter, and the punitive patrols of Paullinus, were things that had never been. Except, of course, that Julian stood high above it all with a small army that Paullinus hoped would prove very punitive.

" The dogs lie quieter than buried bones," said Sulla out of his twisted mouth.

" Aye, but with all ears to the ground," said Julian. " They will know we are here."

" Would that we could smoke them out and run them into that valley below," said Sulla in his slurring voice. " That would settle the issue once for all."

Julian made no response to that. He knew why Sulla bore such fearful scars. It had not taken him long to obtain the story from men who had served under the centurion. He fancied Canis would be disappointed to hear that Sulla had not burned to a cinder. He spoke to another centurion.

" They lie as well hidden as a thousand leaves beneath ten

thousand other leaves. You may turn them all over and find none. But they are here, I am sure. That is a vaster and quieter forest than all others. What did that Belgic informer say? ' Put your nose to the west of the forest when the wind blows from the east, and you will smell them.' I have smelled none, but I have sensed them."

" I also have a feeling, tribune."

" I am committed to it," said Julian. " Now, wherever they break out they must at some point turn west. That is obvious and unavoidable, but still leaves us guessing. We sit on a tall tower commanding a large arena and are blind."

" Not completely blind, tribune, for we have our outposts. They are our distant eyes."

" Which Canis will put out at a moment of his own choosing, if he has a mind to," said Julian. " Well, they have been warned to be sharp. And I hope if Canis strikes at them, they will be sharp enough to escape him."

" He will need to be even sharper to escape me," said Sulla, sounding as if his mouth was full of ashes. " I have a score to settle with him."

" There is more than one man with unfinished business on his hands, perhaps," said Julian coldly.

Sulla turned pale, protuberant eyes on him. Julian turned his back.

On the plateau, the Roman camp was a great square—intersected by straight lines of tents, each tent equi-distant from its neighbours. The scene was martial, glittering, orderly. To the west side of the tented area was the compound containing the cavalry horses. In the centre of the camp, stood the pavilion of the tribune. Banners fluttered. Julian went thoughtfully to the pavilion to study maps. They brought him intelligence of the local geography, but no nearer to Canis. He mused with distaste on his terms of reference. An armoured guard entered to announce that the Iceni maid, Cyella, petitioned for audience.

" Again?" he said wryly.

He had brought her this far, as he had promised; but during

139

the months of his slow, methodical search, she had not been as patient as himself. He suspected she thought he was merely humouring her, dragging her along on a prolonged march that would eventually take him back to his starting point.

" I will see her," he said. He rose as she entered. She was clad in a clean tunic, over which she wore a woollen cloak dyed red. It gave a glow to her fair, calm beauty; and she carried herself as proudly as always. There were Romans who would say that Cyella's pride, looks and independence counted for nothing against the simple fact that she was a barbarian. Julian thought he had seen far more barbarism in certain women of Rome than in Cyella.

" The sun is upon you, tribune," she said in greeting.

" Mistily," he said, " as if its promise is weak."

" Is your own promise weak?" asked Cyella.

" What promise is this?"

" Did you not promise to return me to my father? Though I know he is nearer to me now, I am no nearer to him. Your army is between us."

" Cyella, what I said was that I would take you with me. I did not say I knew how to deliver you to your father—and I still do not. Are you sure he is nearer to you than he was?"

" You know he is," said Cyella bravely. " You have used spies and men greedy for gold to find out where he, and Canis, and all the others lie."

Julian regarded her with a slight smile.

" You yourself, Cyella, is this not what you wanted me to do?"

" It is what you were commanded to do," she said, " and now you are here and devising how to suck them out of the forest and bring them to battle. But you are doing nothing about re-uniting me with my father."

" When it can be done, it will be done," he said.

" Which is more of nothing," said Cyella.

" Meanwhile, stay and eat with me," said Julian.

" Do you command that of me, tribune?" she said.

" Do you think me so graceless?" he said.

She flushed at that, and looked unhappy with herself.
" Oh, I am sorry," she said, " you are never graceless, only perhaps a little forgetful of why I am here."
He let that pass. He was not forgetful. He was waiting for other men with an itch for gold. None had come to his camp here yet. But he was still patient. He had food and wine brought in, and Cyella sat with him to eat, but drank only a little wine. He spoke of everything except how he would have her taken to the Britons, so in the end she said, " Is it impossible for you to send me to my father?"
" How can I reach your father?"
" You mean I must still wait. Why can you not send me with an escort to the edge of the forest? I can be left there, I will be quite safe."
" I will do no such thing," said Julian grimly. " You are not to be dumped on the edge of a forest like an unwanted pot. Nor am I the man to dump you. The forest harbours as many dangers as it does friends. I will not permit any foolish maid to be left there. Eat your food and say no more about the matter."
At that Cyella put on such an air of pretty scorn that Julian found it difficult not to smile. She finished her meal in silence, thanked him, and begged leave to go. She left his pavilion with her red cloak flowing in disdain, or so it seemed to Julian.

*　　*　　*

The Britons were in conference, their subject the Roman force that lay in wait for them.
" It sits up there like a dog of the hairy ones," said Hywel. " A dog with many heads all turned in every direction."
" We can lop a head or two," said Canis. " It is the dog itself that troubles us." He took a sharp stick and drew in the dirt. " See now," he said, " their army is here, and their outposts set up along the full length of our western boundary. Yet until we make a move, they are without initiative. They can only sit and wait."

"Waiting men grow dull heads," said Hywel.

" I would not count on that myself," said Andudo.

" If I were Julian," said Cea, " I would in some way keep the enemy locked in until high summer, and then set fire to the forest."

" Oh, that is not to be thought on," said Lydia.

" Julian is patient," said Grud, " but not idle, I warrant. He is not Marcellus. He has a head. Marcellus merely has a lodging place for his helmet."

" This is the season of mists," said Canis thoughtfully. " The high ground on which they camp sits above the mists." He made other marks in the dirt. " Here, to the north of their camp, is the plain of twisting streams. And here is the valley of thorn and scrub. And here, half a league north of the valley, is the track used by our horse traders in happier days."

" Aye, when we drove the horses north and west for trading," said Andudo.

" A poor track," said Hywel cheerfully, " and not to be compared with the roads we Trinovantes forged for our grain waggons."

" A horse is not a waggon," said Andudo.

" The track will take laden horses and people," said Canis, " and leads up to the southern border of the Brigantes."

At the mention of Brigantes, Andudo rolled spit.

Grud mumbled, " The track is overlooked by the Romans, and watched by patrols from their outposts. But what is done under the very eye is often that which is never noticed."

" When the morning mists have lifted," said Canis, " the Romans will certainly notice a cavalcade of horses and people, but how will they come at us? From their camp there are two routes. One, a lengthy ride over easy ground skirting the forest. The second, a shorter but rougher ride, that will bring them straight down into the plain of twisted streams and through the valley here." He pointed to the marks in the dirt. " There is no third way. How will they commit themselves? If they take the route that skirts the forest, they will lose sight of their camp and of us for a considerable time. They

142

may not regard this as important. Say now, Grud, if you were an intelligent Roman commander instead of an old goat, what would be your choice?"

"Either as an old goat or any commander," said Grud, "once I had you in my eyes, I would not let go of you for any time."

"If Julian came straight down from the heights," said Canis, "then his eyes would never lose us. But he will weigh the choice. He will know that if he can see us, we can see him. Yet by the faster and easier route, where neither can see the other, he may suspect ambush. To come straight down at us is the obvious way. He will know that we know it to be too obvious. Perhaps, therefore, he will consider we expect him to come the other way, where he will be out of our sight. If so, then that is when he will begin to think about an ambush."

"Ah," said Andudo, which meant he was confused.

"We are to make an ambush?" said Hywel.

"At the moment," said Canis, "we are making guesses. We will march in a few days. And then we will have to make a decision."

*　　*　　*

"Bring Cyella," ordered Julian.

She came to his pavilion, where he received her. Several of his centurions were there, including one with a distorted mouth and scarred face that aroused her pity, though she did not like his eyes. There was also a Briton in attendance, who seemed a cheerful fellow. His friendly countenance showed broken teeth, as if perhaps an offended Roman foot had kicked him there.

"Cyella," said Julian, "today you can go to your father."

Her pleasure was plain to see, though after a moment it was dimmed a little by uncertainty and hesitancy. Then she said, "How am I to go, tribune?"

"We have found a diligent, honest man," said Julian, "a Trinovante whom you see here, called Bada. He bumped

143

rather carelessly into one of our patrols, and we might have sent him as a gift to Paullinus, for I suspect he has been a warrior and active against us, though this he denies. But as the only people who can get through that witch-haunted forest to Canis are Iceni or Trinovantes, I am having this man escort you. The brave fellow has no doubts that he can safely guide you."

"But I am Iceni and can do as well for myself in the forest as he can," said Cyella, who for some reason decided she did not like the look of the broken teeth.

"Jupiter's truth," said Julian, "after plaguing me for days are you now saying you would rather not go?"

Cyella, in fact, did not know what she wanted to do. She did know that Julian had been kind and very patient, and that she had been sensitive and proud. She thought of her father, of Canis, and of her Iceni people.

She said, "It is only—" She stopped, wishing there were no centurions looking and listening. "I will go, tribune," she said.

"Come, then," said Julian, and took her out into the bright day. Sulla watched them leave the pavilion, his marbled eyes contemptuous of a Roman tribune who could not put a barbarian chit in her place. Bada, the Trinovante, followed in the steps of Julian, and waited at a distance while the Roman spoke his farewell to the girl.

"Cyella, Bada will take you as soon as you are ready."

"I shall not be long," she said, her eyes on the ground.

"You are a sweet maid," he said.

"Oh," she said, and bent her head lower.

"Though perhaps you chide a man a little unreasonably at times," he smiled.

"Oh, I do not," she whispered.

"What does it matter? You have been sweet company. I give you my blessing, and I hope you will find your father and your people. Will you take word to Canis from me? Say I give him friendly greeting—but am, alas, bent on venture not at all friendly. Say that no matter how the gods decide the issue, I

144

will not forget what obtained between us in the past. Say also that I trust he will give Bada hospitality, and let him go where he will, and not hold against him the fact that he has lately spoken with a Roman, namely myself."

"I will tell him all this," said Cyella, her fair hair full of the sun, but her eyes sad with shadows.

"And if my sister Lydia is with Canis, as I do not doubt, tell her that though I find her incomprehensible I love her yet. Lay this upon her cheek for me."

He placed his hands on Cyella's shoulders, and pressed his lips to her face. A deep flush suffused her.

"I will do this also, tribune," she said. "Oh, it is cruel," she whispered.

"It is not the best of circumstances," he said. He knew what was in her mind. The inevitability of battle between her people and his. Her hair was spun by the breeze. It flirted and danced. Her eyes were on the forest. "Your gods go with you, Cyella," he said, "and keep you sweet with life."

"It is you who are at risk," she whispered, "and I will pray for you." Breathlessly she added, "Oh, I do not know any Roman my gods would favour more than you." Then she ran from him with her eyes moist.

A little later in the company of Bada, the Trinovante, she left the Roman camp, clad in her red cloak. Julian watched her descend the sloping track, treading lightly and gracefully, the sunshine putting gold in her hair. Not once did she look back; and eventually the brightness of her hair was lost, and the red of her cloak gone, as she and Bada disappeared amid the foliage of thicket and bush.

Julian returned to his pavilion in some sadness.

*   *   *

It was bright evening. The Romans stood patiently containing the long western border of the forest. The Britons, now numbering two thousand, lingered in the forest, putting the final touches to newly-forged armour and weapons, and waiting for the moment to break out. Neither Romans nor Britons could see each other, but each had a sharp sense of the other.

On that evening, Canis said to Lydia, "Why do you not name the child?"

"Why do you not name her, Canis? Are you not her father?"

Canis regarded her. She was vividly beautiful, her hair lustrous, her green eyes full of haunting shadows.

"How was your mother named?" he asked.

"Julia. We will not name her after my mother, for my brother Julian was so named and that is enough. Canis?" She was almost shy. "Canis, shall we name her Dilwys?"

The grey eyes of Canis took on their own shadows. Dilwys had been the younger daughter of Boadicea, impish and teasing, and had been tragically slain when fleeing the Romans after her mother's defeat.

"Is this your own wish, Lydia, and not merely a desire to please me?"

"It is my wish," she said, "and all my desires are to please you."

"Then we will name her Dilwys. Lydia," he said, her dark beauty putting him in mind of Cerdwa, his joyful warrior maid who had also died, "you are like Cerdwa reborn. You turn the head of every warrior, and Hywel is moonstruck. Will you not let the one who loves you best speak for you?"

Colour rushed agitatedly into her face.

"Oh, you do not know the pain you put me in at times," she breathed. "I could bring no joy to any man, nor any man to me, except you. Do I encumber you with my love? Do I hang so heavy around your neck? No, I do not, I stand as much at a distance from you as any woman here!"

"Not quite as much," he said, "which is something to consider. To look at from a distance, one tree is very much like another, one leaf indistinguishable from a thousand others. Therefore, when a woman is as beautiful as you, it is a greater pleasure to see her in front of one's eyes than it is to peer and pick her out from a group of women at a distance. I will not push you into any man's arms, Lydia. That would do no good to my eyes at all."

Lydia laughed in delight, for he was so wry in his self-truths.

But there was no delight about Princess Cea when she heard a few minutes later that the babe was to be named Dilwys.

"Dilwys? Dilwys? Oh, Canis," she said angrily, "sly and devious is that Roman hussy. She has done this to soften you, and weaken me. I will not have it, I will forbid it."

"You would not forbid so sweet a name as Dilwys," said Canis.

"Would I not? My will is like iron, I tell you."

"Iron?" Canis did not know who intrigued him more—his young and precious Princess, or his green-eyed Roman woman. "Iron, you say?"

"Iron," said Cea resolutely.

"You are not for yielding?"

"Never."

"Then I shall kiss you until you are mute and undone," said Canis, just as resolutely.

Cea retreated hastily.

"That I do forbid," she gasped, "for it is not the kissing by which I am undone, but that which follows, and oh, we are not even wed. Canis, stand off—oh, sweet villain, there are people gaping."

She escaped him with her knees knocking. Grud found her flushed and full of laughter at herself.

"Ah, Wolfhead has been around you," he said.

"And I am undone," she said in rueful amusement.

"Ah?" Grud's round, innocent eyes surveyed her.

"There is nothing to see, old bowlegs, I am not undone in that way."

"It is all the same in any way," said Grud.

A few minutes later two hairy ones arrived, bringing with

147

them a cheerful-looking Trinovante and a girl in a red cloak, carrying a pack.

" We found them in the western part, lord," they said to Canis, " to which they had come from the Roman camp. The maid says her father is with you, and the man says he was commanded by the Roman tribune to protect her. They are accordingly yours now, to deal with as you wish. For our part we have no quarrel with them."

Canis considered the man and the maid with interest. The man returned this interest with some of his own, admiring the demeanour of Boadicea's general and observing the activity in the camp. Cyella could only look at Canis silently; not because she was awed, but simply because she had long wanted to see what he was like. He was as tall as she had heard he was; and his strength was not only in his lean physique, but in himself. But he was not, to her eyes, as engagingly handsome as Julian Osirus—

She stopped her thoughts.

" You are Canis," she said simply, aware that the scene was drenched by soft light and evening greenness. There were timbered huts, cooking fires, frisking children and so many people, so many brown-faced warriors and warrior maids.

" I am Canis. Who are you, my fair one?"

" I am Cyella, and my father is a chieftain who serves you, I think. His name is Andudo. I was taken by Romans when they slew my mother, and I have come to be with my father again."

Canis put out his hand. She took it, placing hers into it. He smiled, and Cyella from that moment was in his service too.

" You will be like a bright sun to Andudo," he said, " for he thought you cruelly dead like your mother. I will have him brought to you." He spoke to a warrior, who hastened away. Bada the Trinovante made himself heard.

" I am Bada," he said, " and was asked by the Roman tribune to escort and protect this maid."

" Ah," said Canis. The activity was absorbing Bada, who

148

saw strange-looking devices mounted on small wheels, and the glitter of piled weapons. Canis saw what the man saw. He smiled, though not in the same way he had smiled at Cyella.

"I bring you greetings," said Cyella, "from the tribune."

"Name him," said Canis.

"Julian Osirus," said the girl.

"By whom I am direly constrained," said Canis whimsically, "for he sits astride my outgoing ways like a many-headed dog, as a man called Hywel has said."

"Oh, the circumstances are unhappy," said Cyella wistfully, "but he is not that kind of a dog, truly he is not."

His eyes encompassed her thoughts and her heart, or so it seemed, and pinkness crept into her cheeks.

"Aye," said Canis, "I know he is not. He is a fine servant to Rome, and faithful to her. He is also a man without prejudices. In the past, he has always been kind to Britons. He has been kind to you. So be in no worry, fair one, I will take off all his heads save his own."

"He will not let you do that too easily," she said. "I am to tell you he cannot help himself in his unfriendly venture against you, and that whatever happens he will not forget the past. He also said he hopes you will receive Bada kindly and then let him depart in peace."

"Aye, that is fair payment for Bada's own part, and fairly expected of me," said Canis agreeably. "You have come all the way with Julian and his men?"

"Oh, I beg you will not ask me to tell you too much of what I have seen of his force," said Cyella a little anxiously, "for since he gave me kindness, I cannot repay him except in the same coin. Indeed, I walked with my eyes to the ground most of the time and observed little, though I will say he has nearly three thousand men. You will not question me beyond that?"

Her divided loyalties were in conflict and a worry to her. He understood why the division was inevitable. Julian had a way of making most people like him. Cyella was in soft earnestness that she should not be made to betray him in any way, that Canis should accept the issue to be of his own solving. He thought the daughter of Andudo likely to become very endearing.

"Cyclla, there are no questions," he said. To Bada he said, "Not every man would venture into this forest, but you have done this to help Cyella. So our hospitality is your honest due. Wanda shall take care of you and see to your comforts, until you wish to go." He sent for Wanda. She was nearby and came in her own way, peeping smilingly through her curtain of hair.

"What is your wish, lord," she asked.

"Here is a brave Trinovante, Wanda, who has helped to bring to Andudo his lost daughter. Give him what he wishes in the way of food and rest, and then he may stay with us or go, as he freely decides."

"I serve people above my own self, lord," said Bada, and showed his broken teeth to Wanda in a friendly smile.

"He came with Andudo's daughter from the Roman camp," said Canis.

"That is intriguing as well as brave," said Wanda, "I will look to him."

The Trinovante went with her. Andudo arrived in haste and wonder. Cyella gave a cry, and ran to him. Andudo stared, opened his arms and she flung herself into them and wept. Andudo shed a few tears of his own. Joy and tears are always close companions.

Bada returned to Canis within an hour, requesting that he might depart; and Canis said he could. So he did. Two warriors took him into the forest, whistled up some hairy ones, and the hairy ones escorted him safely to the forest's edge.

Back in the Roman camp, Bada spoke with Julian.

"They will leave the forest in two days, tribune, emerging at dawn. This I had from one of them who spoke strangely of vengeance."

"There are always disgruntled ones," said Julian. "At which point will Canis emerge?"

"Alas, this I cannot say, for the one who informed me knew only the day and the time."

"The information is enough, and as good as I could expect. Here is your gold, Bada. But be in no hurry to go, for gold given for information is not truly earned until the information is proved true."

"Then take back your gold, tribune," said Bada, "since I do not want to be paid for that which may prove false by reason of a whim. In this land, whims can come about because of shadows passing over the face of the moon, or because of the way grass leans in morning dew. Whims mean changes of mind. Who is to say Canis will not change his mind, and so make me seem a liar?"

"It is a risk you take by virtue of your calling," said Julian, "and your life hangs on such."

Bada took the gold. He slept under guard that night. His mind was uneasy, his sleep restless. Had the bright-haired Wanda given him false information? In his own shrewdness concerning people, he had not thought so, even allowing that as a woman her whims were all her own. He was relieved when he was aroused at dawn, but dismayed beyond anything when they hanged him. He would have been full of self-pity as well, had he known he was the first and only long-nosed one whom Julian had hanged. But his information had been infuriatingly false, for Canis and his Britons had emerged from the forest this very day and well before dawn. Julian had intended to use this day to dispose his force in a way that would ensure Canis did not steal a march on him. But before dawn, before Julian had stirred, there galloped into the camp an exhausted survivor of one of the outposts. Julian was awakened. He flung a robe over his body and heard what the cavalryman had to say.

"Tribune, all outposts and patrols on our northern watches are beset. And all, I fear, are now slain."

"Not all," said Julian, "for you are here—and though you sweat, you have lost no blood."

"I alone made an offering to Mars before I bedded,

tribune. And though the barbarians were at my throat, the god intervened. By his favour alone, I made my escape."

"By the favour of the Wolfhead, you mean," said Julian impatiently. "Who sees better, or contrives better in the dark, than these Britons? They would not have let you get away, unless they meant you to. They were at your throat, you say, and did not even scratch you? They spared you, so that you could bring me sad tidings. Therefore, sad tidings in this case are meant to deceive."

"By my life, tribune," said the weary soldier, "I swear that only by brave defence did I win free."

"And I swear," said Julian, "that by you Canis seeks to fool me. We are meant to hasten blindly northwards in this grey dawn and meet them as they march on a north-west route. They will not be there, I will swear that too."

Sulla was biting savagely on his twisted lip. He said, "Tribune, are you sure this is deception?"

"Canis would not have let any Roman escape to bring me news that was hot," said Julian, "his wolves would have been at this man's heels until they rode him down. So; he has destroyed my northern watches. Am I to march there to see what he is at, while he emerges on our southern flank?"

"South, then? We will move south?" Sulla was burning for action.

"We will not," said Julian, "we will wait. We will not move in any direction but the right one. Send my servant to me with hot water. There will be time, I think, for me to scrub my chin."

He seemed calm enough. Nevertheless, he fretted. And the whole Roman force fretted. The dawn mists were thick, and the camp on the plateau seemed suspended above them. No word was received from any other northern outposts, and Julian grimly accepted the possibility that he had indeed lost them all to the Britons, in the eerie darkness before dawn. He sent other detachments to replace his considered losses, and he sent gallopers to find out what was happening in the south

152

and the east. Two hours after dawn, no galloper had returned; and the new northern detachments were silent.

He stood thoughtful at the northern exit of his camp, isolated for the moment from his restless centurions. He knew he could well have sent those replacements and gallopers into certain ambush. But it had had to be done; he would not commit his army until he had heard or seen something of the Britons. He had to be certain of where they were. The sounds of the camp rang clear in the sunshine; but below, the silent cloak of mist still covered the ground. By all the gods, he should have thought about the morning mists, but there was always so much else on his mind. His force, numbering fifteen hundred cavalry and over a thousand infantry, stood in armed and horsed array, ready to move as soon as he gave the order. But he could give no order yet, he was blind.

At last the mists lifted, uncovering tracts of wild country on all sides. But still nothing was heard or seen. Then a soldier, riding hard, his mount lathered from its upward climb, burst into the camp to bring news that the Britons were moving north. Julian took that a little bitterly.

"One is entitled to expect a man of guile not to do the obvious," he said.

"They are moving, tribune, along the old track of the horse traders, the northern track to Brigantia."

"They are in sight?"

"Aye, our new detachments will not lose them, tribune."

Julian called for his horse. Another rider appeared, one of the gallopers he had sent south. The man reported that all their southern outposts had been taken by the Britons in the night, that every Roman was dead and all horse captured. And that Britons were swarming in the area.

"The night, the night," said Julian. "He has used those hairy forest friends of his. No men are more invisible outside of day. Now," he said to his centurions, "now has Canis put us in several minds at once. Which way does he intend to send us? North or south? He has sat and conceived deception, while I have sat and conceived nothing except a way of exchanging bright gold for indifferent information. But none of his deceptions will convince me he has split his force, so my obstinacy will not let me split mine. He is going only one way, not two. I will move north or south, but not north and south."

And while his centurions sat restlessly on their horses, and Sulla chewed savagely on his scarred lip, Julian sent gallopers to ride hard north, and further gallopers to the south. The latter returned quickly to report that no Britons could be seen. Julian did not wait on the return of those sent north. He moved north. If the Britons were still on the horse track used in bygone days his army could reach them by late afternoon, or at worst follow on and catch them the next morning. There was the direct route, over difficult terrain but quite negotiable, or the easier but longer route that skirted the forest.

It must be the direct route. Whatever the advantages of the easier way, the direct route at some stage would bring them into sight of their quarry, already being watched by the new northern outposts—if Canis had not by now destroyed them too.

And so the Romans moved glittering and purposeful in the sunshine. They met the returning gallopers from the north, who confirmed the Britons were well clear of the forest—by more than a league, for all their unwieldiness—and were marching towards the kingdom of the Brigantes. They were beyond a valley which Julian could now hazily encompass. It was marked by a green hill that formed its eastern side. Aye, he could reach that point by late morning, his infantry marching with quick, tireless stride despite the rough going. They headed directly for a plain which streams made lush and green in summer and marshy in winter.

The infantry marched, the cavalry trotted. Julian, with two of his centurions, rode ahead, some distance behind his foraging scouts. Had it not been for that prolonged mist, he would have spotted the Britons from the camp itself, always providing they had emerged at a point within sight. And he

154

felt they had, he felt they had simply taken the quickest way possible to reach that horse track, which traders had pushed through terrain totally unsuitable for battle. He had to catch up with them by not later than the morning, or his pursuit of them would be a thing of piecemeal sorties and murderous ambushes.

They marched two leagues, first over descending ground, and then over ground anything but flat. The banners fluttered and danced, accoutrements jingled, and for all the heat and the sweat the sense of purpose kept morale high. Julian strained his eyes constantly. They were near enough to the route taken by the Britons to have seen them, but none came to the eye. They must have moved quickly and kept at it, despite any old people they had with them; and Julian wondered how far along that northern track they had advanced. He approached the plain veined by winding streams, and here his scouting patrol came doubling back at speed. A hot but exultant cavalryman pulled up beside him.

"Tribune! They are there, less than a league in front, and look to be waiting for us. They are grouped at the northern end of a hard valley."

"I know that place," said Julian, "and it not a place I would choose to stand. I might be squeezed to death. So what now, what more is in his mind?"

He went on. He had to. No wonder they had seen no Britons. Those who had taken the track had probably been the women, the widows, the young children and old men. The warriors had obviously diverged long since and gone to cover by that valley, behind the hill on its eastern side. And now they had massed in the valley and were waiting for him.

He reached it. In compact, disciplined array the Romans entered the valley. Its hard, flinty bed threw up only scrub. And there at the far end they saw the assembled warriors of Canis, almost fifteen hundred strong. Well over two thousand people had marched out of the forest, and all who were not too young or too old bore weapons. Burnished swords, spears and javelins flashed in the afternoon light. Women, children and aged were some distance north-west. So was Lydia. Canis would not have her see him in bloody conflict with her brother.

Since misty dawn the Britons had been there; and in the time granted to them by the confusion sown by Canis, they had not merely sat in idle contemplation of the coming battle. They had worked until the mist lifted, they had then gone to cover; and now they were there again, and waiting.

Julian, bringing his full force into the head of the long, wide valley, halted to make his survey and his dispositions. The Britons stood six hundred paces from him. They looked to have about five hundred horsed men. "The better part consisting of Roman horse, no doubt," he said ruefully to himself.

Sulla rode up. His protuberant eyes stared glassily at the Britons, searching for one who was taller than most.

"We have the dogs, tribune," he said.

"We have not caught up with them, they have waited for us. Think on it," said Julian. He surveyed them, assessing their number. They were not armoured as Romans were, they relied mainly on their round shields of wood and leather. He saw warrior maids. They stood out by reason of their vivid tunics and bare, gleaming legs. Julian judged his troops to be reasonably confident, but knowing Canis he did not think victory would come too easily. Fifteen hundred Britons under the command of Boadicea's general were not waiting there merely to bravely die. No matter. From the moment Paullinus had thrust the command on him, Julian had never thought his campaign would be anything but difficult. It had been hard, grinding patience up till now; and now it was going to be hard, grinding battle.

He saw why Canis had chosen this valley. Its walls were too steep to permit wide, flanking manoeuvres. His tactics, reckoned Julian, would be defensive. He could not afford to lose men in attack, especially against a superior force. On the other hand, the Romans could only make direct frontal assaults. To get behind the Britons, Julian would have to turn

156

back and make a wide detour, during which time the Britons would melt away. Then would begin the exhausting dance in chase of them, which Paullinus had contemptuously dismissed.

He wondered why the Britons had not melted away in the morning mists after destroying his outposts. There was only one answer to that. Canis did not want Romans forever at his heels. He had decided he preferred to give battle.

Julian rode slowly forward, his horse stepping daintily around patches of scrub, two mounted centurions behind him. He came close enough to the Britons to make himself heard. They stood silently. So did the Roman troops.

"I am Julian Osirus," he called, "and I command for Paullinus this day. I will, if you will, speak first with your own commander, whom I know. Will he come before me?"

There was movement in the rear of the warriors and Canis, mounted, rode through them. His horse stepped as daintily as Julian's had, though not for the same reason. He dismounted when he had gone twenty paces, and then came forward on foot. Julian also dismounted and advanced to meet the Briton. It was the first time they had seen each other since the day Canis had left the house of the Roman more than a year ago. He had been in bondage to Lydia. Julian, resplendent in his armour, gave Canis a whimsical smile. He looked no older, thought Julian. There was no touch of grey in his thick, brown hair with its glint of copper, though he was now thirty-six.

"I am here, you see," said Julian, and to the surprise of the Britons and the astonishment of Romans, the tribune and Canis put out their right hands and clasped each other by the wrist.

"I have not forgotten you," said Canis amiably.

"Nor I you," said Julian. "But you must know I am here to destroy your force, and to take you to noble Paullinus, our Imperial Governor. You have heard of him, no doubt. Why did you not dwell in peace? Had you done so, I should not have had such a scurvy command as this."

Canis answered with a smile on his face.

157

"I have heard of the illustrious Paullinus indeed. He is a man who allows none of us to dwell in peace."

"Will you not disband your warriors, Canis, and give yourself up?" suggested Julian.

"If you are here for battle, Julian, so am I."

"Well, I would just as soon give you battle as deliver you to Paullinus," said Julian. "Where is my sister?"

"Not here," said Canis. "What is her fate?"

"Pardon, if I take you," said Julian. More quietly he added, "And if I also take Princess Cea."

Canis, who had been participating amiably in the dialogue, did not lose his good humour.

"Paullinus must also have his ghosts now?" he said.

"If I deliver neither you nor the Princess to Paullinus," said Julian, "if I only take Lydia, then my sister is sacrificed."

"Well, you must find her first," said Canis. "Will you attack us now?"

"I would just as soon you ran at us," said Julian.

"We are neither disposed to, nor equipped to," said Canis, "and it is your battle more than ours. Julian, be of good cheer, as I am. We are both favoured. You have Caesar to inspire you. I have Boadicea."

"Then you are the more favoured," said Julian.

They clasped wrists again, and separated. Canis returned to his warriors, unaware of the eyes of Sulla burning his back, and Julian to his lines.

He did not waste time in deciding his tactics. Canis would expect him to wedge his infantry and attack to split the Britons, then advance his cavalry to cut them down. It was a classical and traditional Roman manoeuvre. Against a man like Canis it needed to be reversed, and Julian knew his cavalrymen were itching to take advantage of the bold run the wide and lengthy valley gave them. The stunted scrub was no problem.

And so the Roman cavalry, fifteen hundred of them, grouped for assault, every man skilled in the use of lance-like spear, and effective with the sword when spear was gone.

They rode out, the hard ground echoing to the clatter of the horses. They formed, they advanced, and as they kicked their mounts into the gallop thunder rolled. Dust and scrub flew beneath the iron charge and the sun painted Roman helmets with golden light. Julian sat quietly in his saddle, watching his cavalry deploying over the full width of the valley and running in massed might at the standing Britons. Manes tossed like a dark sea, iron-shod hooves pounded the ground, and the bright day was sundered by the cataclysm of galloping assault. The vengeful arm of Paullinus reached to smite the Britons.

But the moment when it seemed that the thunder would engulf their ears, the Britons' vanguard rolled swiftly back, and their defence in depth was gone, empty. They leapt in lightning retreat, and sped through scrub to turn in on their rearguard and stand elbow to elbow with them. And in the ground they had vacated, which they had hidden from Romans, reared a network of iron and timber stakes, driven firmly into the ground and angled viciously. The oncoming Romans, so near had they been at the moment the Britons sped back, saw the cruelly pointing stakes too late. Nor could they leap them, their depth was too great. The stakes seemed to rise swift and sudden at them, and a hundred of the foremost riders plunged into the forest of sharp iron and timber.

Horses screamed as spikes gutted them, and Romans pitched headlong from agonised animals to impale themselves. Worse, the whole body of cavalry was carried by its own impetus into the wreck of the vanguard—every man expecting not the piercing shock of static spikes, but the yielding impact of enemy bodies. It was a hurtling, massed charge into two thousand merciless points. Within seconds the sea of cavalry was a sea of mangled flesh and running blood, lashing, frenzied horses killing and maiming fallen riders. The screams of the horses mingled with the screams of men. The network of stakes covered the width of the valley, and the deployed Roman cavalry lay writhing, dying and grounded from flank to flank. More than five hundred men and mounts died in a few, savagely cruel minutes. Others did not die but continued to scream.

The fervour and the solidity of the charge had been its undoing. Survivors were in shock and turmoil, wheeling before the horror of it. With Roman trumpets still sounding advance and attack, turmoil became red, roaring confusion in front of that bloody sea of spiked flesh. At this moment the Britons opened ranks and rushed forward small, mobile catapults on wheels, the wheels speedily blocked to render the machines static. They began to whir and crack like whips, hurling masses of iron fragments, sharp and jagged, at the plunging, disordered Roman cavalry. Men pitched from their horses as if struck by the fiery bolts of Vulcan. Others who had been flung into the network of stakes, but had miraculously escaped impalation, were staggering dazedly about. The wounding rain of iron showered on them.

The savage hail increased. The Romans floundered, the maddened horses reared and crashed, or broke free and bolted. And when the roaring confusion was at its worst, Canis flung in his own mounted warriors. They skirted the spikes on both sides of the valley to come at the reeling Roman cavalry from each flank. They rode tightly, heads down, leaping scrub, and above the brassy din and shouting tumult rose their cries of war. The Romans heard the throaty yells of the men and the singing cries of the warrior maids. The catapults quit the conflict as the mounted Britons joined issue with the floundering Romans, charging like demons into the battered enemy. To make his counter-attack doubly effective, Canis sent in foot warriors to give bloody and swift quittance to unhorsed Romans and to spiked Romans not yet dead.

The maimed cavalry staggered anew. The lightning, two-pronged assault of the mounted Britons swept or smote them from their horses. Fierce, supple warrior maids, hair swirling and streaming, used sword or short stabbing spear with relentless joy. It paralysed a Roman to see a warrior maid laugh as she smote him to death. He died in numbed astonishment.

The Romans were in chaos, the Britons in smiting triumph.

Princess Cea, not to be denied her place any more than her mother when her warriors were at war, watched with Canis from higher ground as Julian's cavalry was hammered into defeat. She saw the reeling tangle they were in. They had never recovered from their plunge onto the spikes. Canis, drawing the axe of Cerdwa from his belt, caught her eye. She drove her horse in front of his.

"Never! You shall not!" she cried. "Only when you are the very last man left will I permit you to court death. You shall not torment me in this way as you tormented my mother. And see, we are in triumph already, look how they fall. What need is there for you to swing Cerdwa's axe, or do you hear your wood-witch calling on you for Roman blood?"

"There was the ghost of a call," he admitted, "but yours is a louder one, Princess." He replaced the axe.

"Mine is the true one," said Cea, auburn hair burning in the westering sun. "And look, look, they are falling back!"

The Roman trumpets were calling, and mauled remnants of their cavalry were fighting to disengage and retreat. Those which did escape were not pursued. Canis did not want any battle-infected warriors to run headlong into the rageful Roman infantry. He had the horns blow loudly to remind his mounted force to stay where they were. Bitter Romans streamed back to their lines. Of that proud, bright unit of fifteen hundred men and horse, less than four hundred survived. In one savage and merciless encounter, Canis had virtually destroyed Julian's cavalry. The reddening sun picked out the gory armour of the survivors, and made starkly hideous the baleful arena of pointed stakes, within which lay masses of slain men and dead horses. Blood oozed wetly and odorously red, and the mangled bodies and carcasses so covered the ground that it was as if the Roman god of war himself lay sprawled in gigantic death.

"They will come again," said Canis.

"After this? They cannot," said Cea and shuddered.

"They must," said Canis.

And they did.

Not immediately, but as soon as Julian had collected himself. He was as bitter as the sweating, broken cavalrymen. He had not embroiled his infantry in that turmoil; they would have had to fight their way through their reeling cavalry and their mass of spiked dead. The centurion Sulla was among the survivors; he had participated in the bloody engagement with red mist clouding his vision, hacking insanely and almost unseeingly at laughing warrior maids driving him mad. He sat panting on his horse, twisted lips flecked with froth.

Julian knew he must commit his infantry. The Britons had drawn farther back, this time uncovering a wide ditch dug across the valley. Their hairy friends, long and mighty of arm, had dug it for them in misty dawn light. They retreated over this ditch on rough bridges of timber, pulling up the bridges when they had crossed. This meant the Roman infantry would have to negotiate not only the breastwork of spikes and their massed slain, but also the wide, deep ditch. Beyond the ditch, within the ranks of the Britons, Julian saw the catapults. Sulla rode up to him, his face fiery and livid.

"Tribune—"

"Tribune? I am more of a dead man than a tribune," said Julian. "I shall be hanged if I return to Paullinus with only half my force. I wonder, shall I be hanged any higher if I return with no force at all?"

"Put me at the throat of that thrice-damned Briton with no more than a hundred men, and I will take him," said Sulla like a wine-drunk demon, "so bid our foot soldiers advance, tribune."

"How will you cross that ditch?"

"Over our dead," said Sulla.

"I prefer sound methods to fiery heroics," said another centurion.

"Use the living," said Julian, "have them jump into the ditch and build bridges of their backs and their shields for those who follow on. Cover this expedient with pila, assailing most of all the Britons who have charge of the catapults. Ye gods, they must have been at their work all night."

So the Roman infantry advanced, compact, disciplined and purposeful; but with fury running fiery in their blood at the cruel death of so many of their mounted comrades. They reached the massed array of stained spikes; they climbed over their slain cavalry and fallen horse; and the waiting Britons watched in silence, warrior maids kissing their bright spears. Their war cries sang out only when they attacked. They really preferred attack to defence, but their ears and their minds had long been buffeted by the forceful advice of Canis, their war lord. They knew now when to stand, and wait, and stand.

As the Romans advanced to the ditch, the Britons began to fill their iron catapults, which were like large round pots mounted on sprung levers. They filled them with hot fragments of iron, which they took from fires burning within iron frames, using long-handled ladles. As the Romans began to leap into the ditch, the catapults whirred and white-hot iron pellets rained down on them. They warded these off with uplifted shields. Quickly more Romans surged forward, taking the bombardment of fiery missiles on their shields. They jumped into the ditch to join those already there. But those already there were lurching and staggering, for the floor of the ditch was lined with straw, and beneath the straw was thorn, brushwood and bramble, cut and hacked from the sides of the valley to make as cruel a bed for the heavily armoured Romans as Canis and his hairy ones could devise. Feet and legs sank deep into the thorn, and the staggering Romans lurched and fell, and the hot iron showered them.

And the iron was as hot as the fires from which it had been taken. Raining on keeling shields as the Romans staggered, it ran smoking and fiery from the shields into the ditch and onto the men. And with it began to come glowing, resinous knots of wood. The straw in the ditch was dry. Tiny wisps of smoke curled, and oncoming Romans stopped to look down on comrades reeling and buckling in the cruel thorn. Here and there, straw began to ignite. It became touched with flame and the flame began to spread. Sulla, close by, stared in madness, his eyes almost bursting from their red-rimmed sockets as he saw the flames and smelt the fire.

From their side of the ditch the Romans hurled their pila, their short throwing spears. But harassed by the expanding rain of glowing iron, and by the necessity of pulling scorched and bleeding comrades from the smouldering thorn in the ditch before they were burned alive, their curses flew thicker than their pila. Fifty catapults flung far greater menace. The red-hot embers of iron tore into flesh, burningly pitted arms and legs and ricocheted from shields and breastplates. Men trapped in thorny brambles beat frenziedly with swords at the darting tongues of fire that ran through straw to ignite the bramble. And still the rain of fire continued.

The Roman infantry began to break before that ditch.

At this, Canis signalled his mounted warriors. They broke out of their standing comrades and charged at the fiery ditch. Again the valley filled with the thunder of flying hooves. Singing, the mounted warrior maids leapt the ditch side by side with their men, at points where it had been narrowed for just such a manoeuvre. The Roman infantry found themselves besieged by the horsed Britons, who rode them down, burst through them, galloped on, turned and galloped back again. They thundered in on that bright Roman glitter, and left spears skewered in Roman flesh. In the ditch the flames in places began to roar, trapped men screamed. Sulla, dismounted, ran about like a madman, his nostrils full of smarting smoke.

Canis let his standing warriors move. They streamed towards the ditch, laid their timber bridges over it, and crossed it. Flames reached with long tongues to lick fierily at the bridges. Beset by the mounted Britons on one side, the Romans now had to withstand the leaping, bounding foot warriors on the other. They were hemmed in, they were squeezed, and the Britons exacted some repayment for being so squeezed themselves on the day of Boadicea's defeat.

Julian knew the battle was lost. The tactics of Canis had always been fierce and quick. That was how he had commanded great victories for Boadicea. He did not believe in protracted, attritional battles. He manoeuvred for speedy victory and minimum loss.

Julian rode with re-grouped remnants of his cavalry to cover the retreat of his broken infantry. Many dead and dying men were left in the ditch and in front of it. Those who were screaming in the fire were mercifully despatched by the Britons.

The full force of warriors smote and battered the retreating Romans, and at this moment Canis, heedless of the angry cries of Cea, rode at the heels of the conflict. But he was not intending to join the fight. He was out to discover whether a Roman tribune, one who had spoken in brave defence of Queen Boadicea at Venta Icenorum, had become dangerously embroiled in the tumbling Roman retreat.

As Julian indeed had.

He found himself suddenly surrounded by Britons. The now outnumbered Romans were fighting and dying, many doing so whilst they courageously covered the escape of others. Julian, with only a few of his cavalrymen around him, fought with them to break out from the ring of Britons. Elsewhere, he saw only that which presaged utter defeat—the British warrior maids wildly exhilarated as they exacted vengeance for their many sisters who had died so bravely on the day of Boadicea's only defeat.

Some Roman cavalry and a few hundred infantry did escape, but Julian and those who fought with him became inextricably hemmed in. He had been right. Canis had not wanted to march westward with Romans forever at his heels. So he had decided to accept battle. He had begun his manoeuvres in the night; and he had chosen the battlefield, prepared it and brought the Romans to it.

" Oh, feckless, fickle Mars," spoke Julian's bitter mind, " my patient contriving apart, you have seen my proud campaign last only the space of this one unhappy hour."

Then he saw Canis, riding a thrusting way through his warriors. Julian urged his snorting horse forward. Britons opened up and then closed in. Canis shouted at singing warrior maids who leapt to drag Julian from his saddle. He crashed earthwards. There was a dart of savage pain, an explosive redness and engulfing blackness.

And as escaping Romans rushed south in retreat, the Britons annihilated all who were still committed in that red valley with its fiery ditch.

They carried Julian, bleeding and unconscious, from the field.

* * *

At a point north-west of the battle, waited the women, the children, the old ones and a number of protective warriors: the latter chewing frustratedly on their lips. It was not what they liked, playing nurse to women and children, when all other warriors were fighting the Romans of cold-eyed Paullinus.

Lydia and Cyella were among the waiting women, Lydia almost as frustrated as the warriors. She had not wanted to see her countrymen die, but she had wanted to be with Canis. If the battle went against him, how could she endure not knowing what would follow? She had listened to his summary command to go with the women, and had been as defiant as the Lydia of old. Had she not been with him in many moments of danger, and had she on any of these occasions borne herself less bravely than others?

"That is not the question," he said. "You will go with the women to the place I have arranged. It will be safer for you and Dilwys."

"Dilwys will be safe enough but I do not crave a hole in a wall myself. What is that to me? I am not to be treated like a humped old woman, I am not!"

It made no difference. He would not take her with him. She could have wept. She had had to go. They knew nothing of the battle at this distance, so how it had gone none could say. They were to wait. Cyella, a little highly-strung because of everything, had bitten her lip until a spot of blood showed. Lydia hid her emotions, but Cyella could not hide hers.

"It is so cruel and needless," she said, "and it is all because of Paullinus. He will wreck all Britain in his desire to nail Canis to a cross."

A little shiver took Lydia.

"Paullinus will not do that," she said. "He may wreck all Britain, but he will never take Canis." She spoke as much to convince herself as Cyella, whom she liked for her pride and gentleness. "Do you worry for your father, Cyella? Put it aside. Andudo is no reckless youth, and now that he has found you he will return to you. He will not risk himself foolishly in any battle."

"There is not only my father," said Cyella, as they stood in the grass not far from the overgrown track they had traversed. "There is Canis and Princess Cea. And," she added, as if in afterthought, "there is your brother Julian."

"No harm will come to any of them." Lydia, her face honey-brown, essayed a reassuring smile, though her uneasy heart beat erratically. "Cyella, it cannot. Canis must survive, he must, for without him we are nothing. We cannot be nothing. No gods would permit this. As to my brother Julian, I have prayed for him, and Diana will guard him."

"If you prayed for Julian, did you not also pray for all his Romans?"

Lydia remembered a desolate morning, a girl child abominably slain and Roman soldiers who looked on without pity while it was done.

"I can pray for Julian and for Rome," she said, "I cannot pray for too many Romans."

"But you are Roman," said Cyella.

"I was born of Rome," said Lydia quietly, "but here is my life, here are those I love."

"You are unlike all Romans I have met," said Cyella impulsively, "except perhaps you are not unlike your brother. There is also your Imperial Procurator, Julius Classicianus. He too is kind."

"Cyella," said Lydia, "it is true. Not all Romans have the face of Paullinus or the vileness of Sulla Petonius."

Who Sulla Petonius was Cyella did not know. Emotionally

167

she said, " I might have borne a spear and fought with the warrior maids today, but my father would not allow this, and so I have been left with old women."

" If I am one of these old women," said Lydia with a slight smile, " then I know now why I too was not allowed to be at the battle. But, Cyella, would you have carried a spear against Julian, when you say he has been so kind to you?"

The Iceni maid expressed sudden visual interest in a bird that swooped to alight and peck the ground. Then she said, " I will wish that although it may go well for Canis today, it may not go too hard for Julian."

Lydia might have commented on this, except that Marcellus came to her eyes. Around a fire, women were preparing a cooking pot. Marcellus, who seemed to have slipped the escort Canis had put on him for this day, strode past the women in search of Lydia. There was something about him that made her hasten to meet him. The warriors assigned to look after the women and the old ones glanced curiously at him, but did nothing.

" Marcellus?" said Lydia.

" I have seen that woman, Wanda," he said. " She has fled from the battle. It has gone against your infallible Briton. She speaks slightingly of him, yet one might also say she was disturbed for him."

Lydia turned white. For a moment her world rocked.

" What has happened to Canis?" She flung the question anguishedly. Cyella was there to put a hand on her arm, as the look on the face of Marcellus froze her and clamped icy fear around her heart. She forgot her child, gurgling happily in the arms of Feola, who had become its nurse. " Marcellus, what has happened?"

" You had better come, and quickly," said Marcellus.

Lydia, frantic, went after the tribune as he began to hasten along the track. Cyella followed. The women looked at them, the old ones wondered about them. They passed the bored warriors. Marcellus said nothing but went on, Lydia and Cyella at his heels. Marcellus left the track, made rapid progress

168

along the bank of a stream, and went with its course as it wound to enter a small wooded valley.

"Marcellus, what are you at, what are you taking us to see?" Lydia tried to come up with the Roman as he quickened his urgent stride. "If anything has happened to Canis, what is it to you?"

Marcellus plunged into the trees, and only stopped to answer when he reached a tethered horse. It had belonged to his escort, who now lay dead in a nearby thicket.

"If Canis has been taken," he said, "and I have not redeemed myself, then I will be taken too and returned to Paullinus in ignominy."

"What talk is this?" Lydia pushed back her raven hair. "It is about ifs, it is not about Canis, it is about yourself."

"What man is there who is not chiefly concerned with his own fate?" said Marcellus. "In truth, madam, whether Canis and his barbarians triumph or not, either outcome does nothing for me. But if I take to Paullinus something he is not likely to get if Canis triumphs, namely your person, then what I lost by reason of your trickery I shall regain by my own. You shall come with me now."

"If you dare attempt this," breathed Lydia, falling back, "Canis will kill you—oh, you fool!"

She turned to escape. Marcellus, desperate for self-restitution, smote her from behind. The blow closed her mind and dropped her to the ground. Cyella sprang at the Roman with a wild cry. Marcellus threw her savagely off, and she rolled helplessly down the slope into the trickling stream. Marcellus stooped, lifted the limp body of Lydia, threw her over the horse and mounted. He rode furiously towards a point that would bring him south of the field of battle, a battle now over.

He had indeed seen Wanda. She had ridden from the battle, had looked for Marcellus, found him and told him the Britons were destroying the Romans.

"So there is less than nothing for you this day, Roman," she mocked him, "unless your gods contrive a speedy miracle,

169

or unless you console Paullinus by taking Lydia to him. Give it quick thought, Roman, for it would not only console Paullinus, it would also turn the fruits of victory sour for Canis, the true cause of your humiliation. Lydia is the mother of his child."

That could not be denied.

And so, as Wanda rode away with a strange laugh, Marcellus made a decision. It was not a difficult one. He had two or three scores to settle with Lydia.

* * *

Lydia came to, a buzzing in her aching head. She lay on hard, inhospitable ground. She opened her eyes. Anguished remembrance rushed. Someone stood looking down at her. It was a man with a face lividly scarred by fire. His armoured uniform was thick and foul with dried blood. But it was not the blood or the puckered, repellent distortions which set her limbs shivering. It was the stony, protuberant, red-rimmed eyes. She had looked into those eyes on another day.

They were the eyes of Sulla, the centurion who had broken and murdered an innocent child.

" So," said the hateful voice that slurred its consonants, " it has been a bad day for your house, Lydia Osirus. Your brother has lost a battle he should have won, and you have gained company you should have avoided. The tribune Marcellus Mercurius will, with my help, deliver you to Paullinus. You do not represent a victory, but you should give him some consolation for a defeat."

A few hundred Roman troops, all that had survived, retreated south in bitterness and fury. With them went Lydia, and in the end Marcellus and Sulla delivered her into the hands of Paullinus.

170

7

Lydia entered the presence of the Imperial Governor like a woman already dead. Paullinus, beside himself with icy rage at news of defeat, invested her with bitter, biting abuse. Lydia made no reply, spoke no word. For a while she did not even hear him. She was numbed by the realisation that they had at last torn her from her world.

Diana, oh, do not forsake me now, do not.

What was this thin-lipped Roman saying?

". . . and so, traitorous sister of incompetent brother, here you shall remain until you are taken by ship to Rome. There you will come before the magistrates of Caesar, charged on my deposition with treason, and they will be well acquainted with every item relevant to your iniquity. Take her away."

She did not even know where they took her, only that they put her in a room with four walls and each wall pressed unbearably on her soul. She collapsed on a couch and wept. But a sound outside her door made her shake the tears fiercely away. She would not weep before gaolers, no, not even if her heart broke. But no one entered, and she sank down again, the anguish a physical pain. The joys and dangers she had shared with Canis were gone forever. All had gone from her.

Oh, Diana, let him understand my despair.

She had given him a sweet daughter. And the daughter was lost to her also. Dilwys, Dilwys, you were my most beautiful gift to your father. He will not let them take me to Rome, he could not. He will come for me and take me back to you.

Her thoughts ran feverishly, tormentedly, her despair the worse because of the four oppressive walls.

She did not know how long she lay with her mind so unendurably burdened, before again a sound at the door penetrated her misery.

"Mistress?" It was a soft voice. Lydia sat up and hid for a moment green eyes that were drowning. Then she looked round. She saw a Roman girl, one with warm eyes who might understand the tears in her own. The girl came in, quietly closing the door. "I have been told we lost a battle," she said.

"I have lost my life," said Lydia.

"You are Lydia, sister to Julian Osirus, who commanded the battle we lost? I have seen him here in days gone by, and am sad for him. For he is a man to command friends, even if not victories. They say the Britons have Julian, and that we have you. I do not think any good will come of it. My kinsman Paullinus will in his new anger so conduct the outcome that there will only be more suffering. You have lived close to the man called Canis the Briton, have you not?"

"Who are you?" Lydia, though her despair overrode all, warmed a little to the girl's soft eyes and sweet sympathy. She was dark like herself, Roman like herself.

"I am Claudia Justian," she replied softly, "and I dwell here with Paullinus, my uncle, until my father comes from Gaul. Alas, Paullinus is so much the stern soldier, he has forgotten how to be an understanding man. When I was a child I remember he smiled often on me. I have seen him smile on no one since I have been here. I have seen Canis smile."

Lydia's anguished heart lurched.

"You know Canis?" she asked.

Claudia looked upon this Roman woman who had become renegade. She saw a woman whose vivid beauty could not be despoiled by tears, or mitigated in any way by the short, kilted tunic she wore. It was the kind of tunic worn normally only by the Britons, both men and women, in this region. It was, thought Claudia, a little shameless on such a woman as Lydia. It showed smooth, brown legs and full, graceful thighs. Claudia had heard much of Lydia Osirus—how she had given up her wealth, and had forsaken Caesar to go with Canis the Briton.

And Claudia had also heard some strange tale of how by trickery and deceit Lydia had contrived to fool the tribune Marcellus Mercurius. Yet she did not look like a woman to whom such faults were common and everyday. There was, through the dust and strain of forced travel, much about her which had to do with far nobler things than deceit. But O, the woe in the drowning green eyes, the paleness that lapped the honey-brown.

"Once," said Claudia, "I talked with Canis. I found him a strange man. In a little while will you not perhaps be in some pleasure to be with your own people again?"

"If you have talked with Canis and if he has smiled on you," said Lydia, "you must know the answer in advance of the question. I cannot endure it, I cannot, for they are sending me to Rome."

"My kinsman has sworn to do this many times," said Claudia, "but I beg you, pay his animosity no great heed, for in the event that you do come before the wise magistrates of Caesar, they will not condemn you for that which was entirely of your heart."

"That will not arise," said Lydia dully, "for I will die long before I reach Rome."

"You must not speak so," said Claudia earnestly. "You are still young, and surely there is much you may still live for?"

"All that I wish to live for is lost to me, which is Canis and the people of Queen Boadicea."

"Hush," said Claudia, even more earnestly, "do not speak that name here, nothing offends my kinsman's ears more than the name of that wanton widow."

"Claudia, she was no wanton widow," said Lydia, "she was a great queen whom we grievously wronged. I saw her cruelly scourged and heard her utter not one cry, and yet I spat on her. That is why the gods, even Diana, are putting this unbearable punishment on me."

"Hush," said Claudia again. She sat on the couch beside Lydia and put an arm around her. Such sympathy made Lydia

173

tremble, but although she knew she had found a gentle friend here it did not ease her sharp anguish.

During the days that followed, Claudia was as discreetly defiant of the wishes of Paullinus as she could contrive, and gave Lydia what comfort she could. She brought her robes and shifts; she brought her little things; and when she could, she took her to the household bath. In the matter of the bath, she was forced to forgo discretion and stand up openly and valiantly against her kinsman, declaring him to be unforgivable for denying Lydia use of cleansing water. Paullinus wished Lydia to be confined permanently to her room, in order to avoid all risks of losing her. He did not wish to have her moved to any other lodgement, for further fear of having her escape.

And so Lydia was imprisoned for the most part within her four oppressive walls. Her room was in the rear of the spacious but austerely furnished villa of the Governor, this villa also being his headquarters. Through the spirited intercession of Claudia, she was free for an hour to come and go in respect of the bath, but never could she put one foot outside the place. Even if she had, the iron restraint imposed by the watchful guards would have prevented any attempt to escape. Paullinus was unshakeably resolved that a woman who had been as false to Caesar as Lydia should be returned to Caesar. Nero would be intrigued to see her. Her inevitable death would bring some solace to Paullinus for the reverses she and her brother had put upon him. And such solace would be better savoured by the fact that he himself had not given her death. No one would be able to say it had been Paullinus who sentenced a high-born Roman woman to be torn to pieces in the arena. Nero, master of music and verse, would look upon her as the lions pounced, would think compassionately about her and in the evening he would compose a sad but sweet song about a young life gone.

" I decided to return her to Rome," Paullinus would say, " for I myself did not wish to both judge her and condemn her."

Lydia visibly languished. This gave concern to Claudia, who held her in growing affection. The green eyes that daily seemed

174

to grow larger in the paling face held a strange mourning, which Claudia felt was not for her possible death in Rome. The girl brought wine to the captive one evening.

"Lydia, if you will not eat even as much to keep a mouse alive, at least let this wine give you some strength and comfort."

"I am forgotten," said Lydia. Though the evening was warm, she was full of shivers. "I am forgotten, Claudia, and that is even more unbearable than being forsaken."

"By whom are you forgotten?"

"He has sent me no word. Surely he could have done this. To forsake me, held as I am by Paullinus, this I can understand, for who could wrest me from the grip of such a bitter Roman as this? But to forget me, this puts me in such misery, such pain—"

"Lydia," said Claudia firmly, "is this your faith in one whom you profess to be your only joy? If only half of what you have told me is true, Canis is not the man to forget you. True, to deliver you from my kinsman's iron ring is beyond most men, but Canis will not forget you. No, never."

Lydia lay on her couch, wrapped in Claudia's warmest robe. But she still shivered. Her long black hair framed her pale face, its honey gone. Her strength, her vitality and her courage were ebbing day by day. Nor could she sleep at night. In the darkness, she lay despairing and praying.

She took a cup of wine from Claudia and drank feverishly.

"Claudia, you seek to comfort me. You do comfort me, and never think I do not cherish your sweet company, for I do, I do. But each day I die. There is no word from him, nothing. He has forgotten me already. Is this not shallow, in a man who is the father of my child?" She gave a softly bitter laugh that distressed Claudia. "Is it not?"

"It would be if he had so forgot, but he has not," insisted Claudia, who was intensely intrigued by the relationship between this beautiful Roman woman and the man who had bitterly mocked her uncle. "I have seen Canis only once, but I am sure he is a man who will keep faith with everyone he loves."

" I do not even have Dilwys to hold and whisper to," said Lydia. She paid no heed to a sudden rapping on the door. It was Claudia who went to admit a soldier, stiff and formal in his armour.

" Mistress," he said to Lydia, " you are summoned to attend on his Excellency, the Imperial Governor."

Claudia insisted on accompanying Lydia. Paullinus frowned to see her at the side of his prisoner. A centurion, brown and weathered of face, stood immobile behind the Governor.

" I did not summon you," said Paullinus to Claudia.

" Yet I am here," said Claudia bravely, " for it is no more than Lydia's right to have no less than her equal in support."

" Not under all circumstances," said Paullinus, " but stay if you must. Heed me, madam," he said acidly to Lydia. She stood quietly before him. Her courage did not fail her on these occasions, for it was not the Governor or Rome or death she feared, only the possibility that Canis was indifferent to her fate. " Madam," continued Paullinus, " your barbarian paramour who calls himself Canis has sent me impudent word concerning you."

Lydia's paleness receded before a tide of rushing blood. Light animated her eyes, and within the blue robe her body trembled.

" Oh, in such mercy as you have, quote me that which he writes," she breathed.

Paullinus smiled thinly, cruelly. He took up a tablet.

" I will quote him, madam, word for word. In this wise. 'Paullinus. You hold Lydia, sister to Julian Osirus. I hold Julian, lately commander and defeated tribune. Return Lydia to me, and I will return Julian to you.' "

Lydia's hands flew to her burning face, and covered the wild glow in her eyes. Paullinus smiled again.

" There is more," he said. " Listen carefully, as I quote. If your consent to this does not reach me within two days, then Julian, lately commander, will become late commander, and I will forgo all interest in Lydia, who is despite all else a Roman and belongs more to you than to me.' "

Lydia stiffened, then violent tremors beset her. The colour ran from her, drained from her and left her deathly white.

"What might I do with Julian of the house of Osirus?" said Paullinus. "Have I not a sufficiency of incompetents about me already?"

"Shame on you," cried Claudia, in passionate suffering for Lydia. "Aye, I cry it again—shame on you, kinsman! Return her to Canis! Oh, you are godless to let death come in this way to Julian, and to give more cruelty to Lydia—"

"Hold your besotted tongue, impudence!" The voice of Paullinus was like the hissing of a whip. "Take the renegade from my sight. She is for Rome. Look upon her, dimwits. Think you there is any joy for her in returning to Canis now? Does he not say she belongs more to us than to him? Does she not now realise she is only a false and faithless woman, who has been used by that cunning, barbarian dog? This was no message requesting her return, this was message to flaunt the dog's victory, to tell me he has not only given bloody death to my soldiers, but is now about to make an end of Julian. Take her away, I say, for in six days she will take ship to Rome. I fancy her incompetent brother is to his own fate."

The eyes of the silent centurion flickered to see the pain and agony of Lydia, to see with what tremendous effort she fought that which threatened to drop her in a swoon. Warmth touched him as he saw her straighten her back. Paullinus nodded, the centurion moved to escort Lydia; and with Claudia he took her back to her room. Lydia walked like one blind, but did not falter until she reached the door, when momentarily she staggered as if her knees had suddenly become treacherous. The centurion's arm went swiftly around her.

"Hold, mistress," he said quietly, "I know the house of Osirus, I knew your father, and I know there is no member of this house who cannot stand straight and proud despite any torment."

He was a soldier, a veteran campaigner of the Empire, but he had never lacked compassion.

"I do not know your name," said Lydia in a whisper, "but

you are one to remind me I once loved Rome. Will you forgive me that I forsook her?"

"Each of us to our own, mistress," said the centurion, "and for your comfort, do not forget that your brother Julian makes friends, not enemies. I warrant you Canis will not despatch him. Canis only has a talent for tormenting our noble Governor. Though we cannot love the Briton, yet there are some of us who understand him, and even some who admire him, for he is the greatest warrior in all Britain. I would that he were for us and not against us. I bid you restful night, mistress, and may Diana herself lay gentle touch on your eyes."

"I will remember you," said Lydia huskily. He went, and Claudia brought her to her couch. Lydia collapsed over it, in greater anguish than she had ever known. "Oh, Canis," she whispered brokenly, "I did not think you so cruel as to utterly destroy me."

"Lydia, do not," begged Claudia, almost weeping, "do not rack yourself so. They were but words, they had no meaning except for my kinsman. Come, drink some wine. You must, or you will spend the night sleepless and tormented. You must be strong, Lydia, you must endure, for Canis will come for you, I know he will."

"Once before, when Romans took me, he came for me," said Lydia distraughtly, "but now he has given me to Paullinus. Oh, Claudia, all this time he had no love for me, no sweet regard for me. He only suffered me. Claudia, I am so cold, I am encompassed by ice."

"Drink," insisted Claudia, almost forcing the wine upon Lydia. She stayed for as long as she could, in an attempt to bring comfort to the desolate woman; but in the end departed for her own room, something of determination overlying her pity.

In her room Claudia spoke to Dinweda, her personal servant and slave girl.

"Dinweda, you are Iceni, are you not?"

"It is no matter, mistress," said Dinweda, "I am here to serve you, and do so willingly."

"Dinweda, you are Iceni. I am Roman. Speak true, would you trust me?"

"I would, mistress, for I have never known you aught but kind to me."

"Dinweda, how may I meet Canis the Briton?"

"Who is Canis, mistress?" asked the slave girl, combing Claudia's long black hair.

Claudia turned her head to look up at the girl, who was of her own age. She saw the girl's eyes were veiled.

"Look into my eyes, Dinweda, and speak me again. Would you trust me, aye or no?"

Dinweda looked into the soft eyes of her young mistress. She knew Claudia to be a strangely innocent and unspoiled Roman maid, who admired honour and courage in men, fidelity and compassion in women.

"You are kind and gentle, mistress—but are of Paullinus, your kinsman."

"Because I am of Paullinus, that is why I ask. Dinweda?"

The veils lifted from the eyes of the slave girl. She said, "Aye, mistress, I will trust you."

"Then how may I meet Canis? Do not ask me again who he is, for you know. Dinweda, Lydia is his beloved, she has borne him sweet child, and who will tell Canis she will put herself to death unless he comes for her? Help me in this and tell me, where is Canis?"

Dinweda drew long breath. Her mother, to save her, had sold her to a Roman official, who had sold her into the household of Paullinus when Claudia had arrived. Dinweda, as a slave in this household, was luckier than some. She looked again into the entreating eyes of her young mistress.

"Canis is here, mistress."

Claudia was on her feet, gripping Dinweda's slim shoulders.

"Here? In this house?"

Dinweda shook her head, the suspicion of a smile on her face.

"No, he is not as near as that. But he is here. Mistress, if Lydia comes to harm either here or in Rome, Canis will slay your kinsman in such a way it will take him many hours to die. Because of your kindness to me and to mistress Lydia, I will help you all I can. Give me your message, and it will be in the ear of Canis within the hour."

"Ask him only where I may see him. Dinweda, I have seen him before, he will remember me, so tell him that by his own gods he may trust me. And Dinweda, is it not cruel world where so much may be spent merely in two people coming to trust each other?"

"Is it not the world as we make it, mistress?"

*　　*　　*

Dinweda woke Claudia when the night was black, to tell her of Canis. How the slave girl had contrived to make contact with the Briton, Claudia did not know or ask. In whispers, the Iceni girl told her that Canis would meet her at the temple of Diana, at sundown on the morrow. Claudia was to look for a man in Roman armour, but with the trappings of a Belgic auxiliary.

"Oh, Dinweda, he is here indeed. At the temple of Diana, you say, and in the guise of a Belgic auxiliary. He is truly himself, is he not?"

"There is but one great general in all this land, mistress, and he is Canis the Wolfhead."

"But in the guise of a Belgic auxiliary, Dinweda—is this not courting unecessary risk?"

"Canis once served in the legions of Rome, did you not know?" whispered the girl, and was gone in the darkness. About the villa were the soft sounds of velvet night, and the measured tread of sentries. Claudia lay pondering.

At sundown the following day, she put on a blue robe and left the stronghold of her kinsman for the temple of Diana. She went unaccompanied, which would not have pleased Paullinus; but to others she was his kinswoman, and might come and go as she wished. Paullinus had his villa in a sternly military town, its atmosphere and orderliness reflecting the austere discipline engendered by the autocratic Governor. There were never more civilians on the streets than Roman soldiers. Nevertheless, there were always more than a few women who came to pray to Diana. Outside the small, colonnaded temple a soldier sat on the steps, his helmet by his side, his long limbs comfortably disposed, the cloak of a Belgic auxiliary about his shoulders. His face was in the shadows but Claudia knew him at once. She went into the temple, saying as she passed him, " I will pray for you first, O reckless one."

He smiled but spoke no word. When she emerged, it was dark and he was no longer on the steps. But as she looked around, he appeared at her elbow to give her escort. They began to walk, she trembling a little. She was wholly unused to plots and assignations. Moreover, she could not help remembering the circumstances of their first meeting, how he had smitten Paullinus senseless and laughed at her distress. Yet as they walked, she thought that perhaps they looked no more conspicuous than any Roman girl in company with a soldier.

" Do not speak my name," said Canis, " but call me Arquebane if you will."

Suddenly she was whisperingly voluble.

" You cannot let her die, you cannot. She is in such despair that I fear when the time comes for her to be taken to Rome she will kill herself. I know not how to comfort her, how to ease her anguish. I was in such impetuosity to tell her you were here, but I dared not for fear that what she might expect you to do for her you could not. And if you could not, she would think it was because you would not."

" Could not, would not? Is this brave and beautiful Lydia you speak of?"

" Oh," whispered Claudia breathlessly, as they made their way through the increasing darkness, " she is in truth so beautiful I am in envy of her. But she is in such torment and speaks such wild words, she thinks you have forsaken her, forgotten her and cast her aside. And she mourns so for her child."

" She is strange Roman. Not so long ago her sole concern

was for the laxity of Diana in not peopling the world entirely with Romans. Now she will not live with any kind of Romans. How is a man to understand so complex a woman?"

"She is not complex. She is like the clearest water. She is wholly devoted to you, and I know not how you can speak so lightly of her when she is in such lonely anguish that she cannot even sleep."

"I will not let her die, sweet Claudia, nor will I let them take her to Rome. She is under the iron restraint of Paullinus, is she not?"

"Wholly so," said Claudia, "for my kinsman will not let her even breathe the air." She stiffened as he put his arm about her shoulders, then realised as they passed two strolling Roman soldiers that the gesture created the illusion of a Belgic auxiliary being casually affectionate with his love. Claudia felt strangely burning because of his light embrace. "If you have contrived to look for her," she said as his arm dropped away, "that is why you have never glimpsed her. I am to call you Arquebane? Then, Arquebane, you have to know that in five days they will take her to a ship and return her to Rome."

"Should this happen, despite my intercession, much good will it do your kinsman," said Canis impassively, "for I will take him in time and give him to my warrior maids. It will soon be as dark as we might wish. You come and go as you please, Claudia, but Lydia may not move?"

"I am free. Lydia is a prisoner."

"In darkness friendly enough and in such robe, you might be Lydia unless your face were seen. I will take Lydia with me this night. When we come to the gate I will enter with you as a Belgic auxiliary of the Fourteenth Legion, come with despatches for Paullinus. You will take me to your kinsman—but if the commander of the guard will not give up this privilege, even to you, argue no point with him, but consent as if it were of no importance."

"Is this how you will enter?" Claudia was suddenly fearful, and a little unimpressed. "Oh, it is too simple, it lacks cunning. I thought you worthier of better and subtler plan. The house guards will not let any man enter the villa unless they are sure of him."

"They will be sure. I shall be with you, or with both you and the guard commander. You will know me as Arquebane, a Belgic auxiliary you have met before, and are uncommonly fond of."

"This is not true," said Claudia in some confusion, "but I will let it go. Although my heart is pounding in fright already, I will contrive to do what you wish as best as I can. It will be for Lydia. But if you fail—"

"No harm to you, sweet one. As kinswoman to Paullinus, you are my surety above all else. But in the event of failure, I will not be your friend of whom you are so uncommonly fond, but a renegade auxiliary who accosted you and put a dagger to your ribs. You will say you were thus forced to lead me into the villa, so that I might hang Paullinus for a multitude of reasons. But if we do not fail, and I escape with Lydia, then you will tell a similar story and also say that not only did I have a dagger to your ribs but I also left you bound and speechless. As I must. So now, lead on, brave Claudia, and put up the hood of your cloak to cover your head."

Claudia did so. She was conscious of his air of assurance and his quite uncompromising intent to do all for Lydia. If necessary, he would not merely crack heads. He would destroy. The night was on them now, but she could see his profile beneath the helmet he wore. She thought he was even smiling. It made her feel he was not thinking so much of Lydia at that moment, as Paullinus. He was going to lift Lydia from under her kinsman's sensitive nose. Suddenly Claudia wished Canis well from the bottom of her heart.

Men should be honourable in their conduct and towards women they should be understanding and protective. She did not know whether Canis was honourable. She doubted it in a man who had torn down sacred Roman temples. But she was sure that towards a woman he would be all that the woman desired. He had neither forgotten Lydia nor forsaken her.

183

They came within sight of the high wall surrounding the large villa. It loomed formidably, lit at intervals by torches. There seemed to be more soldiers than usual, but then usually she scarcely noticed them. They were part of the daily pattern. Now they seemed very watchful as well as numerous. But Canis was entirely at ease as he approached the gate with her, only his tallness setting him apart from the other armoured men. With heart thumping and knees weak, Claudia spoke to the guard, but not before she had made a silent prayer. She knew she was betraying Rome and she needed the gods' understanding and forgiveness.

" Who commands here?" she asked.

" I am that one," said a man, stepping forward from within the open gate. He saw Claudia, her head covered by the hood, her face in its shadow. " What may I do for you, Mistress Claudia?"

" Here is Arquebane, known to me. He bears despatches from the Fourteenth Legion, and I am taking him to the Governor."

" He has come on foot?" The guard commander could not resist a sarcastic smile as he looked at Canis. " He is certainly long in the shanks, but it is still something of a walk for all that."

" I am an auxiliary of the Belgic company," said Canis, " and have stabled my horse in friendly quarters where they will pull the burrs and thorns from his coat with gentle hands. Claudia, will I wait here while you advise the Governor of my arrival?"

Oh, clever and cunning one, thought Claudia. His easy command of his part gave her more confidence in her own.

" Indeed no, Arquebane," she said fondly. At which the guard commander looked a little enviously at Canis, for Claudia was entirely personable. " I cannot be as inhospitable as that, and since it was my good fortune to meet you I will not let you out of my company quite so soon."

" If it will not offend you, Mistress Claudia," said the guard commander, " such are my orders that I too must

184

accompany this Belgic galloper who cannot trust his horse to our stables."

"I am not offended in the least," said Claudia, speaking in the light, casual way Canis had advised, though she was still full of palpitations. With the guard commander escorting them, they walked over the wide tiled way illuminated by torches set in iron cages along the wall. When they reached the villa, Claudia was dry of mouth and constricted of throat, so that her breathing seemed to her to be a series of painful and perceptible gulps. A sentry in shadow looked on as the guard commander entered, Claudia and Canis following. Here the commander stood aside to allow Claudia the courtesy of preceding him. Through the lamplit passage Claudia walked, her heart hammering. Behind her she heard the softest thudding sound and then what was surely a sigh into oblivion. Almost at once, Canis came forward, bearing the unconscious body of the commander in his arms, and whispered in her ear, "Take me to her."

Claudia went quakingly but bravely, hastening, fearful of discovery and hot with trepidation.

Lydia lay on her couch in a dark room whose walls pressed upon her, mind and body. She asked for no lamps, for it was only in the darkness that her tormented mind could shut out images, only black night which could make those walls invisible. She dwelt in desolation on that which had gone, and on that which lay ahead. It was life itself which had gone, for life itself was inseparable from the wild freedoms of the forests, and from that which she thought had existed between her and Canis. She had been faithful to him, and to Diana. But Diana had rejected her and Canis had relinquished her.

She was unloved.

But she would never reach Rome. She would not even reach the ship. She would open her veins before they came for her.

With what cruel, jesting indifference he had relinquished her.

She heard Claudia's voice, softly calling to the sentry outside. She heard the sentry move, but no other sounds followed, nothing that told of the noiseless shadow which moved to darken the sentry's back and induce him into mindlessness. Claudia would perhaps come with wine. If she did, she did. If she did not, what matter?

There was another sound, faint, and the lightest of rustles. Then a subtle change of air brought about by an opened door. Had welcome death come in the shape of an avenging Roman, outraged by her desertion of Rome? She would willingly lift herself to the dagger thrust.

She stiffened, then every numb nerve in her miserably frozen body leapt into life as to her nostrils came that which was so familiar and dear to her. It was the rich, sweet scent of forests, the smell of a man who had lived long in them; and suddenly her blood was tumultous in every vein, and although her flesh took fire her skin rose taut and hard with icy, rapturous cold.

Oh, Diana, he was here, Canis was here! She knew. The joy of his unseen presence took ecstatic hold of her mind and body. Her heart soared like a freed bird taking wing, and then his strong hand was upon her, over her mouth, smothering her wild longing to cry out.

" Lydia . . ." It was a whisper, a caress in the darkness, a joy in her heart. Her lips moved to kiss the hand that stifled her and the tears sprang to prick hotly at her lids. " Speak no word," he breathed, " but when we are ready take Claudia's robe and sandals, putting the hood about your head. We will then go, I as a Belgic auxiliary who has delivered despatches to Paullinus and you as Claudia. You will walk bravely, as Claudia did, and if I hear your knees knock even lightly, I will buffet you senseless. Lydia, did you think I would let them take you to Rome? No, never."

He removed his hand and was gone from her. He bound the sentry and guard commander with their own leather. Both men lay inert inside the door, both still unconscious from the deadly blow each had received on the side of the neck. For a moment Lydia lay in utterly beautiful bliss. Then she rose silently, though her limbs trembled violently. In the darkness a helmet dimly glittered and a Roman girl gasped. Lydia heard the softly harsh sound of tearing linen and strained to hear her Briton's whispering voice again.

"For your sweet courage, Claudia, I can only give you hurtful bondage, but be sure I bind you only of necessity, as I said, to foil your kinsman's malice concerning Lydia and any suspicions he may have concerning you. By reason of your collaboration, you have saved his life for him, so content you with that. The bonds will give you a badge of innocence and so save you from his temper."

And he bound Claudia with twisted strips of linen torn from her shift, and with a cruelty that made her gasp the more. Yet she understood. "I will remember you, brave Claudia," he whispered and stooped to lay his mouth on hers, and in such a way that a bitter, haunting sweetness rushed on her. But that which he then thrust into her kissed mouth and between her teeth to gag her into gurgling muteness seemed so infamously unkind after so sweet a gesture. She knew its necessity, but it left her feeling she had been treated a little ungenerously.

Worse, he then thrust her backwards onto the couch and bound her feet, and Claudia could not hold back the tears at being so ill-used when she had served him so well. But his hand came to touch her face, to lightly caress her cheek and ask her forgiveness, and if she could have spoken she would have said, "Will you come again, will I see you more?" But because of the gag she could not. She wept just a little.

He had taken her robe and sandals, which he now gave to Lydia. Lydia, fearful for him, but full of the wildest joy, put them on while Canis also thrust gags of linen into the mouths of the trussed sentry and guard commander.

She was ready. She put the hood of the robe up over her head as he had told her to. It would shadow her face.

"Come," he whispered at last, though it had all taken only a matter of minutes. Lydia moved, then thought of Claudia. Involuntarily, she stooped above the couch to murmur a farewell to the girl.

"Truly, sweet Claudia, you have so much of my love that I too will remember you." And she kissed the cold wet cheek of the Roman girl, then silently but with fast-beating heart she went with Canis, skirting the bound, limp bodies on the floor. They left the dark room with its oppressive walls. The household sounds were muffled and indistinct, but were there all the same, and were enough to bring cold fear to Lydia. However, no one came to question their going as they hurried through the frescoed corridor. Coming to the arched exit, Canis took on a lack of hurry, whereupon Lydia simulated a leisureliness very much at odds with her sense of desperate urgency.

She glimpsed the sentry. Canis showed no haste. He strolled. She matched his casualness. The sentry, who had seen three go in, now saw two coming out, the Belgic auxiliary and Claudia Justian (or so he thought). The guard commander, it seemed, had been detained by Paullinus.

With Canis, Lydia passed the man at leisure, hood hiding her face.

They trod the wide, tiled path, and still Canis sauntered. Lydia felt the eyes of the sentry on her back. She tried to walk as Claudia did, with the buoyant spring of youth. She did not know how she stayed her urgency, as she and Canis passed in and out of the light and shadow flung by the caged torches and high wall. She was feverish with both rapture and fear. One joy rode above all fear. That of knowing Canis had come for her. At great risk he had come for her. But they were not free yet. Anything could go wrong. A meticulous guard might ask to see her face. She did not clearly know how they were to get out, but if death did come to her now it could not alter the fact that she had had a moment of purest bliss when she had known he was in that room. So far she had not spoken one word to him. She knew she must not until he spoke first.

A little way from the turn which would bring them to the gate, when the sentry on the door could no longer see them, Canis stopped. Lydia halted with him. Flickering light showed him to her in his Roman armour, his crested helmet giving him the splendour of Apollo himself. He was formidably composed, or seemed so. Her love for him became wildly extravagant. He whispered for her ears alone.

"We will walk to the gate and go through it in the same way. But only I will talk, for though you look like Claudia in this robe of hers you speak in a different key. I will say all that is necessary, so that you need say nothing. Only remember you are Claudia, kinswoman to Paullinus, and may come and go as haughtily as you please."

"If you say anything which might be amusing to her," whispered Lydia, "I will do my best to at least laugh as softly as she does."

"When did you ever fail me, sweet Roman?"

The almost imperceptible endearment scalded her eyes with tears. His hand pressed hers. Hers clung compulsively and passionately for a moment and then they went on to the gate. Sentries loomed. Lydia shivered. A torch in an upright spigot flared, but Canis walked so that Lydia was partly in his shadow. The gate guards, two of them, with others nearby, turned to observe the couple. Lydia, affecting little consciousness of the soldiers, was listening to Canis.

"And if I come again," he was saying lightly, "let it be with despatches of a more welcome kind, for your august kinsman did not seem happy with those I brought tonight." They were passing through the gate, the sentries giving way, and Lydia was walking as Canis had commanded, with the light ease of Claudia, but still unhurried. To copy Claudia's walk was not difficult, for Lydia had her own grace, but how she managed to walk at all without her knees knocking she did not know.

The hood kept her face out of the light and Canis was still talking of Paullinus. This kept the ears of the sentries more attentive than their eyes. But what was there to see except two people who had lately gone in and were now on their way out?

"Mistress Claudia, had it not been for your friendly sympathy and your knowledge of how I have served Rome, I

189

do not think the august one would have allowed me to depart as peacefully as this, for he is hardly disposed to give a man comfort at times, no matter how innocent the man's heart or brave his deeds."

The sentries, grinning a little, let them wander on.

"Also," said Canis cheerfully, "he seemed to mislike my face."

Lydia laughed softly and they walked on in their leisurely way. The sentries thought the Belgic auxiliary a windy fellow, like all Britons; and how sweet Claudia Justin could stomach any man in such conceit of his wordiness, they did not know. Again they heard her soft laughter. One sentry remembered something.

"Wait, fellow," he called, "where is Maxilius who went with you to the Governor?"

"Since you ask," said Canis, halting and turning, "I left him at the sharp end of the Governor's tongue, for what reason I know not, only that the Governor seemed to mislike his face even more than mine."

And he turned back to Lydia and they continued on their way. The sentries heard him remark jestingly on the misfortunes of Maxilius. They also heard another soft laugh.

"I like not that Belgic babbler," said the first sentry.

"Nor I," said the second, "and I wish the lady Claudia might find as much in my babble to sweeten her ear as she does in his."

"Go," said the first sentry as Canis and Lydia became shadows in the night, "attend on her return, whether she likes it or no, for Paullinus will not commend us if we let her return alone in this darkness."

"And if she is exchanging moist kisses with the Belgic cockerel," said the second man sourly, "am I to wait on her dalliance? Call her servant and let her dance to her mistress's tune."

"Go," said the first sentry, "or when Maxilius returns from having his face re-shaped, he will make you dance to his tune."

But by the time the grumbling man had taken his first step, Canis and Lydia were far in advance of his ponderousness. The sentry returned after some time to say the lovebirds had surely found a warm nest somewhere. And so, for the moment, both sentries and other members of the guard thought no more about it, except in its less palatable aspect, which was that Claudia's favouring of a windy Belgic auxiliary could not be considered agreeable to a true Roman.

In silent, urgent flight Canis and Lydia came within sight of the city gate. It was closed and guarded. They withdrew and vanished into the blackness cast by the city walls. Aided by jutting buttresses, they climbed the stonework. Canis went up in his sure, sinewy way; and Lydia, forgetting the privations of her captivity, climbed tooth and nail like a warrior maid. Wonder, effort and prayers took her up. Once at the top of the wall, Canis permitted himself a smile as he extended a hand to her. She was high-born and patrician, but she could climb a wall. He laughed softly as she dropped to the ground with him on the other side.

"So," he murmured, "this is my Lydia, whom Claudia said lay feeble and wilting. Is it Diana who has suddenly lent you wings?"

"Your Lydia? Oh, Canis—" His name burst from her, but his hand flew to smother her again, to enjoin her continued silence. Oh, she thought, you may speak but I may not, though I must speak if I am not to die from sheer restraint. However, when he took his hand away she was obediently silent. All that mattered for the moment was to get as far from Paullinus as possible. Now she desired wings in very truth, as she ran by the Briton's side in the darkness.

"Swiftly, sweet Lydia," he whispered, urging her to faster flight.

The new endearment impelled her forward, and on wings of excitement she flew through the night with him. Their eyes grew used to the darkness, although it was hardly like day. He did not search for the way, he knew it, and in a little while led her off the road. How he also knew the way through dark, bushy thickets made her marvel, but then this was his land, his country, he had been born here. Unseen branches tugged at her robe. She would have spoken then, for surely no one was near enough to overhear, and there were so many words bursting to come forth. But she swallowed them.

They were skirting a black-looking wood. He had taken off his helmet and was carrying it. Her heart was full, her gratitude intense, and her conscience just a little stricken. She was free again, free to live in the forests again or in the western mountains. And she had doubted him, she had even doubted Diana. But she had been so desolate. He would forgive her, and Diana already had.

He went on, tirelessly and silently, she hurrying behind him as he tracked the way for her. Once Lydia's escape was discovered—which because of the absence of the guard commander could not be long—he knew that Paullinus in bitter fury would not wait until morning to despatch patrols in every direction. The Governor's men would for once brave all night dangers, if only to get away from his uncompromising anger.

The dark wood on their left seemed to Lydia to be alive. She knew that the plains of Britain were silent at night, except for the wolves, but the woods and the forests were never silent, least of all after sunset. The spirits of long-forgotten forest gods were always making themselves heard. She could hear rustles, whispers, murmurs, calling to her as they did to all people close enough when the night pressed. But she was not afraid. She was alive and in wonder, she was going back to Dilwys. The sky was a vast black canopy jewelled with tiny stars.

Canis took such sure strides. She was beginning to stumble. All her exhilaration could not quite sustain her. Her legs ached, and she felt now the weakness brought about by eating so little during her captivity. Canis heard her laboured breathing. He stopped and took her hand. It gave her sweet comfort and renewed strength, and she went on with him, their hands linked. She wished they might halt, just for a

192

moment, just long enough for her to kiss him a thousand times, despite Cea.

But on they went, and in a while Lydia did not know how her legs carried her. And the dark woods were still there, still whispering, and bush still tugged. Then under his breath Canis began to count his footsteps. Sloping ground was beneath them. It came unexpectedly to Lydia, and she would have pitched forward but for the strong arm thrown around her. They descended until she felt a moist coldness under her feet. Pebbles slithered and scraped beneath her sandals. She heard the little sounds of flowing water. Canis stopped, lifted her and carried her in his arms. He bore her along the course of the shallow, winding stream. He had replaced his helmet. He would not discard it in case its subsequent discovery gave notice they had passed this way.

"Canis?" She could no longer contain herself and whispered his name.

"Be content," he said, knowing that in her woman's way she wished to unburden her tongue.

"I am content, dearly so. I only wish to say thank you."

"Well, you have said it."

"And that I love you and that I am out of all my senses with bliss and that—"

"And that is enough."

She sighed, her dark head on his shoulder. She heard the splash and scatter of water as he carried her, and she realised they were in the wood. The stream ran through it. About him was his own warm smell. It was of forests and heathlands, of wood fires. It was of sun and rain and the sweat of effort, of worn leather and burnished belt. It was of himself. She knew no more comforting smell. She locked her arms tighter around his neck.

When at last he set her down on dry land, they were deep in the wood. He helped her to climb the sloping bank, and she found herself standing amid lofty, spreading sentinels whose leafy branches shut out the night sky. She was still not afraid, but she was a little nervous. It was so black.

"This way," said Canis and went into the blackness. She kept close to him. After a while she felt they were entombed.

"Canis?" she said a little fearfully.

"There is no harm here," he said, "the boars have long since outwitted the wolves. And in a little while we will be with our friends."

She rushed into entreaty at that.

"Then pray stop a moment, only a moment, so that I may speak to you."

"Do you wish to speak of Paullinus? There is no need. I know you have taken hurt, but he will not lay hands on you again—"

"Oh, no, no, no," cried Lydia, "it is not that, it is this!" And she threw her arms around his neck, and in the whispering darkness she pressed her mouth to his. Her lips clung, her warm lissom body clung, and her kiss imparted feverish gratitude and passionate love. "Canis, I was in such despair." She seized his hand and kissed that too, then pressed it to her full, round breast. "I thought myself forgotten and I would have opened my veins. I thought never to see you again, never to see Dilwys again—oh, tell me of Dilwys."

"She has been fretful for so small a baby, aye, even with Feola. I think she has missed you, as I have myself."

"You have missed me?" Her green eyes glowed in the darkness.

"Should I not have?"

"Did it give you just a little torment of your own? Oh, say it did, even if it did not, for if you say it I will tell myself it is true."

"Why else did I come?" he said.

"Canis," she said breathlessly, "I knew you were there before you spoke. I could not believe it, for when you sent word as you did to Paullinus I thought myself unloved and forsaken."

"It was only to bait him and to leave him in some complacency about you. I did not want him to put a full cohort around you.

"I did not know this. How could I? Your message was so cruel and gave me so much pain. I—"

"You thought I would let them take you to Rome?" He seemed almost grim, and her knees shook.

"Oh, I thought—I thought because of Cea you might have let them—"

"How could any man forsake the mother of his child?"

"Some men might, but you did not. Oh, do not be angry with me because of my doubts, how could I bear that? You do not know the despair I was in—"

"Lydia, enough," he said gently. "I came for you because in simple terms I cannot now be without you. I came as much to bring you back to me and Dilwys, as to save you from Paullinus. Nor did it need Grud to mumble in my ear."

Oh, Diana, he loved her!

"It is joy to hear you say that," she whispered. "I am to go with you to the west, am I not, and to be dear to you always? Promise me this, promise me."

"You shall go with us, Lydia, and be dear to all of us," he said. Her hair was night-back, her eyes brilliant. How like Cerdwa she was at times. "You are a strange Roman and I have seen none more beautiful."

Radiant Diana reached out to invest Lydia's night with glowing brightness.

She said huskily, "Then may I not be kissed? I so long to be."

He bent his head, his helmet off again. He kissed her and the forest was a whispering caress now. Her eyes closed. The sweetness rushed at her. His kiss was of love, surely of love. Her physical need consumed her. Sometimes at night that need made her burningly restless. But she had never complained about his denial of her. She had promised him, long ago, when she begged to go with him to help his people, that she would never complain. And there was always Cea standing between them, Cea who was becoming as beautiful as her mother.

But now her longing was violent. She held on to him. He

unclasped her. She swayed. He put his arm around her shoulders and they went on, Lydia burning.

He is to wed Cea. But he is not wed to her yet.

Their rustling feet disturbed the night creatures. Once, far off, Lydia heard the long, drawn-out complaint of a dismal wolf, but it did not disturb her. She was locked in the heart of the world at night with Canis, and the earth and the sky were asleep.

In time the dark, towering trees gave way and fell back, and they stood within a large circle of clear ground. On top of a huge, roughly-hewn stone obelisk lay another stone, precisely and immovably balanced. She looked up and saw that the sky had awoken. It glimmered with stars.

"This is the place," said Canis and whistled. Once, twice, thrice—as clear as a blackbird. A minute later, he repeated the call. Faintly but unmistakably, Lydia heard the call answered in the same fashion. Then Canis surprised her by sinking to the ground to lie comfortably on his back. Lydia went down on her knees beside him, her eyes caressing him. He had saved her oh, so many times.

"He has gone for our friends and our horses," said Canis, "and they will be here in less than an hour. Take your rest, Lydia."

The helmet was discarded but the armour he still wore had a sombre glitter to it under the star-encrusted sky. They called him the greatest Briton since Caratacus, who fought Caesar but won favour of him in Rome; but Lydia did not like this armour he wore.

"Canis, tell me of Boadicea."

The shadows reached to mask his eyes.

"She was a queen," he said, his voice murmurous, "she lived like a queen and died like one."

That was all he would ever say about his beloved, magical Boadicea.

"She loved you also," whispered Lydia, "but no more than I do." She leaned over him and brought her warm lips down to his. He lay quite still, as if asleep. She fought her

196

trembling. "I wish you were rid of this," she said, her hand on the metal breastplate. He looked up at her, his eyes dark, haunted, his face carved, it seemed, from weathered stone. She unbuckled the armour that kept him from her, and drew it off. "Canis?" she sighed. She was close above him, her glossy hair all about her.

"You are like Cerdwa," he said.

"I am Lydia and I am burning. Will you not love me? There is no one to see or to know, and I would cherish it so."

"Oh, strange and wilful Roman to cleave to an ancient barbarian when young men are on fire for you," he said.

"Ancient? Barbarian? Canis, no!" She had called him barbarian in the beginning. It distressed her painfully to hear him mock himself so. "I will not let you say such things, I will kiss you and kiss you—so—and so—"

He drew her down, enfolded her, and he laid his mouth over hers in his own way, so that fire and sweet pain swept her. She felt irresistible desire to be possessed, to bring him into her burning, hungry body.

Diana, give him to me now.

Diana or the stars or destiny gave him to her. Flame encompassed her. She was possessed. Here was her world, here the one man. And his possession of her enraptured her. The night sky drew back. There was only glowing radiance, and the ecstatic miracle of Lydia and Canis merging.

Life. So sweet, so sweet.

She lay quivering, the tears seeping through her closed lids. He covered her from the eyes of the night, and the feel of her robe and shift caressing her limbs again brought new emotion to her. She caught his hand and kissed it in tender acknowledgement of his gesture.

"Oh, that was such sweet embrace, Canis, was it not?"

He was not without his own tenderness, even if his smile was a little sly.

"Perhaps I am not too ancient, after all," he said.

She saw his smile. Amid her tears, which were only because it had been so beautiful, she laughed softly.

"I think you will last the night out," she said, and she lay in wonder, for her day of hopeless despair had ended in unforeseen joy.

Not long after, their friends came—emerging from the darkness in the wake of the whistling message of the blackbird. Led by a hairy one who had picked up the original signal, came a dozen warriors, all highly delighted to see not only Canis but Lydia as well. Among them was Andudo. They had needed a patient head to restrain their hot ones during days of waiting.

"We were not too worried," he said, "but also we were not exactly unworried. For several days we have waited, as you instructed, patrolling the area at night so that we should not be too far from you whichever way you came, and the time has not gone quickly. Some said it was impossible for you to lift Ludicca from the cold eagle, and some said not. Well, you have done it, and it is a pleasure to see Ludicca here with you."

Andudo might also have said that Princess Cea was in a fretful temper about it all, and was likely to box Lydia's ears and scratch Canis to death when they next saw her.

"The horses?" said Canis.

"They are here, lord," said Feneda, one of the three warrior maids among the band, "close by the stream."

"Then let us go," said Canis, "there is no time to loiter. Look to each other, and especially to Lydia. Her day has been long enough already, but we cannot delay. We must reach our forest as soon after daybreak as possible."

"We are going to the forest? But where are our people?" asked Lydia.

"It is safer for us to go through the forest, not around it, to get to them. Come."

They had to reach that massive but friendly forest for the security it would give them, and then track their way through it with the help once more of Agra and his friends. After that, they would ride to catch up with the march of Princess Cea. With her warriors and people, Cea was making for a densely-wooded area on the southern border of Brigantia, ruled by Queen Cartimandua. Cartimandua was reviled by the Belgic tribes of Southern Britain for having betrayed their Prince Caratacus into the hands of Romans, many years before Boadicea rose in revolt.

The small band of Britons reached the horses, then rode cautiously over sloping ground until they were able to make their way over the sandy, pebbled stream bed. In this fashion they emerged from the woods. The night was still dark as they travelled at a steady pace over open country, the muffled, rhythmic beat of every hoof sweet music in Lydia's ears. Paullinus might still contrive to claw her back, but her heart was singing. Canis had loved her under the night sky.

They did not travel by any road or known track, but crossed the uncultivated countryside, always at the same steady pace because of the hazards of the ground in the darkness. They asked no more of their mounts than the animals could give, and had to halt only once to let them blow foam and gather wind. Lydia fought the weariness that began to creep into her bones. In former days, she would never have attempted such an arduous night journey; but her existence with the Britons had given her the same physical resilience that they had. It was the mournfulness of her captivity which had sapped this resilience somewhat. She was grateful for the short rest they took a little before dawn, and for the meagre ration of food the Britons shared with her. She ate her portion ravenously, then flushed as she saw Feneda looking sympathetically at her.

" Among friends," said Lydia, faintly smiling, " one always eats with relish, especially if one is hungry."

" Friends," said Feneda, " make one hungry for life itself."

Lydia shook her head as the warrior maid offered some of her own hard bread. But how hungry she still was and how blissful did the thought of sleep seem. Canis, however, was under no illusions about the resourcefulness of an infuriated Paullinus. Once advised of Lydia's escape, the Governor would not have wasted a moment. Immediately he would have had detachments ordered out to scour every corner of the night, making use of roads and paths which the Britoᴧs did not dare to use. And so, after the short rest, Canis took his band on again just before daybreak. They were going at their steady pace when dawn broke pinkly grey, and at their backs the eastern horizon gradually became a glory of flushed, rising colour. The air was fresh, the portent of rain later.

At the first real light, they began to ride harder, making for the distant haven of the forest they knew so well. Once there, the Romans would never find them.

It was an unexpected halt Canis called after they had ridden for an hour. He wheeled and came trotting back to warriors who rode as flanking escorts to Lydia. Her face was pale, her eyes huge within dark circles of strain, but their green was a melting one as she looked at Canis. His expression was wary, questioning.

" Andudo," he said, " will the earth echo for you as the sky seems to for me?"

Lydia knew what this meant. Canis had sensed Romans. Andudo slipped from his horse and lay full length on the ground. He embraced it and put his ear to it, to the earth which was the mother, the provider, the communicator. Lydia could hear nothing but the murmur of a light morning breeze flirting around bushes. There was no mist, and the rising sun showed clear above an horizon of pink radiance. Every blade of grass and every undulation in the rolling terrain seemed sharply defined by the light, so that despite the cloudless sky she knew there would indeed be rain later. She breathed in air cool and sweet.

Andudo rose. His rugged face was sombre as he pointed due south, adjacent to their line of progress.

" They are on the road," he said, " but going at no great pace."

" The road has been their advantage," said Canis, " and they know that in one way or another we must travel west." He looked back the way they had come. Andudo nodded.

" They have picked up our scent behind us also," he said.

Strangely enough, Canis smiled. He was bareheaded, having

200

buried the helmet, and the morning sun fingered the dark coppery tints in his hair.

" Lydia," he said, " Paullinus holds you in such esteem that he has spent the night searching for you."

" Do not let him take me," she begged, " kill me rather, and leave him only my body."

" Shall we so dispose of our own Roman?" asked Canis of his warriors. They were heated from riding, they had travelled through the night and eaten little. But in answer to Canis, the warrior maids laughed and a man spoke.

" Aye, when Rome is only a stone sepulchre."

" Ludicca is of us," said Feneda.

" My warriors can ride," said Canis to Lydia, " and now so must you. For you must indeed, sweet Roman."

Lydia's green eyes caressed him extravagantly and shamelessly, and she said, " Dearest lord, I will be at your heels forever."

He laughed, he slapped his horse and led them all in streaming, galloping file, with Lydia immediately behind him and his voice calling on them to keep head to tail. He rode directly for the distant forest that stretched greenly and thickly dark beyond the rolling downland. They entered a long, wide, shallow valley, flecked with bright golden gorse. Canis took them in as straight a line as he could, skirting bushes high or wide and leaping all others. The gentle downward slope of the extensive valley was enough to give accelerating impetus to their drumming ride; and well they needed this acceleration, as a troop of pursuing Roman cavalry, accompanied by an impressed Belgic tracker, began to mount the ridge of the higher ground they had left.

The Romans broke the summit minutes later. They halted, outlined against the sharply clear sky. They surveyed the ground before them, saw the wide valley and the movements of their quarry in the distance.

The centurion who led the troop of thirty men drew a sharp breath. His eyes gleamed and his teeth showed between his distorted lips. It was Sulla. He had ridden out in pursuit less than an hour after Lydia had fled with Canis. Discovery had come when the guards, suspicious and uneasy about the continued absence of the guard commander, had ventured to enquire. Paullinus, at the news that Lydia had escaped, was like ice cracking under intolerable heat. Sulla had nearly burst with fury, for the man who had passed himself off as a Belgic auxiliary had undoubtedly been Canis, the man for whom Sulla nursed a hatred so uncontrollable that his sanity was forever on the brink.

Seeing the mounted Britons, tiny at this distance as they moved through the green and gold valley, the gleam in Sulla's eyes made them look like polished stones. With an invective movement of hand and arm he signalled the advance, and the Romans plunged down from the ridge. As soon as they found suitable ground, they followed Sulla in a disciplined gallop. The Britons rode in single file, Canis bruising a path for his band, so that they looked like a serpent of many humps foraging and slithering through the green and gold. The Romans fanned out behind Sulla and raced through the valley with each man able to pick the going that seemed easiest to him.

The pursuit took on a relentless momentum. The Roman cavalrymen rode with trained rhythm and a love for such a gallop as this. The Britons rode low over their horses, offering minimum resistance to the wind. The ground vibrated, the echoes of their gallop flung far and wide, only to roll back from the sides of the valley to merge with the vibrations and sounds that minutes later marked the passage of the Romans. A banner fluttered, helmets glittered in the sharp sunlight, accoutrements jingled harshly and leather strained, creaked and sweated. Rushing horses threw up clods, and ever before them the Romans saw the snaking file of fast-riding Britons.

The mounts of the Britons were of Roman stock, captured from Romans, but the Iceni, famed breeders of horse, had trained them to their own ways. Each man and each maid knew his or her own mount, and the love, which was mutual, was that which only obtains between man and horse, for no two creatures command more affection for each other than these.

Canis led his men and women in file simply because he would not have them fan out and scatter, risking an unhorsed warrior being too far removed from the aid of another. Nor would he have Lydia ride alone without a following escort. Hearts pounded, lungs sucked in air, knees gripped on the woollen blankets that covered the wooden saddles. And they galloped on. Canis took his horse through undergrowth, where Lydia behind him saw no way until he opened it up for her, his impetus scarcely checked. Constantly she fought the urge to turn her head and see how far or how close were the pursuing Romans. Her heart thumped wildly, painfully, her fatigue again forgotten in this final desperate endeavour to escape. Wholly and completely, she was committed to this bruising, rushing charge through the valley, the golden gorse so beautiful but so cruel, the bush so swift to reach and pluck. She kept her eyes on Canis and followed him devotedly and courageously; and where he leapt, she leapt also. The vegetation thinned for a space, and Canis increased his speed, his horse shining wetly with sweat. Lydia dug in her knees, asking for similar speed of her own mount. Behind her rode Feneda, calling encouragement to her. Through the rush of wind and the thunder of hooves, she heard the other two warrior maids in the galloping file, singing their urgency to their straining, foaming horses.

"On, oh lovely fourlegs! What, do you need wings as well? Never! On, oh sweet greycoat, or Canis will have you set for supper!"

Lydia, in the hammering, thudding tumult of heart and mind and body, wondered at the joy in their singing voices, when the moment was so dire and perilous and the noise of the pursuit sounded like the echoes of their own charge. But was there not exhilaration and joy in such turbulent movement?

There was.

And it was she, Lydia, they were riding for, she whom

Canis had come for, she whom they were all risking so much for. She would follow him into the halls of Apollo, or even into the black waters of the Styx, according to fate.

He looked back and she saw his face, and he too seemed in exhilaration.

"Ride, Lydia! Ride, Feneda!" His voice soared and sang back to them.

"On, lord, on!" called Feneda. "We follow, every one!"

The creaking, sweat-stained leather, the movement of the woollen-covered saddle, the flying, kicked-up earth, the pounding violence of the gallop and the singing cries, all were part of that which beat at Lydia's throbbing head.

On, oh sweet horse, brave horse, fly and you must, but on, on! Do not lose him, but follow, follow!

Andudo, riding last in the file, threw a backward glance. He saw the Romans, the sun reflected by flashing armour. They galloped in fanned, purposeful pursuit, determined to ride the Britons down—if not by speed, then by economical perseverance. Sulla galloped well in advance, going like a madman, but if he chose to ride so, let him. It was not in the nature of Roman cavalry to ride a horse to death. Nevertheless, they did not lack speed, their disciplined gallop compelling the Britons to maintain their wild pace.

And Canis took them on, rushing and thrusting, concerned only with the necessity of bringing them to their objective by the shortest line. He swerved around the high impenetrable bush, and leapt spurs or clumps of prickly gorse, taking his warriors and his Roman woman along the long sloping floor of the seemingly unending valley, making for the short but steep ridge in the distance. Beyond the ridge was a downward slope that would take them to the road. Across the road, and a little beyond it, lay the eastern edge of their forest.

What of the Romans Andudo had heard on the hard paved road? Had they passed the point where the Britons would cross? The road ran roughly parallel with the left side of the valley and continued in a broad, sweeping curve that cut across the Britons' line of gallop. Would those Romans hear the thundering chase, or would the valley contain such sounds? The thoughts ran at Lydia, and fear struck. Might not Canis ride straight into ambush? Oh, the gods forfend. Oh, Diana, great goddess and mighty huntress, look down on us who are now the hunted and save him, I beg you, and if you have tender inclinations, save all of us. It is true I am no longer of Rome, but I am faithful to you and beg you to take no heed of words Canis has spoken in mockery of you. Heed only the prayer of Lydia, your most devoted servant, and I will make such offering as to light your eyes. Did he not come for me despite all my doubts?

So ran her desperate and most prayerful thoughts as blindly, with sweat in her eyes, she galloped in the wake of her Briton. He rode so recklessly, so bruisingly, but his every endeavour was for her and she was out of every sense in her love for him. The wind caught at her hair, which streamed and whipped and tossed, and the same wind tugged at her body, but she galloped achingly on, gripping the wet flanks of her horse with robe-protected knees, her long sun-browned legs flashing, her hand cuffing her mount's neck.

Oh, take wings, dear horse, do not fail me, oh do not!

Canis leapt gorse. Lydia took her animal in a desperate rush, and it did not fail her, it leapt and soared. Behind her each Briton leapt in turn, one after the other, like so many great birds, the high singing cries of the warrior maids lifting their mounts up and over. Lydia heard the voice of Feneda close behind her.

" Ride, Ludicca, ride! "

The sweat was streaming into Lydia's eyes, stinging them. She dashed them away, and her heart plummeted in shock and dismay as she saw the gap that had opened up between her and Canis. She dug in her aching knees, she kicked with her heels, she urged and cuffed her horse and spoke gasping words of love to him.

" Oh, brave creature, your name I know not, but I love you well and will bring you to the tenderest grass I can find—but on, go on, go on! "

"Ride, Ludicca!" Feneda's voice was in her ear.

"Oh, Feneda, do not stay for me," she cried, "ride by me, I must not burden your pace, so ride by me."

But Feneda, only called, "Ride, Ludicca! Canis will surely burden you and all of us with something crueller than pace if you do not run on his heels. So ride, ride, for you are as brave as anyone here!"

Lydia rode with galvanised desperation then, though her body was racked with weary effort. Feneda distanced her, rode by her side and struck the rump of her horse with a switch cut at early morning from a bush. The horse snorted and Feneda struck again. The animal leapt into faster gallop, foam-flecked mouth showing red, heaving tongue, taking Lydia on, Lydia with her legs and knees numb and cramped, but digging in to prevent herself rolling. Feneda thrust the switch at her, Lydia groped for it, took it and used it, begging forgiveness of her great-hearted mount.

Feneda dropped back. She called.

"On, Ludicca! You are taking wings again!"

She was on the heels of Canis once more. Sweat-blinded and limb-tortured, she thought to hear echoes that were not their own echoes, their own galloping vibrations. But she did not look back. She dared not. There was such pain in her thighs and knees, it crucified the numbness, but she rode her brave, beautiful horse close in the wake of Canis, and heard Feneda calling joyously.

"On, Ludicca! We are with you!"

Reverberations like muffled rolls of thunder assaulted every ear, the Britons riding, riding, the Romans coming on apace, Sulla frenziedly leading their charge. And then Canis was at the steep ascent, his horse taking it in snorting upward plunges, Lydia and the others following. She did look back for a moment then. She saw them, a glittering array of armoured cavalrymen in wide formation that made them seem a scattered body. But their gallop was a relentless one, they were riding fast down the richly green, gold-flecked valley and oh, Diana, so close, so close.

Up, up, dear horse, follow him, go up, go up!

The ascent was rough as well as steep, but it gave the animals footholds for each plunging leap to the top. Hooves gouged the grassy earth and Lydia's every bone was shaken, but she took her horse up and up behind Canis. The other Britons, breaking file, each found a separate way up. Canis was on the ridge, Lydia with him, her breast heaving, her open mouth gulping in air. Canis checked, his horse blowing. And as the others came to the crest, they saw what he had seen. A picket of Roman cavalry was on the road beyond the ridge, a picket of ten men. They were in the act of dismounting.

"Oh, Canis!" Lydia was in shock at such tragic disappointment.

"We will take them, we must," he said. He glanced back at the pursuing Romans who were riding hard for the ascent. "Look to Lydia," he said to the warriors, "for if we do not cheat Paullinus of her now, we will have lost all when all was nearly won."

Lydia saw the axe of Cerdwa in his belt. Andudo had brought it. He also had a Roman sword. So she reached quickly and took the axe. His grey eyes held hers for a moment. She had always said she would never harm any of her own countrymen. But times exceptional could not always be avoided.

"Ride, then," said Canis, pointing to the green and brown fringe of the forest beyond the road, "let us go and call on Agra and his friends."

He led them in a savage rush down the slope to the road, Lydia and the others close-packed behind him to bring maximum weight and impetus to bear. The Roman picket, already sniffing the air, heard the noise of the charge before they saw it. They stared at the bunched band of Britons riding headlong down the slope towards them. They sprang to horse, meaning to scatter, to deploy and then engage. One man, quicker than others, detached himself and rode at a furious gallop down the dusty road to alert the main troop of foraging cavalry. The nine remaining men were in their saddles and wheeling about as the Britons came at them pell-mell. Before they could scatter, the Britons were on them.

Such was their impetus that they smashed into the picket with almost irresistible force. The outnumbered Romans spilled and crashed. A hail of murderous blows beset them. Canis took one man clean from his floundering horse; and Lydia, in strange exhilaration, felt the axe of Cerdwa alive and vibrant in her hand. She heard a singing voice that was like the music of a forest when the birds rose at dawn. Her arm swung. The axe, bright and sharp, rose and fell, and a smitten Roman dropped from his saddle.

Amid the sounds of the Britons playing havoc, came shouts and cries from the troop of Roman cavalry descending from the ridge and riding for the road. They were in charging triumph, Sulla leading the assault. But his shouted words were like screams as he saw the Britons burst through the destroyed picket. The brief engagement had been like the scattering of corn by a battery of sickles. The picket was sundered and smashed aside, and the Britons rode through the Romans and over them to gallop their exhausted horses towards the embrace of the forest. None had been unseated, and only two or three carried minor scratches.

They heard the furiously charging Romans of Sulla behind them, but Lydia was sure they were safe now. She galloped in heady exultation, the axe swinging in her hand, warrior maids by her side. Sulla's troop crossed the road, rushing through long grass in seething frustration at seeing their quarry so close and yet, because of the forest, so near to escape. Sulla was seconds too late. The Britons plunged in and melted away within its leafy denseness. Beside himself with frenzy, Sulla pulled up, his men sweating and wheeling about. His eyes were bloodshot with near-to-bursting veins. He swore oath upon oath. By every god who countenanced just vengeance, this was intolerable. And no god would commend him if he accepted it.

He lifted his arm and gestured. The mouths of his men fell open. They were to enter the forest? What was the madman about? The madman hissed his command, they obeyed him and they followed him into the forest.

Their advance was completely inhibited by their uncertainty and their surroundings, the undergrowth thick and tangled. Trunks and branches began to separate each man from the next. Sulla halted, his twisted mouth working, his saliva running. His livid face was like an obscene mask. He lifted his hand, commanding silence. He listened, as they all did. They heard nothing but the uncanny whispers in high branches. Under their patient, standing horses not even the driest leaves stirred. Above their heads the roof of the forest shut out the sun.

A blackbird whistled. Once, twice.

Sulla put his horse to a walk and went on. His men followed. Now the disturbed leaves rustled and whispered. There were no other sounds. Everything was blanketed and muffled.

" Madness," whispered one man to another.

" Aye," whispered the other, " but would you be the one to acquaint Paullinus with the news that Canis slipped our net just as we were about to cast it?"

" None of us is likely to carry any news to any man if this madman leads us into the arms of the hairy ones."

A red, writhing mist of fury blinded Sulla as he went deeper into the forest. To be so baulked when he had nearly had the dog. But the dog was here. He could not have gone far, not with horses. He was around somewhere, with the rest of them and that accursed Roman woman. Otherwise he would have made himself heard.

The Belgic tracker called softly. Sulla halted. His men gladly stopped. Again they listened. Again nothing. But the Belgic tracker was pointing to a narrow defile, summer dry, and loamy with perished leaf. Hoofmarks abounded, showing the tracks of horses which had moved through the defile. Sulla licked his lips. The Britons were using this ditch to penetrate the forest. Sulla rode his horse down the soft bank and along the loamy gully, his men following one by one. He led them as fast as he could, his eyes on the many hoofmarks, his savage desire for vengeance overriding his caution. He went on with the blood still red in his eyes. Beyond a sharp turn in the defile he ran into the long trunk of a tree ancient and dead. It spanned the waist-high chasm and was used as a bridge by the hairy ones when the defile ran deep with spring or winter rains. Sulla's mount reared and the men following on were brought to a sudden and confusing halt. And the halt brought death to many, for out of the trees dropped a horde of hairy ones, and from the deep cover of trees leapt the warriors.

The Romans, helpless to manoeuvre in the defile, were dragged from their horses. The wiser ones leapt from saddles to fight on equal terms or to run for cover. But equal terms were quickly unequal. The hairy ones had had their ears to the ground all morning, and were speedily on the spot when Canis arrived. There were two of them to every Roman. And the soldiers who dismounted to fight had their hamstrings slashed. They toppled and were slain. A few escaped. Sulla, still in his saddle, hacked and thrust. Out of his red mist, he suddenly saw Canis and the Roman woman. The red mist exploded into roaring fire. He came down from his horse and rushed with the fury of the deranged at the Briton.

Lydia saw the glaring, protuberant eyes. She remembered a fair girl child. In her hand she still held the axe of Cerdwa, and as Sulla hurled himself forward with sword raised to strike, the burnished blade of the axe rushed in flashing descent. Sulla took it full in the face. It smashed bone and eyes and flesh.

He lay there. He felt no pain, only discomfort in his throat and lungs. He was conscious of the green forest gradually darkening and drawing him into blackness. There was a gurgling in his throat. His lungs filled up. He died from the blow of an axe that drowned him in his own blood.

Lydia had completed the unfinished business and avenged a slain child.

The rain came later. It washed away the blood. The bodies were carried off by the long-haired wood-witches in great glee.

* * *

Paullinus could not completely rid himself of suspicions concerning Claudia's story of Lydia's escape. It was a possible but improbable story of a soldier who accosted her, put a dagger to her ribs and made her bring him to the villa and to Lydia Osirus. Claudia freely confessed she had recognised the soldier, that it had been Canis, and that he had also recognised her. She told her story simply, and at the insistence of Paullinus she repeated it. He could not disprove it, yet there was so much about it he did not like, perhaps because there was something about her which he did not understand. She showed bruises, she showed the red weals of tight bonds, and when they first discovered her, the signs of tears. But even so, what she did not show was dismay at the escape of a traitorous woman faithless to Rome.

She only said, "If the Briton has her, it is what she wishes."

It was Dinweda who guessed why Claudia was lacklustre.

"This is for you, Dinweda," said Claudia the day after Lydia's escape, and she pressed a trinket into the slave girl's hand.

"Mistress, you are always kind, there is no need of this gift."

"It is yours, Dinweda. We are friends." A sigh. "Dinweda?"

"Mistress?"

"Does Canis command much love in women?"

"He is cruelly irresistible, mistress, and was so even to Queen Boadicea, who was beautiful above all other women."

Silence save for the soft, swishing caress of the comb as Dinweda plied it through Claudia's silky hair. Then "Do you think him handsome, Dinweda? He is not prettily so, is he?"

"It is his eyes, mistress. You must never look into his eyes. For there you will see the earth and the waters, the darkness of night and the brightness of the sun."

211

" Oh, fie, Dinweda. How can one not look into his eyes?"
" By looking above them or below them, mistress."
Another sigh.
" Of course, it is absurd to consider his kisses—" Claudia
stopped and blushed.
" Mistress?"
" I did not say anything. Dinweda, where does he go?"
" To where he and his people may be safe, mistress."
" Where is that, Dinweda?"
" Mistress?"
Claudia turned soulful eyes on her cautious servant.
" You may trust me, I swear, Dinweda."
" He goes to the western mountains, mistress."
" So far? Oh, Dinweda, so far? He will not come back here
again, then?"
" Alas, no. Mistress, do not think too often of him. Yours
is a sweet life, and it has nothing to do with Canis."
But Claudia, young and wholly innocent and romantically
idealistic, thought of that which had brought Canis to Lydia
at such great risk.
" Dinweda, is not Lydia the most fortunate of women?"
" Mistress, you are the sweetest and kindest, which is
better than being fortunate."
Claudia picked up her burnished copper mirror, but it was
not her own face she saw in it.
Oh, you were cruelly hard to leave me, so cruelly hard to
rob a maid of her happiness. I wish you had not kissed me
as you did.

8

Princess Cea was in a temper. She was also out of her mind with worry. The Britons had made a temporary camp in a forest close to the land of the Brigantes. It was a vulnerable place compared with their previous haven. Andrasta help them if the Romans found them. And the great Father himself help them if Canis had been taken. Oh, reckless he was to have gone, and an idiot Lydia had been to be duped and carried off by Marcellus. Cyella wept when telling the story. Canis, unbelievably grim, had gone the following day, saying that Lydia could not be left to the ungenerous mercies of Paullinus. Cea begged him to send others, to send Hywel, but he would not. He had gone himself, taking twelve warriors with him. That had been many days ago. But how could he and twelve warriors bring Lydia out of the iron hands of Paullinus, who was a fortification in himself?

If word came that Paullinus now had Canis too, Cea told herself she would take all her Britons and march on that cold, implacable fortification and invest it in fury. For if Canis had to die, then better that she and all others died with him.

But a different word came in the end. It was brought on an afternoon when there had been much rain the day before, and by a hairy man who was all grins in his bush.

"They are on their way, Princess, and will be here in an hour."

"Canis? Lydia? All of them?" Cea was in joy, in agitation.

"All, Princess."

The joy and relief allowed her the luxury of dwelling on how she would pull the ears of Canis from his head. He arrived, in an hour, with Lydia, the warriors and with some hairy ones, including Agra, who had travelled from his own forest in genial escort. Within the leafy camp, they were immediately surrounded by overjoyed Iceni and Trinovantes, Hywel thrusting vigorously forward to help Lydia dismount. Some of the returned warriors bore wounds, but were modest about them. They had been tickled, they said, by a Roman picket.

As Canis dismounted, Cea had an urge to run to him. But she was a princess and a flouted one. He had caused her more worry than he had a right to. Therefore she would not run to him, but wait for him to come to her, by which time she would be satisfyingly mettlesome. She watched as several warrior maids flung themselves at him, and shamelessly and smackingly kissed him.

" You have done it, lord, you have lifted her from old cold-nose! "

Oh, the villain, thought Cea hotly and jealously, he will bed with one of them before my eyes. Then her quick Celtic temperment turned itself about, and she laughed. He saw her and tumbled the warrior maids aside to walk to her. She put her laughter aside, and received him with her nose sweetly in the air. It enchanted him.

" Sweet day to you, Princess, and how good it is to see you in such pleasure at having us return so soon," he said.

" So soon? So soon?" Cea could not get her indignant breath for a moment. " We have seen a multitude of suns since you left. I thought you taken days ago. Oh, the ups and downs of my heart. And now you come as if you only left yesterday! Oh, now I know why the Queen my mother was so put out of temper by your wilful comings and goings. Canis, do not smile, do not dare to, or I will have your teeth drawn one each day until you will not be able to smile without gaping like an old man."

" You were a proud princess when I left," said Canis warmly, " and are even more so now. What sits more proudly on any princess than a fine temper and an inclination to pull a man's teeth out?"

Cea stamped her foot. Her kilted tunic swirled, a shapely thigh flashed.

" I will not endure such jesting, I will not! "

He took her hands, raised them and kissed each palm.

" Cea, it was not a wilful endeavour," he said, " it was that which we had to do. If I had not gone, in time you would have held it against me."

Cea, declining for the moment to be sweetened, though she did not know how she refrained from kissing him, cried, "I would not! Am I to encourage you to fly to that Roman hussy each time she disappears? Aye, and a specious talent she has for it, constantly letting herself be carried off by her uncivilised countrymen, so that she can vastly enjoy the haste with which you run to her."

" I had not thought of it in that way," said Canis. " but then I am not able to see any woman as other women see her."

" As you are," said Cea, " do you see me?"

" Always," said Canis, " and with love."

She melted. He drew her close. She blushed.

" Canis, the people—"

" Here are my kisses," he said, " one for each day I have been gone, and one—"

But Cea escaped them all, not because she did not want them, but because she did not want people to see her yielding to them. And she knew she would yield, warmly and immodestly. So she escaped his embrace and stood back from him, laughter in her brown eyes.

" You are too bold," she said, " but Lydia is not, it seems. See how she comes with her eyes cast down. That is to hide her satisfaction with the way you deliver her from the spite of Romans. She *is* a hussy."

Lydia had joyfully received Dilwys from Feola, hugging her four-months-old infant to her breast. Then, after handing her back, she approached Cea with her dark head bent. She simply did not know how to look into the eyes of the Princess. She still felt the warmth of the flame lit by her rapturous union with Canis under a black sky strewn with tiny jewels of light. She thought she would surely betray herself if she lifted her eyes to Cea. So she kept her head lowered.

" Forgive me, Cea," she said.

" Forgive you? What is this?" asked Cea.

" I was foolish," said Lydia in a subdued voice. "I let myself be deceived by Marcellus, and no one could be more foolish than that. The consequences put Canis at great risk, and you in fear for him. Forgive me for this, and other things."

" What other things? Why do you hang your head, Lydia?" Cea was puzzled rather than suspicious.

" She is weary," said Canis, " she has had little rest since we slipped Paullinus two days ago. And there was no great risk, Cea, only a question of waiting patiently for fortune to favour us. I will tell you about it. Meanwhile, give Lydia what she asks—a sweet welcome."

Cea gave him a look that plainly told him: she would if she would, but not if she was commanded. He smiled at her. She was truly in so much relief that he was back safe and sound that she let his smile command her charity.

She said, " Lydia, it has not been easy to wait here thinking the worst would happen. But there, it is not the worst, it is the best—and I am happy for you, if you are happy too. Your brother Julian is here, and in seeing you he will be even happier. For he too has been worried."

" Julian?" said Lydia vaguely, and lifted her head. She looked as weary as Canis had said. The journey, even though full of moments of joy, had been an ordeal after her long days of captivity. Even so, it seemed to Cea that she still looked disturbingly beautiful, and much more than she had a right to. She still wore Claudia's blue robe, but it was dirty and creased, and there was dust in her hair and on her feet. Her green eyes showed strain and fatigue, and were dark-rimmed. Why, then, thought Cea, grinding her teeth, does she not look just a little unattractive?

" Aye, Julian, your brother," she said, " he is here, did you not know that?"

Lydia did know. Canis had already told her that although Julian was wounded, he was doing as well as he could. Lydia

216

had realised that after his defeat, her brother would do as well in the hands of the Britons as in the hands of the infuriated Paullinus. She was conscience-stricken now for having let him slip from her mind.

" Where is he?" she asked.

" Come," said Cea.

They went with Canis through what to Lydia seemed swarms of Britons, many of them giving her a warm welcome. They reached a bowery shelter, built of branch and leaf to protect from the elements a Roman who lay there with a broken ankle and a gashed thigh. The wounded thigh was healing, the fractured ankle bedded in moss and bound. The man himself sat propped against a high pillow of heaped fern covered by a soft skin. He was pale and drawn, but making a healthy meal of meat.

The Britons had a warm regard for Julian Osirus, for in defiance of his countrymen he had spoken in brave defence of Queen Boadicea as Romans prepared to scourge her. He had condemned the scourging, called it infamy and outrage, had been clubbed senseless and later risen to give the suffering Queen his cloak to cover herself. The fact that he had commanded the recently defeated Roman force did not lessen the respect the Britons felt for him. They also had a place in their hearts for his sister Lydia.

He looked up as Canis, Cea and Lydia approached against a background of excited people. His dark eyes glinted as he saw Canis. He felt exasperation, bitterness, but no malice. He knew the Briton too well, knew his tragedies as well as his triumphs. However, a man was only a man, and Julian could not help wishing that Canis had taken himself elsewhere long ago.

Princess Cea he had seen before the revolt, but he had never met her until now. He found her a sweet edition of her proud mother, with an occasional little tantrum remindful of Boadicea. There was a woman with her at this moment, a woman with black hair running wild, whose supple grace seemed to have little to do with her dirty blue robe. She did not look like an Iceni or Trinovante woman. Ye gods! Julian sat up and smiled as he recognised his sister.

"By all that pertains to voluptuous Venus," he said, "never have I seen you in such shabby disregard of her, Lydia. Shabby? Why, you are grimy."

"Julian, oh, how sweet to see you," whispered Lydia, and dropping to her knees beside him, she put affectionate arms around him and kissed him emotionally. His platter of meat was overturned.

"That will not please Cyella," he said, making light of his own emotions. As if she had heard him the Iceni maid arrived. She had been down to the stream to fill a water jar, and it slopped as she halted in startled consternation at what she saw, a woman embracing Julian. Then she recognised Lydia. She flung back her fair hair, saw Canis, danced in joy and slopped more water.

"Oh, such pleasure to see you again," she said, "and you have brought Lydia back to us, as I knew you would. And my father Andudo also? Is he safe?" Canis nodded. "See," she said to Julian, "did I not say so, did I not say Canis would return with her?"

"You said this so many times," said Julian, "that not only have I suffered by what Canis has done, I have also suffered a surfeit of what he might do. But no one told me that so mighty a man would bring back my sister looking as unwashed as a charcoal burner."

"I had no time to dip her," said Canis.

They had not seen each other since the battle. Julian had lain unconscious for some while; and when he had come to in somewhat feverish condition, he found himself a prisoner of the Britons. But a well-treated one. He had been attended by Grud, a physician of not inconsiderable skill, and had been nursed by Cyella. Cyella had pointed out that it was no more than she ought to do for someone who had been kind to her.

Julian knew why Canis had been absent, and had been in grim anxiety about his sister's fate. He sighed. He knew himself in debt to the man who had defeated him so cruelly.

" Julian," said Lydia, " it is such joy to see you again. Are you not just a little pleased to see me?"

He kissed her. The Britons slipped away. Alone with her, Julian thought how much his sister had changed. Up to the moment when she realised she was in love with Canis, she had been wilful, selfish and unmanageable. That was all gone. Dirty and grubby as she was, her beauty had a more haunting quality to it now. He had once likened her green eyes to those of a cat greedy for cream. They were softly luminous now. Her raven-black hair, which she had had so proudly dressed, had grown lustrously wild. It framed her face and caressed her shoulders in unruly disorder.

Perhaps she was less of a Roman than she had been, and more a woman trapped by all the pain and mystery of her sex. " Julian?" She was anxious. " Why do you look at me so? Am I not still dear to you?"

" When were you not, even in your most capricious days?" he said.

" Truly, I am not as unlovable as I was," she said, " and I am distressed at your ill fortune. You are hurt, you are a prisoner here, you have lost all favour with Paullinus. He speaks so bitterly of you now."

"He makes much of my incompetence, no doubt," said Julian drily, and went on to say somewhat ironically that in the hands of the Britons he was under much the same advantage as Marcellus had been, in that he was out of the range of the vindictiveness of Paullinus. And Paullinus was surely in a worse state now that Canis had robbed him of Lydia. Also, Princess Cea could not have been kinder, and though the unguents and potions Grud conjured up for his relief were vile beyond anything, his gashed thigh was mending apace. For the moment, therefore, he did not burn to hobble off.

Lydia told him there were rumours that Paullinus would be recalled to Rome, for his administrators were complaining about him. She thought if this were to happen, then Julian

219

could happily return to Calleva Atrebatum and fight Britons no more.

"Would you go with me?" asked Julian.

She flushed a little. She heard the sounds of life, the activity of the people, the murmur of song, the laughter of boisterous children and the whispers of leafy branches swaying in the wind. She remembered a dark room with four thick walls.

"I cannot," she said, hiding her eyes. Julian lifted her chin, but her lashes dropped. "Julian, I cannot."

"Do not hide what I know is there, sweet sister. I am not the one to deny your wants and wishes, however foolish. But you are young, Lydia, you are Roman, and for you your life now is so much waste."

"Waste?" Lydia shook her head and her hair flew. She breathed in the smell of leafy earth and tang of wood fires. She remembered her hours of anguish and the joy of the moment when she knew Canis had not forsaken her. "Julian, I belong to these people, I belong to Canis."

"But he does not belong to you," said Julian, "he belongs to one woman alone, and will never wholly cleave to another, not even to Cea. This I think you must know by now."

"I know he belongs to Boadicea," said Lydia quietly. "But she is dead, and a man like Canis cannot bind himself in life to any woman who is only a whisper in the night. He is for enduring life and love, for warmth and joy, for these things he gives to others. They are what he has given me. Whatever the dead were in life, however beloved, they cannot rise from their graves to make a living man warm and joyful on a cold night. Boadicea was a great queen, oh I know this, Julian, but she herself would not ask of Canis a denial of all his sweeter needs."

"Are you his sweet need, Lydia?"

Warm blood rushed to her face.

"Whatever else obtains," she whispered, "he is mine, I know he is mine."

"If you are content to be a barbarian's concubine—"

" Oh, you are unkind to call him so! " she flashed.

" I have never called him so," said Julian, " I only repeat what you yourself have said."

" Never, I would not," she said, although she knew she had been guilty. " He is a man to make Caesar himself look ordinary. He is born to command men and women, warriors and princes. Such a man is never a barbarian, never."

" I will put it another way, then," said Julian. " If you are content to be a Briton's concubine, I am not enraptured for you. My sister was born for better than that."

Lydia shook her head and laughed.

" I am not his concubine, I am his love," she said.

" Come about," said Julian, " think with your head."

" I am my own mistress and know my own mind."

" Senseless one, you let him get you with child. I have seen the infant."

" Then you have seen the most beautiful babe, have you not?" She was shamelessly proud of herself. " Canis dotes on her."

Julian sighed. He had found his sister and lost her again. She was more bewitched by the Briton than ever. Here she sat, resting back on her heels, her dark-rimmed eyes betraying strain, and smiling as if she possessed all the riches of life—instead of only a dusty robe.

" Have you no distaste for your lot?" he asked.

" Distaste?" Lydia laughed again. " Oh, Julian, never did I think that my agreeable brother would become pompous. Is my robe so dirty? Am I so dirty? This comes from circumstances, not habits. I scorn your Roman disdain."

" Do you?" Julian smiled and thought of Cyella, who was also quick to scorn this or that in a man.

" It is true we do not have the advantages of Roman baths," said Lydia, " but I have come to know warm baths and heated rooms do not give a person greater wisdom or more tolerance. Indeed, immersion in a cold stream is infinitely more stimulating—and at the same time, infinitely more chastening."

" First I am scorned, now I am lectured," said Julian.

"Lydia, you are my sweet sister and I can only wish you joy. I will not order your life for you, nor check your deeds or frustrate your whims. It is a fine child you have given Canis, but you cannot be wholly content."

"Who can have more than what each day brings?" she said, and looked up as a long shadow fell astride her. Canis had returned to bring her food and drink. There was no bread, for the Britons lacked flour at the moment. But there was meat. She took the platter, and Julian saw how she caressed Canis with her eyes. His heart was wrenched for her. Canis would eventually wed Cea, and what joy would his sister get from that?

"You brought Lydia to bed," said Julian, a little grimly.

"I think," said Canis pleasantly, "that she will tell you it was contrived by her goddess Diana, whom she says has a talent for such things."

"Was it Diana who got her with child?" asked Julian.

"She is all things to some Roman women," said Canis.

"An honourable man would wed the mother of his child," said Julian, at which the red suffused Lydia's face.

"A free man would find great joy in taking Lydia to wife," said Canis, and that brought sweet tears to her eyes.

"Any man is free who has not yet taken a wife," said Julian.

"If he can discount his promise," said Canis, "he may be free, but cannot call himself honourable."

"You are a describer of artful circles," said Julian, "and a wager of cruel war."

"He is not as cruel as Paullinus," said Lydia, beginning to eat.

"Ah, you love him, do you, for defeating me as he did?" said Julian.

"He is my dearest lord," said Lydia, relishing the meat.

"By every patient god," said Julian, "you look like a Briton, you stuff your mouth like one and you speak like one."

"I count myself one," said Lydia, "and I am to travel with Princess Cea and her people. Canis has promised me."

"Then you must rest when you have eaten," said Canis, "for we march at sundown and go through the night. But, Lydia, since your brother is here, and since we can get him to a place where he may be taken safely to Calleva Atrebatum, will you say if you are in any mind to go with him? No one here will deny you this wish and desire."

"Ah," said Julian, "bread is cast before the meat-eater."

Lydia, incredulous, looked at her platter, threw it aside and leapt to her feet.

"Oh," she cried at Canis, "to dissemble so! I will not, I will not! I am to go with you! Oh, you do not understand me even now." She threw back her hair, showing eyes big and fierce. "To go with Julian is one thing, to return to Roman ways is another, and I do not know how you can lay tongue to the suggestion. I will speak to Grud, who would never promise me one day what he would take back the next. Nor would he imply, as you do, that I am in doubt about my wishes and desires!"

"This is my true sister," murmured Julian, shifting his leg to ease his still painful ankle, "so go to it, Lydia."

"Lydia, get to sleep," said Canis, intrigued and not discomfited by her fierceness. He had never favoured spiritless women. "You need all the rest you can find, if you are to go with us at sundown. You can go in company with Grud, and mutter all the way with him. No, do not twist my ears again. I merely thought you might have wished to go to Calleva with your brother, and cosset him a little on the way."

"I have never cossetted Julian, nor would he let me now," she said.

"I should have come for you at Calleva," said Canis.

"Oh," she said. She went off with her eyes swimming a little. Canis watched her go, his smile not without tenderness.

"She is like Cerdwa was," he said.

"I have heard of Cerdwa," said Julian.

"Once you saw her," said Canis; then he ventured to ask whether Julian had received any information concerning the movements of the Britons prior to the battle.

223

"There was a Trinovante," said Julian frankly, "a man called Bada. He informed me you would emerge a day later than you did. For such false information about so critical a matter, we hanged him. We hanged none of the others who laid us false trails. I should have known, with Bada, that the fox in you was at work. But I thought, having used him to help the girl Cyella get to her father, that you would not be so ungrateful as to use him yourself."

"I used another, whom we ourselves might hang," smiled Canis. "Julian, if you are not too feeble, I can arrange to get you safely back to Calleva."

"For Paullinus? Not so," said Julian. "I must be as practical as Marcellus Mercurius was, and lie outside the reach of our Governor for a while. And since you are responsible for my injuries, what you shall not do is place me in charge of warriors who may be gaily careless with them. You will have to take me with you until I am well enough to make my own way, at least."

"My house is yours for as long as you wish," said Canis, "but its roof is the sky."

He went, and on his way Cyella shyly detained him.

"Lord," she said, "we are to leave here at sundown?"

"We are, Cyella," he said. He knew what was in her mind.

"Will it be desperate?"

"Only when we have to fight. We will not have to fight every day."

Cyella in the most casual way mentioned the tribune, Julian Osirus, saying he was a kind man, and that it would be uncharitable to leave him in this place when he was so crippled. Canis remarked that he had offered Julian the help of warriors, so that he might reach Calleva Atrebatum.

"Will I go with him, lord?" she asked. "His wound is still sore and his ankle troublesome. I will not consider it a great hardship if you command me to go with the warriors so that I can attend to him."

"He has refused my offer, Cyella, and is coming with us."

Cyella, looking at her hands, said that perhaps that was

best, and that although Canis smote Romans cruelly he was not wholly unkind.

"It is not my kindness that affects this, Cyella, but my responsibility, as the tribune will tell you."

"He has that kind of tongue," said Cyella, and smiled as she went on her way.

Canis found Hywel and asked him to fetch Wanda. Hywel did so, bringing her before Canis. In curiosity other warriors looked on.

"Wanda," said Canis, "why would you avenge your kin who died in battle against Romans?"

The smile that was no smile peeped from her curtain of golden hair.

"Why? Because my kin did die, lord."

"Who were your kin?"

Hywel, who did not like Wanda, saw her hesitate. Then she said, "There was but one. She was named Cerdwa. She died that you might live. It was a cruel and unjust death."

"So you would be avenged on me, Wanda?"

"That is foolish, lord," she said.

"The man Bada, who came to our camp with Cyella, returned to the Romans, giving them information concerning us. It was not the right information. For this they hanged him."

"That is the price men like that have to pay at times," said Wanda.

Canis regarded her in a way that made her chew her lip.

"You alone conversed with Bada," he said, "and the information he carried to the Romans, he received from you. You thought, as others did, that we would break out of the forest a day later than we did, for that is what I said we would do at the time. That was to protect from greedy ears what we would really do. Also, I think you induced Marcellus to carry Lydia off. Since you were kin to Cerdwa, who was the bravest of all forest maids, we will not hang you, Wanda—but give you as bride to the hairy ones."

Wanda turned white. Everyone knew the hairy ones took

no true brides, only women whom they shared and kept in the darkest caves in their forests; the only women the hairy ones treated equally with were their daughters, the wood-witches. Wanda screamed, and screamed again later when six delighted hairy men arrived to take her—after receiving word from Canis that there was a lustrous bride in the offing. Canis told them to deliver her to Agra.

"Say to him that as he has done so much for us, this woman is the least we can offer him."

"Lord," said one of them, "Agra will be in great pleasure at such a gift. He has not enjoyed a golden-haired tidbit like this one for a hundred years. But he is not a greedy man, he will observe the custom and share her with all. She will bear us many daughters, for she is strong, healthy and young. For such generosity we are your servants always, lord. May the sun and the rain be your sustenance, and the earth your friend. Now we will take the prize and run hard with her to catch up with Agra."

Agra had already departed to his forest. His friends bundled up Wanda and carried her away. It was a long time before the sounds of her screams were completely lost. They carried her far, to the forest in which Agra lived. They reached a place in the forest where the trees were so thick and had such a mighty spread that day was like green night. Agra, who had not long arrived, was highly tickled to receive Wanda, who was hysterical as the hairy ones unbundled her. Then rage consumed her as the tickled Agra tickled her. She drew the dagger from her leather garter and sought to slit his stomach. Agra picked her up as if she was no more than a ruffled chicken, and tossed her into the arms of his friends.

Spitting and scratching she lost her dagger, the hairy ones using it to slit her garments. They stripped her and eyed her in delight. Agra drank three brimming cups of mead to fortify himself, carried her into a cave blacker than a fox's burrow, and there gleefully fought with her, wrestled with her and subdued her. Outside the hairy ones capered to her screams. She found Agra stronger than a bear, and with more arms than an octopus. And though she still scratched and clawed as he claimed her for bride, Agra discovered she was a shapely and sweet tidbit indeed. Discounting her nails, he was tender with her. Wanda sighed, yielded and stopped clawing.

Within a few weeks, several of the hairy ones bore scratches and bruises, but went about grinning and happy, nonetheless. And Wanda, a forest maid, though a strange-minded one, accepted her fate. Indeed, one step outside her restricted perimeter, and the wood-witches would have her. So though she continued to excel at spitting and scratching, the tenderness of the hairy ones in their enjoyment of her made her a sighing, yielding bride. And in due time she was delivered of her first fair girl child, though who the father was none could be sure. But that was of little consequence to the hairy ones. And of no consequence at all to Wanda by then.

*　　*　　*

Some while after Wanda had been taken away, the camp of the Britons was astir with people ready to march, and only Lydia was still asleep. They would not wake her until the last moment. Canis, Cea, Grud and Andudo studied a roughly-drawn map on a piece of soft leather hide. It showed the country of Brigantia, to which they were close. The problem was still Paullinus. He was not going to let the surviving Iceni and Trinovantes, now numbering almost three thousand, escape him. It was not beyond him to commission another force to find the Britons and bring them to further battle. Every route to the west would be closely watched, and every man disposed to carry word to Romans of the movements of the migrants would be encouraged to do so by Roman gold.

Canis indicated a route that would take them first to the eastern border of Brigantia, and then across that country to the west. Here the stumbling-block was Queen Cartimandua. Of all the client-monarchs in Roman Britain, she was the friendliest to Rome. It was she who had betrayed Prince Caratacus of the Belgae to the Romans, after Caratacus had bitterly fought the invasion by Claudius. It was she whom the Romans had helped when her divorced husband, Venutius, had mounted civil war against her. With this Roman help she had decisively beaten him.

But perhaps, suggested Canis, Cartimandua might give help to friendly fellow Britons on this occasion. In one way or another.

9

I t was a lonely field, dark under the gloom of poor evening light, the dying sun blanketed by heavy grey clouds. Bergotix of Vamachelle Ford unhitched the horse from the wooden plough and wiped his sweating face. Horse and man began their welcome plod home. A tall man emerged from the shadows of a tree. He too led a horse, though not one that had pulled a plough.

"Greetings, land man," he said.

"I know you not," said Bergotix, too weary to take any real heed of the stranger in the gloom. His woman would be waiting in their simple dwelling with hot, tasty food and perhaps a cup of mead.

"I have come from the south," said Canis.

The south was the land of the Belgae, and Bergotix thought little of the Belgae.

"Then return there," he said, "for what we can offer here would raise the status of few men."

"I seek a way of entering into the service of your Queen," said Canis.

"If you are willing to place your neck in jeopardy, then who am I to dissuade you? Eburacum is that way, stranger, and I wish you joy of it." Bergotix grumbled, shrugged, then continued: "If you wish a bite, then come. It will not be much, but I must offer something to a man who seeks of his own free will to serve Cartimandua."

"Queens are more than other women," said Canis, "and there are few women who can be called ordinary."

"My woman is all of ordinary," said Bergotix, "and I bless her for that. Let me tell you, stranger from the south, I have known only one queen who was above all expectations, only one queen I served heart and soul, and she not my own monarch. But I was younger then, though it was no more than two years ago. Look at me now, I limp along before my time. I work from dawn to dusk seven days each week, and what I grow on six days is not for my own table, but Cartimandua's. If you have come from her to spy on me—"

"I have not. I do not even know her."

Something about the stranger made Bergotix less unreceptive.

"You look like a warrior," he said. "Ah, there is a life for a man. Once I was quick for strife and battle. Aye, fought for Queen Boadicea, I did. There was a woman for you, as well as a queen."

"You served Boadicea?" The voice of Canis was a gentle persuasion to the tongue of the Brigante.

"Aye. We thought she would rid all of us of Romans. And came near to it, she did, as near as anyone could. Many Brigantes slipped away to enlist with her armies—and I, Bergotix of Vamachelle Ford, took her my own spear and my own band of twenty men. You mark how I limp? I took a Roman thrust at Verulamium, and by virtue of that could not fight for her in her last battle. So I escaped, where thousands died. That is not to say I might have won the battle for her, yet at the time I was sore in heart to miss it. Ah, what a campaign she waged, what battles her general fought for her. Aye, beautiful was Boadicea as a woman, and inspiring as a queen. Show me another like her, and I would put aside my limp and fight for her. It is good to be a man in the service of Boadicea, or one like her."

"I also escaped where thousands died," said Canis.

The track was rutted, and in the gloom Bergotix limped awkwardly, peering more keenly at the profile of the tall stranger.

"Were you of Boadicea?" he asked, feeling pleasure at perhaps being in company with one who had shared the exhilaration of those brave, tragic days.

"When was Canis not of Boadicea?"

Bergotix halted, drawing quick breath. How quiet the evening was. There was nothing about its atmosphere to suggest that the moment was out of the ordinary. Why, if this man were truly Canis, the general of Queen Boadicea, surely the clash of cymbals would have preceded his arrival? But no, it had been lonely and unspectacular for the past hour and more. He put out a hand, taking Canis by the arm and turning him.

"You say you are Canis?" He was disturbed, excited. " I knew the man called Canis the Wolfhead, who served Boadicea as her general. I saw him not once but many times, so I cannot be deceived. Let me see you." He stared full into the face of his man. " Oh, by great Andrasta, Boadicea's own goddess, you tell no lie, you are Canis!" Bergotix flung his arms around the Queen's general, and would have wept on his chest, but Canis was not a man to stomach an excess of emotion from another. He broke the hold.

" The occasion is not as momentous as that, friend," he said.

" Lord," said Bergotix, " the occasion is the happiest since you received me and my Brigantes within your command. I have heard rumours that you still plague Romans, but I did not truly know if you were alive or dead. Come, you shall have more than the small mouthful I spoke of, and more than one miserable measure of mead. This evening we shall empty the jar. My woman will be all grumbles, for she has railed often at me over you. This is because I have sometimes talked of how under your command we scattered Roman legions like so much chaff, and because she is a woman who cannot bear to listen to any talk of battle or bravery. Aye, even boxed my ears she has, and roared at me to close my mouth. ' This Canis,' she has said, ' I have heard more than enough of that miracle worker, who in the end did no more for his so great Queen than I could have done myself.' A woman is not to be argued with, since she will either turn the argument into a loud quarrel, or use it as an excuse to kick a man from the bed. Therefore, though all we have is yours this night, do not

231

answer her back if my shrew does not show the same regard for you as I do. For all that, she is a fine pot-stirrer and the food will be hot, I warrant."

"Friend Bergotix," said Canis speciously, "you are right. An argumentative woman is so dangerously contradictory that it is like trying to reason with a double-faced tigress. One face smiles at you, while the other bites your head off. It is better to keep your tongue between your teeth and look at the moon."

"Lord, you own the way of it," said Bergotix amiably. "But why do you seek employ with Queen Cartimandua? She is no Boadicea, and you will not prevail on her to fight Romans. She fawns on them. Having served such a queen as Boadicea, why do you seek to serve one as inferior as Cartimandua?"

"Politics, Bergotix."

"Politics? They are even more confounding than a woman."

It was a long walk to his dwelling, and it was dark when they arrived. It was a hut of stone and wattle, thatch and lime. There were others like it nearby, all built within a small Brigante encampment. There was no door, only a covering of heavy skins to keep out the wind. When Bergotix and Canis had seen to their horses, they entered.

It was like a thousand other humble encampment dwellings, with a smoke-blackened far wall where a fire burned. A hole in the roof drew out the smoke. An oil lamp gave light, and skins on the floor served to warm feet. There were crude stools to seat inhabitants and visitors. An earthenware pot hanging from an iron tripod bubbled on the fire, and the aroma was of hot food. On hearing them enter, a woman came from the only other room, pushing aside the dividing skins. She was tall and looked graceful. She bore a second lamp, a small baked clay vessel holding oil and wick. The lamps and the flames of the fire cast moving shadows, and in lifting the lamp she held, the better to observe Bergotix and the visitor, her own face came into the light.

She did not look like an ordinary woman. Even less did she

look like a quarrelsome shrew. She was handsome, of some thirty summers, her woollen robe aged but clean. Her hair was striking, a flowing cascade of soft copper.

" So, man of the plough," she said to Bergotix, " you have found one more wandering stranger. And he, no doubt, is also of your noisy fraternity of iron shields and brass trumpets." Her voice was not grumbling, however; it was a quiet and pleasant voice, underlined by soft humour.

" She means to say," said Bergotix to Canis, " that I have sometimes invited other men to sup with us, when they had tales to tell of how we waged war for Boadicea."

" One day," said his wife, speaking to Bergotix but viewing the stranger covertly, " you will bring a man who favours a Roman ear more than your own, and then, sweet fool, the Romans will hear from him how you fought for the rebellious Iceni Queen. Then they will come and take you. Miserable will be your end, especially as it will come about through your own indiscretion. Tell me," she said good-temperedly, " who is today's stranger?"

" I am from the south," said Canis.

" He is more than that, Caleda," said Bergotix triumphantly, " he is a man I have often spoken of."

" What man is that?" asked Caleda. She lifted the lamp higher, and looked up into the face of the tall Briton. She saw him clearer then. She saw wide grey eyes tinted by the fire flames, and compulsively she returned look for look as he smiled at her. A strange weakness took her. Despite his shabby cloak and the tunic showing worn where cloak parted, he had about him a presence which seemed to her to place him above other men. If there was a little slyness in his eyes, there was also resolution and knowledge. Her normally calm blood ran a little confusedly. " No," she said wonderingly, " this is not the man you have often spoken of, Bergotix, this is not the man called Canis. For you have always said that Canis was a man whose mouth issued flame, and whose voice commanded fifty thousand warriors like a battering iron. This is not Canis, therefore."

Bergotix blew out breath.

"Woman," he said, "did I not look upon Boadicea's general myself many times? Do I not know him? Have I not said he could be King of all Britain if he wished—save only for accursed Romans? And did I not also say—"

"In all you have said, in all you have told me," interrupted Caleda, "you have, dear fool, painted only a man of clattering iron and voice of brass."

"When we razed Londinium to the ground," said Bergotix, "I saw Canis advance in his chariot, and with him Cerdwa of the axe—"

"Enough, O windy acolyte of war," said Caleda. She set the lamp down on a crudely-hewn table and said to Canis, "Come, seat yourself and let my foolish man buzz in his own ear. I will bring you cool water and warm cloth."

She disappeared. Canis seated himself and Bergotix also drew up a stool. The Brigante launched into an apologetic reasoning of the foibles, whims and miscalculations of his wife, at which Canis nodded or shook his head or smiled. Caleda returned bearing a wooden bowl of water and a clean square of linen. Canis and Bergotix laved their hands and Canis put water to his face. Caleda moved about, serving food from the pot into earthenware bowls, the while casting swift glances at the man her husband said was Canis. When she had served them, she went into the inner room, taking one of the lamps, and there she looked at her face in an old mirror of burnished metal.

She returned to serve herself, and when she sat down to eat with them she moved the table lamp so that its light did not betray the roughness of her hands. She did not speak, she listened to the talk of the men. Although Bergotix could lay his tongue to no other subject but the brave campaign of Queen Boadicea, and Canis spoke only of small things that were insignificant against the bold canvas of Bergotix's colourful discourse, yet she listened as she never had before. From beneath lowered lids she cast her covert glances at the man Bergotix had so often sworn was a warrior of the most fearsome mettle, as mighty as Cyantillus, the Celtic god of war, also known as Camulos. Such compelling eyes he had. They glimmered at her husband's lusty outpourings concerning great battles and heroic marches. If this man was truly Canis, he was no roaring battle fiend, not with eyes such as he had. He could not be a mere commander of blood and death. That was the trade of loud and vainglorious men.

She noted the regard her husband had for him, and the way he spoke to him. "This was the way of it, lord." Or, "Lord, how could any man have seen Queen Boadicea run her chariot at Romans and not followed her against Caesar himself?" The light in Bergotix's eyes was something she had not seen before.

Bergotix interrupted her musing.

"It is beyond all reason, Caleda, but here is Canis come to Brigantia to seek service with Cartimandua. Argue with him, for he says he will contest anything except a woman's tongue. We would not wish him to put his head into Cartimandua's house, so argue him out of it, Caleda."

"I will argue in no way with him," said Caleda, "for he is not a man to be set aside from his purpose, least of all by me."

"You see?" Bergotix spread his hands before Canis. "Did I not say she would give you only scant regard?"

"I did not quite see it that way," said Canis. "Answer me a question if you can. What is Queen Cartimandua's greatest desire?"

"She is all desires, all greed and all whims," said Bergotix, "and I know no other answer than that."

"I know another," said Caleda, her hands in her lap, "though I do not know if it is the one you want. Her greatest desire is a man called Ancastus."

"How do you know this?" asked Bergotix, looking as if a sacred hare had popped out of his wife's mouth.

"Because while you are a great talker, Bergotix, I am a keen listener," she said.

"The way of it in this dwelling," said Bergotix to the

235

ceiling, " is that I am so frequently bested I am better out of it than in it. Is there some mead for us, O woman of light wit and keen ears?"

Caleda fetched the jar and poured the dark mead into homely clay cups. Canis took the one she gave him, thanked the Brigantes for their hospitality, hearth and company, then drank to their long life.

" For the honour you do us in being here, we are privileged," responded Bergotix in the traditional manner, and he drank to that. Caleda did not drink at all, she only waited silently for what Canis would say next. He had not, she thought, said a great deal so far.

" Who is Ancastus?" he asked.

" A lion of a man," said Caleda, " whom Queen Cartimandua wishes to tame and bring to her bed, where she will draw his claws and tangle with his virility. But he will not be tamed, or go to her bed, for he says there is nothing so dangerous as to bed with a woman who has as many whims as Cartimandua and is also a queen. While she cannot have him, she suffers him, courts him and begs him. But should she prevail, when she has sucked him dry and tired of him, she will give him to her hornets and have the weary lion stung to death."

" There is a whimsical queen indeed," said Canis.

" Also," said Caleda, " besides her great desire, she has a great weakness. This is vested in her daughter, Princess Venturia, on whom she dotes with sickly possessiveness, but who is as venal and sensuous as her mother. A man who is a man and can be recognised as such may find, if he seeks to serve Cartimandua, that he will also have to serve her daughter. But this same man, if he has enough cunning about him, may perhaps find a way to use the weakness of the Queen to his own good purpose. I know not too much of men and women myself, and rely more on what I hear of them, than what I know of them, to make up my mind about them."

" Tonight," said Bergotix, " you make speeches instead of argument, Caleda. How has this come about?" But his eyes were merry in the shadows and the light, and he laughed at the pink that touched his wife's cheek. The faint colour brought a glow to her smooth face, but she still kept her hands hid.

" Tomorrow I will go to Eburacum," said Canis.

" I had better go with you," said Bergotix, "for to a stranger it is a place full of villains, as are all towns."

" You have your field work," said Caleda, " so I will go. Indeed, we have some produce to sell."

" Nought of any consequence, and not tomorrow," said Bergotix, as if that were the end of it.

" There is always some produce to sell," said Caleda, as if she had only just come to the beginning, " and although I do not think Queen Boadicea's general incapable of finding his own way, it would be discourteous if one of us did not accompany him. You cannot leave the fields, husband."

" By all the talkative harpies of Britain," said Bergotix, " have you not said more than once that if Canis ever did come your way you would douse his roaring iron with a bucket of pigs' water?"

" And have you not said a thousand times that he had a voice like a hundred brass trumpets?" said Caleda placidly. " You are a great talker, husband, but alas, no great painter of men."

Bergotix grinned. He had known her for many years. She had been the only child of a lesser underling of a Brigante chieftain. Bergotix had owned the land called Vamachelle Ford. He was of the same age as Caleda, had spoken for her many times, but always she had said no, she would not leave her father, a widower. Her father, given to roistering, would have gladly parted with her; but Caleda, who had had a happy childhood, would not, as she put it to others, " Leave him to roister himself into a bottomless marsh on a black night, he is too merry a father to come to that kind of end."

She grew to be quite old for an unwed woman, and seeing she was adamant in her continued refusal of him, Bergotix, a natural warrior, gave up the joys of fruitless courtship and sought instead the joys of combat under Queen Boadicea. He

237

went off with twenty other Brigantes to fight for the Iceni Queen. When he returned with one leg slightly shorter than the other, he found that Queen Cartimandua had dispossessed him of his land. She said there was a law entitling her to claim the land of all absentee owners. As soon as Caleda found Bergotix had a limp and no land, she left her father and wed her erstwhile suitor. She thought he should have something, even if only a wife. Bergotix argued that he was now poorer than any man, and no catch for any woman; but Caleda argued far better than that, and they were wed. Cartimandua graciously allowed him to farm the land that had once been his. The produce was shared, one seventh to Bergotix and Caleda, the rest to the Queen.

As Bergotix had said, Cartimandua was no Boadicea.

In the matter of accompanying Canis to Eburacum, Bergotix did not argue further with his wife; so on the following day she went with Canis to this chief town of Brigantia. It was a little over a league away. With her, she took a basket of produce, which she said she hoped to sell in the place where those who grew food bartered with those who made cloth or pots or tools. Canis rode his horse, and Caleda perched behind him, modestly tucking her legs within her best robe as she dangled over the animal's rump. Her basket she balanced on her knees.

"You will not ride fast?" she begged, for she was a little nervous of horses, or even more nervous of what the wind might do to her robe if he galloped. She did not want her naked legs gaped at.

"We will step daintily all the way," said Canis. He trotted gently, in fact, and Caleda bounced gently. For all that, she vowed she would arrive at Eburacum with her stomach in her head. It was not so bad when they reached the road, except that when they passed a small Roman outpost there was the usual to-do about who they were, where they were going and why. Canis passed himself off as a Belgic man from the south, who sought service with Queen Cartimandua, at which the Romans looked at him as if he were touched in the head.

They were not to know this was Canis, for whom Paullinus was everlastingly searching. They did not even have him in their minds, for although they had heard of him, his exploits had never touched this northern region. Nor did they know that his three thousand followers lay securely hid in the land of the Parisii on the eastern border of Brigantia, where they would wait in all quiet until receiving word from the Wolfhead.

The day was a little sharp, and on each side stretched the mystic wonder of moorlands, darkly colourful and sometimes darkly forbidding. In such country, a man and a woman might find all the solitude they wanted, but little on which to sustain themselves. Even then, they would have to fight the wolves for it. Outlawed Brigantes did dwell there, and their sustenance was mostly extracted from those who, whether they could spare it or not, were forced to give it up.

Coming eventually upon the approaches to the town of Eburacum, Canis and Caleda caught up other people making their way. A red-faced buxom woman hailed Caleda with a laugh and a loud word.

"Ah, you are up with a new man, Caleda. Is Bergotix pitched into the well at last?"

"I am with a man who, liking my face above yours, Ergola, took me up on my way," replied Caleda.

"How might he have come by such liking, since he has seen my face only this moment?" laughed the woman.

"I told him of it," said Caleda as Canis trotted by, "and so he took me up lest he met you later and his courtesy was above his incredulity."

"Oh, shrew you are, Caleda," shouted the laughing woman after them, "and how any man could get joy of you I know not!"

Eburacum was a crowded place. Here Caesar's men had a main stronghold, and the streets were filled as much with Romans as Brigantes. There were buildings of native stone, and fortifications of stone and brick. There were places of busy barter. Canis remembered Venta Icenorum, the soft

239

wildness of the country seen from the escarpment of Boadicea's palace, and the wide streets. But he did not make comparisons, for what made one town fair or ordinary to some people, had a different effect on others. He had seen Greece, Gaul and Rome itself. Each to his own. And no one could say that Eburacum did not have the square grandeur that Roman architecture brought to so many of their main strongholds in time.

As for Venta Icenorum, the Romans had razed it to the ground after Boadicea's defeat. It had vanished. It was easier to blot out stone than memories, however. None could take the image of his Queen from him. Would there never be a lessening of his deep, inner yearning for the beauty of his magical Boadicea? How many knew of the moments when a particular word or gesture, or a head of tawny hair, brought her sharp and clear into his mind, so that the dagger of pain struck? How often had he drawn her out of the night and filled his dreams with her Celtic beauty? And how often, when evenings were quiet and soft, had he heard her voice, as murmurous as the sigh of the wind? He had loved her from the day nearly ten years ago when he had come to her palace in Venta Icenorum as the son of Callupus, the Queen's most loyal chieftain. He had been sent by his father to serve her. He had seen her, tall, regal and majestic, and he had said to himself, " There in all honesty is a queen." She had captivated him, commanded him, and she herself had found him more of a man than all others. She came to love him so fiercely that it was unendurable to her pride, and she found a pretext to banish him. For seven long years he was gone, and though Boadicea's proud spirit bore his absence, her heart nearly broke. When Canis returned, her husband King Prasutagus, was on his deathbed. She had been a faithful wife to Prasutagus, and his death made a certain day poignant and mournful; but she had Canis within her house once more; and never, she vowed, would she allow him to raise his pride above her own again or ever leave her again. She intended that he should wed her a year and a day after the death of

Prasutagus, and meanwhile could scarcely bear him out of her sight.

Canis lived in ignorance of his Queen's tempestuous love, but not out of hearing of her possessive voice.

"*Canis, though you are a villain in your disregard of me, you are committed to my house, to me and mine, so do not venture to slip away or I will put chains around you.*"

How often had she said that, or its like?

So many times.

She had been so proud, so fearless, so rich with life.

Cerdwa had spoken true, for she had said that Britain would not see the like of Boadicea for a thousand years.

Caleda came to his ear, saying, " Do you sleep amid so much traffic and bustle?"

" Where will I put you down, Caleda?"

" Here, O man of roaring iron."

He dismounted and helped her down. He smiled at her. The street was indeed full of traffic and bustle, people and noise. Two stalwart Roman soldiers, standing sentry at the entrance to a prefect's headquarters, looked boldly on her smooth, handsome face and shapely figure. She was no mere flighty girl, she was a mature woman; but her looks were still such as to make some men turn their heads.

" Caleda, if anyone should ask you what man I am, say nothing about how I roar—only that I am Belgic, and have come to seek service with your Queen."

" And I will also tell them your name is Herco, which was my father's name," said Caleda. Her father had died peacefully enough a year ago.

" I could not own a better—so Herco I will be."

" I go now to barter our produce," said Caleda, " you go to the Queen's house. Bergotix will be sorry not to see you again."

" Why, will the Queen despatch me so quickly?" he said. Caleda, about to say she did not mean that, saw the laughter in his eyes. Her every bone melted.

" Oh," she stammered, out of calmness for once, " I only

241

meant that our dwelling is humble, and you are a lord of the Iceni. It is not to be thought you will come again to visit us. And see how red my hands are."

And she showed them to him, as they stood by the quiet horse. Canis lifted her hands, and the Roman soldiers saw him lightly kiss the left palm and then her right. The gesture, which bestowed friendship, left Caleda flushed and a little bemused.

"You are no ordinary woman, Caleda, and few men give more to life than any woman. Your dwelling is above any other I have had in many months. It is not humble, but warm and hospitable, as you are. So I will come again, if I may, for in Caleda and Bergotix I have found friends, and life itself has nothing sweeter to offer than friendship."

The bustling street, so familiar to Caleda, suddenly seemed strangely unfamiliar.

"Perhaps you should not come again," she said in soft distress, "for though Bergotix miscalls me and is sometimes foolish, he loves me and I cannot and would not be unfaithful to him."

"I did not have that in mind," smiled Canis.

"But I did, and would—if you came again," she said breathlessly, and she fled, her basket clutched to her.

Canis did not go to the Queen's house in the light of day, but waited until evening.

*   *   *

The hall of the Queen's house was stony. It was walled and flagged by stone, and surrounded by squared casing of stone. A formidable stone wall bounded the gardens. The fire that burned in the hall warmed only those who sat near enough at the long table, on which were huge platters and bowls of food. Queen Cartimandua sat with her back to the fire. A woman of forty summers, she was volpine and voluptuous, with full lower lip and white heavy lids to her eyes. Her straw-coloured hair was piled and coifed; and she looked down the table from its head with discontent simmering. On her right hand sat her daughter Venturia, who looked much like her mother and would, in a score of years, be a replica of what her mother was now.

Brigante nobles, men and women, crowded the Queen's table. They were a heavier, broader people than the Iceni, but were no less hardy and no less immersed in their own age-old customs and cultures. They had suffered Roman overlordship more stolidly than the Belgae, and more expediently than the Iceni, who had risen up in rebellion not once, but twice.

Cartimandua sat on her throne by favour of Romans, and would not give it up. She had divorced her husband many years ago, and when he had tried to wrest her crown from her, she had enlisted Roman aid to defeat him and slay him. She was wholly representative of her times, when such were the circumstances and the ways of life, and such was the subtlest distinction between cruelty and heroism, that while some people would have said Cartimandua was gross and treacherous, others might have said she was bold and cunning. If she did not draw upon herself the love of her people, as did Boadicea, Cartimandua herself would have said, "I am not for loving by sorry vassals, I am for loving by men lusty enough to dare."

But the man she passioned after had no mind to dare, though he was lustier than all others. Ancastus, Brigante chieftain of an ancient tribe, sat lower down the table, his big, brawny figure coming often to her brooding eyes. His teeth were comparatively white, his face brown, his moustache the envy of Vikings, and his laugh a deep musical melody in the ears of the avid Queen. He was younger than her by nine years, but what of that? Her fulsome body was still ripe enough to be coveted by nobles as great as himself. Because of his temerity in rejecting her favours, she would have crushed him, debased him and poisoned him. But she dared not, for two reasons. Firstly, she desired him above all other desires. And secondly, Ancastus was too powerful, and the

Roman procurator of the province would not have tolerated the disposal of such a figure without asking awkward questions and worrying the heart out of the matter. He would have said that the reason for this was political, and would have worked his way round to judging it inimical to Rome.

Whenever Cartimandua caught the eye of Ancastus this evening, she could only discern arrogant masculine independence and not a jot of affection. He was loyal enough to her crown, but it was his weakness for her body she wanted to feel and encourage. She was bored by all who sat at her table, saving only Ancastus and her own sweet Venturia. To Cartimandua, Venturia's greediness was merely a thing of happy impulse in her lamb. She saw Venturia as her sweetest comfort, though Venturia mocked her mother as often as she wheedled her.

A lackey entered through the far door, stamped thrice upon the flagstones with his heavy staff of office, and lifted his voice.

"A stranger in your house, O Queen. A man who begs the custom of your table, O Queen."

The custom was that a stranger should be given the best of her table and her hospitality for a month and a day—if accepted. If not accepted, it could be painfully bemusing for him and hilarious for the guests.

"Let him show himself," said Cartimandua.

Canis entered to stand by the side of the servant. He had a confidence, an air and a quiet smile. Venturia raised her head. She looked idly at the stranger, bit her lip in sudden interest and sat upright. Her eyes began to glow. He was tall, he had hardness and lean strength, he was firm of mouth and quietly at ease, surveying the hall, the guests and the serving men and women without humility. All this, despite the fact that his cloak was worn and no bright metal adorned him. Masculine he was, thought Venturia, and incontestably so.

"Gods of love," she whispered to her mother, "a very

244

man has graced us this night. Bid him welcome, O my sweet mother, and look you, he is mine. Throw Cervax from his seat."

Cervax was a mulish young man who sat next to her.

Cartimandua, richly garmented in a red robe, rose in accordance with custom. Canis saw her, sallow of face, pale of eye and sensuous of lip.

"I am Cartimandua, Queen," she said, "and you are welcome, stranger. You may have a place in my house and at my table for as long as a month and a day. Come, sit here. Cervax, go feed my dogs."

"Your dogs are fed," said Cervax.

Cartimandua lowered her glance, looking at him with her mouth redly spiteful. Cervax was mulish enough, but not witless. He rose and went, and the dogs howled when he thrust unwanted meat down their throats. Canis came to take the vacated seat, the servants looking at him curiously, the guests boldly. Venturia clapped her hands plumply and prettily, and servants came running to attend to the wants of the stranger. He wanted nought that was not already on the table, and helped himself to bread and meat. Cartimandua resumed her place, and the table was momentarily quiet, save for the sounds of those who had not allowed the acceptance of a stranger to disturb their eating.

"A stranger in my house," said Cartimandua, viewing Canis under heavy lids and judging him, from his garments, to be a man of little consequence, "may not only dwell here for a month and a day, eat until he can eat no more, but he may also keep his name and his secrets fast to himself. However, if you will, speak your name and tell us your secrets."

Canis looked up from his platter. Venturia, seated on his left, drank in the brown, shaven countenance and the compelling grey eyes. How unlike other men he was, how unlike the heavy, fleshy men she was used to seeing at her mother's table. He had no moustache, but his brown hair was long and thick, and tied at the nape of his neck with a strand of leather.

245

Venturia had long sought a man who would be more of a man than all others, for just such a man would complement her unequalled beauty. Venturia did not doubt her own beauty, her mother had long ago convinced her she was fairer of face and form than all other princesses. She looked upon Canis and thought him assuredly the man she had dreamed of. Gods and goddesses, what a mouth he had, and what subtleties glimmered in his eyes as he raised them to her mother.

Everyone listened as he responded to the Queen.

"Cartimandua, Queen, I have no secrets. My name is Herco, I am a Belgic man and am kinsman to a prince who lives in Rome. He also has no secrets and his name is Caratacus. Is there salt on your table, Cartimandua?"

The Brigantes sat dumb. Only Ancastus grinned a little. The Queen sat in fury. Venturia sat in longing. Aye, this was a man indeed. To have said that to her mother. To have looked her mother in the face and said that. No one ever spoke of Caratacus in this house. No one dared.

"So you have no secrets?" said Cartimandua, her voice at its sweetest—but her eyes hooded with malevolence. "And your name is Herco, and your kinsman is—say again, what is his name?"

Venturia knew this was to dare the stranger to repeat it.

"Caratacus," said Canis, addressing himself to his meat. "He is a Belgic prince and knew the friendship of Claudius, Caesar. He came by such friendship on account of his tongue, for he was always an orator who compelled the ear of listeners, though it is said there was one notable occasion when his voice fell on an ear regrettably deaf." He looked up from his food to regard the Queen in all amiability again. Cartimandua, seeing his friendly humour, knew not whether this showed him to be a fool, or cloaked villainous impudence. Venturia was sure he was mocking her mother. She sensed the challenge that went with the mockery. If her mother accepted it and an accident befell him, all here would know her mother had contrived it. Such an accident would be in unforgivable

246

violation of the custom of the royal house. Stranger accepted was stranger inviolable.

It had not taken Canis overlong during the day to discover what customs obtained here.

New fury took hold of Cartimandua. The heavy white lids dropped to hide the flame in her eyes. Here was a shabbily-cloaked stranger, a man who called himself Herco, who had secured safe lodging within her house because her daughter had begged it, and in gratitude almost his first words had been to remind her of her betrayal of another guest many years ago. She did not lift her lids until the flame had died. There were other ways of dealing with a man as insufferable as this. She noticed the broad grin on the face of Ancastus, and was hard put to it to restrain new anger.

She said, her voice sounding wet, " If you have no secrets, Belgic man, yet you possess an abundance of ignorance. Did you not know that my ear was the deaf one?"

" Ah, was it you?" said Canis. He smiled. " There was some queen who became involved. But which one it was is of no consequence now. My kinsman knew many queens, and it might have been any of them. You did him a great favour, though perhaps not intentionally, for how many other Belgic princes have been honoured by a Caesar? None. What favour might I do you in return?"

She said, " By saying, when you go from here, that Queen Cartimandua gives the comfort of her house and the best of her food to any accepted stranger, be he simple fool or impudent villain."

There was some laughter at this. Under cover of the noise, Venturia whispered to Canis, " Pay her no heed—for though you may be impudent villain, I swear you are no simple fool. You may become a man after her own heart, for there is no other man here, save Ancastus, who can do much more than eat his food loudly. What is sweeter to a woman than the embrace of a villain who is also impudent and chews his meat quietly? I like not loud men or fawning men, or men who think they come by manhood only through the luxuriant

247

flowering of their moustaches. I like you, Belgic man, though you have no moustache at all."

She passed her wet tongue over her full bottom lip until the lip glistened. Canis observed her, misliking her too soft face, her plump chin, her white fleshy throat. Caleda would make a far handsomer princess than this one. This one was surely born to milk goats. He drew her pale eyes to his, smiling upon her, and Venturia was mesmerised. She emitted a soft moan, and put her hand on his thigh. Shudders shook her greedy body. She felt as if she were bedded with him, and the noise of the table and the great stone hall faded into nothingness. Her face grew red from pulsing blood, and then paled to exhausted whiteness. A voice, quiet but resonant, came to her out of the receding mists.

" Princess, have you eaten too much meat?"

She could only stare in enraptured numbness at him.

Then there came a singer, who bored Cartimandua to tears and also interrupted the malicious progress of her thoughts. Her thoughts were all about what might fatally befall Herco of the Belgae. She stood up and hurled a ragged bone at the minstrel.

" Begone, wailer," she shouted, " begone, for when you do not wail you croak."

The minstrel grinned in his beard. He went happily enough. It was all one to him whether he sang to the Queen and her court or not. Indeed, he preferred to sing to the slaves, rather than to Cartimandua and her feasting nobles—for the slaves listened entranced, where the Queen and her nobles only gobbled on.

" Mayhap you sing?" Cartimandua shouted at Canis. He responded mildly.

" Cartimandua, Queen, my ears are sound, I am reasonably possessed of all other senses, and suffer no physical infirmity save that of advancing maturity. Why, therefore, do you raise your voice so?"

Ancastus broke into roaring laughter. Venturia, her body weak but blissful, gazed open-mouthed at Canis. Assuredly, incontestably, this was the one man she must have, would have. If not, she would pull the house down.

Cartimandua's lips drew back to show her teeth.

" For that, stranger, you will sing, whether you have the art or no," she said. " You will raise your voice in song—and if we find you tolerable, so much the better for you. But if we do not, I will have you bruised and buffeted from my house."

Ancastus rose, sternly reproving.

" You cannot," he said to Cartimandua, " it would violate the custom. Herco has been accepted, and unless he himself offends by striking a blow must be given fair hospitality."

Cartimandua, though desiring Ancastus as she did, could have killed him then.

" If this Belgic man comes unmusically to my ear, that will be offence enough," she said, " and he will pay for it by the rods or the whip."

Ancastus, defying her glare, said again, " You cannot. Queen or no, you cannot. And if he sings, it should be from choice, not command."

" I will sing," said Canis, " if the Queen will find me a lyre."

They brought him a lyre. He strummed it for a few moments, found it well-strung, and sang this song.

Where is the love of my sad, sad youth,
Who tangled her curls in branches of oak?
Where is the love of my beardless years
Who dipped her feet in the dew of morn?
Where is my love whose eyes were bright,
Whose voice was a sigh o'er green, green hill?
Where is the love of my life long ago,
Who danced each day in the dew of morn?

Gone is the love of my sad, sad youth,
Who tangled her curls in branches of oak.
Where did she go, my sweet fair love?
She went from me to wed a man.

249

So gone is the love of tenderest youth,
Gone her voice and her trailing curls,
And heavy is the pain of my sad, sad heart,
For like a fool I wed a shrew.

Venturia, ecstatic, clapped loudly. The company, boisterous, applauded generously. Only Cartimandua was unresponsive. She sat silent and sullen, brooding on the way Ancastus had defied her. The Brigante chieftain's voice, deeply rich, smote her ear.

"You cannot bruise the stranger for that, Queen," he said heartily, "for it was a fine song well sung, and came musically enough to me."

"Then mediocrity is what you favour," said Cartimandua. She shrugged and went on, "But perhaps I cannot say it was not tolerable. Yet you have far better voice, Ancastus."

"What, do you favour croaking frogs, then?" asked Venturia of her mother.

That was enough to bring laughter to everyone, including Ancastus himself—and even to Cartimandua. Smiling at her daugher's wit, Cartimandua patted her arm fondly.

"I will allow myself to be bested in song," said Ancastus, "but only in song. Song is gifted to frivolous minstrels, not to men."

Canis let this pleasantry pass as if he had not heard, but Cartimandua's eyes gleamed. There were ways of dealing with a villain that might not go against custom. Ancastus might contrive a most painful end for him, even if the laws of hospitality demanded that she could not.

After supper Venturia took bold possession of Canis. More than one of the Brigante women there would have been glad to lay claim to his company, and not because of his gift for song. But none dared compete with Princess Venturia. She had most unlovely ways of venting her spite. That she might be alone with Canis, she prevailed upon him to see the gardens of the Queen's house spread silvery in the moonlight. She stood with him in the lee of a buttress, while from the royal house of stone came sounds of noisy revelry, where Cartimandua had only eyes for Ancastus and her teeth bit on her lip to see him dallying with other women in his usual flamboyant way.

However, if the Queen's blood ran in anger and heat for Ancastus, outside in the cool night air Venturia's blood pounded in unquenchable greed for Canis. Being of twenty-one summers, she was no innocent—but felt in his presence like a shivering maid racked by the first fearful pangs of unmentionable desire. Her mouth was dry, her body hungry and burning.

"Why did you affront Cartimandua so?" she asked, and her voice sounded in her own ears as if it were cracked.

"Cartimandua your mother," said Canis, "is a queen who will treat with a man only if he has the measure of her strength and she has knowledge of his. She will listen to a scheming man, and use him for what he is worth to her—but will contempt him if he is only a schemer and nought else. She drops her eyes before mine, and so will return favour for favour, for that is how she is made."

Surely, thought Venturia, only gods would know so much about a woman.

She licked her lips and said, "If you wish her to do you a favour, ask it first of me, and I will procure it for you. For she can deny me nought."

"Will she give me five hundred horse, one hundred chariots with horse, one hundred sacks of flour and one gold Brigante crown?"

Venturia thought him godlike but quite mad.

"No, ask for one horse, one chariot with horse, one sack of flour and aye, even one gold Brigante crown, and I will procure all these for you, Herco. But five hundred horse! One hundred chariots with horse! One hundred—"

"So. She will not, even for you, fair Princess."

Venturia coloured and looked palely pink in the moonlight. How agitated her breast was, how she longed for bruising, hurting contact.

251

" All that you have asked for," she said faintly, " would be as much as a dowry."

" Ah," said Canis, observing the moon.

" With one hundred gold crowns more—if it were a royal dowry."

" Could any husband be worth so much?"

" Herco," said Venturia breathlessly, " it would be insufficient when weighed against some husbands."

" Ah," said Canis again, transferring his observance of the roundness of the moon to the roundness of her face, " what man could ask for so much, and also for you, Princess?"

" If it were the right man, it would be his own just due and my own demand," she said even more faintly.

" Might a man who is Belgic and kinsman to a prince content himself by asking only for that which will put him to sweetly dreamful sleep?"

" And what would he ask?"

" This, O fair one," said Canis and drew her close and put his mouth to hers. Venturia moaned, swooning. She clung to him, and trembled. She let the shaft of rapture pierce her again.

She opened her eyes. He was gone. She put her back to the stonework, else she would have fallen. She had no bones, no strength, only a panting sickness. Was he a god? Everyone knew that Cyantillus, god of war, often appeared in the form of mortal man, driving his fiery chariot from encampment to encampment, from town to town, looking for the one mortal woman fit to be his magnificently beautiful consort. It was said he had spent a thousand years looking in vain, and that though he had found many beautiful women, all had lacked some little perfection. Indeed, many beautiful maids and women had sworn to fathers or husbands or sweethearts that it was Cyantillus who had got them with child. All remembered being snatched by him from their beds when they were innocently asleep, and returned when he had had his godlike way with them. They had also sworn that he had robustly enjoyed their perfections, without giving the faintest hint of what imperfections they had. Fathers, husbands or sweet-hearts could only say that although Cyantillus was a great god of war, he had a scurvy way of behaving when he took the form of mortal man. But the women said—though only to each other—he served as a great boon to them, and eased many of them of certain worries.

Oh, thought Venturia, was tall Herco of the Belgae the god of war? And was she his woman of matchless perfection? If so, he would take her, make her immortal, and she would live for a thousand years. And the thousand years would be one vast, unending night of fiery love.

Venturia moaned, and subsided to her knees.

The next day she followed Canis about in hopeless, in-fatuated longing. He was kind enough to her, save that at times he would make her silently scream by asking, " Where is the light of this house, the fair Venturia?" She would be almost at his elbow, and would feel a violent urge to kick him, god or no god, at his pretence of not seeing her. Instead she would say, breathing heavily, " Has my light so failed that I have become invisible?" Oh, the torment he gave her, as with his mocking grey eyes he bewitched her.

Canis had been housed comfortably enough in a small room in the Queen's house. This, Venturia had insisted on, lest her mother consign him to sleep with slaves or servants in poor dwellings adjacent the royal house. Canis slept soundly enough the first night, but lay awake and alert the second. When the great stone was still, and the night was advanced, he heard the soft sound he had been waiting for. She came into the room, Cartimandua herself, a flowing night robe over the voluptuous, insatiable body, a lamp in her hand. He lay on the couch amid a warm pile of skins, clad in his tunic.

" Why are you here, Belgic man?" Her voice was a slow, hissing whisper, her straw-coloured hair uncoifed and loose, her tongue wetting her lower lip. Venturia had the same nervous, sensual gesture.

" To bring you your heart's desire, Cartimandua," replied Canis.

253

She came close to the couch and hissed, "Who gave you leave to uncrown me? I am Queen here or anywhere. Name me so, villain."

"Your title is empty, for what is any queen who cannot have what she most desires?"

"Beggar, I have all I desire."

"Except a certain man."

Her pale eyes glimmered in the light of the lamp. "What magic do you have," she sneered, "that my wisest men cannot emulate? What can you, a wanderer and a peddler of poor songs, do better than they?"

"I am not a man to dispense potions."

"Impudence is what you dispense. How dared you speak of Caratacus to me?"

"He wished it so," said Canis, "when I saw him in Rome. 'Say to Cartimandua,' he said, 'that to be betrayed by a woman is man's destiny, but to be betrayed by a queen sets him as high as a king.'"

"What did I owe any covetous Belgic prince?" she spat. "He was a fool to wage war against Rome. There was an even greater fool—Boadicea. What is she now but rotting bone? At least Caratacus did not lose his life."

It may have been the flickering lamp flame that was momentarily reflected by his shadowed eyes. She did not know. He spoke agreeably enough.

"There was a true queen for you," he said. "Aye, you own not half her stature, Cartimandua—for though you command fear and obedience in your people, you cannot command a certain lusty man. But let be on this argument, for I concede your kingdom is larger than any."

"But what of this man? Can you, beggar, command him for me?"

"Beggar I am not, for I am high-born in my own domain," said Canis, "and I will win your man to you, if you burn enough for him."

She was suddenly shaken by lustful thoughts of Ancastus. She put the lamp down and sat on the edge of the couch, her bold features flushed with heat. She looked down at Canis as he lay unmoving on his back. She was a queen, but for all the villain showed in the way of courtesies, she might have been a graceless wench. However.

" I do burn," she said, " so come, boastful stranger, acquaint me how you might win him to me."

" You have a kingdom as rich as it is large, Cartimandua."

" I have enough and will reward you, never fear."

He smiled and told her what he wanted. She choked, fury struggling with incredulity.

" What, you long-shanked idler! Five hundred horse, one hundred chariots with horse! One hundred sacks of flour! And a gold crown? Oh, your modesty anent a solitary crown is well taken, but go up, huckster, trickster! I know an impudent jest when I hear one, or do you wish to add more to your meagre demands?"

" Only your daughter," he said, as if Venturia were the least of it."

Cartimandua almost fell from the couch.

" Only my daughter? Only my daughter!" Her head went back and she choked again, this time at the effort of stifling hysterical laughter. " Oh, now will the very sky fall, now will every stone in my house crumble and the walls tumble inwards and outwards. My daughter, quoth he. My lamb, my flower, my innocent, my sweet boon. My Princess. For you? Belgic rogue, custom or no custom, Ancastus or no Ancastus, I will have your impudent eyes put out, your insolent tongue slit. You will have to grope for the food you seek at my table, and you will sing no more."

" Ask your daughter."

Cartimandua gaped. Then convulsions overtook her, and her hands clenched and unclenched. She said spittingly, " You lie, you dog. It could not be, not in so short a time as this. Never, I say, never!"

" I am not an ordinary man, Cartimandua. I am kinsman to Caratacus, a prince."

" A pox on Caratacus. Venturia, my own innocent sweet-

255

ling, my helpless lamb, to wed you? Will wed you? You?"
"Ask her," said Canis, unmoved.

She rose, her shaking hand took up the lamp, she swept out and bore away to her daughter's night room like a soft, plummeting bird. Venturia's couch lay in rumpled disorder, as did Venturia herself. Her arms were flung wide, as if in her sleep she was suffering either stress or ecstasy. Cartimandua shook her awake. Sleepy eyes opened, eyes full of hot enchanted dreams. Misty disillusionment came at once when she saw it was only her mother who stooped over her.

"Venturia, wake, my lamb."

"Oh, go to your bed, mother," said Venturia pettishly, "and take my forgiveness for waking me from my sweet dreams. I was his goddess and was in his arms, we were wed—"

"To whom were you wed?" shouted Cartimandua.

"To whom?" Venturia stretched her arms and her body in bliss. "Why, to Herco, and soft clouds were our couch and the stars our bright roof."

"Sweet fool," seethed Cartimandua, "the villain has bewitched you."

Venturia sat up, shaking sleep from her. Her face was hot, her breath came quick and warm.

"He is mine," she said hungrily, "so procure him for me, Cartimandua mother, or your lamb will cut her own throat and thus sacrifice herself. Yours will be the blame and the responsibility, and the gods will take you cruelly for failing your own daughter in such a matter as this."

"What magic is this he has?" Cartimandua spoke in strangled whisper. "He has spoken for you, Venturia. He has asked for you, for five hundred horse, one hundred chariots with horse, one hundred sacks of flour and one gold crown."

"I am wooed, won and wed!" Venturia gave herself up to writhing paroxysms of sensuous delight, then stretched again in sublimest ecstasy. He was hers. And although he looked as a god in mortal form should look, despite his lack of glitter and metal, he was no god, no Cyantillus. Cyantillus would not

256

have asked for anything. Perhaps there was some relief within her at this conviction, for had he been Cyantillus he may have found some little imperfection in her that she herself was not aware of. In that case he would have taken her, only to return her before the night was out. She would have borne him godlike child, as, it seemed, did all women he snatched dreaming from their beds. But she would not have seen him again. The godlike child would have been poor consolation, for it was said of the babes fathered by Cyantillus that though they were indeed godlike at birth, they grew up as ordinarily as others and became as ordinary.

Ah, Herco.

A thought flashed into her blissful mind, and she sat up in sudden affront.

" What, a single crown! And I a princess? Never! Is he out of his mind? He must ask for a hundred. He knows this. I cannot take him a dowry of a single crown."

" But there are also five hundred horse, one hundred—"

" Tidbits," said Venturia.

Cartimandua was in shocked turmoil. She fumed, she begged, she pleaded; but Venturia would not be denied the smallest part of that which she wanted. She wanted Herco and she wanted the full dowry. And Cartimandua, the doting mother, could not do aught but concede these wants. She understood that Venturia desired the Belgic man above all others—but did she have to wed him?

" Oh, the furies," breathed Venturia, "would you have me be his concubine, and see him one day wed another? Out on you, stupid, and have him contract to me with all speed. For I swear I am in such longing I can scarce contain myself."

Cartimandua fondled her flushed lamb. Her flushed lamb bit her. Cartimandua returned to Canis in seething confusion that quickly became rage. Nor was this because Venturia's teeth had been spitefully sharp. It was because the man was asleep. The dog! Venturia was in turmoil, and he was at peace! Furious, she woke him.

" So, infamous Belgic villain, you have won my lamb. But

never, unless you win Ancastus to me, will you take her and all else that you ask for."

Canis mused on this for a moment, and then said, "Ancastus said he could only be bested in song. Can he throw a man?"

"Like a lion." Cartimandua's teeth gleamed. "Do not provoke him to try a fall with you, or he will break your back. It would be all one to me, but not to Venturia. She would slit his throat, and thus mother and daughter would both have lost the men they most desire. Though how any woman, least of all my fair Venturia, could conceive desire for you, is beyond my understanding. Yet she has. Herco, if that is your name, what magic do you bring with you that my daughter is so addled in so short a time?"

"No magic," said Canis, "only knowledge imparted to me by another. Tomorrow, Cartimandua, if you still wish to have Ancastus, provoke him into essaying a throw with me. As Queen, in fact, you may command this of him at least."

The dog was so impudent he was almost intimidating.

*　　*　　*

The men and women who were Cartimandua's closest adherents, counsellors and advisers gathered on the square of emerald-green grass behind the Queen's house the next day. They were there to watch Herco of the Belgae and Ancastus the Bold contest a play of strength, holds and throws. The play would go on until one cried quits or, mayhap, was accidentally strangled. Cartimandua did not hold back from persuading Ancastus to challenge the conceit of the Belgic posturant, for though the side issues were all in all to her, yet if Ancastus should strangle Herco or hug him to death, it would give her so much pleasure that she would be able to bear Venturia's grief and wait for a less frail magician to win Ancastus to her.

Ancastus was a man of brave heart and robust living, and a lover of sport. He was by no means a braggart, only a man of self-confidence; and on hearing Cartimandua speak of the

258

stranger possessing far more manly gifts than those of song, his ruddy face broke into an amiable smile, and he ventured to ask what these other gifts were.

"He can, he says, throw an oak," said the Queen.

"I am not an oak," grinned Ancastus, "but let him throw me."

"If you break his back, be ready to slip the dagger Venturia will draw on you. She is smitten by the fool."

"Aye, she has been short of breath since she first clapped eyes on him."

"Ancastus," said Cartimandua coyly, "why do you not seek my favours?"

"Because your favours as a woman put me at the mercy of your whims as a queen."

"What are whims when love is so strong? Ancastus, I would have other men killed for defying and denying me as you do."

"I know," said Ancastus, "and that is the heart of the matter, Queen."

"Accept my favours, Ancastus," she pleaded. "And then if you kill the Belgic knave, I will protect you from my daughter's vengeance."

"I will best him, not kill him. If perhaps I break a little bone or two of his, it will be without malice."

What with the impudence of Herco, and the imperturbability of Ancastus, Queen Cartimandua thought that one day she would take great pleasure in slaying all men within sight.

The two men, Canis and Ancastus, made ready for the contest in agreeable rivalry. The sun danced through clouds as Cartimandua, with all who attended on her, watched them prepare. Venturia watched also. She had spent the morning looking for her confusingly elusive Herco, wanting to hear him declare his burning love for her. She had not found him. But he was here now. A pulse was beating in her plump white throat, her lower lip was pinched by her teeth, and excitement flushed her face. She felt no fear for her betrothed, only a sensuous eagerness to see strong men give each other hurt. Ancastus was broad, muscular, and formidable; clad in jerkin and kilt. Canis was tall, lean, quiet. He wore his familiar tunic, his legs strapped by the leather leading from his sandals. Venturia thought of hard masculine bodies striving in combat, breaking within iron holds; she thought of the agony one man might put on the other, and her saliva ran so that her teeth slipped from her wet lip. She shivered. She felt the pain that her grey-eyed Herco might feel. The pleasure it brought was erotic. How hard her breasts were.

Cartimandua was silent, her heavy lids drooping, as in the centre of the sward of long green grass Ancastus reached for his opponent. He took him and swiftly turned him. There was a suppressed sigh, so soon would the agile, brawny Brigante break the Belgic man. But as Ancastus turned him, Canis went adroitly with the turn, and himself turned again. Suddenly Ancastus was lifted from the ground to soar through the air like a levitated giant. He thundered onto his back, and for a moment lay stunned and bemused.

"Ye sweet gods," he said breathlessly, and shook his head. He came to his feet; he crouched, and came in swiftly and no less confidently. He feinted an upward hold, then swooped downwards to fold his arms around the stranger's legs. But his arms closed on nothing, and a hand came to smite the back of his neck. He pitched. He thudded to the grass face down, air bruised from his lungs and mouth emitting gasping grunt. Venturia softly moaned. Cartimandua burned. Ancastus lay quite still for a short while, then lifted his head. His teeth showed in a grin.

"You are a very dog," he said, but without animosity.

"I have a little of the art," said Canis, "it was imparted by a Greek."

Ancastus came up gingerly and cautiously this time. However, he found a hold and closed triumphantly with his man, winding long arms of iron around him—to exert a pressure which, when it was sufficiently increased, would crack ribs one by one. He grinned into the face of Canis.

"Go tell your Greek," he said, "that I am no novice myself."

The watching men and women felt a quickening of their blood to see Herco of the Belgae locked fast within the lion-like hug of Ancastus. But Herco did not seem unduly discomforted.

"Ancastus," he said, oblivious of the loud panting of Venturia, who stood nearer than any, "you are only lacking in the art of pleasing your Queen. Her bed is yours for the taking, yet foolishly you sleep in your own."

Ancastus goggled. His opponent should have been sweating, straining and groaning within the iron band, but was not.

"What is this?" he breathed. He tightened his hold, increased the pressure, then puffed, "Come, confess it, your breath is painful to you at this moment, is it not?"

"A little," said Canis, finding space that Ancastus thought did not exist between their bodies. The hands of the sinewy Briton slid upwards over the Brigante's chest until his elbows were hard against it and his palms cupped the Brigante's chin. "Ancastus, if you will not be Cartimandua's man, then I must cripple you. But if you will, then I will only bruise you."

"I am not for her bed," said Ancastus, and sought to bend and break the ribs of his man. Canis exerted a pressure of his own, thrusting with his hands so that the chin of Ancastus pointed skywards. Back went the Brigante's head, there was pain in his throat and at the back of his neck. His locked arms strained to hold their grip; but as his chin was forced higher, the pain became unbearable and his arms fell away. There was a sensation of uncontrollable movement, the sky swung, the earth fell away and his body whirled. The sound of his fall was brutal; and when the red mist cleared, he was on his knees and another's knee lodged agonisingly hard in the middle of his back. An arm was around his throat, and he was bent backwards from his knees like a strung bow. A voice whispered in his ear.

"Come, Ancastus, a broken back is not for you. So think, my friend, will you be the Queen's loving man, or no?"

"Oh, you are a demanding dog," groaned Ancastus, "and a scurvy one, to ask that of me."

"She has given me a warm room, her best food, and has promised me her only daughter."

"Gods' light," gasped Ancastus bravely, "you will get little joy from Venturia, and no satisfaction from me."

"I owe Cartimandua a favour," said Canis and applied enough pressure to make the helpless Brigante choke in pain. She is hot for you, my friend—and must have you. She might even wed you."

"Break my back, I will not bed with Cartimandua," gasped Ancastus, while Venturia turned red, and hot breath escaped over her glistening lower lip.

"Must I?" Canis increased the pressure, and red lights danced in the Brigante's brain. "It will not kill you, Ancastus, but bed you in pain for life. Cartimandua will only bed you for so long. Come, be as wise as you are brave. Even Cartimandua is preferable to a broken back."

"Oh, very dog indeed," choked Ancastus. His Queen and his Queen's daughter thought to hear his spine snap at any moment, so great was the anguish he showed. His hands clawed at the iron arm pressing his throat. "Oh, you are no friend to Ancastus. I yield, then, and will take Cartimandua. You have my word on it."

Canis released him. Ancastus drew in breath, lightness coming to his tortured body, relief to his racked spine. He knelt sweating. Cartimandua hastened to him, concerned for his suffering.

"Oh, that Belgic dog," she cried, "he has tricked you into grievous hurt."

Ancastus lifted his head. The sun beamed weakly from the receding rim of a cloud. In its light his ruddy, handsome face was pale. But he managed to smile.

"There must be better things in life than a cracked spine,"

he said, "so I will take your favours, Queen, for surely your embrace must be softer than his."

"Ancastus!" She knelt beside him, vibrating for him, and murmuring words for his ears alone. "Oh, is your love so hot with your body so bruised?"

"I would that I had been content to remain bested in song," said Ancastus.

*   *   *

"Herco!" Venturia's voice was as hot as her face, every plump curve eager as she burst into his room. He had taken a bath and lay musing on his couch. "All day you have avoided me, even when I ran to embrace you after you had so cruelly grounded groaning Ancastus. It gave me such excitement to watch it. Why do you avoid me when you have spoken for me, and Cartimandua my mother has promised me?"

"Since Cartimandua has promised you, what is there I need from you, O fair and impulsive Princess?"

"My lips," she breathed, "so come, take them, bruise them."

He took them, she bending low over him. She swooned, and fell ecstatically upon him. He threw her off. She screamed as she tumbled onto the rush-strewn floor. What a man this one was! No other would treat her so. She sat up, eyes glowing, breast heaving, her robe in what she knew was sweet disarray.

"This is not how Belgic princesses behave," said her betrothed.

The reproof only further intrigued her. Gods and goddesses, how she passioned for him.

"A pest on all Belgic princesses," she cried, "it is I who am to wed you, not they."

"Only if you observe my customs, and not your own," he said.

"Is it your custom to throw your betrothed Princess to the floor?"

"That is never a custom, only a necessity. That which

obtains between us now means we must remain apart. In this way my eyes will not dwell hotly on your royal ripeness, until we are ready to make the journey to my father's house in Aquae Sulis."

"But when wed, when?" she asked, consumed by the fever of frustration. The more he stood apart from her, the more she wanted him.

"When we arrive there, and your mother and her court arrive also—which will be seven days after my own arrival. Fear not, lamb of fulsome mother, I pant for you most assuredly. I must, however, pant in patience."

"How can any man pant in patience? I cannot."

"You are not a man, O shapely dove. You are a finely discriminating princess, with sweet niceties, and do not pant at all."

"Jester, I pant all the time."

"Then hide it from me, lest I blush for you," he said.

Venturia, on her knees, vibrated with mirth. She threw back her head and let laughter issue. He thought the curve of her pale, fleshy throat made her look like a soft plump pigeon.

"Oh," she giggled, "you are an uncommon man, Herco, and have tickled many a maid into laughter, I doubt not. You did not tickle poor Ancastus, however. You treated him ill, yet whispered to him like a loving brother. Will you buffet me if I vex you, and will you then whisper to me?"

"Whenever I buffet you, O tender lamb, you will be deaf to my loudest roar."

Her eyes gleamed, her breathing became heavy, she looked into his eyes. They mocked her, caressed her. She felt herself pierced again by that shaft of rapture, and the redness came to overlay her plump pastiness.

After a while, with her voice sounding strange in her own ears, she said, "When do we journey to your father's house?"

"When Cartimandua has assembled your full dowry. I cannot journey home with a poorly-laden bride, especially if she be a princess."

264

*　　*　　*

Venturia found the waiting period almost unendurable. Her strange, quirksome, masculine love insisted in uncompromising fashion that what he had said was true—that according to Belgic custom, his eyes must not look upon her until he took her to his father's house. They met often enough under her mother's roof; but each time this happened, he would look over the top of her head and say, " Cartimandua's dove has escaped her cote. Let someone fold her wings and put her back."

It maddened her. It also increased her devouring hunger.

Cartimandua herself was in a state of bemused generosity, though her heart ached at the thought of losing her lamb, for Ancastus had been as good as his word and had bedded her. He had proved the very incarnation of potent love. Never had her sumptuous couch been so lustily companioned. Ancastus, having committed himself, was not a man to let the bitterness of calculated impressment wreck his pride in performance.

Cartimandua, her voluptuous body in content these days, gradually assembled the dowry. Five hundred horse, one hundred chariots with horse, one hundred sacks of flour and one hundred gold Brigante crowns. All were procured, and only the chariots, machines used for sport, were a little hard to come by. The Brigantes possessed none of the heavier chariots of war, for the Romans would not have countenanced this. The required racing chariots had to be obtained for the main part from miserly nobles or niggardly landlords. Cartimandua had to hang one or two of the more miserly. How dared they deny either her or her blissful lamb? If she could bear to part with Venturia, then they could and would part with their chariots. And also with their heads.

Venturia spoke artfully on the matter of the future.

" Do not think he will master me in any way but love. In love I will be all to him. Other than this, Cartimandua, he is not a prince, only kinsman to Carat—"

265

"Do not speak that name here," said Cartimandua sharply.

"It is I who am royal," said Venturia, "though that is not to say I would rather have him a prince than ten times a man, which he is."

Little sweet goose, thought Cartimandua, a man is only ten times another man when he is as lusty and vigorous in love as Ancastus. What was a man's muscle to a woman, except in the especial way he applied it to her? Ancastus applied his in the most satisfying way. That long-shanked Herco might by trickery best Ancastus in grunting wrestle, and by the same kind of trickery even uproot an oak, but what was that to a woman wanting love?

"However," Venturia was saying, "since I am to be Queen of Brigantia after you, here to Eburacum we will return before the year is out, and here I will make him King if it pleases me."

"I am not dead yet," said Cartimandua, patting her daughter's cheek.

"As King he will look magnificent," murmured Venturia, "and because of my own beauty, we will make the handsomest monarchs in Britain."

Her bottom lip grew wetter day by day.

10

I t was the evening before Canis was due to leave Venturia on
his journey to the land of the Belgae, where the Romans lay
thickest. Bergotix had heard strange rumours.

He sat at his table and mused on them.

Quietly Caleda filled a jar with mead, and brought it to him.

"Aye," he said to her as she filled his cup, "they say a
man from the south, a Belgic man, kinsman to Caratacus, is to
wed Venturia. What kind of a head does he have, not to know
that her appetite for gobbling men is as ravenous as her
mother's? I have heard that everywhere rumours buzz about
him."

"These are not rumours," said Calenda, "for everywhere,
deaf husband, they have been proclaiming the true details."

"None have come to my ears," said Bergotix, "but then I
work for Cartimandua, and have no time to stand and listen."

"On account of Cartimandua," said Caleda, "you will
drop into a furrow one day, sweet husband."

"Sing a happier song, sweet wife."

"She is not the best of queens," said Caleda.

"Nor I the greatest of men," said Bergotix. "But this
Belgic man, do they say who he is, O woman of fine hearing?"

"He is your man of iron," said Caleda, moving towards the
fire. She seated herself on a stool beneath the smoke-blackened
ceiling, and looked dreamingly into the flames.

"You mean he is Canis? Canis?" Bergotix stroked his
moustache, then pulled on it. "Aye, it would be. But what is
he at? Venturia will wed him, tire of him, and eat him."

"Venturia will not wed him or tire of him or eat him," said
Caleda, who had of late been rubbing oil into her hands before
retiring at night. "There is more to your man of iron than

267

iron, and though I do not know what he is at any more than you do, I will swear he is not for having that plump limpet fasten herself to him."

She looked up then. Not at Bergotix, but at the hanging skins that kept out the rain and the chill. Canis was there, parting the skins and insinuating himself into their dwelling as noiselessly as a fox entering the domain of its prey. How tall he was. The roof seemed to become so much lower. His eyes flickered to see her. She looked away from him and into the fire again.

"Lord," said Bergotix, rising, "I am in pleasure to see you again. Our hearth is yours, there is food and also a jar of mead."

"I will drink mead with you and gladly," said Canis. He removed his cloak and sat at the table with Bergotix. In light and shadow, he seemed as sombre as Caleda.

"Will we drink to the Queen's daughter?" asked Bergotix as Caleda rose and poured the mead.

A smile came to lighten the Briton's seriousness. Caleda took her place by the fire again.

"Let us at least drink to her dowry," said Canis, "for much of it will expedite our journey." He did not say which journey. He and Bergotix drank, but Caleda did not. "Bergotix, once you were life and death for my own Queen, once you were for Boadicea. Are you still for her?"

Bergotix said, "I fought for her, and other Brigantes I knew died for her. We thought she would rid us of all Romans. She was a majestic queen and, ah, who can say why it was that the gods served her so ill against Paullinus? Alas, I was not there, but lay crippled elsewhere. Yet you were there, lord, and as her general. How was it we lost when all seemed won?"

"We let them stand and form on the highest point of the valley, Bergotix. We let them so command the field and the battle that we could neither break their front nor turn their flanks. And, as I have said to others, we came at them that day with our hearts, and left our heads in our waggons."

Bergotix shook his head sadly.

"Cruel it was, for she had the dogs eating each other up till that day."

"That day is done, friend," said Canis, "and we are looking to another—if you are still for Boadicea."

"How might I serve a dead queen?"

"Through her people, such as are left." Now Canis made plain to Bergotix and the dreaming introspective Caleda, how it had come about that he was where he now was, and how he was seeking to lead the surviving Iceni and Trinovantes to the mountains of the west. He spoke of the mountains, and how the people who lived within them stood fast against Romans. He spoke of the intent of Princess Cea and her people to live there, to build a new kingdom that they would hold secure against Paullinus. He told of desperate affrays, of how in ones and twos and families, his warriors and his people had escaped the Romans and had become a full three thousand. He told of battle, trickery and endurance, until the eyes of Bergotix were glittering and excited. Caleda held her peace and let her husband ask the inevitable question.

"But you are alone here, lord. Where are these three thousand people you speak of?"

"Close to your eastern border, in a forest in the Parisii country not so far from Eburacum. Bergotix, will you, this night, take them a message from me? I have it writ here on parchment taken from the house of Cartimandua. I may not go myself, I may not absent myself for so long. Do you know an encampment called Parridium, lying south-east across your border from Eburacum?"

"I know it," said Bergotix, "a poor place. The Parisii never build higher than a man's shoulder, and crawl in and out of their dwellings for the most part."

"Beyond Parridium lies the forest where Princess Cea and all the others are hid, awaiting word from me. Take the track from Parridium until it turns to run in line with the forest, and at this point whistle three times like a blackbird. Can you whistle like a blackbird?"

"Aye, for it was the only whistle used by warriors during Boadicea's campaign."

"It will take you four walking hours to reach them. I would spare your limp and let you take horse, but while a man with or without a limp may make himself invisible, a man with a horse may not. You will have little time for sleep when you return. Here is the message. Princess Cea can read and so can another, a woman called Lydia."

"I know my own name," said Bergotix, "but nought else."

The message Canis had inscribed on the parchment of fine, dried skin was this;

"*Cea, Princess and Beloved. I came here only in hope, and met two who were honest and out of the ordinary. By their friendship I conceived that which may bring us through this land well-equipped. At noon tomorrow, I journey from the house of Cartimandua with item: five hundred horse, one hundred chariots with horse, one hundred sacks of flour and some gold. Item, also: Cartimandua's daughter, Venturia. We are to journey to Aquae Sulis wherein, so I have said, lies my father's house. And there, so I have said, Venturia and I will wed. Ask the bringer of this message not what I am about concerning the daughter, but in the darkness make your way with eight hundred warriors and maids to Eburacum, and at daylight enter the town as the servants and attendants of Herco, who is myself—saying if any should ask, that you have come from his father's house to escort your lord Herco and his bride and dowry to Aquae Sulis. Eburacum will be full tomorrow with many people, all come to see Herco—who is myself and kinsman to Caratacus—take Princess Venturia on our journey. Command Andudo and Hywel to ask for me as my stewards. All others—warriors, women and children and all—must make their way to the road going south out of Calcaria, there to wait as inconspicuously as possible, half a league outside the town. If accosted by Romans there, they must say they wait to give greetings and fair wishes to their Princess Venturia and her beloved Herco, myself, when we*

*pass. Do not fail, but come with the eight hundred to Ebu-
racum, and all others to the road outside Calcaria. When I
appear in Eburacum with my sweet dove, raise your voices
joyfully for her, who, as I have said, is to be my bride; and
shout also in acclaim for myself, your lord Herco. By daylight,
many people will be on the road to Eburacum. Mingle freely
with them, and so come freely into the town with them. Thus
I will see thee anon, sweet Princess, and kiss thy soft nose.
Greetings to thee, and all others. I give you my mark, Herco
—who is myself for the moment."*

Bergotix took the tightly rolled parchment.

" I will carry your message, lord, and gladly," he said,
" and do not fear that I will lose it, or let it fall into any hands
but those of Princess Cea." He went into the inner room for a
cloak, and returned to say, " Your people will endure, for they
have a true Princess, and they also have you." He muttered a
little, and shifted his feet about. He pulled at his glossy
moustache. " Caleda and I are Brigantes, and lack that which
Queen Boadicea gave her people. It is not to be thought—that
is, you have enough which is burdensome without having
more—yet it is true I fought willingly for Boadicea."

" Speak clearly, Bergotix, for you have little time to hop
about here," smiled Canis.

But it was Caleda who then spoke, and for the first time,
though she did not move from the fire, nor did she lift her
head.

" My foolish husband can only speak clearly when he is
discoursing on clattering iron and loud battle. In all else he
mumbles. What he wishes to say, lord, is that if you will have
us we will go with you, and so add two to your three
thousand."

" How came this to your mind," said Bergotix to his wife,
" when it has only this moment come to mine?"

" Do I not know you better than you know yourself?" said
Caleda. She raised her eyes. Her face was smooth of skin,
placid of expression. She addressed herself to Canis. " What
is Bergotix to do when he returns?"

271

"Take what rest he can," said Canis, "and then come to Eburacum before I leave with Venturia."

"And I, what am I to do?" she asked.

"Come to Eburacum with him. And when I leave you, he may follow if you so desire. If I bring to Princess Cea two people who are out of the ordinary and make uncommonly brave friends, then she will welcome you with more than ordinary pleasure."

"Lord," said Bergotix, a light in his eye, "we will follow you, never doubt. Crooked leg or no, I make light of travel and can still throw a sharp spear. I will—we will—be in Eburacum anon." And he kissed Caleda affectionately, then with the message secure on his person he went.

Canis, left alone with Caleda, observed her. She still sat by the fire, still looked into the flames. There was a grace and a handsomeness about her which stirred him.

"Caleda," he said, "if you wish it, I will dissuade Bergotix from pursuing this other matter. He is not so obstinate that he cannot be made to see the disadvantages of his impulse."

"It is no impulse," said Caleda, "he would like above everything else to go with you, and serve under your command again. I will do what he wishes to do, but my hands shame me."

"What is that to do with going or staying? It is only to do with being a woman, is it not? Caleda, the hands of Princess Venturia are soft and damp, they fasten on a man like clammy tentacles. Strange is that which ordains what we become, when one born to milk goats finds herself a princess and one who works from sunrise to sundown would make a more gracious queen than Cartimandua. Come from the fire, Caleda."

She rose and went to him. He was slightly stooped because of the low ceiling. He took her hands. They trembled a little. She dropped her eyes.

"Bergotix and I both work in the fields," she said, "but I did not think about my hands until you came. Now they shame me. Is it because you are a king, though you come to us like a homeless wanderer? Lord, are you a king?"

272

"I am no king, Caleda, nor even a prince."

"Yet you look as I would expect a king to look. When Bergotix and I go with you, will I cook for your warriors? Bergotix will tell you I make a fine pot out of the meanest fare."

He smoothed the hands that so strangely troubled her.

"Bergotix is a warrior first, a farmer only by circumstance," he said, "and he wishes for the chance to be warrior again. Your hands are finely-shaped, Caleda, with long fingers. They are not for stirring cooking pots. You shall be a warrior also. Many of our maids and women are warriors, and I know no braver ones in all Britain. Or more joyful."

"I? A warrior woman? To fight for you and yours? To be of clattering iron and clanging brass? I?" She was in whispering amazement.

"I will swear to it, but only if you wish it, and only if you are of a free mind to come with us. For my part, you have had more than enough of bending in bitter fields and stirring pots. You were born for more than that. It will be hard and desperate, and unlovely at times, but there will be freedom and joy also. You will make handsome warrior, Caleda."

He bent his head; and as he had done once before, he put his mouth to the palm of each of her hands; and when the sweet tingling had passed he had gone, leaving her not unfaithful to foolish Bergotix, after all.

She knew of the warrior maids of Boadicea. They had outnumbered the men. She had heard all there was to hear of their wild ways. Bergotix had painted his own riotous pictures of them for her, and now her disturbed mind seemed to be filled with the echoes of their singing cries, while from the flames of the fire her bemused eyes drew images of their long limbs and streaming hair.

"A warrior woman? I?"

She sat looking into the dying embers.

11

Lydia had taken fever. The privations and destroying anguish of her captivity, and the exhausting ordeal of her flight to safety, might have been responsible for her momentary lack of resistance when the chill caught her. Nor at the time was she the soul of cheerfulness, for Canis was in Brigantia, contriving the gods knew what, and had refused to take her with him.

Bitterly she had said, "You did not lack to use me at Durvulavum, to have me risk myself and my unborn child too. Am I of no consequence now?"

But he would not take her, he said they must think of Cea. So she had been left with the Britons in the forest, close to the eastern border of Brigantia. There, out of sight, they waited for word from Canis. To Lydia every hour dragged, every day seemed interminable. Nor could she help thinking that Romans would get to hear of their whereabouts.

She knew she was unwell. She fought the sickness. But coming from the forest stream one morning with Dilwys in her arms, she staggered and would have fallen, but for the ready arms of women. Within an hour, her fever was high. Grud was full of concerned mutterings at the quickness with which the burning engulfed her. He wrapped her in the warmest coverings he could procure, but Lydia shook and shivered without let. He dosed her with the vilest of potions, only to find that by the hour the fever increased. And for all that she burned, her shivering consumed her. She lay in the most protected place Grud could find, and women came to stand near and softly whisper.

As night fell she slept but cried out. She woke and rambled, the fever raging. Grud sat with her in the darkness. He listened to her cries, her delirium, and he knew that in her burning sickness she was reliving again and again the desperate gallop from pursuing Romans.

"I hear them, I hear them," she cried, "but ride, Canis, ride! I follow, you cannot lose me. See, I follow, I am up with you. On, sweet horse, fly for me. Up, up, do not fail me—oh, brave horse, there rides Canis, so follow, follow!"

"Sweet mistress, none can say that what love you have had from the Wolfhead you have not earned," whispered age-old, young-eyed Grud to his feverish, burning Roman woman, as she tossed and turned within her coverings. He had taken her to his heart. "Hold on, sweet Roman, and you shall come through to kiss him for many years yet. Hold on, hold fast, let the soft night cherish you, not devour you."

But she was no better by dawn, and even worse by noon. Julian limped painfully to see her. He sat by her, his handsome face distressed. For all that she had plagued him in her wilful days, his sister was dear to him. And dearer now, because of many things—in especial because, he thought, she would not face reality. He bathed her dry, fiercely-hot forehead with wet linen. She stared up at him with eyes great with fever and did not know him. The women whispered, some tearfully, for to them Lydia was no haughty Roman, but a warm woman who drew laughter from their children and soothed their hurts, who took joy in them because they were the future strength of Cea and Canis. But there was one gloomy woman who said, "She will die, for Romans when they ail in this fashion take on the sickness of their tainted blood." The warrior maid Feneda, who had ridden so hard with Lydia during their relentless gallop, and who came often to ask how she fared, turned fiercely on the woman.

"If she was born of Rome, she is not of Rome now. She is of us. She has served us and endured much for us. She is Ludicca, and there are none braver. She will not die, her blood is not tainted but rich and quick. But if she does, then woe to you, with death on your tongue, for it will have been your voice that called the dark spirits to take her. And when

275

Canis hears of it, he will take your tongue from you and feed it to the blackbirds. Away with you, away, I say."

The crestfallen woman, who had spoken as she had merely because she was of the kind who took melancholy joy in pessimism, went humbly away.

Cea came many times to see Lydia.

" Grud, how does she do?" she asked each time, to be answered that Lydia burned. And when she came again an hour before sunset, on the second day of the fever, Grud muttered fiercely and in a way uncommon to him.

" There is a fire upon her which I cannot put out, I cannot."

Lydia lay there, shapelessly bundled within thick coverings, the heat perceptible on her face, her eyes dryly, strangely bright and whispers gasping from her throat. Cea's brown eyes were misty. She put a hand on Grud's arm. Although three thousand people filled this part of the Parisii forest, there was such a quiet that only these gasping whispers could be heard.

" Grud," said Cea, " I do not wish her to die, she has given too much of herself for us. Do not heed my jealousy but save her, Grud, do not let her die."

" You are a sweet princess," said Grud, " and have found that jealousy is not the worst of a maid's emotions. Go to your rest. I will stay with Lydia and fight the dark spirits with her."

When the sun was at its lowest and the forest was red, Lydia came out of her fevered whisperings.

" Grud . . .?" Her voice was faint. He knelt beside her. Her hand was dry and hot as he laid his own upon it.

" I am here, mistress."

" I give him sweet child, Grud."

" Aye. He knows this."

She seemed to struggle for breath.

" Is the sun . . . is it gone, Grud?"

" It is warming to its night couch."

" Grud . . .?" Fainter yet.

" Here is my hand, sweet one. Hold fast."

She held, burningly.

" He is not like other men, dear Grud."

" Nor are you like other women. You are as brave as Boadicea."

The last light of the sun reached through the silent trees to put flame upon her face and fire into her unseeing eyes.

" It has been so much joy, Grud . . . so much . . ."

Her fingers slipped from his.

Grud rose. He went to Cea, who fretted for Canis and worried about Lydia. She was not asleep, and in the purple light she caught her breath to see his face.

" Grud, is it the worst?"

" Not yet." Grud muttered." I am going as far into the forest as I must. Give me one who will carry a bright torch for me. I seek a plant that may grow here or may not, that may wrest her from the dark spirits or give her to them."

" Grud, it may poison her, you mean?" whispered Cea.

" Or save her. But her blood is clean and she is brave, so I must lack no courage myself. It is a plant with a root that must only be taken from the earth at night, for it shrivels in the light of day. Give me a man and torch."

" I will carry the light, Grud. Aye, and Feneda also, for she is weeping for Lydia. And we must throw out a wide circle of warriors so that they may take any Parisii who see our lights and wonder about us."

They went deep into the forest, Princess Cea and Feneda, lighting the way for Grud with flaring torches. They were screened by a far-flung circle of warriors commanded by Hywel, much distressed by Lydia's sickness. The warriors moved in darkness, but had eyes now for any forest at night. Grud hunted with his nose close to the ground, his bow legs swift and restless. In the end, he found what he sought—a tender plant, but bitter in its content. This he dug up with infinite care, so that its long, tapering root was neither broken nor bruised. He returned to the camp with it, and over a fire he cleaned it and then boiled it. He poured away half the water, and with a pestle ground plant and root within the

277

residue, until the pot contained what looked like thick soup, as dark in colour as the earth from which the herb had been taken.

When it was quite cool he took it to Lydia, who lay comatose, except that faint shudders seized her from time to time. Cea lifted her. Grud needed to devote himself to the necessity of giving Lydia every drop of the muddy liquid. The fiery heat of her body appalled Cea, but she raised her and supported her. Grud mumbled and muttered, as he forced Lydia's mouth open and gave her the bitter potion. It took so much time that Cea ached. But finally Grud closed Lydia's mouth, almost fiercely, holding on until he was sure she had swallowed every drop. Cea laid her back, and Grud covered her again.

" Take your good rest, sweet Princess, I will tend her."

Cea spoke prayerfully to her Iceni gods, and went. Grud, who could do nothing now but sit and wait, did that.

How she burned, the Roman woman.

Her fevered fancies returned, she moaned and shivered. Grud sat silently. For him, the course of her life was ordained. His medicine could only speed her the quicker to destined death or destined recovery. He hoped, but he did not pray. The dark hours went by and the fever seemed hotter upon her. No symptoms of gradual change preceded the sudden change that occurred. One moment Lydia was highly feverish, the next she sank into quietness, her tormenting and disordered dreams running from her. She still shivered a little, but she was quiet.

Another dream came, a clear and radiantly bright dream.

A woman was there, a woman with wondrous, shining hair and sweet wide mouth and strange glowing beauty. She had come to Lydia in another dream, long ago; and if only her eyes had been uncovered, Lydia would have known her. But there was a mist before her eyes. In a rich, musical voice the wondrous woman spoke, so clear, so clear.

" You are the Roman woman," she said.

" I was," replied Lydia. " I am not now."

278

" No woman can deny her heritage, neither queen nor Roman."

" My heritage is of Britain."

" Foolish one, you have lost all you were born for."

" I was born for Canis the Briton, and am in his heart."

" One alone is in his heart."

" I am that one, I am! "

The mist wreathed, the sweet wide mouth curved to a mocking smile.

" You are still Roman."

" Only by birth, no longer by heart. Who are you to doubt me and question me?"

It seemed for a moment as if the mist dissolved; but before Lydia could see the eyes, it wreathed again to hide them. The bright hair was a cloud of tawny light.

" I am one you know, Lydia Osirus."

" I only know you came to me once before, when I was in torment for his love. You spoke to me strangely and truly, yet mocked me."

" Did I not tell you to let him go?" The musical voice was vibrant.

" And I did let him go, I did! "

" But clung to him and put the chain of your desires around him." The mist deepened. " What is your destiny, Lydia of Rome?"

" I do not know my destiny, only my longing, which is to be with him and serve his people, and through them to serve his Queen also."

" His Queen is dead."

" Boadicea cannot die. She lives in the hearts and minds of all who knew her."

Again the woman smiled, but this time her mouth curved sweetly, though the mist still covered her eyes.

" All, Lydia of Rome?"

" All. I am of Britain now. She is my Queen also."

" She is more than that, she is your spirit and endeavour, and through you Canis will find her again. The child you bore

279

is her child, for when she was conceived his Queen was in his heart and mind, not Lydia of Rome."

" Oh, speak—who are you?"

" I am his life and his death, as he was mine. I am one you know. Look upon me and see your destiny, Ludicca of the Iceni."

And the mist lifted, and in the warm clear brilliance of her dream Lydia saw the magical blue eyes and majestic beauty of a face she had looked upon in the palace of Queen Boadicea at Venta Icenorum, and had spat upon in the courtyard of that same palace. And the voice came again to her, this time like the murmur of softest summer.

" I am your destiny, brave Ludicca."

In her sleep, the faintest sigh broke from Lydia. Grud heard it. He put out a hand to touch her brow. It ran with perspiration. In the shafted forest moonlight, the eyes of Grud —round as the eyes of all innocence, and dark as the eyes of every night—brightened. His ears pricked to catch her breathless, joyful murmur.

" Oh, now I know you . . . you are Boadicea . . . and Queen . . ."

Grud smiled.

12

All was in happy confusion at the house of Queen Cartimandua. It had been ten days since the marriage contract had been drawn up and agreed, and now Princess Venturia, quite beside herself with delicious anticipation, was impatient to leave. The only one who was not ready to smile cheerfully on her departure was her mother. Cartimandua had become quite woeful during the last day or two. Venturia's insistence that she would not stay long in her husband's domain, but would return to Brigantia as soon as she could, bringing Herco with her (and by the ear), could not alleviate the fond mother's woe. It would not have been so bad if Venturia had been going elsewhere than among the upstart Belgae, or with any other man than that Belgic magician. She made so much of his faults and his indifferent splendour that in the end Venturia became spitefully unlamblike.

"Ah, I see through this, Cartimandua. You want him for yourself. Oh, that my own mother should be so shamefully covetous."

"I? I want that sly, mawkish Belgic snake. Are you out of all your senses?"

"Mawkish, you say? Snake? My Herco? To miscall him in this way is to betray yourself. You do want him and are tired of Ancastus already. Such is your love for me that you would rob me of him, and I your own daughter."

This accusation had an hysterical and frenzied effect on Cartimandua, and she and her lamb almost came to scratching and clawing. But on the day of departure, she and Venturia had forgiven each other—though Venturia, even in her sense of giddy excitement, watched her mother closely. She knew Cartimandua's appetite for men only too well.

The only person who did not seem to be rushing here, there and everywhere was her betrothed, whom her eyes hungrily devoured, whenever he came into her sight. How unobtrusively commanding he was, how much a man. She trembled at the anticipation of discovering just how much. It would take her some time to bend him to her will; but what rich delights there would be in the sustained, prolonged contest of nerve and wit; and what rapture would be hers, even when he beat her. He had said he would if she vexed him. Constantly Venturia was beset by erotic imaginings and amorous shivers.

Midway through the morning, Canis had said to Cartimandua that if she would so favour him he would borrow as many Brigante servants as she could spare to his aid. Although he had sent word to his father's house for Belgic servants, he had received no reply and did not think that if any were on their way they would arrive in time. And he could not, he said, carry away under his arm five hundred horse, one hundred chariots with—

"Did I think you could, fool?" Cartimandua interrupted, unable to contain her ill-tempered gloom at the imminent departure of the daughter so dear to her. "You may take what servants you wish. Speak to my steward Medwyn. In truth, I mistrust your magic, even though it won Ancastus to me, and I will be in no sadness to see you go—if only you were not taking my sweet lamb with you."

"The roses that blush in your cheeks are not for me, then?" he suggested.

"What woman who has Ancastus could simper over you?" she said maliciously. "Be content that you have had from me far more than any other man might. I have given you the fairest princess in all Britain—aye, Venturia is fit bride for Caesar himself—and I have also given you—"

"Has Caesar himself asked for her?" interposed Canis amiably.

Cartimandua responded to that so spittingly that tiny flecks of her saliva dappled his tunic. Not only Caleda, thought

282

Canis, but any of my warrior maids would make a more endearing queen than Cartimandua.

Towards noon, a servant approached as the Queen was listing for Canis the comforts he must procure for Venturia. She had already listed her daughter's virtues, not the least of which was her unsurpassable beauty. The servant shifted about, until Cartimandua sharply bade him speak.

"There are two men, O Queen, who say they are the stewards of my lord Herco, and are here by his father's command from Aquae Sulis."

"Ah," said Canis non-committally, as if he would have preferred to have heard more of Venturia's virtues. But then he said, "So be it. I will see them. And if your virtuous lamb who is my true delight comes skipping in further impatience, tell her to skip back again and change her robe for another."

Cartimandua's eyes followed him as he went with the servant. She could not understand how it was that he had arrived like a beggar, and from that moment had commanded all his wants like a king. She could not restrain the smile of malice about her mouth. Whatever he was, he would not find her lamb was without teeth.

"In the end," she told herself comfortingly, "she will eat you, impudence."

At the lower entrance to the Queen's house, Andudo and Hywel awaited Canis with an air of composed beatitude—as if by their presence here they gave blessing to this great day. Yet their hearts thumped a little when they saw Canis. He seemed so remote from the swarming activity of the place. There were all manner of gaudily-attired Brigantes about, men and women, and all coming or going, chattering or buzzing. A Brigante noble hailed Canis as he approached, stopping to voice a jesting whisper.

"Is your gold counted, Herco? If it is, then take it, every crown. You will earn it, for your lamb is a hungry one, and will eat you down to your bones."

"You are a formidable jester, friend," said Canis heartily, and smote the man's back so jovially that he entered the

283

Queen's hall as if he had plunged from a chariot. Cartimandua had him flung into a pond for being too drunk too soon. Canis went up to Andudo and Hywel. " So," he said in the hearing of people passing in and out, "you are here at last. You are not the swiftest of stewards. Go now, and with the other servants who came with you take up the horse, the chariots and the hundred sacks of flour that await attention. They are in charge of one Medwyn of the Queen's household here. Seek him out and make known to him that since my own servants are here, it is my command that he delivers all these items into your hands. Count them, every one."

Those who heard him smiled. This Belgic man would not journey forth with less of the dowry than he was entitled to. Even though it was her own daughter's dowry, Cartimandua might not resist the natural impulse to cheat a little.

"Aye, my lord Herco," said Andudo solemnly. But he was hard put to it not to burst asunder in wonder and disbelief, while Hywel could scarcely meet the stern eye of Canis (who here called himself Herco) without his gift for merry laughter betraying him. However, they went as instructed and found the steward Medwyn, acquainting him with the lord Herco's commands and wishes. The Brigante steward's disdain for the robust rather than distinctive appearance of Herco's stewards had little effect on Hywel and even less on Andudo, who had never seen such a mincing popinjay. They confounded Medwyn with this robustness of theirs, the confidence they had seen in Canis giving them more than enough of their own.

Eburacum was squeezed with people, all come to crowd around the Queen's house on three sides, though only those who stood before the wall gate could see anything of the activity and bustle within. But the dowry of Princess Venturia had been assembled in an open space a little distance from the royal house, and there it could be seen in all its generosity, apart from the gold. People came to gape as much at the dowry as the Queen's house. Andudo and Hywel, with the supercilious Medwyn, came to count it.

For many Brigantes, it was past all belief that Princess Venturia was to wed a Belgic man. Surely everyone knew that the Belgae were the least commendable but the most acquisitive of men. What kind of a Belgic man was it, then, who had won the hand of the voracious, demanding Venturia? That gurgling man-eater would not wed less than a man and a half.

"Do you know him? Have you seen him?" So asked a round-faced woman of a maid with hair that showed auburn tinted with gold beneath the hood of her robe.

"Have I not fed the dogs in his father's house for many a year?" returned Princess Cea, for Cea it was indeed. "And have I not come with many other servants to escort our lord Herco and his bride and the dowry to his father's house?"

"You are Belgic?" The round-faced woman could not be unkind to one with such soft brown eyes, even though she was of the upstart Belgae.

"As are many of us here," said Cea, not knowing how she hid her fluttering excitement and trepidation, "and a long and weary way we have come to give our help to our lord Herco on his journey home."

"Ah," said the woman, "I thought there was more ungentle jostling than we are used to here. Is he a commanding man, your lord Herco—one to take the eyes of a princess?"

"He stands so high," said Cea, "which is neither too tall nor too short. Nor is he too round or too thin, and while I myself would not say this or that of him, lest I were deemed too flattering or too critical, I will say that to see him is at least to know he is not a woman."

"By all the Queen's own men," said the woman, "that is to say nought about him at all."

In the jostling crowd two lean, sunburned men hemmed Cea between them and discreetly milled about to remove the precocious Princess from her gossip.

"My lady," whispered one in her ear, "I beg of you, do not invite overmuch of chatter. Enough is enough."

"I am in a little flutter," murmured Cea, "but also in exceeding high spirits. I cannot wait to lay my eyes on my

285

lord's newest love, whom I will stretch from tree to tree as soon as I can put my hands on her."

Lydia was among the crowds also. She had been up four days, and although Cea and Grud had pressed her to go with the women and children and other warriors to wait on the road outside Calcaria, as Canis had instructed—Lydia would have none of it. She was pale from her illness, but her blood today flowed swiftly and strongly again, and what physical weakness she still felt she was able to forget amid the noise and bustle of crowded Eburacum. She saw many Romans. Even they were curious, though only in their glitteringly superior way.

Grud was by her side, spritely watchful. So was Feneda. If she wearied, they would have her out of the press in a twinkling. But she was not wearied, she felt quick and alive, a warm woollen robe about her, her green eyes bright. Grud knew the reason for the brightness. She was not here to see Eburacum, nor to see the people. She was not even here to see Queen Cartimandua.

"I have seen Boadicea," she had said to Grud, "what other queen is there?"

She was here to see Canis and to look with burning curiosity on Princess Venturia, of whom Canis had made such strange mention in the message brought by a Brigante called Bergotix, a man with a limp and a rugged, likeable face. The message had aroused wonder, confusion and incredulity at first; but so lucid did it sound when read a second time, and so assured, that there had been no question of not following the instructions to the letter. And when Bergotix had described the sender, they knew the message was indeed from Canis.

But, thought Lydia, he was the dearest rogue to have wooed Cartimandua's daughter and to carry her off to— where? And the dowry—surely this could not truly be as he had described? Even if it were, the Queen's daughter could not be other than squint-eyed and fat-nosed. Or was she beautiful? Had he kissed her, had she known his embrace, his lean muscular body? Oh, he would not have been such a rogue as that. Or would he? Aye, maybe he would if it were necessary. Beloved Diana, let her not be beautiful. It is enough to bear that Cea should have such soft bewitchment.

Feneda touched her arm. Lydia turned. Feneda was supple and graceful, as were all the warrior maids. Although in Eburacum this day, they all wore cloaks or robes to hide their short tunics and weapons.

"You look so intense, Ludicca," said Feneda. " Shall we go from this bustle and all these sharp elbows?"

" Is there undue bustle, Feneda? I had not noticed," said Lydia. She felt nervously high of spirits, but not because of any weakness. She had woken the morning after her clear, radiant dream and had felt such sweet, blessed relief within her body that she had wept just a few tears of happiness. Now she felt only this nervous wonder at what Canis was about. She looked around. There were so many people. How heavily moustached the Brigante men were, how sturdy the women looked, and what an austerely handsome place Eburacum itself was, with its weathered stone and its Romanisation. She saw the Roman soldiers, most of them showing more interest in the Brigante maids than in a man who called himself Herco and came, so it was said, from the south. South or north, east or west, what was the difference? To the Romans they were all barbarians, some more so than others A little further north they still painted themselves when they came on their raids. However, some of the Brigante maids were shapely enough.

Lydia's heart leapt suddenly as she saw Andudo and Hywel. There was a Brigante man with them, a spruce little man. Had they seen Canis? If so, what was afoot now? Andudo pushed his way through to the gate leading to the Queen's house, and climbed the square stone post to look down at the crowds. Drawing air into his lungs, his speech came as a bellow.

" Hear me! All who have come from Belgae and are servants to our lord Herco and his father, end your roistering and dallying, for there is work to do. Hear me! When our lord and his fair Princess appear, all must be ready for departure. So

287

come forth, skulkers, idlers, carriers and drivers. Leave the Brigante maids to their own sweethearts and follow me. Come forth, women who belong under my stewardship, and be ready to give escort to Princess Venturia, so that she may not say she lacked courteous Belgic attendance on her journey. Stop your kissing and come forth."

The Brigantes of Eburacum became noisy with merriment at this, and good-humouredly made way as men and women and maids began to edge their way through the crowds. The Brigantes were there in great numbers, as many as three or four thousand; and the eight hundred men and women warriors of Canis had mingled unobtrusively enough with them up to now. But the Brigantes began to gape a little as they saw just how many servants there were making their way through to attend on the requirements of the lord Herco. It did not need more to tell them then that the man who had won the hand of Princess Venturia was of high estate, for by what better standard could a man's position be judged than by the numbers of servants or slaves he owned? They seemed countless.

Andudo and Hywel, together with the fussy Brigante steward, Medwyn, began to lead the seemingly endless column of servants to the open place, where all that Cartimandua had assembled now awaited them. The Iceni and Trinovantes, playing their parts with as much servitude as they could simulate, took up the stations allotted them by Andudo and Hywel, though they could scarce believe their eyes at the multitude of horse and chariots they saw. All these! And a hundred sacks of precious flour, of which they had had so little for so many months. They stood by every horse, they stood in twos by every chariot, while a hundred men each hoisted a sack of flour and carried it to load it onto a nearby waggon. Princess Cea had told them of the immensity of the dowry they were to take charge of; but a man needed to see such a dowry before being able to finely appreciate it. True, some of the small, shaggy horses were indifferent-looking to the eyes of the Iceni warriors, but it would be foolish to say so.

There were three waggons. The first would carry Canis and

288

Venturia, together with the gold and some of Venturia's more personal belongings. The second was piled high with the remainder of all that she was taking, and on it would ride two of her tire-women, who would look to her whims and wants on the way. The third and larger waggon took the sacks of flour. Escorting the waggons would be a score of Brigante warriors, members of the Queen's own bodyguard. And because Cartimandua was a client-monarch under Caesar, the Roman legate at Eburacum had offered a courtesy escort of Roman soldiers as far as Legiolium. This was to show that the daughter of Cartimandua had Caesar's favour, but only as far as Legiolium.

Princess Cea, with Feneda and Lydia, stood outside the Queen's house. They endeavoured to look like house servants assigned to attend on Venturia during the journey south. Cea and Lydia were in a ferment now. Would Canis never appear with his sweet love?

He would and did, and at last.

Amid the buzz and din of the many curious people, they came from the house of the Queen. Venturia, looking as gaudy as a peacock, came first, accompanied by the no less gaudy Cartimandua. Canis was behind mother and daughter, and the Brigante people saw him, a tall man without either beard or moustache, and clad in a kilted tunic beneath a grey, fustian cloak. If the people expected him to shine with metal and bright colours, they were disappointed. He did not dazzle any eye, yet eyes were drawn to him nonetheless, and more than one Brigante maid sighed to see how quietly commanding he was. Walking next to him was Ancastus, bold, flamboyant and as colourful as any woman could wish.

Cea and Lydia in the forefront saw them coming. Cea's eyes sought quick confirmation that Canis was among the Queen's procession, then turned immediately upon Princess Venturia. Lydia's eyes, having alighted on Canis, lingered compulsively on him. Boadicea herself had told her to find her destiny, and Canis was part of that. He was so brown that his grey eyes looked blue in the light. But what an air of complacency he feigned, like a man who had indeed won himself a royal bride and a royal dowry. Devious he was, but so dear to her. Had she been in his thoughts? Did he know she had almost died of the burning sickness?

Her green eyes strove to tell him of her presence, but he did not look her way. She felt a foolish, almost childish disappointment, and reluctantly turned her gaze on the princess he had wooed. She stared. Why, she thought, although Venturia was neither squint-eyed nor fat-nosed, yet beside herself and Cea and any of his warrior maids, Canis had surely found himself a new love who was no more than plump, pasty partridge. That which had been in her mind, a fear that Cartimandua's daughter would be beautiful, laughed itself joyfully away. Oh, Canis, you have never kissed this one and had rapture of it, never.

Venturia was smiling, and though the day was cloudy and the light soft, her bottom lip glistened. Ancastus too was smiling, but not for the same reason as Venturia. His was rather a rueful smile, as if he were still not quite sure why the wheel of fortune had spun for him in the way he had least expected or intended. A man, after all, could govern much of his own destiny if he were determined enough. Ancastus had been immovably determined but he had still ended up in the Queen's bed.

Lydia, thinking of Boadicea and her slim, strong majestic beauty, was wholly unimpressed by Cartimandua. The Brigante Queen was a glitter of gold and copper, but was entirely without beauty or majesty. Out-of-doors, her voluptuousness was only a pale, heavy unhealthiness. Also she was in maternal glumness. The joy of her eye, her dearest Venturia, was being taken from her. But only because Venturia so desired it was Cartimandua permitting it.

The men of the Queen's bodyguard broke open the crowds to make way for the principals and all the following men and women of the court. The people were noisy enough at seeing them; but even Venturia's most charitable friends would not have said they cheered at the sight of her or her mother. It was the noise of curiosity, rather than joy. There were few

Brigantes who did not consider Cartimandua and Venturia dangerous rather than lovable. It did not do to cross either of them. Cartimandua, candidly, did not care whether her people cheered or not, and Venturia was quite unaware of anything except the loud song of blissful triumph in her head. But she began to see how people who were close enough stared at her tall Herco. There is a man for any of you, she thought, and he is mine. Where is the maid or woman anywhere who could capture such a one as this one? There was only her beauteous self.

They came through the people to come to the open place, where all was now ready, including selected escort men of the Queen's bodyguard. The Queen was addicted to bodyguards. More than one attempt had been made on her life.

Caleda and Bergotix were not in Eburacum, after all. Caleda had said it would not do, there were too many who might recognise them and ask about the bundles they bore, and why they placed themselves among the servants of Herco. So they had gone instead to place themselves among the remainder of Princess Cea's people, who waited on the south road outside Calcaria. Among those people was a Roman tribune. Julian still had an obstinate ankle and an obstinate mind.

Cartimandua began to embrace her daughter, smothering her with her amplitude. Venturia felt that to be suffocated by her own mother on a day such as this was beyond anything. Indeed, not only was Cartimandua bosomly engulfing her, she was also dinning her ears with every kind of final lamentation.

"Oh, the gods protect me from more of this," Venturia cried in a muffled voice, and violently disengaged herself.

"Oh, my lamb, my little one," groaned Cartimandua. She looked matronly and colourless, for all her jewels and glitter. Her heavy lids seemed waxen white. She looked mistily around as if seeking that which would keep Venturia with her, but her moist eyes quickly dried as she saw how five hundred horse were ready and mounted, how one hundred chariots each bore two people, and how a hundred others were grouped in escorting array on each side of the waggons, making her score of Brigante bodyguard men look meanly small. "How is this?" she asked Canis. "Are these your people or mine?"

"My father's house is not a small one," said Canis, "and I am myself kinsman to a prince, as you know. I would not have my father send insufficient servants, or do less than justice in any way to our blushing lamb."

Venturia endeavoured to bring pink to her cheeks by holding her breath, but only put more plumpness into her face. She giggled.

"Herco," said Cartimandua, "you came like beggar, and said you had no secrets. Each of your many servants here is a secret, and all of them imply that a man who owns so many men and women does not need one hundred gold Brigante crowns."

"The gold, Cartimandua," said Canis, "is to help me build a house even larger than my father's. Our sweet Venturia deserves no less. What say you, most radiant one?"

Venturia could not restrain a further giggle.

"I say you are a man with a most beguiling tongue," she said. As servants came to assist her to mount the seat of the waggon, she cast her mother a knowing glance. "Farewell, Cartimandua, Queen and mother, until you come to us in seven days and see us wed."

"The gods give you happy, safe journey, O my daughter."

"I will be more than safe with Herco and so many of his people," said Venturia, "but I will not lack when we are wed to see you again as soon as I may."

"That meeting, if not marriage, will be even sooner," said Canis, but only to himself. He said farewell to Cartimandua, thanking her, though not effusively, for the gift of her daughter. Cartimandua, having seen his multitude of servants, was less inimical and suffered him to put his lips to her cheek. Mounting the waggon beside Venturia, he saw Cea, Lydia and Feneda nearby. They were to ride on the second waggon in company with Venturia's two tire-women. "Ah," he said in lordly manner, "you are not here to stand and gape, but to ride in the following waggon. So up with you, wenches, or grass will grow around your idle feet."

" Oh, the villain!" Princess Cea spoke the words in a hissing whisper; but Lydia understood, and from under her hood her eyes looked up to kiss him. When they were in the waggon, with Cea still in a fine temper, Lydia whispered so that the tirewomen should not hear.

" He is a villain indeed, Cea, is he not?"

At which Cea could not restrain bubbling laughter.

With the score of escorting Brigante warriors, there were also the same number of Roman soldiers. The escorts were all mounted, the Romans being officered by a decurion. They gave martial pomp to the procession. There were last farewells.

"Depart in good fortune," called Ancastus to Canis, " though you came to change mine."

Canis smiled. Ancastus was by no means an unlikeable man. The crowd quietened as they saw Venturia's promised man stand on the waggon to address them.

" As I take your Princess," said Canis, " so must you take my thanks. And if you have this day lost one who was dear to you, I am not a man to be deaf to your woe. Your bright jewel will come again to shine among you, never fear."

Dutifully the Brigante people acknowledged the words of this Belgic man, although most of them thought he was sadly insensitive to their true feelings if he imagined Cartimandua's daughter was dear to them, and that they were in woe to see her go. One man bold enough to raise his voice, shouted: " Our woe is not to be your concern, lord, keep her to be your constant joy."

Canis laughed. Venturia laughed. The crowd buzzed and laughed. And amid this laughter, Canis drove the waggon forward at a walking pace to carry Venturia from Eburacum. Cartimandua groaned to see her heart's joy being taken from her under the bold banner of Belgic impudence, and she glanced around to see if Ancastus was close enough to lend her aid, if in maternal anguish she should swoon. But Ancastus, oblivious of her suffering, was gazing after the waggon. He was shaking his head as if he still did not clearly understand who it was who had come among them, and now went taking not only Venturia but so much prize as well.

As Canis unhurriedly took the waggon along, the horse plodding steadily, the other waggons following, the people pressed more closely around the cavalcade—but because of the escort, did not impede it. Falling in behind the waggons, came the Iceni and Trinovante warriors, mounted on the dowry horses, or riding the chariots or walking. Thus, apart from the gold, stowed securely away in the first waggon, the Brigante people saw the vast dowry and how it was being ridden or carried away. They saw the third waggon piled high with sacks of flour.

"Flour," quoth an amazed woman, "flour! Are they so wanting in Belgae that they need so much to make bread for them?"

There was some hilarity around her at this. The Brigantes were in good humour—not because their Princess went to be wed, but because she went.

Canis took the road to Calcaria. He still drove at walking pace, not only to allow people on the road outside Eburacum to see all that they wished to see of the procession, but because he did not want to appear in any undue haste. But when the way became open on all sides with spreading moorland, and those who walked mounted up behind comrades on horses, he went at a jog-trot, which was as fast as the waggons could be pulled in any event. The waggon containing the flour was twin-yoked. The road, not long re-surfaced by the Romans, was kind enough.*

Not until they had had gone beyond Calcaria would they see forest land. The clouds began to break, the day became sunny and fine, Canis was in the mood to please his betrothed, and his betrothed was in mesmerised content and excitement. He spoke drolleries that made her giggle and gurgle, so that frequently

* It should not be thought that the Britons did not build roads. They did. In many cases Roman roads were British roads re-surfaced by Romans.

294

her eyes turned on the Roman officer who rode by the side of their waggon. It was as if each glance said, "Oh, dull one, stiff one, have I not found a man to make even your fat Caesar laugh?"

She was in high spirits, but wished the journey were not so long. She did not like being absent from her usual comforts.

"When do we reach your father's house, when?" she asked.

"In four days," answered Canis, "as I have already said."

"I only ask again in the hope of hearing it will be less," she said prettily. She was not concerned with the wild beauty around them. She did not even see it. "There will be a great welcome for me. It is not every man, even one kin to a prince, who brings home a Princess of Brigantia. I dare swear your father is so amazed at your boldness and good fortune that he is in some trepidation. But since he has sent all these, his many servants, to escort us and my dowry, he need not fear I will be too distant with him. I will be as sweet to him as my position allows."

"Knowing my father," said Canis, pleasantly aware of the cavalcade, and who rode in whispering laughter in the waggon behind him, "I dare swear myself that he has sent all these to take as much care of the dowry as of you. It is my father's opinion that the true worth of any bride, be she a princess or a field woman, can be better judged by her dowry than her manner."

"As to that," said Venturia pertly, one hand clutching his arm as the waggon rumbled and creaked along, "is it my dowry that will give you joy in bed? Is it the sacks of flour that will make you beg for my favours on a cold night?"

"How, on a cold night which is also dark, will I know you from a sack of flour, O perfect one? How?"

"Impudence," she giggled, "you will know me well enough."

She shivered excitedly at how his knowledge of her would come about. She longed for bruising, wrestling overture to love, to the moment when this would become wanton compliance on her part and compulsive passion on his. She was no innocent, nor did she deprecate that by her fair beauty she would in the end inflame Herco to feats that would make her gasp and swoon.

The Roman officer rode closer in, to ask Canis how far he proposed to travel that day, and whether he would take rest in any town.

"We shall ride until we reach Calcaria," answered Canis, "and when we have passed through Calcaria, we will rest under the night sky. There is no town sufficient to quarter our many servants and escorts, or our horse, but no matter—for what will fit our mood better than warm earth and night sky? We have a comfortable tent for the Princess."

The Roman officer looked down his nose; and Venturia, a little pettish, said, "Under a night sky the earth is cold, not warm. I am not the kind to complain, yet I am also not the kind who should be given cause to—Oh!" It was a sharp gasp as the thumb and forefinger of her beloved applied an admonishing pinch to her arm. She flung him a furiously quarrelsome look. He responded with a smile which had something so calculating about it that she knew he would pinch her even harder if she raised her voice in the presence of the Roman decurion. Ah, he had no compunctions. He would indeed violate her flesh whenever he thought it necessary. The alarm she felt was akin to sensuous rapture. She moved closer to him and fell into entirely pleasurable contemplation of the prolonged battle of wills there was to be between them— when they were wed.

They reached Calcaria in four hours. This was another Roman stronghold, and the prefect of the town gave Venturia formal welcome. While she rested within Roman quarters, her tire-women in attendance on her, Canis went to see that all was well with his servants. They were well enough, what there were of them. Most of the Iceni and Trinovantes had gone on to rest outside the town, taking horse and chariots with them. Canis wasted little time in seeking out Princess Cea. She was resting with Lydia, Feneda, Grud and others, in the centre of the town. There were some civilians about, regarding with curiosity these people they thought were Belgic, and there were also the usual knots of Roman soldiers.

Cea would have greeted Canis with joy, but wisely forbore to. Lydia caressed him with her eyes. Canis thought Lydia a little pale, but did not at this moment comment on it.

He said, " I knew you would not fail me, Cea. Are all the others waiting for us outside Calcaria?"

" If they have obeyed you through me," said Cea, " they are. Hywel has gone ahead to make sure all is well with them. It was arranged that they should make their way there in groups and families."

" There are many people on these roads today," said Canis, " so our people will look like any other."

This was true enough. People from Brigante towns and encampments had emerged to see Venturia's procession go by at a number of places. Because of the circumstances, one could expect people to be on the roads or to be congregating at various points. It was not every day that a Brigante princess journeyed through the land as the promised bride of a man from the south.

" Is your loved one restoring her beauty?" asked Cea coyly.

" Is there need?" said Canis innocently. " Is she not one whose beauty at all times shames the freshness of dawn?"

" She is one who is remarkably like a plump, pale-faced shrew," said Cea, " and if you do not tell us what you are about, I shall burst."

" Did I not tell you? I journey to Aquae Sulis with Princess Venturia, where I am to wed her in the sight of her mother and my father. Cartimandua is to follow us in seven days, and we are to be wed seven days after Cartimandua's arrival."

" If that is to be the true way of it," said Cea, " then I will have Andudo slay your plump one at the first onset of darkness. It is to your shame to have her ride with you and put her greedy hand on you, as she does constantly. But because I know that out of this you are contriving to bring us safely across Brigantia and into the mountains of the Deceangi, my temper is contained, as you see. Yet it grieves me to see your conceit in your cunning show so plainly. It puts irritating

297

complacency on you. Tell me the true way of it at once."

Canis assumed an air of modest sobriety. Lydia, however, saw the laughter in his eyes. Whenever Princess Cea was in spirited or haughty mood, he took sly delight in her. However, he told them the true way of things, as Cea had demanded.

In the first place, the expedient of travelling north and then turning west to cross Brigantia was to make it harder for Paullinus to keep track of them. The Governor would assuredly be looking for them on all known ways south of Lindum. He would not anticipate them going so far north, and then moving across the middle regions of Brigantia, a country whose Queen was friendlier to Rome than any. But had they made this move without subterfuge, their numbers, even if they kept to the most difficult and uninhabited ways, would quickly have come to many eyes. Their presence would have been made known to Cartimandua or Romans or both. They would not have been left unmolested for long. Roman garrisons within Brigantia would have been alerted, and would have marched to contain them.

So, how to cross Brigantia as openly and as freely as possible? By first contriving to outwit Cartimandua, and then crossing under her patronage. The whole of Brigantia now had either rumour or news that the Queen's daughter was journeying to Belgae to wed a Belgic man. Princess Venturia was the key that would turn each lock, and was also the guarantee that Cartimandua would not be treacherously disposed to cheat them.

" Think you she would have let us journey farther than a league with the horse, chariots and flour, before she sent her Brigantes to dispossess us and kill us, if I had not claimed her daughter also? The horse, chariots and flour, with one gold crown, were her gift to me for what I did for her concerning a man called Ancastus. When I claimed her daughter, she increased one gold crown to a hundred and named the whole as dowry. Had Venturia not been wooed and won, that which I had from Cartimandua for the favour I did her would have been reclaimed by her a few hours after we had set out with it.

Ancastus was her greatest desire, Venturia her greatest weakness. So said Caleda, wife of Bergotix, the man who brought you my message, and so it proved. It has not, so far, been difficult."

Cea said, " I like not your conceit, it will undo us yet." But her brown eyes glowed.

Lydia only said, " Alas, poor Venturia." She could entirely understand that which had made Venturia leave her house, her land and her lamenting mother.

Canis was observing Lydia. The sun was about to begin its late afternoon descent, and in the soft golden light he remarked again her paleness. In a month it would be autumn and the land would be full of leaves whispering and falling; but it seemed as if winter had touched Lydia, when the sun was still full of summer warmth. Grud was muttering.

" Lydia," said Canis, " do you ail?"

" Ail?" said Grud to the sky. " There is a word for a woman, and she one of many without any food to speak of since morning, to say nought of her nearness to death and her worry over a certain child who is with Feola. Feola is where the others are, if they are where they should be, and who knows whether they have lost their way or not? I am nothing, so I cannot say."

" What is old mumchance muttering about now? What is this about Lydia?"

" I am well enough," said Lydia.

" She has had the burning sickness," said Cea, " and it took her fiercely. How she came out of it I know not, save that she bravely wished to continue the hard, weary way you press upon her."

" I was there," said Grud, " and was not entirely useless."

" Cea," said Lydia, a little distressed, " Canis presses nought upon me. It is my free choice to go with you." She would have protested her good health, but could not, for suddenly her blood was tumultuous. Canis was looking at her in such strange way, his eyes almost darkly brooding. A man did not look at a woman like that unless he were in pain for what so nearly

299

might have been—did he? Was his love strong for her? Was it? O Diana, let it be stronger than the unbreakable chain Jupiter put around Prometheus.

"Nonetheless," Cea was saying, something of regal reproof about her (for she was not a princess unaware of her proud lineage), "Canis is not innocent in the matter. My mother the Queen knew him well. And he has won the heart of another poor, misguided maid. You may well say poor Venturia, Lydia. I doubt not he has whispered to her, kissed her, deceived her and altogether bemused her."

Feneda let a bubble of laughter escape.

"Aye," said Lydia, "is it not merry? Is it not, Cea? Did you not see her greedy mouth and plump covetousness? I will laugh amain to see her take the kind of tumble she least expects. It will be more than merry then."

Cea's eyes sparkled. Her mouth quivered. She laughed. There were Romans about, but none took a great deal of notice of the merriment.

"Softly," said Canis, as they stood in the lengthening shadows of stone buildings, "the jest has not been fully played yet. Hear me further how we shall contrive our going, and then I will give you enough gold to procure all the food you want."

He spoke of the rest of their warriors and people waiting beyond Calcaria. The cavalcade would come up with them not long after they left the town, when Andudo was to slip away and go among them, bidding them follow as soon as darkness prevailed. They were to greet the cavalcade as if they were Brigantes, raising joyful cheer for Princess Venturia, and were not to forget Herco either. The cavalcade would pass on, travelling south from Calcaria, for the south road was the one which would bring them to Aquae Sulis in the shortest time. But in the night they would turn back and go north-west across country to avoid Calcaria, and strike the road going south-west. This would bring them at length into the country of the mountains and the Deceangi. He finally spoke of that which was to be done after they had made camp for the night.

At which Lydia said again, " Alas, poor Venturia."

And Cea said, " But oh, Canis, are you so sure of yourself and your cunning? Will this truly bring us safely out of Brigantia with all our people, and without fighting Romans?"

" It will bring us first to the northern border of the land of the Cornovii," said Canis, " and not until then will we encounter Romans who will be looking for us for what we are. But I doubt if Paullinus can bring force strong enough to contain us in the little time we will give him. If, however, we have to accept battle, why, we will bring them to a place of our own choosing, as we did before. And this time we will give them speedy, rushing, offensive battle—for we have five hundred more horse, and one hundred chariots with horse."

" And flour," said Cea, " of which we have had so little for a year and more, save for that which we took from Durvulavum. Oh, that was truly inspired thought, Canis. What other man would ask for a dowry to include one hundred sacks of flour?"

*　　*　　*

They rode out from Calcaria with the sun sinking on their right, a merry, jingling procession that carried the mesmerised, beguiled Princess Venturia into the night. The reddening sun struck wild purple from the moorland on one side, and tipped the roofs of forests with fire on the other. The Roman and Brigante escorts rode immediately behind the three waggons for the most part, though two Romans and two Brigantes took their place in the van of the whole. It was a matter of courtesy.

Half a league out of Calcaria, waited all the other warriors and people. There had been no incidents. They had come to this spot by various ways, with warriors in confident command of each small or large group. It had been a day of weary travel for all, but it had also been day when the country buzzed to stories of how Princess Venturia was journeying south to wed a Belgic man called Herco. It was said she travelled with one hundred waggons loaded with gold given to her as a wedding gift by Caesar himself. It was also said that her Belgic

man was clothed in raiment of gold given to him by Cartimandua. So the country was astir. Which roads did she travel?
Where could one see the hundred waggons loaded with the
gold of Caesar?

On any other day, the groups of Iceni and Trinovantes would
have been suspiciously obtrusive, but not this day. To any who
stopped them, whether Romans in their officious way, or
Brigantes in curiosity, they only said they were going to see
Princess Venturia pass by because they were no less loyal
subjects of the Queen than others.

In the end, all of them had arrived safely at this place by
the road going south from Calcaria. Here, many of them rode
or walked a little further to take shelter in the adjacent forest.
It hid from suspicious eyes the fact that there were more than
two thousand of them. Hywel had come up with them, but had
avoided answering all questions from the Roman tribune,
Julian Osirus, as to what Canis the fox was up to this
time. Hywel found avoidance easy, for he simply did not
know.

When the cavalcade reached this point, numbers of Cea's
warriors and people were still hiding in the forest; but hundreds
of men, women and even children rose up from the sides of the
road to call greetings to Princess Venturia, and to lay their
astonished eyes on the length of the procession. The sun was
low, its redness had burned out, and it was now no more than
a dull yellow disc shedding half-light over the land. But it was
more than enough for the people of Cea and Canis to clearly
see the Princess of Brigantia, and they raised their voices as
they had been told to, greeting her as if they were truly her
own subjects.

" Dove of sweet light," said Canis to Venturia, " even here
your people stay from their beds to come and give you fond
farewell. Ah, what is any princess who is not well loved?"

" They are a ragged lot," observed Venturia petulantly.
She had no feeling or liking for people whose shabby indigence
was too obtrusive. She could only respond to her own well-fed
kind. Nevertheless, she acknowledged the clamorous rabble

here with a careless wave or two of her hand, and felt that her graciousness in the matter pleased Herco.

She wished Herco might have been more concerned with pleasing her. She was not at all enamoured of his desire to have her tented under the night sky. She would have preferred to arouse burning flames of jealousy in him by dallying with the Romans at Calcaria, for she was sure that they coveted her proud beauty and were in some awe of her status. In Venturia's book, it was nowhere writ that the daughter of Cartimandua should be afflicted with false modesty. Nor was it writ that the Romans thought her the undistinguished daughter of a barbarian client-queen. " Why could we not go on to Legiolium, and be quartered there for the night?" she asked, as they began to leave the cheering rabble behind. " Is a soft couch not my due?"

If he had answered that her due this night was a prickly bush, Venturia in her bemused infatuation would have lain in a prickly bush, providing he lay with her. But it was not in her to wholly restrain her petulance, even though her body was constantly on fire at his nearness, and the anticipation of sensuous pleasures to come an ever-present deliciousness.

" Fair one," said Canis, acknowledging the last of the roadside greetings as carelessly as Venturia, " there are too many of us and I would not, in any event, give up the joy of the earth and the sky for the cramped quarters of Legiolium, with Romans falling over my feet at the sweetest moments."

Venturia's bosom heaved.

" Oh, Herco, you will madden me with such words, for you never follow them with the actions they promise. Have not my lips been yours since we first met? Yet you have only taken them twice."

" In truth," said Canis, " I have been tempted by night and by day. In resisting my ardent desire I observed our custom. But on such a night as this, what is any custom when your lips are so sweet and my desire so earnest? I have only the resistance of one man, not ten thousand."

Venturia was almost overcome. She gave him a glance of

intense longing. How uncommon a man he was, how devious his ways, how hard his body. And such was his way with words that he made her bemused mind spin dizzily. Her blood tingled, for when a man was so uncommon, his ways so devious and his strength so physical, even the only daughter of Cartimandua could not be expected to bend him to her will without quite a deal of rapturous suffering. What was in his mind now? Was he thinking to take more than her lips during the night as she lay in her tent?

Heat rushed upon her, her knees felt weak, she jolted on the seat of the waggon and pressed closer to him. For her comfort, the seat was draped with soft coverings; but being the kind of princess she was, she still found it villainously hard.

Andudo slipped silently away from the cavalcade at dusk, to make his way back to the waiting people of Cea—all of whom had now hidden themselves in the adjacent forest.

Darkness came, and coolness.

"I am cold, beloved," said Venturia as plaintively as a sensitive virgin maid, which she was not.

"So much the better," said her devious lover, "for what is sweeter to a man than the pleasure of turning cold lamb into burning flesh?"

"Oh, Herco," she panted, and she shivered; and every tremor was carnally ecstatic.

They halted; and in a sheltered level place, some distance off the road, they camped. From one of the waggons a tent was unpacked and erected for the comfort of Venturia. There was food and wine in plenty, and much of this was also unpacked. Fires were built and ignited. Food was distributed among the Roman and Brigante escorts, and Grud also gave them wine. The eight hundred warriors, whom Venturia and his escorts thought were Herco's servants, had their own fare. They had purchased it in Calcaria with the gold Canis had given to Cea, who had then given it to Andudo.

Feneda sat with Lydia and Cea around a fire warriors had built for them. Ostensibly they were there to give feminine company to Venturia, but Venturia had turned her nose up at all but her own two tire-women. However, Feneda was not thinking about Venturia, but about Lydia and Hywel. The Trinovante captain, esteemed for his courage by Canis himself, was so merry and handsome. If Lydia were to wed him, he would make her the kindest and most agreeable of husbands. Feneda did not doubt Hywel's feelings in the matter. He was frankly enamoured of the beautiful Roman woman. But Feneda knew Lydia had eyes for no man save Canis. And Canis was to wed Princess Cea. Even so, Feneda doubted if that would induce Lydia to wed Hywel. It was very sad. Poor Hywel. Surely he was handsome enough for any woman, and rode a horse like a wild young god.

Cea was biting on her lip more than on her food.

" It is well enough so far," she whispered to Lydia, " but where does Canis sleep until it is time for us to do our work? And with whom?"

" Cea, not with that plump chicken," murmured Lydia, who was still full of sweet relief that Canis had not found himself an irresistibly beautiful love. " You cannot think that. He would not, not even to give every last one of your people freedom and peace."

" He would, if he thought it would serve his purpose. He would shamelessly close his eyes and his mind to the fact that it would dishonour me, to whom he is truly promised. He can be an unscrupulous, heart-breaking rogue, Lydia, can he not?"

" Perhaps, when it is a means to an end, he can," said Lydia.

Canis sat with Venturia, she constantly reaching out her hands to warm them at their own fire. In courtesy, Canis had invited the Roman decurion to sup with them. It was Grud who had distributed wine among the other Romans and among the Brigantes, and it was also Grud who served wine to Venturia, Canis and the Roman officer. Canis, in his easy way, drew the Roman into companionable converse, and brought wine-dreamy talk from Venturia. They dwelt long by the fire until the wine began to lie heavily on their senses and conversation was ousted by the languid but insidious desire to sleep. The Roman officer

305

withdrew to his own place for the night, and Venturia felt only voluptuous content as Canis lifted her and carried her to her tent, where her two tire-women disrobed her and wrapped her in a warm, woollen night shift.

She lay in dreamy, befuddled languor within her coverings, waiting for Herco to come and claim her. He would take pleasure of her, and give her intense pleasure in return. He would groan and pant to find her so beautiful. She would enslave him, for was she not fair indeed of face and form, and a princess as well?

How warm, how drowsily slumbrous and how willing she felt.

*   *   *

She woke. Her head was heavy, her eyelids weighted and her body listless. There was a taste in her mouth as if all her teeth were bad. She was not concerned with wakefulness, only with a desire to prolong her inertia, but after a while she was disturbed by a vague but growing realisation of an uncomfortable strangeness instead of consoling familiarity about her surroundings. Where was she? Had there been too much indifferent wine at her mother's table last night? Her heavy lids opened wider, and the strangeness of her surroundings resolved itself into the likeness of a tent.

A tent? How was this?

It was hard to put her dulled mind to work. Enlightenment crept hand-in-hand with dragging lethargy, so that it was some time before she began to remember.

Herco! She sat up. The movement brought momentary pain to her aching head. She groaned and sank back again. She pressed her temples. Herco. Ah, he had said he would make her cold body burn, and that indeed he must have done and with a passion that had reduced her to this racked exhaustion. Yet how bitterly galling to have been left with no exciting remembrance of his kisses, his embrace and his body. Assuredly, he had been on fire for her—but oh, how unreconcilable it was to her avid senses not to know how hot his

306

fire had been, and with what ardour he had possessed her. Her coverings were loose, untidy. Yet not by this alone did Venturia know a man had lain with her. There was that which told her that her body had indisputably had knowledge of a man not an hour since. Moreover, her night robe lay discarded and she was naked beneath the coverings. Herco, if I slept so heavily because of the wine, why did you not wake me when you lay with me in the night and took pleasure again at dawn? I did not think you so devious as to cheat me of my bliss whilst you revelled in your own. I cannot remember either the beginning of any embraces or the end. Oh, laggard body, nor can I remember all that was so ardently encompassed betwixt each beginning and end.

Herco. Thief of love. Robber, trickster. You wined me and seduced me. You took my senses from me, and the night which should have been ours was only yours.

He would pay dearly for that. He would more than recompense her. In her inertia, she lay there sensuously musing on how she would exact this recompense. He was a sweet, magnificent villain. She had met none like him. She stirred at last, aware that it was bright day outside, and she called her tire-women. They did not come. She called again. It did not make her head feel better to raise her voice. Suddenly she was aware that there had only been silence since her first waking moments. She sat up, throwing off her coverings, mewing petulantly at not being attended, and making a face at the sour dryness of her mouth. Slipping on a robe, she called a third time for her tire-women. There was no answer. Angrily she dragged her heavy body upright, she licked her bottom lip, thrust aside the hanging flap of the tent, and looked out.

She screamed. It sounded in the bright day like the hoarse croaking of a lost and frightened frog.

The sky was full of white, moving clouds, the sun partially hidden; but she knew from its position that she had slept all through the night, all through the morning, and that it was now afternoon. And now there was nought to be seen but the distant road, the spreading landscape and the cloud-littered sky. No sound came to her ears, there was only ominous, quiet stillness. The splendid magnificence of her following, the waggons, the escorts, the gilded Romans, the chariots and the mounted servants of Herco, and Herco himself, all had vanished as if they had never been. All that remained in this place was herself. And a tent.

Incredulity took hold of her reeling mind.

Herco. Vanished with all else. Gone. There was nought but emptiness. It could not be, it could not. She was dreaming. She closed her eyes, then fearfully opened them again.

It was no dream. There was only herself here, standing before her tent in her night robe. She screamed again.

As the echoes died away, she heard a voice behind her.

" Ah, you are at last awake."

She swung round, and there sitting on the ground to the rear of her tent was a man. He rose to his feet and came towards her. He was a young man with long fair hair and untrimmed beard. He wore a cloak so old that it was a patch-work of many pieces. He carried the staff of a shepherd. He halted before her, leaning on his staff. He had a bluff, weatherbeaten simplicity about him, though his eyes were not unknowing, and his simplicity did not disguise his lustiness.

" Come," he said in the slow fashion of a man who did not have the quickness of speech of those who lacked no opportunity for conversation, " since you are awake, I will take you now to Calcaria, and return you to your family there—as I have been instructed. The man who decamped with you against your mother's wishes has overnight been in great repentance at abducting you. I was brought to him by one of his servants last night and he gave me a gold crown to watch over you and bring you safely home as soon as you awoke."

" What man was this?" Venturia cried hoarsely.

The simple young shepherd described him. He had not gone far with his laboured picture before Venturia knew that he spoke of Herco. She fell to the ground, she foamed and kicked and screamed. When the shepherd would have lifted her, she struck and clawed him. He grinned.

" So-ho," he said, " is this why he lost his eagerness, and desired me to return you to your family in Calcaria?"

" Fool," she raged at him, " I am daughter of Cartimandua, Queen. I am the Princess Venturia, and have been deceived, tricked and deserted by the foxiest villain in all Britain. I will have his head, I will impale him!" And she rolled about, tearing at the grass, at her robe and her hair.

" Come, girl," said the shepherd, "I will allow you may have been tricked and even deserted, but not that you are a princess. Princesses do not tumble about in the grass and spit. Rise up, and I will take you to Calcaria."

Venturia sat up, her robe soiled, rent, crumpled. Her straw-coloured hair was tangled, her mouth and throat working convulsively as she sucked in air.

" Aye, Calcaria, then," she said thickly, "and with all speed."

" It shall be as fast as our legs will take us," said the shepherd.

" Legs?" she screamed up at him. " Legs? I am to walk? Walk?"

" I will escort you, as I have been paid to and as I have promised, but I will not carry you. Come, girl, and bring what you want from the tent."

Princess Venturia flung herself back over the ground. She laughed as if no man had ever come as mirthfully to her ears as this uncouth simpleton. The sounds of her laughter were like uncontrollable bursts of hysteria, and birds rose up from bush and tree to wing a frightened way into the sky.

In the forest on the western side of the road, a Roman officer, a score of Roman soldiers, an escort of Brigante warriors, and two Brigante tire-women, lay in heavy sleep from drugged wine. Grud was mysteriously efficacious at mixing potions that took a man's senses from him for many hours. Even when they came to, they would be shamefully immobile during the hours of daylight, for all of them were naked, even the two women. Not until darkness came to clothe them, would they want to return to Calcaria—and it would be a burning but shivering business for the comely women.

It was three leagues to Calcaria. Princess Venturia was in hysterical ferment most of the way, and proved a great trial to the young shepherd, who thought far less of her in the light of day than when he had given her his protection during the night. He did not, however, mention this. Her rageful lamentations, constantly dinning his ears, were not the kind a man wanted to hear more of. He was not surprised that by the time she tottered into Calcaria, she was momentarily no longer able to wag her exhausted tongue, even to demand for the Roman prefect. While she was still swallowing and gasping, mottled of face and grimy of habit, the shepherd slipped away. He had a feeling that plump though she was, she had the spitefulness of a shrew; and he did not doubt that in the end she would take little account of the way he had brought her safely home. And perhaps her family might consider his part in the matter a little questionable. Moreover, the fact that she was out of her mind in her talk of queens and princesses might—if the family were as ungrateful as she herself was—be laid at his door.

So he slipped unobtrusively away, while Venturia tottered about hoarsely calling for Romans to take her to the prefect. He preferred the quietness of his sheep. He did not travel by road, but across country; and as he walked in tireless vigour, he hummed a song of the northern shepherds, and occasionally he grinned.

Venturia, almost prostrate, was given wine. She was in the house of the Roman prefect of Calcaria. The wine dribbled from her slack mouth. The prefect was there with his wife; but even as Venturia was about to hoarsely acquaint them with the story of Herco and his treachery, there leapt into her mind the numbing, astounding truth of the whole escapade. It so stunned her that her mouth fell agape, and was for a while unable to close it.

310

Oh, fool that she had been, not to have guessed this truth as soon as she came from her tent and saw that Herco and all else had vanished. Fool that she was, not to have realised then that it was all as she had first thought, when Herco had come in such strange fashion to her mother's house.

Herco was no Belgic man, no kinsman to Caratacus. Nor was he mortal. True, he had the image of a mortal man—but he was, of course, no mortal at all.

He was Cyantillus.

Cyantillus!

She, Princess Venturia of Brigantia, had been snatched from her mother's house and bedded by the lusty, roaming god of war, who was brother to Andrasta, goddess of victory. Only Cyantillus, as magnificently cunning as he was virile, could have contrived to possess her in this devious way. He had looked down at her from his fiery domain, had seen her beauty and her perfection, and had assumed mortal form in order to claim her. Last night he had bemused her, bewitched her and lain with her. Oh, he had lain with her in very truth, far into the night and morning. She had not been mistaken about that.

She had won the lusty god of war, and had also lost him. He had returned her to her own world, using the medium of a simple shepherd.

And even the shepherd had disappeared.

Had he been Cyantillus in yet another mortal form?

Oh, the shame, the mortification. Despite her beauty, she had—like so many others—been rejected. Some imperfection, unremarked by mere mortal men, had been discovered by Cyantillus; and had caused him to deny her a thousand years of unimaginable bliss as his consort. She could not think what that imperfection was. She could only think of the wonder of having lain with a god, and of the unendurable fact that he would not lie with her again. Why, she had not even been conscious when he had lain with her.

He was gone from her, never to return.

Venturia moaned and swooned.

311

She came to, groaning, unable to find any words that would adequately explain matters to the Romans, who worshipped other gods. The prefect, dissatisfied as he was with what he considered her inarticulate stupidity and the wholly suspicious nature of the matter, could not, however, do less than hand her over to his wife. His wife, not altogether enamoured of her either, got rid of her as quickly as she could, by seeing the bemused suffering Princess to a couch for the night.

It was well past midnight, when Venturia had at last dropped off to sleep—before her erstwhile escorts of Romans and Brigantes, and her two tire-women, returned to Calcaria to report to the prefect. They were clothed in foliage, and begged the awakened prefect not to have more than one lamp lighted. All they could tell him was that they had lain down to rest the previous night, and had known no more until they woke late in the forest that afternoon.

The prefect sent a detachment of cavalry to Eburacum the next morning. Venturia went with them. She could not contain herself on arrival, and ran screaming into the presence of Queen Cartimandua.

"I am in woe and decline! Oh, Cartimandua, it was not Herco—it was our god of war, Cyantillus. He took me from you, he snatched me from our house, he has lain with me, and I am with child!"

Venturia knew, as did all other Britons whose god of war was Cyantillus, that all women who told how the god had snatched them up and lain with them never failed to bear him a child. She babbled hysterically of what had happened, and Cartimandua was beside herself—until, having finally been able to separate facts from fancies, she realised just what had befallen her sweet lamb. At once, rage began to convulse her, so much so that her daughter's constant reiteration of how the god of war had lain all night in a tent with her became an unendurable irritation.

"Besotted child! Hold your foolish tongue. You are bemused with fantasies. This is nought to do with Cyantillus.

312

It is the work of that knavish Belgic magician. He has tricked us both."

"I am with child and will bear a godlike son," moaned Venturia.

Cartimandua boxed her daughter's ears.

"Hold your tongue, I say! With child, indeed. How can you know? Give me the plain truth of the matter, and then if I must I will surely rouse Ancastus and warriors and Romans to scorch the heels of the fox. The truth, foolish daughter, the truth."

Whatever Venturia saw as the truth, and whatever Cartimandua interpreted as the truth, there was no denying the calamitous fact that some weeks later the Queen's own physicians confirmed Venturia was indeed with child. In the end, a godlike boy child was delivered. Proudly but sadly, Venturia said he was as like Cyantillus (or Herco) as he could be. Assuredly, the child seemed out of the ordinary, as do all babes in the eyes of fond mothers—but he grew up looking remarkably like the simple but lusty young shepherd who had watched over Venturia that night, and escorted her to Calcaria the following day.

But things being what they were, and people and gods being what they are, none could truly say Venturia's son did not look like his father. What was said out of her hearing had no substance except that of everyday cynicism.

*   *   *

At the time Princess Venturia had first woken from her drugged sleep, the cavalcade, now led by Canis and Cea instead of Canis and Venturia, was many leagues away. They travelled not on the south road, but the south-west one. By the time Cartimandua and the Romans had organised a pursuit that would take them in a futile chase along the southern route from Calcaria, the Britons were already well on their way westwards. Canis, in crossing this region of Brigantia, had chosen almost the shortest breadth of Northern Britain.

313

As soon as they had disposed of Venturia, her tire-women and the Roman and Brigante escorts, all by means of Grud's doctored wine, they retraced part of their progress from Calcaria to within half a league of the town. Then they left the road to break across favourable country in a north-west direction, until they reached the road running south-west from Calcaria to Cambodunum. Here, they were a league from Calcaria. The night hid them, the darkness muffled them. Cea rode in the guise of Princess Venturia, with head and face hooded. Andudo wore the uniform of the drugged Roman decurion, and other warriors wore the uniforms of the dispossessed soldiers. Women and children rode on chariots or up behind horsed warriors, and as the Britons now owned thirteen hundred horse in all, as well as a hundred chariots and three waggons, there was room for a great many of them to ride. They travelled at a steady pace, reaching the outskirts of Cambodunum by dawn. News of the journey of Princess Venturia had reached most Roman strongholds in Brigantia, but only a few Romans turned out at this hour to salute her as the long procession rode through the town. These few gaped to see the extent and the numbers of the Princess's following. The leading Britons noisily cried, " Make way for the Princess of Brigantia and the lord Herco of Belgae." Since there were only a handful of Romans about, it seemed somewhat unnecessary to cry a way for the procession, but Canis thought it more in keeping for the proud procession to noise its way through, than for it to slink through quietly and furtively.

The clattering of iron wheels and the sound of laden horse woke many a sleeper, who cursed the interruption and stuffed fingers into ears to shut out more of it. The long cavalcade passed through entirely without incident, and went on to Mancunium. They took a rest lasting some three hours, snatching what sleep they could before going on to enter this town. At this important stronghold, the Roman legate would have pressed upon the principals the hospitality that was their due, but Canis said so much hospitality had been theirs already that more of it would be enough to confound Bacchus himself, in which case no one could say when they would reach his father's house. Upon the legate commenting that it was as well for them to know they were taking the longer not the shorter route to Aquae Sulis, Canis said, " I must avoid the latter, for it takes us through the land of the Coritani people, and I was once pledged to a princess of theirs. The fact that it came to nought was no fault of mine, but nevertheless the Coritani do not love me, and the less they see of me the happier they are."

The legate smiled. Canis, standing down from the waggon, smiled also. The legate, however, felt in courtesy bound to renew his invitation for the Briton and his betrothed to take food and wine with him and his household. When he received a further refusal, couched in the friendliest way, he forbore to delay the cavalcade longer, and saw it on its way. His eyebrows rose as he remarked its extent and its magnificence, and the bystanders gaped as much as others had. The cloaked and hooded woman on the leading waggon was the Briton he surmised as Princess Venturia, and he raised his hand in salute as she threw him the sweetest smile. Even though her face was shadowed by the hood, she should not have taken the risk, as Canis was quick to tell her; but she was a spirited Iceni princess, and in her impulsive way, so much was she her mother's daughter, she could not resist the challenge.

It did not put them at the risk it might have done, for the legate had never seen Princess Venturia.

" By fairest Cupid," he said to the prefect, as he watched the jingling army of escorts and followers, " I have been told the Princess Venturia was not one to inspire any great reaction in a discriminating man, but I will surely give the lie to this hereafter. She has the sweetest countenance and the softest brown eyes, and the smile she gave me was enough to melt Jupiter in his sternest mood. By his bride and her dowry, the Belgic man will be as rich as any barbarian I know."

" I have long discounted rumour as being the bearer of truth," said the prefect.

They were not to know then that had they heeded what

315

rumour put about concerning the plump daughter of Cartimandua, and questioned why the hooded maid looked so
unlike all they had heard of Venturia, they would have escaped
the screaming wrath of both the Queen and her daughter. The
simple, generous acceptance of what seems only a pleasant
surprise, can create the most embarrassing burdens for a man.
It did occur to the legate and his prefect that the number of
men, women, maids and children gave an uncommonly
crowded look to the procession. It seemed to be more like a
tribal caravan than a following. But they gave this aspect little
attention, save that of detached curiosity, and thought it must
be typically traditional of cumbersome barbarian custom.
They saw no Roman escorts, as Andudo and the warriors had
by now discarded their Roman uniforms.

For the Roman legate, then, there seemed nought to cloud
the issue. It was merely the barbarians intent on making the
journey a memorable one for the Belgic man and his betrothed.
Moreover, in this part of Northern Britain few Romans had
been directly affected by the bitter affair between Paullinus
and the surviving people of Boadicea. They had been remote
from it.

In this way Canis and Cea and all their followers passed
safely through the great stronghold of Mancunium, and proceeded on their way to Deva, which was some fifteen leagues
from Mancunium. They still carried Julian with them. His
ankle was troublesome and obstinate; but to all suggestions
that he be returned in some way to Paullinus, he turned a
deaf ear. Cyella suspected he travelled with them because he
was far more concerned about his sister Lydia than himself.
She could have told him that the only man whose concern
Lydia coveted was Canis. Julian would have replied that this
was the reason for his own concern.

They passed all minor Roman outposts without halt or
suspicion, although by this time Cartimandua, in fury and
rage, was hotfoot in pursuit with Brigante warriors and Roman
soldiers. Unfortunately for Cartimandua, she was hotfoot on
the wrong road—that which led south from Calcaria, that

which had seen her daughter's greatest mortification. It was not until she reached Legiolium that the perspiring, spitting, purple-faced Queen suspected the Belgic villain had outfoxed her again. The Romans there assured her that he and his followers had not passed through Legiolium, had not even entered the place. Cartimandua returned to Calcaria, and there word came that the cavalcade was travelling south-west. She stormed out to take that road, but was far too late; and when she finally realised that the man who called himself Herco had slipped her, she writhed in demented fury for many days. She threw the leader of the warriors who had provided escort for her daughter into a wild place where hornets' nests hung amid trees like dark clouds, and the issuing clouds of vicious insects stung him to death.

Not even Ancastus could give her solace. This did not seem to greatly perturb Ancastus. The vigorous, flamboyant Brigante chieftain went about with a strangely cheerful grin on his face.

As for poor Venturia, she was prostrate. She spent each night in lamentation and woe, each day in groaning despair. She would never again meet such a man as Cyantillus in the mortal guise of Herco. And it was all very well for Cyantillus. He had had joy of her beauty. She could not even claim the slightest memory of his godlike embraces that night. Never would she know the rapture she had so anticipated, for the god did not visit any woman twice, however beautiful her shape, however slight her unremarked imperfection.

Poor Venturia.

13

The Britons were resting five leagues from Deva. They had long since passed the bend of the great river that was like the long, wide tongue of the mighty ocean beyond, and their journey had been as much without hindrance or incident as they could have wished. True, Cea in pale but resolute necessity, had hanged a man for molesting a woman one night, and Canis had hanged another for incurable thievery. But these incidents had nought to do with Romans. Canis had seen them safely through every stronghold, and past every outpost; and Lydia marvelled at the ease with which his slyly agreeable tongue and his diverting good humour induced every Roman, soldier or official, to see them cheerfully on their way.

They had finally left the road, for it would be courting discovery and disaster to attempt to pass through Deva. Deva was the northernmost gateway to the mountains; and the Romans there, as at all western approaches, would be looking for Canis and his Britons. So they had left the road, and from this point on they would be forced to make their way across country which, though wild and difficult, contained little of the immense forest areas they loved. Now the rest of their journey would be slow, arduous and dangerous. Paullinus would be more than ordinarily alert, for the complete disappearance of the Britons since the escape of Lydia would have fired every bitter nerve in his body; and undoubtedly he would have warned every stronghold in the west to watch for the emergence of Canis and his followers at any point and at any time.

Some distance from the road they rested, they ate and they surveyed the wildness of the country before them. To Lydia it was greener than green, a spreading panorama of hills and lowlands, of soundless, undisturbed verdancy. How lush and beautiful was her adopted land, how soft its mists and its summer rain. It was utterly without the harshness of barren brown, sun-scorched rock and burnt scrub. Here the vista was one of deep, changing greens, of hazy undulations, of soft white clouds merging with vague, transient horizons.

"Canis, is this our land, is this where we will build our new kingdom?"

"Not here, or even there, Lydia. Within any part of this region we would still be accessible to Paullinus. We shall travel due south for a space, and then turn west. It is west of this region that the mountains lie. Can you not see them?"

"I can only see a vast greenness."

"Lift your head higher and look. Look hard enough and long enough, and the mountains will come to you."

Lydia lifted her eyes to far distant clouds. Their whiteness was broken by palest blue. She held her gaze, and gradually they came to her, out of the clouds and hanging from clouds, bluely-white peaks. She drew a deep breath. There they were, at a distance that seemed infinite, the peaks of the mountains that would harbour them and give them security. There dwelt the fierce Deceangi and Ordovices, people whom the Romans could not contain or subdue because of those mountains. It was in far Mona, beyond those mountains, that Paullinus had conducted his campaign to finally crush the power of the Druids; but though he conquered lowlands and valleys, he could not conquer the mountains. Within the lowlands and the valleys, he maintained his communications; but always the Deceangi of the northern heights and the Ordovices of the middle heights constituted a threat to any complete Roman overlordship of the west.

Cea was breathless, joyful.

"Oh, it will be a wild, sweet land—with room for us, and more."

"If the Deceangi do not argue our intrusion too contentiously," said Canis.

319

"They are a fearsome people," said Grud, "and get their pleasure from denying others, rather than placating them."

"Yet we have fought Romans as they have fought them," said Canis, "and they will know of Boadicea, and how she won great victories. Though that may not placate them, it may mean they will consider the wisdom of not wholly denying us. In any event, it is the mountains which will swallow us, not the Deceangi."

"Does this mean we will not have security, that there will always be some strife or battle?" asked Lydia a little unhappily.

"Lydia," said Cea sweetly, "it only means that Canis is to be in as much conceit concerning the Deceangi, as he is with Romans."

"But will we always be lying at night in fear of what the morning will bring?" persisted Lydia.

"No, sweet Roman," said Canis, "not when we have presented the Deceangi with good argument."

For his tender naming of Lydia, Cea administered a cruel pinch and hissed "Trifler!" in his ear.

"Where will we make our kingdom?" asked Lydia, possessive in her adoption of the cause of the Britons.

"Within the friendliest mountains we can find," said Canis.

"The name of the Queen my mother," said Cea wistfully, "was writ upon the face of the sun, in the waters of the river and the mist of the mountains. So some part of the mountains belongs to us, and we will build our kingdom strong and enduring. Then what will we have to fear, with Canis our kingly lord?"

"Only the consequences of my conceit," said Canis.

Cea laughed merrily, but Lydia felt sudden pain, for when they came to their new land and established possession, Canis would at last wed Cea; and each night, while she herself lay lonely and yearning, he would be with Cea. Lydia did not know how she would endure this. It would be mental anguish and physical pain. But she would have to endure, for she could not exist in any world but his, she could only live where he was within her sight each day.

Caleda and Bergotix had travelled with the Britons, Bergotix happily, Caleda in wonder at herself. As they gazed now at what lay before them, Caleda said, " I doubt that where we are going will be like Brigantia in any way."

" Woman," said Bergotix, " did we not know that from the beginning?"

" Will it content you, husband?"

" Aye, it will," said Bergotix, " for I am a man who fought for Queen Boadicea, and worked in my dispossessed fields for Queen Cartimandua, and I know what sets a man down and what raises him up. Yet I would be less content if I did not have you to argue my ears off, Caleda."

" I cannot believe I am here," said Caleda, " but I am. This Canis has a strange, compelling way of divorcing a woman from her hearth."

" He did not compel us," said Bergotix, for whom vigorous life had begun again, " it was our wish."

" Bergotix, husband," said Caleda with a smile, " he came to us, we saw him and lo, foolishly and without thinking, we went with him. But I am not in any regret, I am only in some wonder at myself, for as poor as any woman's hearth is, it is her home."

" I will build you a broader, grander, greater hearth," said Bergotix.

" Aye, but only when you are not limping into some conflict or argument, behind your man of ten thousand brassy voices," said Caleda. The wind was light, it stirred her coppery hair with the gentlest fingers, yet the effect was sufficient to bring a ripple of maidenly youthfulness to her serenity.

" Would that I were a hard enough man to put salt upon your tongue," said Bergotix, " for what Canis would do to you if he could hear you, I know not."

" I will tell him what I have just said about him, and I know he will only laugh," said Caleda. " Bergotix, is it not a

L   321

country to make you blink? It is not in the least like Brigantia."

"So you have already said."

That day the Britons began their difficult journey south into the land of the Cornovii. It was gorged where rivers ran turbulent and deep, and the way was difficult since perforce they had to travel where few others did or would. They had to clear traverses for the chariots and waggons, these laden with all they could not easily carry, as well as with the precious flour. Old men groaned and widows cast wistful glances at warriors, that they might prevail on them to look to babes and small children in difficult places. There were, however, few widows who by now could say they lacked the help and comfort a man could give them. Indeed, this was so much the case that more than one widow was looking towards the time when new babes would be born. Canis, understanding of women, was not inclined to have any of them own a new babe but no husband.

"Wrekin," he said to a warrior one evening, as the Britons lay encamped within the high wooded bank of a stream, "Dinylla is with child. No matter now, for this is not the time, but when we reach the mountains you shall take her to wife. A woman fit to give you joy is fit to be wife, regardless of all else. Is this not so with you and Dinylla?"

"Aye, lord, it is," said Wrekin, a young veteran, "and I am willing, but Dinylla is not. Some women have a strange pride."

Canis told him to fetch Dinylla, and he did so. She was more than comely, even though—as was the case with so many of them—her tunic and cloak grew shabbier each day. She did not hang her head, but looked Canis in the eye.

"Dinylla, why are you too proud to take Wrekin?"

"It is not my pride, but my lack of all else," she said. "I have one child, and he is all I have. See, I clothe myself in rags—not because of my pride, but because of my modesty. If I had pride, I would not wear such things, but rather go naked. Wrekin is brave warrior. Where is my dowry? Shall I

322

go to him clad in rags, and with nought but a child fathered by another warrior who is now dead?"

"Who is the father of the child you carry now, Dinylla?" She flushed.

"It is Wrekin," she said, "for I have not lain with any other man, lord, nor would I."

"Then you shall wed Wrekin, and bring to him the sweetest dowry of all, his own babe. Nor is it true you have nought else save your present child and your rags. You have your own part of all we have—horse, chariots, gold and flour—as does each one of us. You are as rich or as poor as all of us, Dinylla."

"Lord," said Dinylla, "some say you are cruel, some say you are unforgiving, and some say you are compassionate. Perhaps you are all of these things, but I know no woman who does not love you. I will happily wed Wrekin." And she went down on one knee to Canis, took his hand and pressed it to her forehead in the Iceni gesture of fealty.

"I am no prince," said Canis.

"You were Queen Boadicea's general and her prince, and you are mine also," said Dinylla. She rose, she saw Wrekin, she hesitated; and then ran into his arms and wept a little on his shoulder.

In similar fashion did Canis deal with many of the problems concerning his warriors, who had cleaved to widows or other women in a way to conceive children. Yet where there was persistent obstinacy in refusal to wed—either on the part of the man, or woman, or both—he did not press the matter beyond reasonable logic. For he himself had fathered Lydia's child, and had not wed her. He merely did what he could to ensure life was not harder for a woman than it already was, for his warriors, owning a reckless, lusty virility, were inclined to be promiscuous and irresponsible.

They journeyed on, sometimes covering no more than a league in one day, so trackless and hazardous were certain stages of their march. They forded shallow streams and deep rivers, unloading the waggons and carrying their possessions and their sacks of flour high above swirling waters. But day by day they grew happier, sturdier, stronger. There were few who ailed. And for those who did, there were always the vile potions mixed by Grud. It was far better not to ail. Occasionally the old men grumbled in the way they do, saying that if the journey became any worse they might as well return to the Romans, who might deal offhandedly with the aged, but never walked them to death.

Princess Cea, fording a river astride her horse, the animal stepping gingerly as the water deepened, laughed to see an old man clinging determinedly to her mount's tail and spitting his grumbles into the water.

"Up, old one," she said, "or you will drink the river dry."

"So much the better for those who follow," wetly panted the old one, "though I did not think I would be used to help those young enough to help themselves."

Julian, his ankle troubling him no longer, stood calf-deep in the water, shouting at women and children hesitating on the bank. Horses were plunging in, the riders taking up behind them those women and children who would follow, where they clung in excitement or fear or confidence.

"Up with you, all who can find mounts," he shouted, "and in with all others, for by any gods who deal in cleanliness, there is nought these gentle waters will do to any of you that will not be for the better. In with you. The fish bite only the tenderest flesh, and I will wager yours is tougher than any."

The brunt of his good-tempered sarcasm was borne mainly by the elements, for most of his words were lost amid the noise and the splashing. Cyella, riding a horse with a child clinging behind her, put her mount into the water and followed in the wake of others. In the middle of the broad river, the animals were swimming, and so were the more fearless of the men and women. There was a great deal of shouting, blowing and laughter. A line of mounted warriors stretched from bank to bank, facing the tide and watching for any who lost their feet. Other warriors, men and maids both, swam on all sides of the three rafted waggons and the racing chariots. The latter, though weighted by their iron- or brass-bound wheels, were light enough to be forded across when supported by the warriors.

"Tribune," said Cyella as she came abreast of Julian, "you give strangely friendly persuasion to your enemies."

"On with you," said Julian, smiting the rump of her horse. He thought her not unlike a bright warrior maid herself, as she sat astride her mount with her long naked legs showing smooth and brown below her shamelessly short tunic. Her eyes flashed him a teasing glance, and her corn-coloured hair blew in fine strands about her face. "On with you," he said again.

"Do not sink, tribune," she said as she went on into deeper water, "it can be a grievously damp end for the most ordinary man, and a dismal one for a proud Roman."

There was often a little bite in her words.

Canis, with Lydia, Grud and Feneda, was last to cross. Feneda, the warrior maid, had become greatly attached to Lydia, though it was Hywel she worried about. Lydia was up behind Canis, Feneda up behind Grud, and Canis led a third horse. Every moment that enabled Lydia to be physically close to her Briton, as now, when she had her arms around his waist, was bitter-sweet to her.

Canis brought the third horse to Julian.

"Here is a sturdy fourlegs," he said to the Roman, "and you are free to go any way you wish from here."

"In this region," said Julian, "to be free is to be foolish. The Cornovii will murder me for my kirtle. Lydia, where is your child?"

"Hywel has taken her," said Lydia.

"Hywel is not her mother," said Julian, showering spray as he mounted. He went across with them. "Nor is Hywel her father," he said, above the noisy flow of the river. Lydia coloured. Canis only smiled. As to Hywel, the infatuation of the Trinovante captain for Lydia was common knowledge by now. She did not have the heart to discourage him too unkindly. "Dilwys," went on Julian, "has only one father, and

325

that father cannot be changed simply by handing the babe from arm to arm."

That at least Lydia agreed with.

They reached the shallows and splashed their way out. As Canis helped Lydia to dismount, he said in a matter-of-fact way, " Julian is growing into an old woman and may yet outdo Grud in his talent for muttering."

"You have talents of your own," said Julian, " one of which has turned my high-born sister into a ragged wench. Behold your handiwork, Briton."

Lydia stood on the bank, her short, worn tunic revealing tanned legs and thighs wet from the river. Thoughtfully Canis regarded her. Where was the wench? Patched and shabby though her garment was, it did not alter the fact that she was inescapably herself, a woman of dark, green-eyed beauty, her skin honeyed, her form shapely. Indeed, the brevity and poverty of her attire only seemed to emphasise the perfection of her figure and the vivid qualities of her looks. Pink crept warmly into her face at the intentness of the Briton's regard, and her eyes were drawn compulsively to his. All about them were the people, all was clamour and commotion as the chariots and waggons were manhandled up the bank to the assembly point, laughing children scrambling on to the vehicles. And in spite of the fact that Julian was also there, surveying her and Canis in some irony, for a moment Lydia felt the world breathed only for the two of them. Canis's grey eyes were warm, smiling, and almost caressing; and it made the cloudy day brilliant for her. Her whole body seemed bathed by that brilliance, as if she had slipped enchanted into the embracing foam of a sunlit sea.

It was a brief moment of magic for her, a moment when his eyes spoke a clear, unmistakable message of endearment. It told her that even though he was bound to Cea, he would not wed the Princess, not when it was herself he loved. He was the only man she herself could love, the only man great enough to be overlord of all Britain. He could be cruel, as when he had destroyed her brother's army and reputation;

but what was that against his courage and his infinite capacity for leadership? There was no other man like him.

Oblivious of all else, she impulsively put out her hand. He took it and pulled her upwards over the loose, shelving bank.

"Cosset Cea if you must," she whispered, "but deny me no more, for you know I am part of you, as you are of me."

"Lydia," he said, and if there was laughter in his eyes it did not lack affection, "do you know why Grud dared not let you die of the burning sickness?"

"It was because he holds me in gentle regard."

"It was because he knew that if he did let you die I would have hanged him."

Julian watched them. He could not hear what they said above the commotion, but he could see Lydia's face. It was wholly blissful. He shook his head ruefully, unable to understand the completeness of her devotion to a man who, because of his unchangeable destiny, could bring his sister no true joy. She knew this, yet was as obstinate and obsessive in her love for Canis as she had been in her hate.

Julian did not clearly know why he continued to accompany the Britons. He was healed of his wound, and there was only an occasional ache in his ankle. He was free to go his own way, as Canis had said. Though he had a great liking for the Briton, and a generous sympathy for Cea and her migrating people, his life had long been dedicated to the glory and advancement of Rome. But not to the Rome represented by the bitter harshness of Paullinus. That he could not stomach. Perhaps he went with the Britons because he could, as a soldier, serve Paullinus only with rigid obedience. He could not serve him with his heart. To Julian, service was a matter of strict code and true heart; and if the heart rejected its part, where was the satisfaction, where was the inspiration or the pleasure? Perhaps he would return to a Roman environment only when Paullinus had been recalled.

Aye, that was the reason why he still went with the Britons. There was Lydia, of course.

And there was also Cyella, who had once been fair but

mettlesome, and was now radiantly brown and sweetly teasing. She called him tribune, and at times had a strange way of keeping her distance; and at other times she had her own way of fussing over him.

" Tribune, you will never lose the ache in your ankle unless you keep it tightly bound. Sit there and I will see to it for you."

" It is well enough. Cyella, some people may want you as a mother—I do not."

" That is to say I am an old woman, is it not?"

" You are a very young one."

Unpredictably (in the fashion of most young women) she was incensed at that.

" And you are a very old tribune, and as full of the grumps as one so old he has no teeth left to chew on his meat."

And she went from him with a fine show of disdain.

The Britons eventually turned west and forded another river at a point four leagues south of Deva, having crossed the road from Deva to Viroconium in the darkness of a sharp autumnal night. They had heard Roman patrols on that road; and had lain soundless and invisible, all three thousand of them, in bush and thicket, within a league of a Cornovii encampment to the east. They had lain and waited, making no move until the moonless world was wrapped in the embrace of quiet, friendly night. And then waggons, chariots and three thousand people had moved so cautiously, with every axle heavily greased by animal fat, that their going in the darkness was only a soft, shuffling murmur. Having crossed the road, they continued on until they reached the river in the light of day; and there they rested before fording the river at sunset.

That night they camped in a wood flanking a tributary of the river. There was a threat of rain, the air damp and cold. Autumn had overtaken them; but the mountains which had seemed no nearer day after day, no matter how much progress they had made, were suddenly looming, lofty giants of stone and ice.

The Britons improvised what shelter they could for women

328

and children, in case the night sky opened and burst; and they built discreet fires within screened coverts to cook their meal. They had found game in plenty most days. Cyella, as always, cooked Julian's supper of meat, the meat accompanied by bread made from their flour. Julian marvelled at the ability of the Britons to so provide for themselves when each fire on each night was a hazard in itself.

Cyella rose from the small warm fire that Andudo had built for her, and took Julian's food up on a platter. She turned to go to him, only to find the tribune sitting on a flat boulder nearby. She had not heard him come, she had been absorbed; and such sounds as he had made had only been like murmurs amid a thousand others in their camp.

" Oh," she said, " you should not do that."

" I am merely sitting," said Julian, observing her in the glow of the fire.

" You should not creep upon me," she said.

" Nor did I. I arrived—and having arrived, I sat."

" I thought you with Lydia. Here is your food." She had grown in the months she had been with the Britons; her slim figure had become shapelier, her fair hair longer, her legs and thighs smoothly, strongly supple in the tunic she wore like all other maids. Her one robe she only wore when it was cold enough to bring shivers, for she was preserving it in the hope that one day it would adorn her freshly and prettily. What other robes she had brought with her she had given to women who lacked warm wool.

Julian took the food, thanked her, then observed it would be as well for him to cook for himself in the future, since he already owed her more than enough. Cyella thought little of that, and observed in her turn that if he meant her cooking sat heavily on his stomach, he need not fear to say so. Julian amiably advised her that he had only meant that he must in some way earn what he ate.

" Men do not cook when there are women about," said Cyella, " and what man is there who can stir a pot without spilling it into the fire?"

329

"Each of us to his own survival," said Julian, "and I cannot let you do for me what I should do for myself."

Cyella looked critically at the fire, as if she found an offensive fault in it. She then took up her own platter of food, seated herself and said, " I never thought to hear such foolishness from you, tribune. Saving only Canis, I know not any man—"

"Ah, Canis," interrupted Julian. "Let him be to you mightier than all the gods if it pleases you, but no more of him to me. I wonder he does not groan as loudly as Atlas under the weight of adulation thrust upon him."

" Tribune," said Cyella, " what is it that irks you so much? It is not Canis, for he is a man you love well. And he has a great regard for you. If he could, he would put you in Caesar's place. He is not the reason for your disgruntlement."

" Am I not heavily burdened with a wayward, obstinate sister?"

" Nor is it sweet Lydia. She could never be happy if you took her from—if you took her from us. If you did so, you would come to be burdened with your conscience. What is it that irks you?"

" Myself," said Julian. He did not sound irked, and was in fact only soberly reflective. About them was the hum of voices, the whispered laughter of women, and occasionally the sound of softly plaintive child. Warriors patrolled the outskirts of the camp—for never, by day or by night, were the Britons less than alert.

" So," said Cyella, " it is yourself, then. And why not? Assuredly, here you are, aged and bent, sore and suffering, your wit degenerating and your gloom flourishing. I am in sorrow for you, tribune, for truly any man who is beset by all these things can immerse himself only in his own melancholy."

"You are an ungovernable impudence," said Julian, " but readily forgiven, as is any unhibited child."

Cyella uttered a stifled exclamation of fury. She was not given to temper, only to fearless frankness; but now her anger

330

was such that she trembled with it. Julian ate his food without savouring it. He was aware of how he had offended her.

"Come," he said, "I did not mean that unkindly. Forgive me. I cannot leave you thinking I was only notable for my graceless tongue. Without you, Cyella, I would have been a cripple. See, on my heart, you are no child—but a true sweet maid of Britain, and I swear there are none fairer."

"Why do you speak of leaving?" she asked quietly, putting her own food down. Hers had no flavour, either.

"I belong to Rome, Cyella."

"Aye, and Paullinus made you a tribune, so you are prouder Roman than ever."

"I am not disastrously proud, Cyella. It is only that soon or late I must return to my own people."

Cyella rose and rushed away into the darkness. He followed; and came up with her as she flung herself down at the foot of a tree, embraced it and sobbed.

"Cyella." He spoke gently. Until today he had not known, nor had he wished to admit, the full extent of his feelings. He had always supposed he would take a wife eventually, but had never thought she would be other than Roman—and in justice to the name of his house, a high-born one at that. He was understanding of Britons, without ever losing his conviction that the true concept of a strong, united world was one wholly governed by Rome. He shared this conviction with most other Romans, except that he conceived a government dedicated to administering the wisest laws and the truest justice within the framework of unbreachable security. There was a tendency for nations constantly to war with each other. If all nations were under the government of Rome, then Rome would keep them from each other's throats. He could not agree with Romans who thought in terms of conquest and power. He could agree that it was necessary to conquer first; but then should come administration of wisdom and tolerance, so that in time the conquered would accept that the advantages of being the provincial subjects of Rome outweighed all else.

331

He had been sad and bitter about that which caused Boadicea to turn on Rome, and he could not forget the proud, tragic Queen. However, despite his love for the country in which he had spent so many years, he had never thought a maid of Britain would so engage his affections as to make him uneasy about what was right for a patrician, and what was not. Originally he had regarded Cyella only as an impulsive young girl, fair to look on. She was no more than eighteen, and had the high-mindedness of proud youth. But he had come to realise she was no adolescent. She was an extremely intelligent young woman, and her fair beauty took his eye more each day.

He had sought to ignore the implications of his growing awareness of her.

He was a patrician, his antecedents as proud as any.

He would be expected to wed a Roman woman of his own class.

But his awareness of Cyella now was impossible to put aside. What was she saying through her tears?

" I am proud also, tribune, but not as proud as you are."

Cyella also had problems. When she had first seen Julian in the house of Classicianus, she had thought him quite the most handsome and personable of men. Only the fact that he was a Roman constrained her in her attitude towards him. She was Iceni, and Romans had almost exterminated her people.

But Julian was not like other Romans; and it became harder each day to think of him in the same terms as those who had destroyed her Queen and her nation, and slain her mother. Since by reason of his defeat and his hurt, Julian had been compelled to live with the Britons, and since she was the one who tended him, her awareness of him had become sensitive. He was the one she looked first for each morning, his the smile that most affected her. And the love she had for him disturbed her and made her unhappy, for it was not a tranquil love. It was a love that craved his. But he was a Roman and more than that. He was of the patrician class, and the patrician class considered themselves only a few steps

332

down from their gods. For all his kindness, she did not think Julian would look seriously upon any maid, however proud her own family, whom Romans would consider barbarian. Cyella did not regard herself as barbarian, but Rome did. Julian would never return her love. Or at least never commit himself to her, except in the one way acceptable to him and quite unacceptable to her. She would not give herself to any man except as his wife.

But to hear him say he was returning to his own people and was leaving her, this she could not understand. Why must he go? He was out of all favour with Paullinus, and the Governor would be hard on him for allowing Canis to defeat him, and also because of Lydia. Surely Julian could not prefer disgrace to the sweetness of roving freedom? But men were like that. It was always to do with honour or dishonour, glory or death. That was nothing to do with sweetness, only with stupidity. It was no wonder she wept.

" I am not going tonight, Cyella, or even tomorrow," said Julian. " I said what I said because while you are of Britain, I am of Rome. Must you weep and distress me?"

" Do not concern yourself with me, tribune. Leave me. It is not to be supposed that my tears should affect anyone as high as you."

" Cyella, even weeping you own a mettlesome tongue." Julian smiled, then stooped and lifted her to her feet. The night was not so dark that he could not see her tears. They made her look mistily lovely. " Oh, the gods," he said, " you are an endearing chit. And if you are of Britain and I am of Rome, what of it? I have lost my heart to you, and that is the sum of it."

" Tribune?" she said faintly, her hold on her emotions very tenuous.

" Never did I think to lose sleep on account of the daughter of an Iceni chieftain. Sweet witch that you are, you know full well what irked me. What else but my weakness for your bright eyes and scornful voice? If I go, how could I manage without you? I cannot, as you say, even stir a pot."

333

Cyella's tears trembled hugely. Breathlessly she said, "Is this to humour me, because I am weeping? Oh, do not humour me, but say only what is true."

"Have you no love for me, Cyella?" Julian's hands were on her shoulders, his smile tender. "I have a great deal for you."

"Oh," whispered Cyella, drowning in a sea of warm, gushing bliss, "you have been in my heart since we first met, and it has been so hard to hide my love."

He drew her close then, and the sweetest sensations attacked Cyella—so much so that she hid her hot face in his shoulder.

"When I go, wherever I go," said Julian, "I will take you with me and wed you, though only with your father's consent, which I will have, I vow. And with your own consent, which I will have also, or kiss it out of you. Will you wed me, Cyella?"

"Oh, a hundred times," breathed Cyella, "for though I have told myself I could not and would not wed a Roman, I have also told myself it would be foolish beyond anything to commit myself unyieldingly to such a sentiment. Am I truly to be your wife?"

"I know of no other way of taking a wife but truly." Julian's laugh was warm. "I will have you, Cyella, for since you are the most endearing of maids, will you not also be the most endearing of wives?"

"Oh, I am quite without words," she said.

"Quite without any?"

"I am so happy, you see," she said, at which he did what he had long wanted to. He kissed her soft, willing mouth, and her speechless happiness flowered into a thousand words of joy—except that all remained unspoken, because each imprisoning kiss was only the forerunner of another.

It rained that night. The Britons, used to physical discomfort, contrived what shelter and coverings they could, and were not unduly disturbed by the night's wetness. Feneda woke up to find the rain falling on her feet. She tucked them up, wondered if Hywel had wet feet too, smiled and went to sleep again.

Bergotix awoke. He lay with Caleda under a covering of interlaced branches. A raindrop hit his nose. He grinned sleepily, he turned to the warmth of his wife. She was a comforting shape on a night like this. She had a way of disputing confusingly with a man, but who would change her for another? Not he.

Cyella awoke. The rain pattered heavily on her shelter. She thought of Julian, his warm voice and his imprisoning kisses, and she dreamed herself into sweet sleep again.

Lydia's eyes opened. Perhaps the rain had awakened her too, but she was unaware of it. She was conscious only of the all too familiar ache and hunger in her body. They were the symptoms of a need that made her burn. If he were only there, with her, close to her, her hunger would be a sweetness. Did he never realise her need? He might count himself as a reasonably honourable man in respect of Cea, but did any man have to be quite so reasonable?

Had she mistaken what lay behind the look he had given her by the river? Was she loved? If so why, on a night like this, when every body needed the warmth of another, did he not come and warm hers? Why did he leave her aching and hungry?

It was a while before sleep reclaimed her, but when it did it brought the dreams that made her slumbrously sigh. The rain fell and smote her shelter wetly and loudly, but Lydia slept in bliss.

The sky was clear by morning, the air sharp and fresh.

Lydia laughed in amazement and delight when Julian came to her with the news of his betrothal to Cyella, which Andudo, because of the earnest appeal on his daughter's face, had already countenanced, though not without sadness. He had lost his wife because of Romans; it was hard to lose his daughter also.

But Lydia was truly delighted. She flung her arms around her brother and kissed him. Cyella, for all her fearlessness, had

335

been much too shy to accompany him on this occasion; and had pressed him to tell Lydia herself, praying that his sister would send word that she was wholly sympathetic. Julian had said, though good-humouredly enough, that his sister's own position was too vulnerable for her to dispense either condescension or criticism. There was no need for Cyella to worry, he had said. Nor was there.

"Julian, you are above anything in this accomplishment," cried Lydia, "for Cyella is the sweetest maid, and will make you a wife you will be proud of. Aye, more of a true wife than any haughty Roman woman. But you are deserving of her, and I am as happy for her as for you. You are a better Roman than all others I have known. I have never said so until now, but I am so proud that on a day when all other Romans were cruelly mocking her, you gave Queen Boadicea your cloak in such brave compassion. Never will Canis forget this, and never will I. But there, I will kiss you again to show you I love you and understand much more of you now than I did when I was a haughty Roman myself." And she did kiss him again. Julian had never felt closer to his sister than he did then. He lifted her chin, and looked into swimming green eyes. She was his own sister, but he caught his breath at the matchless, vivid beauty she had about her this fresh morning.

"Lydia, each to our own destiny, but what is yours?"

The paleness of her illness had long vanished, she was honey-brown again and with strange brightness in her eyes.

"To be with Canis. Though he weds Cea in the end," she said, "yet I have my own joy, my own moments. I am his beloved. I know it. He cannot deny me, and in my own moments there will be all I desire of life. I know that also."

"And in other moments," said Julian, "there will be only torment."

"I am dear to him," she said, "and will not ask for more."

She was as blind in her love as she had been in her hate. She would not otherwise have compromised on so heart-rending a matter. How strange were the gods, he mused to himself, for they owned perversities far more incomprehensible

336

than the perversities of the most changeable mortals. How perversely they had dealt with his sister, endowing her as a young woman with such unlovable traits that she had made Boadicea's captured general her slave after the Queen's defeat. In truly godlike incomprehensibility, they had then tormented her by making her conceive such an intense love for this Canis that she had given up her house and her wealth and followed him into his wilderness.

Julian was not sure, however, whether he could put all of it down to the perversities of the gods, and said to her, " Lydia, you are too much of a woman for my understanding."

She would have willingly argued that with him, but an interruption came. Into the camp, where the Britons were making ready to depart, burst two mounted warriors. They leapt from horse and ran to Canis, who was with Cea.

" Romans! "

Lydia's heart sank. She looked in anguish at Julian, and saw that he was unhappy too.

The warriors reported that Roman infantry were swarming across the line of the Britons' intended march. Canis had chosen country rugged and heavy which would afford them some cover, and also a route which would keep them clear of all known encampments—a usual precaution. The presence of Romans ahead of them now did not surprise him. They could not expect to avoid them forever in their laboured, lengthy journey. It had only been a question of time before they were called on to fight again. Troops of the 14th Legion were in this area, but how many their commander could concentrate against the Britons in an emergency, Canis did not know.

He had the evening before reconnoitred the area in front of them, as he always did each time they made camp. He had ridden over it with Andudo and Hywel. He had picked the site on which to fight in the event of any brush with Romans. Those whom the warriors had sighted were infantry from Deva, with a few cavalry. A man who had marched and fought with Roman legions in Gaul, who had crushed them as Boadicea's

337

general, he acted swiftly now, despatching a force of four hundred warriors towards the oncoming Romans. They were to march quickly, but as soon as they sighted the enemy, they were to turn and retreat in ostensible panic to the place Canis had selected for battle. Andudo was to lead them, for Andudo knew the place. And no one followed instructions better than the veteran Iceni chieftain.

On the battle site, Canis and the rest of the warriors would await their retreating comrades. The latter would bring the pursuing Romans with them—though how many Romans there would be was in the lap of fortune. The two scouting warriors had reported that it was impossible to judge their strength, though they did not think the numbers too formidable. It would take them, they thought, an hour to reach this particular area. The Britons themselves were not inconsiderable; they could now mount twelve hundred horse, and call upon eight hundred foot warriors. They also had one hundred chariots, a gift from the duped Queen Cartimandua. Given reasonable odds, Canis hoped to destroy the Romans with minimum loss to his own forces, as was his way. Every warrior gave strength to the cause of Princess Cea, and he would not let any die needlessly.

After the four hundred decoy Britons had marched out, all the other Britons marched too, including the women, the children and the old ones, who were carried in the waggons or up behind mounted warriors.

The four hundred marched apace. The country was a rolling wildness of unihabited green, shallow hills and undulating depressions visible on all sides. Evergreens climbed slopes, and deciduous trees showed the turning colours of autumn. White clouds moved ponderously across the sky, and at times the sun came out to blink brightly. In half an hour, the decoy Britons sighted the Romans. There were a thousand and more of them, a small body of cavalry scouting for them. They had been moving all ways, but the general line of advance was eastwards. Someone had laid information, Andudo did not doubt. There was no mistaking the martial glitter of the Romans. The Britons halted, then milled about in alarm and disorder. The clouds rolled back from the sun, trumpets brayed, eagles were hoisted, and the pursuit was on, led by the troop of cavalry. The Britons turned and retreated in haste. The Roman cavalry rode apace —not to come up with the scampering Britons, but to keep them in sight. The Roman infantry formed to march in columns, and at their famed trot. It was not easy over the undulating ground, but the trot was rhythmic for all that.

The Britons, going pell-mell, scattered untidily over wide stretches; and bunched as they poured between converging hills. Andudo roared at men to maintain their semblance of panic and disorder. They tumbled over the slopes of hills, tripped each other each time they bunched, spilled outwards in running confusion when the terrain widened. The cavalry closed up, marking their panic, cantering a hundred paces behind them.

Suddenly at a distance in front of the fleeing Britons, three lumbering waggons appeared. Around and behind them walked women and children, and not just a score or two, but several hundred. The Roman cavalry scouts squinted, seeing them as a moving mass about their waggons. They were obviously travelling westwards in the wake of the warriors who had been marching ahead, but who were now doubling back. The Romans did not need an oracle to tell them these were the warriors and people of Canis.

One cavalryman galloped back to the oncoming infantry. The others cantered on, watching the retreating warriors haring towards the distant waggons. The waggons pulled up. The mass of women and children, dark amid the green of the undulating tors and depressions, seemed to flow and surge around the stationary vehicles. The Romans heard the running warriors shouting, heard the women shriek. They broke away from the waggons; and with the children began to stream back the way they had come, the warriors roaring them into urgency. The shallow hill formations echoed to the shouts and cries, and the long green grass, tipped with the dry yellow of autumn, rustled and stirred. The cavalrymen rode almost at the heels of tardier warriors now. In the distance, the women and children ran in panic, and the three waggons were beginning a lumbering turn to follow them.

The Romans wondered. There were not more than four hundred warriors scampering in retreat, and the cavalrymen knew better than to believe these represented all that Canis had. Reports said he had faced Julian Osirus with over a thousand, and that with these and the use of hot iron and fire he had almost annihilated Julian's force.

Ah. A sigh came from the leading cavalrymen. In the path of the streaming women and children, appeared a second body of warriors. Of course. The women and children, with their waggons, had been travelling under the protection of warriors front and rear. And there were a score of other warriors visible now, pulling at the wheels of the waggons, helping the lumbering vehicles to turn. The mounted Romans fell back a little, riding in comfortable command of the situation. The Britons could not escape, not with so many women and children inhibiting their retreat. The Roman infantry were coming on, at a tireless, jogging trot, and the Britons were abandoning the waggons, warriors leaping down from them and fleeing in the footsteps of the women and children.

The first body of warriors converged on the waggons and spilled around them, going fast over the uneven ground. The second body of warriors, the rearguard, had halted. They now opened up to let the women and children through, urging them on, thrusting at them. In a little while, the original four hundred were there, and all warriors merged to stand and form. A few Britons on horses appeared. The Roman cavalry maintained their steady advance, bringing their infantry on behind them. The rugged quiet of the terrain was alive now with sound.

The mounted Romans pulled up. The armed Britons were standing, presenting a deep wall of defence that stretched between grassy hills. There, obviously, they meant to hold off the Romans to give their women and children time to escape. The advancing Roman infantry changed from trot to tramping march, then were brought to a halt while their centurions surveyed the situation.

Canis, buried in the grass on the summit of a turfy ridge, watched. By his side was Princess Cea. Nearby were Lydia and Caleda. Caleda wished to see how her man Bergotix conducted himself in a fight with Romans; and how Canis, man of brass and iron, conducted the conflict itself. Lydia was there simply because she adamantly refused to go with the women and spend her time waiting again. The Romans were from the 14th Legion, many of them veterans of hard campaigns. They looked bravely caparisoned. Weapons, armour and shields danced and glittered in the light. The Romans brought colour as well as purpose to a battle, so that none could say carnage was not preceded by splendour. There were about twelve hundred of them. Formidable, but not too formidable.

The centurions conferred with their senior officer, and as a single, vast cloud rolled over the face of the sun, the tempering of the sharp light softened the picture of men preparing for war.

" Well, we have found them," said one centurion, " there they stand." And that was no less than the truth. Since the Britons seemed determined to stand and not yield, to block the Roman's passage, the Romans were not inclined to temporise. Paullinus had demanded bold and vigorous action, in the event of any force making contact with these rebel Britons. They must be smashed, and Canis must be taken.

Two cavalrymen were despatched to inform the main body of troops that the Britons of Canis were being attacked. The Britons would either be contained, or defeated; but it was requested that the main body come with all speed, since it was estimated that the rebels numbered nearly a thousand, and it was not to be expected that Canis would fight an unworthy battle.

The troop of Roman cavalry, with the mounted centurions, led the infantry into the attack. The infantry went at the trot to bring weight, force and impetus against the British front, to scatter their lines and cut down their flanks. They passed the abandoned waggons, and there before them stood over eight hundred Britons, some horsed men in their rear.

A blackbird whistled in the hills. The sound was taken up and relayed, and the hills piped sweet echoes. The standing Britons moved and opened up. The whistles ran on, as if blackbirds were in fast flight. Hywel came out from between hills, riding his horse at the gallop, running it at speed towards the ground over which the Romans had passed minutes before. Behind him charged scores of other mounted warriors. From between hills on the opposite side, poured more horsed warriors, going at a gallop, coming at the Roman rear. The advancing Romans heard the soft thunder of a thousand horses pounding grassy turf and ridges. A cavalryman wheeled. He swore as he saw them—two bodies of Iceni and Trinovante cavalry converging to make a massed onslaught on the Romans.

The consequences of accepting what was now all too obviously a trap struck like a hammer blow at the Romans. Nor could they rely on their two gallopers, for several Britons were riding in furious chase of them. From the moment the Romans had sighted the original body of warriors, they had kept their eyes on them alone, instead of searching the hills and depressions as well. But it was not the terrain for ambush, there were no narrow valleys or thorn-squeezing defiles. The ground was open, rugged and gently hilly, that was all. The British cavalry had lain with their horses between hills, all grounded in the deep grass, the animals muzzled with soft leather to keep them quiet.

Before the now alarmed Romans the foot warriors stood. Behind them the mounted warriors came on at speed. The foot and the mounted were all that remained of Boadicea's fighting host; but they were there to avenge Boadicea, and would do so. And the Romans knew they would.

And to complete the impossible odds came the hundred chariots. They ran out from amid the women and children in the distance, and the women and children were no longer running. The wheels of the chariots rushed through the grass, heading in wild, bucketing abandon for the conflict. The Roman advance had been halted. For the moment, they still had the opportunity to break right or left, but either way would mean they would be run down and chopped to pieces. They stood, they formed into a solid, compact square, shields clamping to form four sides of iron. They had to withstand the charge of mounted warriors on one side, the rushing chariots on another. And on the heels of the chariots, the foot warriors would run. A centurion thrust the standard of the eagle firmly into the ground. Orders rang out.

The mounted warriors came in their massed charge, their war cries flung to the sun and the clouds, the warrior maids singing. The standing warriors opened up a wider space; and the chariots raced through, rocking and keeling. Every voice took up the war cry. The quiet was completely gone, slaughtered by the noise of battle. Centurions within the Roman square called on their men to hold fast, so that the chariots would smash and crumple against the iron wall. But the chariots did not ride into that wall, they wheeled and turned at speed and ran across its face; and each man standing beside each driver hurled a heavy spear over the heads of the front line into the massed ranks.

The cavalry arrived, not to charge into those clamped shields, but to cut Romans out from the corners of the square. In minutes, that square was surrounded, the chariots containing one side of it, the mounted warriors containing the other three sides. Charging horse and bucketing chariots created a maelstrom of violent movement and continuous assault. Shock, speed and surprise were the essence of the initial tactics, wild and exhilarated offence the keynote of joined battle. Canis knew well enough that it never paid to fight a sustained battle with any Roman force, for Romans had a genius for turning a lengthy conflict into victory. To go at them frontally, to run one's head against the wall of clamped shields, was costly and wearisome. One could not intimidate Romans with superior numbers, only with the menace of superior tactics. He did not want his wild warriors and his extravagant warrior maids to pound the iron perimeter. They were to cut the corners of it, to hack men out and gradually shrink that square.

He came down from the ridge. Cea cried out in anger. But

343

he was on his horse and he rode into the conflict, to lead a group of warriors into the smashing of one corner of the Roman square. Warrior maids followed him joyfully, Feneda in full cry at his heels. The chariots withdrew, the foot warriors came in. Bergotix, in command of a hundred of them, obeyed the orders given him by Canis. He did not pound the Romans, he and his men contained them, harassed them, pressed them.

Canis had said, " If you lose me more than ten warriors, Bergotix, my friend, I will return you to Brigantia and tender Cartimandua."

So Bergotix fought and commanded as instructed. It was a moment when his blood ran quick and hot again. The tumult became a clashing storm, as if cymbals of brass were being beaten by iron hammers in a raging wind. The foot warriors harassed, the chariots came again, the mounted Britons made their continuous assaults, cutting and hacking as they gouged gaping holes in the iron wall. They disengaged and withdrew, and others rode in, and they began to destroy the Roman force as a repetitive whirlwind destroys a cornfield, angle by angle, corner by corner. The Romans staggered under every hammer blow. They lurched, formed and re-formed as they lost their comrades, ten by ten and score by score. They were boxed in on all sides, their shining armour and brave colour gory with blood. Plunging horses smashed into them, crushed them and trampled them, spears pierced them and swords cut them down. The small troop of cavalry died as it sought vainly for an avenue of escape.

Cea, Lydia and Caleda watched from the ridge, each with faces pale and eyes wide. They saw Canis. He was using Cerdwa's axe. Cea cried out at his recklessness. But his was the endeavour of a man determined to squeeze the Romans to death, and without wasting time. No one knew whether other Roman forces would arrive or not. He had his warriors hammering ceaselessly, and the green grass ran with Roman blood. But Caesar's soldiers fought bravely, and no centurion cried for quarter.

Lydia's ears, numbed by the sounds of the battle, became

344

deaf to the screams of Romans savagely smitten. Her heart fought on the side of her Britons, it could do no other than that. Caleda watched with wide, staring eyes. So this was what Bergotix so loved to talk about. Oh, foolish Bergotix. This was indeed clattering iron and brassy conflict—but oh, the death, the agony and the cruelty. She had long since lost sight of her limping husband amid the movements of the manoeuvring foot warriors, though Bergotix was there and in fine command as he showed the Iceni and Trinovantes that he still knew how to neatly pin a Roman with his long spear.

The constant roar assaulted Caleda's senses, the incessant surge of battle confused her eyes, and a man of iron riding a horse of war was the centrepiece of all. There he was, commanding his cavalry, pointing with his axe, and the Romans were dying.

He had come like a man of peace to their dwelling in Brigantia. But he was not a man of peace, he commanded all the gods of war to his side, and he had put into the mind of Bergotix a restlessness and a desire to be a warrior again. He had told Bergotix to follow him if he wished, and Bergotix had done so. What was it he had said that made her follow too? Caleda could not remember.

He was a destroyer of Romans. Bergotix had spoken true there. But he had said little about the screams of broken men and the savagery of others. Nor had he said how fiercely the warrior maids put Romans to death—he had only said how brave and wild they were. To Bergotix, the bravery of making battle was all. Or perhaps to talk about it was all.

Yet, strangely, something of the exhilaration of those warrior maids found an echo in her heart. They were brave, they smote joyously as well as fiercely, and they followed Canis as if he were the lord of life itself. Or death.

Caleda, her blood rushing, bit on her lip until the blood came.

The whirlwind reaped until there were less than two hundred Romans still standing. Canis offered quarter. A surviving centurion refused, and his men fought on. And Canis, remembering that Paullinus offered Boadicea neither quarter nor honour, destroyed all remaining Romans. These fought in final, courageous defiance, surrounded on all sides. From out of a ruck rode Feneda, swaying on her horse, a wild laugh on her lips and red blood coursing from a gashed arm.

Lydia, from above, saw the warrior maid, the reins hanging loose and the horse with pricked ears and snorting nostrils because of so much blood. She ran down the slope. A riderless horse was tranquilly cropping grass. Lydia flung herself up and rode to find Feneda, who had been such an inspiring comrade to her on the day they ran from Sulla and his Romans. The field of battle was bloody and trampled, littered with Roman dead, and the last of the living were being swallowed up. She saw Feneda where the grass was still green. The horse was standing, Feneda drooping. Lydia rode to her. She leapt down to catch the exhausted and wounded warrior maid as she tumbled from her saddle. Feneda found her feet, and Lydia brought her to the side of a slope and made her lie against the friendly green.

" Oh, Feneda, you are a brave warrior," she said, " and see, it is only a gash. I will bind it. Where is your battle linen?"

" I am in no hurt," breathed Feneda, " so look for Hywel if you will. I saw him fall, and it was then that I was foolish enough to take this small cut. See to Hywel, bring him clear or he may be trampled. If he has taken his death wound, he will be in joy to have you kiss his lips."

A kiss given to a dying warrior brought him or her across the dark river of death with love warm on the lips, and the spirits carried all such kissed warriors tenderly to the dark gods.

But it was Hywel himself, breathless but unscathed, who galloped up at that moment. He sprang from his horse, the heat of battle still about him, his expression quick with concern.

" What is this? Have you taken hurt?" Hywel, however, spoke to Lydia, not to Feneda.

" I am not a warrior maid," said Lydia, " but Feneda is, and she has taken serious hurt. So give your care to her." She

346

knew where the warrior maid's heart lay, so added, "She has a great need of it."

"Hywel?" Feneda spoke faintly.

"Why, Feneda," said Hywel, seeing her blood. From his belt pouch, he took fine, clean linen and herbal ointment, which the warriors always carried into battle. He went on one knee and bound the wound with the smeared linen, tightening it above the deep gash. "Why, Feneda," he said again, seeing her paleness. She was a fair maid and a joyful comrade.

"I am faint from loss of blood, and will soon be gone," whispered Feneda, the noise of battle dying. "Am I deserving of warrior's kiss, Hywel?"

"Above everything," said Hywel in warm grief, and bent to kiss her—at which Feneda wound her arms around his neck and pressed her mouth to his with all the healthy ardour of a maid suffering far more from the pangs of love than a gash in the arm. "Why, Feneda," said Hywel yet again.

"Almost I am gone," breathed Feneda, "so will you kiss me again, Hywel?"

"Willingly," said the handsome Hywel, not unaware of the pleasure of the first kiss. Lydia, sensing what Feneda was about, rose to her feet and mounted her horse, riding away in search of Canis. The battle was over as Hywel kissed Feneda again.

He had not conceived that Feneda's mouth could taste so warm and sweet, or that her arms could keep him from surveying the field of victory. It was very strange. And so sad that she was dying. As for Feneda, although she was fearless, she had no idea how to deal bravely with the sensitive and complicated matter of courting a man, especially one who had eyes only for someone else. She could not speak about it to her comrades, for that would have brought on the kind of raillery to make her blush. She only knew that her feelings for Hywel were extraordinarily disturbing, inducing in her immodest desires to touch him. Also disturbing was his infatuation for Ludicca, though she could not blame him. The Roman woman was uncommonly beautiful. But she knew Hywel sought the unattainable there. Ludicca loved only one man. That was

347

Canis. Feneda did not pine for lack of Hywel's regard, for she was not frailly disposed; but she was frequently sad that he took so little heed of her shape or her bright eyes.

But now, how sweet to be kissed by him. The battle was over and won, she was emotional from it all, and this was tender reward for her wound.

In Hywel's mind was the thought that if Feneda was dying the embrace was tragically sweet.

Dying? With her arms so strong about him?

"Feneda?" He straightened. She was pale, but aside from that looked shyly herself. There was no sign of impending death, only a pinkness that stole to colour the paleness. He laughed. "Feneda, your kisses are remarkably warm for one about to breathe her last."

How strange were those colourful warrior maids. The battle had been remorseless and cruel, with a thousand Romans slain and the earth red with their blood. Yet at this moment Feneda blushed as vividly as a tender virgin, and thought the day quite beautiful in that it had brought Hywel's kisses to her. Hywel laughed again. He lifted her in his arms and carried her away from the gory field, their horses trailing in their wake.

And Lydia looked for Canis. Her needs were always compulsive. Where was he, this man who gave her so much joy and her countrymen so much death? The place was full of horsed Britons, full of foot warriors milling around the tumbled bodies of Roman dead. The violent sounds of savage war and thundering horse were gone, and there was comparative quiet as desolate death showed its fearful face, and triumph paused to draw breath. Britons were searching for any legionaries not yet dead, to give them merciful quittance.

There was Canis.

He rode out from a body of mounted warriors. He was hard of face, bitter of mouth. There was blood on his thigh. His left knee and leg ran red with it. Lydia rode wildly to him.

"Stand off," said Canis, "I will not have you cossetting a scratch and see my warriors grinning behind their spears. Stand off."

Lydia laughed. Her hair spilled and tossed in the breeze. The tragedy of countrymen slaughtered, the acrid smell of blood and the impact savagery had had on outraged senses, suddenly seemed so much less than the exhilaration of knowing victory had been complete, so she laughed like a woman intoxicated. Canis regarded her with a grey, brooding look.

"Canis, was it not a great and speedy victory? Did not your warriors smite well this day for your Queen?"

She seemed, thought Canis, to have taken his dead Queen within the personal context of her own life.

"Your countrymen did not lack bravery, Lydia. They stood to a man, though greatly outnumbered."

He spoke in a grim way that injured her all too sensitive heart. Was he disapproving because she took pride in his victory over her countrymen? But they were not her countrymen, not now. She had given all of herself to him and his people. He knew that. She looked into his eyes, they were a world away, and she knew it was his tragic Queen he was remembering. As he always did when he fought against Romans.

"Oh, that is not a look for me," she protested. "Canis, it was a great victory, it was, and—"

"Victory is the issue of true battle, not slaughter," he said. His hard, brooding expression softened. "She rode with us, did you not hear her?" he said.

She knew he meant Boadicea.

"I heard only the pounding of my heart," she said.

He smiled at that.

"Come," he said, "let us find our Princess."

Cea, on a horse, was among her warriors. She was in brown-eyed brilliance and pride as they clamoured around her.

"Canis," she cried as she saw him, "you are my mother's most prodigious general, and my warriors' most protective one. We have lost but a few while vanquishing a thousand."

"Well, we squeezed them to death as once they squeezed us," said Canis. He looked around amid the triumphant clamour. "Where is Bergotix the Brigante?" he called loudly.

"Here, lord." Bergotix shouldered through, limping and grinning, and stained with Roman blood. Canis leaned from his horse and clapped him on the shoulder.

"Friend Bergotix," he said, "you did as I asked, and did it well. You are an economical warrior and a wily one. So now, forget any weariness, take horse and five other riders, and use your eyes to look for other Romans. Go in the direction where we first sighted these who now lie dead. Be invisible, Bergotix, for any you see must not see you. Return as soon as any of you lay eyes on them."

"Why must this be?" asked Cea.

"Because gallopers may have been sent to alert other Roman troops when our decoy four hundred were first sighted," said Canis. "We took the two gallopers they sent later. I am concerned with others who may have been despatched earlier. Deva is not so far, and there the Romans have their headquarters for this region. Go, Bergotix, and be our eyes. While you are gone, we will clear the field of Roman weapons and everything else we can use to our gain. When we are ready, we will march. We have come most of the way, there are only a few leagues between us and the mountains now."

The mountains, green and blue, with their peaks trailing mist, were close enough to beckon them, or so it seemed.

Bergotix and five other men rode on their way, directly west. The rest of the Britons busied themselves lifting everything from the dead Romans that was useful, especially the weapons. Some would have decapitated a few of the dead and mounted the heads on their spears, but for the sake of Lydia, who begged him not to permit it, Canis forbade the indulgence.

"But, lord," protested one warrior, "the gods—"

"You have won this battle, not the gods," said Canis, who believed in none himself. "If we had time, we should give these Romans honourable burial—for they fought honourably. But we do not have any time, except to prepare ourselves for the arrival of others. We cannot march until we know the way is clear."

He sent warriors to fetch the women, children and old ones.

They had remained at a distance, and were still there. In an hour all were assembled in a depression sheltered by nestling hills, not far from the trampled site now desolate with its heaps of dead.

Canis would not move until Bergotix returned. And when he did, it was to report that the way was not clear.

" By Andrasta herself," he said to Canis, " you are a man to read Romans, lord. There is a cohort of cavalry looking not only for you, I warrant, but for their infantry comrades."

Canis, warm from the endeavours of the day, and from the day itself, nevertheless looked bleak. Then he smiled faintly, as if in philosophical acceptance of what could not be avoided —and what he had perhaps expected. Julian was close by. He had been confined under guard during the battle. Canis, knowing the Roman could be of no help to his countrymen, had thought it preferable for him not to be too closely aware of their destruction. Julian grimly disliked what had happened, and disliked just as much the news that more Romans were about to cross the path of the Britons. Cyella had been emotionally torn by the battle. She had been with Julian, and not known what to say to him during the battle and after it. Julian himself had said, " It is bitter, Cyella, but Canis and Cea must win free. I cannot deny them this, when I think of what has happened to their nation."

However, he now had something else to say, and to Canis.

" Wolfhead, you will find no soldiers more persistent than Caesar's, none more dedicated than those under orders from Paullinus."

" We shall not regard this cohort lightly, tribune," said Canis, " we shall sit in quiet and serious contemplation, while they come in search of their infantry. It is not expected that you will sit quietly with us, so we must bind you and muffle you."

Cyella gave a cry of distress. But Julian said, " Cyella, he must do this as much for my sake as his."

She understood then. Canis was removing from Julian the necessity of making a decision. As a Roman he must, if he could, warn the approaching cohort of the proximity of Britons. Yet he was the Britons' friend. If the Romans escaped, they would bring all they could of the 14th Legion down on the Britons unless Canis quickly retreated east. And such a retreat would be negative and dangerous. Bound and muffled, Julian would not have to wrestle with his conscience or his sentiments. Silence and impotence would be thrust upon him.

So the Britons bound him and muffled him, and took him to a spot where he would be out of sight and sound of what took place. Cyella, suffering because of her divided loyalties, went with him.

The Britons lay low. The women, children and old ones lay lower, prone in the long grass of the depression. Each warrior with a horse muffled his animal. They could have ridden out and destroyed the bulk of the approaching cavalry, but they could not risk having some escape to take word back to Deva. They had to slay every man, and take every horse.

So they waited. They were in advance of the field of recent battle, and the Romans would have to pass them before they could sight their fallen dead. And if this cohort had been informed of the Britons' presence in this area, they needed to think them gone, perhaps running eastward in retreat from the infantry.

The Romans came. First appeared lone riders scouting the uneven country. Some way behind them, the Britons saw the cavalry force. Canis sighed. It did not look like a full cohort; he judged it a body of three hundred. The scouts rode alertly, three of them, marking the tracks of the doomed infantry. Wary and watchful, they came at the trot. The glitter of the full detachment became sharper, brighter. Aye, three hundred, give or take a man or two. The foremost scout began to pass the low, humped hills which sheltered the Britons. He followed the trail of flattened grass, and headed on towards the site of the battle—the folds and the ridges of the ground presenting their own problems as far as a clear view of the undulating green was concerned. The other scouts followed him. Andudo nudged Canis, and pointed.

A black-winged carrion bird, disturbed by the advancing scouts, had risen from the field of dead and was drifting and circling overhead. Another rose. The scouts were disappearing, riding on, but the body of cavalry had not yet begun to pass the Britons. How long now before the scouts found their slaughtered comrades, and came galloping back to warn the detachment? They still had some way to go.

I cannot look, thought Lydia, I cannot. She pressed her face to the cool earth on which she lay. She felt it tremble, and then came the muted drumming of three hundred mounted men. It grew louder. They were passing, and every Briton lay breathlessly still and quiet, hands on the noses of muzzled, grounded horses. Tails swished, lay still and swished again. The drumming was heavy, persistent, the cavalry cantering. Lydia thought there must be a thousand of them, so long did it seem to take them to pass. Then the noise was receding, and the Britons' limbs were like tight springs uncoiling.

Suddenly there was a shout. Faintly, they heard it. Lydia lifted her head. She saw the detachment, she could not see beyond it. Had she been able to, she would have observed the three scouts riding back as if the Gorgons were behind them. Their faces were white because of what they had seen, and they galloped headlong, shouting at the cohort. A centurion leading it flung up his arm; the cavalry halted before they had fully passed the hidden Britons, and the scouts increased their warning gallop.

Canis was up, his horse was up and he was astride it.

" Ride! " he shouted.

The centurion wheeled, the leading scout at his side, gesticulating and horrified. The arm of the centurion described a wide arc, and the cavalry began to move.

" Ride! " shouted Canis again, as he burst from cover and put his mount to the gallop. " Ride, or they will spring free! "

Hundreds of Britons leapt to horse to follow him. The Romans, wheeling, saw the green humps disgorging horsed Britons. The centurion took one look, and without hesitation led his detachment in speedy retreat along the way they had come.

Behind Canis rode Lydia. She had not meant to. Exhilaration had long receded, leaving her sad and depressed. But the instant Canis had broken out, she had impulsively followed. It was Grud who restrained the excited Cea.

" No, hold back, Princess," he said, " this is not your work."

" Oh, Grud, you are full of advice I do not want. And Canis will heed no advice but his own. Is this not how he tormented my mother, and now torments me?"

" His regard for you and your house is his only motivation," said Grud, " and he will brook no Roman interruption of this the final stage of our journey. We must cross to the mountains, and must not be caught before we reach them. He will return to you, sweet Princess, as he always returned to your mother— though many a time she singed his ear for going at all."

Cea stood, her young and mutinous heart in her eyes, as she saw her Britons streaming in pursuit of the Romans. Three hundred, five hundred and more, rode out of the ridges and humps in a wild, abandoned gallop. The Romans rode hard, forsaking the limiting constraint of formation in their endeavour to escape death. Canis was well ahead, followed by Lydia; and as she galloped, her depression lifted and her weariness dissolved. In her short tunic, her supple legs shone and gleamed. She dug in her heels and rode as she had that day with Feneda at her heels, with Sulla in relentless chase. But now the chase was in reverse, now it was the Britons who pounded in pursuit, the Romans who wisely fled. Oh, the wildness of it, the brilliance of the greens, the wind strong in her face and stinging her eyes. The long grass sprang and flowed and rippled, the air vibrating and the thunder of hooves so familiar. Above the noise, she could hear the warrior maids singing their cries. How they loved their galloping fourlegs, how recklessly they courted death, defied it and laughed when it came. There was the joyous Feneda, not with them now because of her wound, but resting happily because of the new-found regard Hywel had for her.

Canis rode like a demon, as cruel and merciless as ever when it was all or nothing for the house of Boadicea, for the Queen's

354

people. If the Romans won free, Lydia knew that soon enough the way to the mountains in this area would swarm with Caesar's men. Savage battle would then take place again, and even Canis could not always win. The mountains which loomed so near were still unattainable, unless the Britons could win passage today and tomorrow. They must disappear from this place without one Roman on their tail.

No people in Britain could ride quite like the Iceni, breeders of speedy and enduring horses, born to the rushing wind of the sustained gallop. Over all that uneven ground, over undulating traverses and giddy slopes, they gained on the fast-riding Romans. The latter, burdened with armour and accoutrements, could not match the Britons' speed, not over this ground. The Britons carried only spear or sword or javelin.

The Romans were in a streaming column, each man riding for his life, each glance over a shoulder at the pursuing Britons inducing greater endeavour. A horse pitched, a rider flew and lay senseless. The long column galloped past him. The rhythmic menace of the pursuers reached into Roman ears, and the Britons saw clearly now the flying tails of the Roman mounts. Kicked-up clods of earth flew in the faces of the Britons. Over the turbulence of wind and gallop sounded the song of the warrior maids, challenging the Romans to stand and give battle. But the Romans rode on until the thunder of their hoofbeats were merging with those of the Britons. Canis shouted his orders.

"Ride! Ride by them, turn them! Do not take their rear! Ride by, flank them, turn them!"

His orders were taken up by those at his heels, and flung back to all. The leading Britons split apart, forming two separate columns on either side of the Romans, while Lydia put her horse into a heart-straining gallop to come up beside Canis.

"Canis! Canis!" The wind, tossing her hair, caught her voice and flung his name aside; but she was up with him, and knew he had heard her. She was conscious of the flash of bobbing Roman helmets on their left, and desperately she shouted. "Canis! Do not kill them—no more death—no more vengeance—oh, I beg you!"

355

He turned his head. The sweat gleamed on his forehead, dampened his hair, but he was smiling, his teeth showing. It was grim, sardonic, but a smile it was, and her heart turned over.

"You are a tender Roman," he called, and she heard him laugh. She kissed him with her eyes and dropped back to let him ride on without hindrance, his warriors pounding behind him as he began to come abreast of the Roman van. On he swept, flanking the right of the Roman column, while the second line of Britons flanked the Roman left. Though aware of this manoeuvre, the cavalrymen did not check their pace but galloped on. The Britons began to squeeze them, but did not engage. On, on, low in the saddle, spears and swords sharp in the light, they drove their horses—until the Romans seemed to be falling back between the two streaming lines of Britons. On, on, men and horse moving in rhythmic communion, until Canis and the leading warriors were riding far in advance of the Romans. Their two columns enclosed the enemy, the warrior maids distinctive adjuncts with their long, flying hair and their brown, graceful limbs.

Canis turned inwards, followed by warriors, and the Romans were faced by closing walls on all sides. Three hundred cavalrymen became a mass of rearing, plunging horse. There were shouts, the glint of unsheathed weapons and a sweating anticipation of bloody engagement. But the Britons were reining in and pulling up to stand in consolidation of their encircling position. Their mounts tossed their heads and spattered foam.

"Who commands?" shouted Canis, as Lydia rode up to him.

"Lyxtus Ceramus, centurion!" came a reply.

"Then say, Lyxtus Ceramus, centurion, are you for life or death?"

"Is there choice?" A man edged his horse out from the ruck. "If death, we will take enough of you with us to even the score in the sight of our gods and yours."

"Ride out, Lyxtus Ceramus, and we will talk."

356

The centurion rode out. He was brave enough, even calm. He had seen too much of the way death leapt to take the best of soldiers to consider himself immortal. Canis sat relaxed in his saddle as the centurion rode up to him.

" I am Lyxtus Ceramus."

" It was a brave ride, Lyxtus, but it is not your day."

The centurion, brown-faced, dark of eye, stared long and hard at the Briton.

" I know of you," he said, " and can tell you that you are much wanted by our Imperial Governor."

Lydia drew a breath. She had seen this man before. He was the centurion who had spoken kind and understanding words to her on the day when Paullinus had given her a message from Canis. He had helped her to stay proud and upright when her heart was breaking and her body faint.

" The Imperial Governor wants me also, Lyxtus," she said.

The centurion, hardy and fearless, turned his eyes on her. She looked like an Iceni maid in her shamelessly short tunic, with her long legs naked. But she was not of the Iceni. Recognition flickered in his eyes.

" I see you, my lady," he said, " and was there when Paullinus heard he had lost you, after all. I was not sorry."

In silence around them, the Britons held themselves motionless, the Romans watching tensely.

Lyxtus looked again at Canis. There was no denying it— he acknowledged that here was a warrior and a man. The face had a subtlety, a distinctiveness. The grey eyes were direct. Lyxtus understood Lydia and her choice.

" I can offer you something better than death, Lyxtus," said Canis.

" Name it," said Lyxtus, " but in the event of it making a coward of me, I doubt if I will accept—for though life is sweet, a man dishonoured is better dead."

Canis put out his hand palm upwards.

" Each of us has his own concept of what is acceptable and what is not," he said. " For some, who put creature comfort first, the sun is acceptable but rain is not. There is life for you

357

and all your men, if another Roman makes a choice agreeable to you. There is my hand on it." He turned his palm sideways. Lyxtus put out his own hand and briefly they clasped wrists. "Lead your men within our escort, Lyxtus, and we will bring you to this other Roman. There you will decide what is acceptable and what is not."

Lyxtus smiled, though his eyes were wary.

"I have heard men talk about you," he said; and then rode back to his silent cavalry. He spoke to them. They sheathed their weapons; and, escorted on all sides by the Britons, they cantered back.

"Canis," said Lydia, riding with him, "you are not always cruel. Lyxtus was kind to me when Paullinus held me captive. I am glad you will give him and his men the chance to go free."

"It is not settled yet, Lydia."

The other Britons were waiting with the women and children, and to the Romans it seemed that the rugged green land had sprouted a full tribe. Canis dismounted and asked Lyxtus to do likewise. Cea was there, eager with questions, but Canis only said, "Where is Julian?"

"They have unbound him and given him back his tongue," said Cea, "and he is now sitting and frowning. Cyella is with him."

"Let us join him," said Canis. Cea, Lydia, Grud and Lyxtus accompanied him. They found Julian sitting in frowning contemplation of the sky, Cyella by his side. He turned his eyes on Canis, regarding him in irony.

"So," he said, "one more victory so soon after the other? Are all of them dead save the centurion there? What is he to you? Your supper?"

Lyxtus, who knew Julian, recognised him, though the tribune's leather kirtle was in a sorry, worn condition and he bore no armour or weapon.

"Tribune," said the centurion, "we served together during the rebellion. I am Lyxtus Ceramus."

"Aye, I know you, old plunder bones," said Julian, and got

358

to his feet. " I am here, you see, and in the same straits as yourself. At the mercy and whims of Canis, of whose name even the sweetest gods must have tired by now. Why has he spared you?"

" He spoke of a choice for me and all my men," said Lyxtus.

" What," said Julian, " has he slain none of you?"

" None as yet," said Canis, " it is all in your hands, Julian." Cyella, in emotion for Julian, prayed that Canis, always hard on Romans, would not be impossibly hard now. " Here is Lyxtus," Canis went on, " and back there are all his men, three hundred of them. They should be enough to protect you from those who would murder you for your kirtle, Julian. You should have no trouble in reaching Deva with them. Take Cyella with you. Paullinus may contrive to diminish you with spite, but if Julian Osirus is not man enough to rise above spite, then who is?"

" That is surely not the whole of the choice for Lyxtus— to provide an escort for me?" said Julian. Cyella thought him quietly courageous in his demeanour and loved him very much.

" Here is the essence of it," said Canis. " Until the night has reached halfway to dawn, you and Lyxtus and his men will search north, east and south for us."

" Where you will not be," said Julian.

" Who can say?" said Canis.

" I can say," said Julian. " This is the choice, then, for Lyxtus. He is to hunt for those he will not find and not return to his headquarters until you are far away and safely away. This is no choice, Canis, this is what Lyxtus must do or give up his life and those of his men."

Lyxtus, however, having briefly considered it, said, " Tribune, where death is the only alternative, life is something of a choice."

" I cannot argue," said Julian. " Ye gods, what else may I do but join you and roam about half the night with you? And what else may you do, Lyxtus?"

The centurion rubbed his chin. He knew the gods did not

359

give a man life for him to throw it away foolishly. And there was an arguable distinction between foolishness and honour. Plainly, he read anguish on the face of the fair-haired maid who stood beside Julian Osirus, and just as plainly he was aware of something almost pleading in Lydia's expression.

He said to Canis, " Briton, how am I to arrive before my legate at dawn tomorrow and explain to his satisfaction what I have been doing all night? You slew a thousand Romans today. My men saw them, and all dead. Am I to say we ran around in blind anger, hacking at the empty air?"

" Go to your legate," said Canis, " arrive before him worn, weary and bitter, and say first that the men we slew made a brave fight of it, as they did. Say next that you spent many hours hunting those who did the slaying, as would any men fierce to avenge their comrades—that you meant to find them and take back word of where they were. And say, finally, that they escaped you. All this will be true. Or almost true."

Lyxtus smiled a little sarcastically. He glanced at Lydia. Her green eyes caressed him, so dearly did she wish him to accept this choice. By Venus, he thought, the Briton had been well favoured in his winning of such a woman as Lydia Osirus.

" It is more acceptable than death," said Lyxtus. " I have three hundred men, all comrades, and all wondering how long it is going to take them to die. They would not thank me for being foolishly honourable. You give them a choice to live and to fight you again, perhaps. That is as sensibly honourable as they could wish. I give you my word on it, Briton."

He put out his hand, and he and Canis again clasped. Cyella's eyes were misty, the strong face of Canis blurred in her sight. She would not see him again—for that had been sealed by the agreement. She would remain with Julian, and the Britons would go. And when Canis and his Britons reached the mountains, they would all be lost to her forever. But she would hear of them, she would hear of Canis, the greatest of all living Britons, for not even those mountains would be able to keep from the world the stories of his further endeavours. She would not see her loving father again, or Princess Cea, proud, sweet and beloved. Lydia too, whom she had such affection for now, would also go with the Britons. Lydia would go with them because of her love for Canis, though she could never possess him. He belonged to the house of Boadicea, to the Queen's daughter. But Lydia would follow him wherever he went, even into the fearsome caverns of the dark mountain gods, adding her courage to his. Oh, Lydia. Cyella turned away, hot tears already spilling.

Canis summoned Andudo and Hywel, telling them to make ready for departure. Lyxtus returned to his uneasy detachment, acquainting them of the conditions of their reprieve. They bristled, squared up, chewed on a variety of words, and then agreed it was something to consider—the chance of meeting the Britons again on a better day.

There was little for Andudo and Hywel to organise, apart from getting the people on their feet. The Britons had been ready to leave before Bergotix had returned from his reconnaissance.

But there was a leave-taking with Cyella for Andudo to endure. Eyes wet, he spent precious time saying goodbye to her, the daughter he had found again and lost again. He would rather have fought Romans. He was only comforted by the fact that in choosing to wed a Roman she had picked Julian Osirus, the Roman for whom the Britons had the greatest regard. Cyella wept as her father left her, and was still weeping when Lydia came to say goodbye.

" Cyella? Oh, do not weep so, for everything is so much better than it might have been."

" I am in sadness," said Cyella through her tears, " for how might I see any of you again? I have been so happy, even though it has been cruelly hard at times, and today was grievously hard. And Julian has been sad too. There have been so many brave Romans slain because of Paullinus, and now to have you go when you have been so sweet to me. Oh, Lydia, truly I have found there are Romans to love and like."

361

"With Julian, you will become a sweet Roman yourself," said Lydia, "so do not weep."

"Lydia, you were born to be my dearest sister, but you are going from us and I cannot help my tears."

Lydia kissed her. Julian came up as they clung together. It had been a day when his heart and his emotions had been torn, and to have his sister depart with the Britons was bitter. She turned to him, her eyes over-bright.

"Lydia, how can I put words to such a parting as this?" he said.

"Say only that you love me," said Lydia.

"Will you not come with Cyella and me? Will you not return home?"

"There is my home," said Lydia, turning her eyes to the mountains. "Julian, do not be sad for me. I have Dilwys. Aye, Cyella, there is Dilwys always to consider. Could I leave her? Could I go with you and not see her grow to beautiful maid? Canis would not part with her, for which I am happy, and nor would he part with me. I know he would not. I have been with him since the day I went with him to find his people. I cannot help my heart, so do not be sad for me, or I will shed even more tears than Cyella."

"You are my most precious, but most foolish sister," said Julian, putting his hands on her shoulders. "May all the gods cherish you, for I know not any woman who needs their guidance and protection more than you. If circumstances allow, if it is in any way possible, send us word of yourself as often as you can. There must, even in the mountains, be some wanderers who carry messages for people, and I will reward all such carriers handsomely."

"Julian, I am your most loving sister," said Lydia, "I am happy for you and Cyella. You have each other, I have my destiny, and I also have Diana."

"Sweet fortune to you, then," said Julian, "and may Diana in the end give you all you desire. But send us word, Lydia, send us word. You will be much in our thoughts."

Brother and sister embraced. Lydia could not hold back

some tears and Cyella wept afresh when at last she left them. The Iceni maid flung herself into Julian's arms. His eyes were also wet.

Lyxtus, after his men had withdrawn into the hills, had a final word with Canis.

" It was a generous choice, Briton," he said, " for you could have slain us all and achieved your purpose that way."

" It would not have helped Julian Osirus," said Canis, " or repaid you for the kindness you showed to Lydia when Paullinus had her."

" You did not know that when you first spoke to me," said the centurion. " I am of Rome, you are of Britain—but in the end, what is that to men? Lydia Osirus was brave before Paullinus. That is what a man remembers. You are a hard warrior. That is what a man should not forget. Go to your mountains."

" Lyxtus," said Canis, thinking of a thousand and more Romans smashed, trampled and hacked to death, " so much blood is a costly way of earning a passage."

" Aye." Lyxtus was sombre. " But a battle is costly in any event. Even if only the blood of one man is fatally shed, it is as costly to him as it could be."

" In battle, then," said Canis, " mark first and foremost the enemy whose desire to live is less than his wish to smite you to death."

" That is how your warrior maids fight. I will remember that if we meet again. Even so, I give you good fortune, Wolfhead."

And Lyxtus rode to his men. The Britons, all three thousand of them, were on the move. Julian came to detain Canis.

" Would you leave without a word for me?" he asked.

" I would not," said Canis, " for where is any Roman who stands higher in my regard? My word for you, Julian, is friend. Farewell now, and be sure that in Cyella you have a Briton who will stand proudly before Caesar himself."

363

"And in Lydia," said Julian, "be sure that you have a Roman sensitive and vulnerable. Look to her, Canis."

"I am not her great Diana," said Canis, "but I will look to her."

"Despite the many other Britons who hold her in affection, she is in your hands alone. You know this."

"She is in our hearts," said Canis quietly.

"Well, though you deal bitterly with Romans you are the man for your people," said Julian. "We will not forget you, Cyella and I. So do not forget us. And cherish my sister."

They took their leave of each other. Lydia, her eyes reflecting the summer green of mountain slopes, rode away with Canis and Cea. Cyella remained with Julian.

Andudo went in quiet sadness.

Hywel went in company with Feneda. Her wound was sore, but her heart was light.

When Cyella, red-eyed, came out from the hills half an hour later to look into the west, only the sun's light lay over the ground. Of the Britons there was no sign. Horse, waggons, chariots and people, all had gone. All had vanished and left no whisper, not even in the tallest grass.

14

The silence in the camp of the Britons that night was of the weary taking hard-earned rest. They had fought a strenuous battle, taken a cohort of Roman cavalry, and then travelled apace to win free of an area too dangerously close to Deva and its outposts. They had made impressive progress, despite their numbers and despite their wounded. They had gone on until exhausted, Canis pitiless in his demands on them, and reached a stage that was only a few hours march from the gateway of their mountain haven.

They camped for the night in the region of tall pine and soft slender fern. Canis was reasonably satisfied, for they had made the most of the evening and did not sink down until midnight. They had lost good men in the battle, and also several warrior maids—more than Cea and Canis cared to dwell on—but this had been inevitable.

Their dead they had buried. Their wounded they carried with them. The silence of the leafy camp was disturbed only by those who could not sleep for the aching pain of broken limbs or the throbbing hurt of gashed flesh. Grud, with Lydia, went from warrior to warrior, both doing what they could for those whose wounds needed attention. The moonlight aided them. Grud had taught Lydia much of his physician's art, much of his herbal potions and ointments, and she had used this knowledge over the months to serve the Britons. Now, because she had endured a long and weary day, Grud continually muttered to her to go to her rest, but she would not.

They found Feneda's wound looking raw and ugly, the flesh redly inflamed around it. Feneda made light of it, though she caught her breath as Grud removed the dressing

Hywel had applied. Grud probed gently at the angry flesh. Then he made a poultice of the entrails of a hedgehog, and bound the warm mess firmly over the wound, bidding her not to remove it for seven days.

" But how shall I live with the smell?" she laughed. " And how will others? Who will come near me?"

" Hywel," smiled Lydia, " though perhaps with nose pinched between his fingers by the end of the week."

Not far from Feneda lay another warrior, needing attention but not demanding it. He had taken a sword thrust in his thigh. It had been bound, but had broken open during the journey—and the blood oozed. Grud berated him for his neglect of it. The warrior grinned. Lydia saw the blood red and wet in the moonlight, and remembered Feneda's blood and Hywel's tender kiss because of it.

" I will see to him," she said to Grud, " while you tend others."

" After this one," muttered Grud, " tend yourself, mistress."

On the edge of the camp Canis sat in silent, sombre reflection, oblivious for the moment of the peaks that soared whitely to the moonlit sky. He was sleepless. Hearing movement, he looked round and saw Caleda. She had come to him earlier in the day, immediately after the battle, to say " It was of iron and brass indeed, lord, and of overmuch blood."

Now she slipped to her knees beside him, and searched his face with softly frank eyes.

" Lord," she said, " it has been a day of great effort, most of all for you."

" And for Bergotix," said Canis, " so go to him, give him warmth and comfort, for he has done well and more than well, and we shall be away from here at dawn."

Her calm, smooth face showed a smile.

" As to Bergotix," she said, " I came to say I now understand my foolish husband better than I did, for he cannot be other than a warrior or a teacher of warriors. But I will not be a warrior woman, after all. It is too noisy and too violent a

366

calling, and the sight and sound of it are still a disturbance in my mind. What else might I be?"

"Yourself," he said, "and when we build a house for Princess Cea, she will need gracious women around her. You shall be one of them."

"Might a Brigante woman with rough hands serve an Iceni princess?"

"One Brigante woman might and will."

She was silent for a moment, then spoke again in her quiet way.

"Lord, I am wife to Bergotix, a good man though given excessively to the joys of warring and to discourse concerning warring. I have also known other men, though not in any guilty way. But I have not travelled before with men of battle and with maids who also fight, and while it is absorbing on the one hand it is frightening on the other."

"There will be no more battles, Caleda."

"I am relieved," she said, "and see, since I left the fields and our humble hearth, my hands, though still rough, are no longer red."

She held them out, and they were palely brown in the moonlight.

"It is strange," said Canis, "that a woman so attached to her hearth, and all that makes life secure and predictable, should leave her dwelling merely on account of her hands."

"Not on account of her hands alone, lord, for you were there at the time. If I have a foolish husband, perhaps he has an even more foolish wife." Caleda paused, then went on. "All are asleep now—except only those who patrol, and some wounded who groan and sigh. And Lydia and Grud. And you. Why, after so long and weary a day, can you not sleep?"

"You too are awake," he said.

"Only in my mind, lord," she said, wondering why there was so much darkness in his eyes.

"In my mind, Caleda," he said, "I think of Cyella and Julian. I think of Lydia and Lyxtus. I think of a thousand Romans, all dead."

Caleda rose, her warm robe softly rustling.

" Then I will send to you a voice that will turn your thoughts into dreams," she said, " and they will not be dreams of battle and death." She went quietly away and found Lydia dressing a warrior's wounded thigh. There was much blood about. She waited until Lydia had come from the warrior. Then softly she said, " Mistress Lydia, all must rest and sleep this night, even you and even Canis."

" He most of all," said Lydia. " What is he doing, if he is not sleeping?"

" He sits awake. He is thinking of Romans. Princess Cea lies in sweet, sound sleep—but Canis sits and thinks of Romans, especially of those who are dead."

" I will talk to him," said Lydia, as if it was of no great importance, " while you go to your rest, Caleda." Caleda turned to go. Lydia put out a hand. " Tarry a moment, Caleda."

" Mistress?"

" Do not call me mistress. I am Lydia. Some call me Ludicca. Caleda, why did you come to me?"

The tall trees, sweet-smelling, filtered the moonlight so that Lydia stood in shadow and Caleda in brightness.

" I only know what others know, Lydia. That Princess Cea is his destiny but you are his understanding."

" Go and sleep, Caleda," said Lydia softly. When she had gone, Lydia went to Canis. Her feet dragged as she approached. He looked up to see why she came so laboriously. She did not speak, only breathed heavily and painfully. Her knees crumpled, and it seemed she had swooned beside him. He stared at her, he saw blood on her tunic, wetly scarlet in the moonlight.

" Lydia?"

She opened her eyes and said faintly, " There—there must be one who is out of sympathy with me—I am stabbed."

He drew in hissing breath. The blood was thickest over her heart. He ripped the tunic, uncovering the short shift she wore, and the shift was also soaked with blood. He tore it and

368

the rent garment fell away. The bright red stained her breast and ribs. Whiteness pinched the hard mouth of the Briton.

"Lydia, who has done this to you?" Using her shift he wiped the blood away to look for a wound. He found none. No wound, no gash, only smooth, warm-breathing flesh of incomparable roundness. Lydia sighed under his touch. His lips compressed into a tight line. Then he said, " I am fooled, I think."

Her arms reached up to lock around his neck and draw him down to her.

"How else might I have won your tenderness?" she whispered. "You have fought hard battle today and been generous victor, but you sit here sleepless. So here is your Lydia, to be your comfort and love. And she herself will be sleepless too, unless you are her comfort and love likewise."

"This was a bitter way to fool me, Lydia."

She drew his hand back to her warm breast.

"I am weak in my love, Canis, you are strong and full of unreasonable resolution. So I must contrive to win your caresses in any way I can. Oh, do not think of Romans, think only of Lydia. See, am I not beautiful? Say I am, even if I am not. All are asleep, all except us, so be sweet to me, be sweet. For though it has been a great day, it has been such a sad one too."

She lay there, her eyes drawing the darkness from his; and in the silence it seemed to Lydia that the world was retreating to leave her and Canis suspended like weightless immortals of the night. His voice reached her, low and murmurous.

"Where is my unreasonable resolution after such a day as this? What is conscience or denial in the face of courage and beauty? Well, since you have fooled me, you must take the consequences of both your deceit and your beauty, though I do not know how sweet you will find them."

He lifted her and carried her, withdrawing from the sight and sound of any who might awake, and he did not set her down until he had reached a place where the night was a bright rim of solitude. And when his arms enfolded her and his body touched hers, the flame rushed and she clenched her teeth against her desire to cry out. But his mouth came to stifle all sounds and to move over her lips in a way to delight her and torment her. Her teeth unclenched and the softest moan broke from her.

Oh, Diana, how could one burn so much and yet shiver so much?

Even so, he was in too much consideration of her weakness, and not enough of her hunger.

" Canis, be not too tender, be strong also."

A sense of physical disunity—what was this? His mouth was gone, his body withdrawn. She lifted heavy lids, and within the radiance of light around them she saw an expression of amusement on his face. Amusement? Oh, how could he dare at such a moment?

" Now how may I know how to truly pleasure you," he murmured, " if first you cry for sweetness, then for muscle?"

" To kiss me is to be sweet, to love me is to be strong," she whispered.

" Then put your mouth to mine, and I will engage with you as satisfactorily as I can. There is your deceit to punish and your beauty to invest, and it will be as much as I can do to combine one with the other—without being confused by new demands."

Lydia's laughter escaped like a murmurous sigh of warm delight.

" New demands? Oh, all my demands are but one, which is constant and changeless. I demand only you."

Her arms brought him down to her, and in his investment of her mouth and body Canis repaid her for fooling him. Such repayment Lydia found breathlessly beautiful. She fought for the sheer joy of being subdued and possessed, she yielded and felt herself no longer earthbound. The brilliant night sky drew them upward, transporting them. There was no earth, no ground, only sensations of winged exaltation. And all that had encompassed her year-long day: the frightening battle, the emotional chase, the heart-breaking sadness and the exhausting march—all were gone, all no more than receding pinpoints of darkness in the radiance of soaring flight. Oh, Boadicea, here is my destiny, my joy, my life.

*　　*　　*

Caleda could still not sleep. She woke Bergotix. He listened in astonishment to her calmly outrageous words.

"You must forget for once that battle is all you desire, husband, and lie lovingly with me this night. I am in danger otherwise of weakly giving myself to another man. It will not help to speak his name, for his name does not matter, only that when he looks at me my very bones melt. Also, it is time we had a child. We must have more than one, for only by children can Princess Cea and your man of iron build a kingdom that will endure. We must do our part. Therefore, make room within your grassy bed, Bergotix."

"I am much more likely to make your head ring if you persist in this kind of speech," said the confused Bergotix. "You have not wished yourself in my arms for many a month, yet when hundreds are lying all around us—"

"Do not argue, Bergotix. I am your wife, and may claim my dues within reason. I wanted no children until now, I did not wish to bring any into our poor life, knowing theirs would be no better. It is different now. I am to serve in the household of our Princess, and I think Canis will make you a captain of his foot warriors. Sweet husband, why do you stare so?"

"Have you not cast off every stitch, shameless woman, and is there not a moon? And are there not a thousand eyes, any of which might pop open any moment?"

"Then hide me within your grassy bed," said Caleda, "for if you will not, then tomorrow or on some other day I will give myself to this other man—and have my child by him."

"Caleda, this tongue of yours, how it rains salt on a man," said Bergotix. "But I see you, and what does your tongue matter when your shape is so fine?"

"Then no more words, husband. I am here and so are you."

She was warmly passionate, so Bergotix could not think why she wept afterwards.

* * *

The mountains were like green and blue hills climbing vastly to the sky, their peaks capped by whiteness or mist. The quietness was such as they had never known. Soundless were the lofty skies, soaring slopes and high ridges. There was brilliance, there was colour and majesty, and there was every shade of green. A solitary, hovering bird began to glide on spanned wing, and that was the only movement that came to the eye. They looked, the Iceni and the Trinovantes, and held their breath. Banked clouds hung motionless above the peaks.

They had traversed lush valleys thick with undergrowth, the dew rich and wet beneath their feet. They numbered three thousand men, women and children, the best and most courageous of the surviving peoples who had gone to war for Queen Boadicea. Those who had remained in the sacked and pillaged kingdoms had been too old or too timid for such a migration, thinking the mountains of the west would surely prove too inhospitable to people born in regions of plain and forest. But three thousand people could not be called inconsiderable—and all of them, even the elders given to finding fault, even the erstwhile people of Durvulavum, had become hardier and more resourceful. They had survived hardships, they had survived Romans. The unknown elements of life among the mountains would not easily reduce them, if at all.

A few had died on the way, and some had fallen in battle; but these losses had been inevitable, and could be discounted against the safe arrival of three thousand. The migration had been slow and wearisome, every league a hazard; but every week had heard a new song born, and every day an old one sung. How they loved these songs, which told of how Ludicca

372

the brave had fooled Marcellus the vain, how Canis had tricked Cartimandua the greedy, and how Princess Cea had endured as fearlessly as her mother.

They had brought with them all they could of precious belongings, and they had also acquired twelve hundred invaluable and lovely horse. The waggons and chariots, having served their purpose, had been pushed over the edge of a high, rocky gorge, to smash piecemeal in hurtling descent— until jagged, twisted metal and splintered wood catapulted into the deep lake fed by some spume-foaming waterfall. Waggons and chariots could not be taken through the wild valleys and defiles of the tortuous ascents to the lower slopes of the mountains. Nor could the vehicles be left where patrolling Romans might find them and know the Britons had passed that way. So they had gone, smashed and plummeting into the lake, and plunder and baggage put on the backs of horses. And as the Britons moved slowly on, traversing the feet of soaring majesty, there was the feeling of Paullinus receding.

This was a world where everything was unfamiliar to them, where the mightiness of stone or granite was like nothing any of them had ever seen, save only Canis, who had campaigned with Caesar's legions for two years and travelled the Roman Empire for five. He had seen even mightier heights, even higher clouds.

The horses picked their way daintily, fussily, but did not blink at the wonders of nature as their riders did. The Britons were travelling in a long, winding column, climbing slowly, almost imperceptibly, it seemed—with Canis and Cea at the head, and Andudo in the rear. Animals used as packhorses showed no ill-feeling, they stepped as neatly as the ridden horse. They were trained to gallop and charge, not to carry bundles, or joggling women or excited children; but they bore it all with such patience that the warriors leading them were always kissing their noses. Women who had lost husbands, and children who had lost fathers, had no lack of the warming company of men now. And as they went on, the old ones

373

gaped and the women stared at near heights, distant heights and vaulted stone.

It kept up the spirits to hear the warriors twisting the beards of the old ones, and to listen to the old ones giving as good as they got.

"Perch up, hoary one, sit lighter on my horse's rump—or you will change his shape."

"Go dip your chin in malt, beardless pup, or say if I might lend you seven whiskers and make a man of you."

If there was a little uncertainty in some minds, it was not surprising—for who could say what their life might be like within these towering walls? Who knew the tempers of these green-clad giants or those blue-slated ridges that broke the roof of the sky? There might not be a Roman at one's door each day, but there were worse things than Romans. It was said that mountains harboured more than fearsome gods. Even the darkest spirits of the forests were not darker than those which howled in mountain caverns. The latter had only to howl in anger and the storm of it would deafen a man for ever.

However, despite little uncertainties and superstitions, the general feeling was not an unhappy one. The three thousand Iceni and Trinovantes—and two Brigantes— had become an indivisible whole. Each knew the other, each had striven for the other, and there were enough comely women and vivacious warrior maids for most of the men to look for the right kind of warmth and comfort in their new life.

Summer had gone. Each day felt the increasing nip of autumn. The trees were tipped with russet and gold. But there were warm cloaks or robes in bundles carried for so long. These would cover the patches and tatters of worn tunics, and protect limbs from sharper nips. Princess Cea wore a cloak of blue as she rode, her auburn hair rich, long and flowing, her eyes full of delight and wonder—as constantly changing vistas of white cloud and distant slopes opened more breathtakingly before her. Three small children rode on the horse surrendered to them by Canis. He walked alongside, with Cea on his left, she regally above him on her chestnut Pegasus. She was more of a princess each day, though cast in a more malleable mould than her mother. Boadicea had been a queen first and foremost, Cea was wholly a woman in her twentieth year of life.

" Canis, is it not awesome and beautiful?" she said. " There must be room for us somewhere here. We cannot build our kingdom on a peak."

" We are still no distance, Cea. We are still treading around the giants' feet."

The ascent they had made had been slow and gradual, through valleys and sloping ways; and now they began something of a descent over a track, which in time broadened to reveal an area dense with evergreens. Here the colours and the trees reminded them of their Iccni forests.

" Oh, this is beautiful indeed," she said.

" But would take us years to clear," said Canis. " We must find land deep in soil to plough and plant. We must go further, climb higher. There will be valleys full of earth washed down from the mountains, and we will find a place too far for Romans to trouble about. But since you are so taken with what you see ahead, we will rest there for tonight and go on tomorrow."

She looked down at him. He was the accepted lord of her people. He had striven so hard for her house, taken much of every burden. He had protected her, been grim with her, provoked her and loved her. Remembrance of love turned her hot. No Princess of Britain should ever give herself to her promised husband until she had wed him. But that was not as much her blame as his. She had gone to him only because she was so unhappy, and he should not have kissed her the way he did. It had quite confused her, as it would any innocent maid. (That which she had suffered at Roman hands, that unthinkable outrage, she had shut from her mind for ever).

She knew, as she had always known, why Lydia was with them. At times it made her jealousy burn like fire. But by her very nature, she could not carry her jealous thoughts beyond the fact that Lydia loved Canis. She could not conceive that Canis would be unfaithful. He suffered Lydia's gestures of

375

possessiveness and her hungry green eyes, because Lydia needed kindness and understanding. Never would he bed with her. He would not be such a villain as that. True, it had happened once, but that had been at a time when two people in their circumstances needed each other. It was painful to accept the child Lydia had conceived on that occasion; but because Lydia had given up so much to help the Britons, Cea could not be unkind. All the same, Lydia was a green-eyed hussy in the way she looked at Canis. If ever she went beyond looking—then she, Cea, would not hesitate to do as her mother would. She would have Lydia married off to a woodcutter.

Lydia, a little distance behind Cea, rode in company with Grud. Behind Lydia rode Feola, possessive and loving nurse to Dilwys, whom she carried wrapped in warm wool. Every horse went at a nodding patient walk, and the child was quite safe. Lydia had a young girl up with her, Grud a small, excited boy who gave the ageless one plenty to mutter about.

It was strange, thought Cea, how Lydia effaced herself at times. Since they had woken and busied themselves for departure at dawn, and during the many hours they had travelled since then, Lydia had not been near her or spoken to her. Cea turned her head to look back. Lydia was there, in a woollen cloak, her face lifted, her eyes on the vast range of evergreens. She caught Cea's glance and distinctly coloured up. She has been up to something, thought Cea.

" Canis," she said, " I do not always trust Lydia."

"Ah," said Canis, regarding the way ahead. Her hand reached down. He took it, pressed the smooth, firm fingers. She spoke so that the children could not hear.

" Sometimes, Canis, I am in doubt."

" Sometimes, Cea, we all are."

" Tell me again I am your true love."

" You are, for who else is of Boadicea?"

" I do not always want to be loved because I am my mother's daughter. I am myself, Cea. Canis, you would not betray me? You would not cleave to Lydia?"

He looked up at her. The white clouds were in his eyes,

obscuring whatever truth was there. Or whatever there was of sly deception.

"I am bound to you alone, Cea."

"Sometimes I am tempted to put out Lydia's eyes that are always eating you," she said.

"You are an imaginative Princess," he smiled. He moved closer to the three children riding his horse, and pointed out broad-winged, fierce-beaked mountain birds wheeling above their nesting ledge, which hung in space.

"I am also sometimes tempted to bite you," said Cea, when he returned within reach of her whispering voice.

"And I to make a meal of you, tender one. Love is a hungry emotion."

She could not resist his way with words, or the smile he gave her. As a child of ten she had loved him. She loved him now. It was the happiest of feelings. She laughed. She was disarmed.

"Oh, you will make a sweet, tormenting husband," she said. "And look, is it not more beautiful yet?"

The mountain ridges stretched into misty infinity, and the light beneath the white clouds, which hid the sun, softened the colour of the evergreens. They went on, through ferns and bushes, making for the trees that would hide them and give them shelter for the night.

"Bergotix, husband," said Caleda, walking tirelessly with him amid the long, winding column of Britons, "this is a strange land, full of high peaks that kiss the sky. Do not stray on that limping leg of yours, or you will tumble over a ledge and never reach the bottom."

"Ah, Caleda," grinned Bergotix, "you are at it again, looking after me in your own confusing way."

They entered the evergreens in a while, and when all three thousand were comfortably encamped and chewing on dried meat and hard bread, Lydia and Grud went the rounds of the wounded, who had had a more trying day than the others. Lydia knew what she might do better than anything else in the new kingdom.

377

"When a dwelling is built for me, Grud," she said, "you will visit me each day and instruct me how truly to minister to the sick and ailing. In this way, I will serve our people as you do."

"Mistress," said Grud, "you are young, and life for you should be rich and quick. You were born for fulfilment, not for stooping and mumbling over old ones with an ache in their bones."

"One cannot help stooping over the sick, Grud, but one does not have to mumble."

Grud, stowing away his unguents, showed what he thought of that by mumbling quite a bit himself. Then he said, "There are lusty sons of chieftains among our warriors here, any of whom—"

Lydia put a warm, slim hand over his mouth in gentle restraint.

"Grud, they are not for me. You know that. Instruct me in the skill of healing, not in how I might be the wife of a chieftain's son. I wish to be your very learned assistant."

"Ah, well, you will make a sympathetic physician," said Grud philosophically. "And perhaps it will be better than being a robe-attendant to Princess Cea. Once you had many to attend to your robes."

"Had I so?" Lydia was indifferent to the reminder. "I cannot remember." She did not wish to. "Oh, this is a sweet and vigorous life, Grud."

The thick mantle of evergreens muted the evening light. But Grud clearly saw the dreams in her eyes. He muttered.

She had not spoken to Canis all this day, or been very near him. But she only had to think of his body and hers in that bright rim of solitude, for her limbs to vibrate as if he were still with her. Nor had she spoken to Cea. She could not meet the eye of the Princess again. Cea, though a woman now, was still unworldly. Lydia, though only two years older, had left unworldliness far behind. But she could still not meet Cea's eye.

It was almost dark when Lydia left Grud. Fires burned, and she sought Hywel and Feneda, who were waiting to share their meal with her, Feneda having begged for her company. Making her way through the crowded, murmuring camp, the twilight about to give way to the night, she stopped as Canis emerged from shadows. He seemed so assured, so invulnerable. She waited for him to speak, her heart hammering, her face hot. His smile was like a softening of the shadows on his face. His eyes held hers. Hers were luminous, his were of the night. But not this night. Last night. A tremor ran through her. Then he was gone, wordless, and she wondered if he had indeed been there, if it had not been her heart and her longing which had conjured up only his image.

*   *   *

The next morning they went on, winding steadily upwards again. Now there was sun as well as cloud, so that sometimes they were dazzled by shining ridges and by vast spaces hanging emptily beneath the sky. The game was abundant, the way difficult in places, tolerable in others. Each turn or bend brought new wonders, new perspectives, to a people born in the encampments of lowlands. The air was crisp and without mist; but as horse toiled and men plodded, they perspired. The old ones grumbled, but went on; for if they could not grumble, what other pleasures were there at their age?

They rested at noon on a friendly strip of green overhung by a vast, jutting ridge of stone. As soon as he had eaten, Canis went on to make a survey of their next stage, taking with him Andudo and Cea, Grud and Lydia. Grud was good at smelling out what was promising and what was not, and Lydia went because ostensibly it was habitual to accompany her mentor. And indeed, she hung a little farther back with him. But Grud knew she was there in case anything happened to Canis, not to discuss the properties of what herbs grew in the wandering mountain valleys.

Canis wished to discover what lay in front of them before asking all three thousand to climb further, and whether there was a suitable place to make their night camp. After an hour he seemed satisfied, though not because the going had been easy. It was narrow and difficult in places. Which was a discouragement to Romans. They could not fight pitched battles in this kind of terrain. The Druids had committed a fatal error in allowing Paullinus to trap them on the isle of Mona, when the mountains had been close enough to swallow them. There were places here where fifty men could hold back a thousand all day, and then vanish at the onset of night.

They trampled on a little longer, winding their way around slopes, and Cea's legs began to ache a little at the climbing they had to do. But Grud rolled upwards, bow-leggedly and tirelessly. It was no great strain on Andudo, and Lydia was supple and agile. They encountered a track, such as it was, and this led them to a broader way. It narrowed again as Canis, leading, skirted a sheer drop on his left, and brushed a high stone face on his right. Negotiating this, and rounding the curving wall, he suddenly halted in his tracks. Cea, following on, stopped too. Her eyes opened wide and she called out.

"Come quickly!"

Grud, Lydia and Andudo joined them, and saw before them a wide, lush valley. It stretched away beyond their sight, and was bounded on each side by gently ascending slopes that extended to merge far and wide with vast, irregular bulwarks of stone rising in serrated formation to the sky. In the distance, the autumn sunlight trapped in the valley seemed to kiss shimmering water, and this indeed was a small lake which, fed by mountain streams, carried its surplus to a rocky gorge and torrented into it. But for that, the whole valley—huge as it was—would have been a lake.

As they surveyed the promise of what lay before them, seeing it virgin and unspoiled, a man watched them from heights fifty feet above. Bold and wolverine were his brown eyes, and strangely flecked with gold. He counted them. Five. Three men and two women, the men in kilted tunics, the women cloaked. The boldness intensified as his gaze lingered on one of the women. She had rich, raven-black hair; and she seemed, from this distance, to be vividly beautiful. Nor, for him, could her cloak altogether hide her shapely form. The man smiled, his mouth showing full and red amid his golden beard.

No one was aware of him, he was silence itself. He could hear their voices, but not what they said.

"Grud, you are as discerning as a man with a thousand years under his nose," said Canis, "so what do you say to pastures like these, old goat?"

"I say we have come a long, hard way to find the kind of land we left in plenty," said Grud, "but there were circumstances to consider which we could not ignore. Therefore we have come to where we are now, and though I am not a tiller of ground or a planter of corn, and though my legs feel as if I have travelled the full face of the earth, there is something about this place which farmers might make much of, if the Deceangi refrain from lopping our heads as we sleep at night."

"Grud, you are a wordy wanderer," laughed Cea. "Confess now, we shall not find a better place than this. And what should we fear from the Deceangi when there are so many of us?"

Andudo said, "My eyes tell me we can find sufficient here for our needs. We have seeds, we have grain, and though we may have to pull our belts in a little for a year or two, there is meat we can hunt. Also, I will admit favouring it for my own reasons. There is the widow, you remember, who was the comeliest of all the widows in Durvulavum. She has a warm heart and two children. She will be happy to wed me, she says, but has been dinning my ears for days with the fact that if we travel much farther there will be nothing left of her legs."

"Tell her," said Cea, "that we have found this place, and that her legs will be saved. Oh, surely Andrasta herself would dew her feet at dawn here. Canis, here is our new domain. It is my wish that we make it so."

It was her wish. Yet it had to be his wish also. He seemed in pleasurable contemplation of it.

Lydia was frankly enchanted. It was not Rome, there were no mighty, man-built colonnades, moulded stone temples, shining marble images or brilliant friezes, and there was not a single house. But then, nor was it under the constraint of

381

narrow laws and fussy decrees, or suffering from argument, judgement and military pomp. Simply, it was soft, green and vast. And untouched. The grandeur was a magnificence, and the land mountain-locked, remote from the heartbreak of bitter conflict. Here, surely, they could live in peace.

"Might it do for us, Canis, might it?" asked Lydia breathlessly.

"There is timber, do you see?" he said, pointing. They would need timber above all other materials at first.

Far down on the left-hand side of the valley, edging the shimmer that was water, and thickly carpeting the slopes, was the massed deep green of a forest. With its timber, with hewn rock and stone, they could build their encampment, found their new kingdom and make Cea Queen. Here the house of Boadicea could rise again. They could build for Cea a palace such as her mother had had in Venta Icenorum, with a lofty and majestic hall, a great and hospitable fireplace and huge winter warmth.

"It will do," said Canis.

"Aye, I have already said so," remarked Cea, not inclined in this matter to be the lesser voice. In any event, she was well aware that meek, assenting women had as much appeal for Canis as sheep. "Indeed," she said to emphasise how independent was her mind, "as soon as I saw it, I knew it would do us very well."

"When the eyes of a woman mark a site suitable for the encampment of a queen," observed Canis, "that woman cannot be less than a princess."

"That is so," said Andudo.

"We will bring our people up tomorrow," said Canis, "and give them a full day to make the ascent. And then a further full day to sit and do nothing."

"Such sweet charity," laughed Cea. She could not disguise her pleasure. Here she would at last wed Canis. Here, when her royal house had been built, she would be crowned with ceremonial ritual and be called Queen. And as Queen she might then, if she so desired, name her consort King.

They made their way back. Golden-brown eyes watched them, dwelling especially on Lydia. The smile was libidinous.

Approaching the bend that led to the narrow ledge and its precarious smoothness, they suddenly encountered an old man. He blundered into them, his head down, his eyes on the track. Startled, he took a step back. He slipped, and might have slithered over the edge, had Canis not taken him quickly by the arm. The old man showed little gratitude; and indeed, what came spilling from his lips in a strange language sounded like irritation for their being in his way.

"Up, old one," said Canis, "and tell us where you are from, and how we may send you safely back there."

The man was grey of hair, which grew wild about his head and face, and he wore a long, ancient kirtle with the dyes so faded as to be lost forever. An even more ancient garment was wound around his shoulders and chest. He cupped an ear, he mumbled incoherently after the fashion of Grud, and he peered up at Canis from under bushy brows. His eyes were rheumy with age.

"Old one, where are you from?" asked Canis again.

The grey old man had a mind that groped to make sense of the question. When he answered it was haltingly, as if rusty tongue had to search for each word.

"I am from anywhere. You are from the east. I came long ago from the east, to wed a maid of the west. Now I am from anywhere. My feet hurt. I have not heard your language for many years."

"What community is yours?" asked Canis. "With what people do you live?"

The old man mumbled some words around without delivering them. He spat; he thought. His tongue took itself in hand, and he spoke again.

"I live with myself, I dwell with none. I am here and there. I have two goats and two sheep. My feet could be better than they are. I lost my maid before she grew to woman. But they will not feed me to their stone-eyed gods yet."

383

" Who are they?"

More searching, before the old man said, " Any who inhabit this region."

" The Deceangi?"

Again the old man spat.

" They deliver all Romans, and all strangers, to the gods who dwell in their bottomless pits. They worship the dark ones, and eat each other. It was said that the dark ones took my maid. But the Deceangi took her."

" Are there many Deceangi?" asked Canis. All about them was space, and his voice hung in the air.

" What is many?" said the old man. " They are all different, yet all the same. They war with each other over trifles. Down beyond over there—" he waved his hand vaguely "—Carriog and his thieves lurk. Up above, you will find Urwin App Erryn and his robbers. The one will not go up, the other will not go down, and so they never meet save when they wish to kill each other. The Deceangi will not stand together against any-one but Romans. The Romans live in stone houses between the mountains. The Deceangi leap from the mountains, destroy the stone and kill the Romans. If I were a Roman in this country, I would go back to Rome. I have seen many others like you down below. Carriog will be watching them."

" And if we bring them all up to the place of forest and water?"

" Urwin App Erryn will watch them." The old man grinned, to show loose brown teeth, and his hair blew about his face. " My feet are not as quick as they were, but they will take me on from here. So if you will make room, I will hop by."

" Bring us your goats tomorrow," said Canis, " and we will give you gold for them, or borrow you and your goats for a while and still give you gold."

" What is gold when a man has goats? Find your own. There are many goats, all for the taking, if you look hard enough. The Deceangi will claim them—but if you are strong enough to argue, they will bargain for them with you."

He shuffled by, close to the drop, his bones creaking. But

384

when he had passed them, he leapt upwards as nimbly as one of his goats.

"The Deceangi," muttered Grud. "Umph."

As they continued on their way back, Lydia prayed that the Deceangi, whoever they were, would not provoke conflict.

15

They began the ascent to their destination the following day. Cea and Canis left soon after dawn, taking with them Lydia and Grud, Hywel and Feneda, Caleda and Bergotix, and an escort of twenty warriors. This advance party was to ensure that the way was clear for the rest. As for the rest: Andudo remained behind to overseer this, the final stage of their journey. It was in his nature as a chieftain to be a stern, efficient and protective shepherd; and with the help of the many warriors, he meant to see that all the women, children and old people, together with all horse, safely reached the site of their intended encampment. It would take many hours to get all three thousand persons up, but Andudo was the man to achieve it.

Canis and his party went on horse. It was not the terrain for any horse; but one more task of the advance force was to find the most negotiable route for the animals, and to mark it for those who followed. There were places where space seemed to fall dizzily away from them, and they frequently dismounted to lead their mounts. Canis carried Dilwys in a strong holdall slung over his back. She was awake, gurgling and dribbling in delight. Cea did her best to act as if the child was not there, but so far forgot herself on one occasion as to reach and tickle her. At which Dilwys opened her pink mouth and blew bubbles.

" Oh, it is very hard," Cea said.

" What is?" said Canis.

" That she is so sweet, that she is yours but not mine."

His smile was affectionate. Cea had become a woman, richly endowed by all that life bestows on a woman in the way of grace, beauty and shape. Rich itself was her dark auburn hair; life itself warm and quick in her brown eyes.

He said, " You have so much time, Cea—enough to have all the children you wish."

" If you will give them to me," she whispered in an impulsive little outburst of warm desire, and then blushed vividly.

" When we are wed?"

" Oh, now, today, tonight, tomorrow—"

" Cea?" There was laughter in his eyes.

" Am I shameless?"

" You are a woman," he said.

" Oh, it is very hard," she said again.

" Now what is hard?"

" To be a woman who must behave like a princess."

" You mean a woman may be shameless, but not a princess?" he said. " Ah well, if you desire it, sweet Cea, I will forget you are a princess whenever you wish to consider yourself only a woman."

" Oh, torment," said Cea, and laughed.

They tracked on in their slow, winding rise. They had advanced deep into the mountainous region since they had first set their feet into its gateway; and now it seemed that space and height had become their giddy new world. But greater space and height stretched outwards and upwards in limitless perspective. They had not ascended all that far about the lower levels. It was far enough, however. They must lay claim to that valley a little way above them. Progress was steady and everyone in fine spirits. Bergotix was manifestly happy, Caleda vibrantly alive. Canis, feeling that he had seen too little of them and owed them more than he had given them so far, had said so and asked them to join this advance party.

" Lord," Bergotix said, " since you have given us freedom, you owe us nothing."

" I owe you for the friendship you gave me."

" That is little, lord," said Caleda, " when set against what we had and what we were, before you put your foot inside our door."

All the same, Caleda was quite unused to climbing dizzy tracks and leading a horse as well. It took nearly all her breath at one stage, but she had sufficient left to inform Bergotix that perhaps the disadvantages of life in Brigantia were not quite as bad as she had thought. Bergotix grinned and offered to take her back there, adding that he would beg the use of two horses from Canis to make the journey as comfortable for her as possible.

" Be a sweet fool again," said Caleda, " do not brush me with nettles."

Bergotix spread his grin. Caleda was more herself than ever. And with looks to make a man proud of her. She had been comely as a maid. As a woman she was handsome. Lately, she had been taking extra care with herself. Her hair shone from the frequency with which she combed it; and she was always putting soft water to her face, and asking for flax oil to treat her hands. Flax oil, where might he get flax oil? She told him to beg it from Grud. He did, and Grud always gave him a little. Except that Grud refrained from saying that it was not flax oil. It did not matter. It served its purpose, and Caleda no longer bit her lip when she looked at her hands.

Feneda, despite her wound and the outrageous smell of the decaying poultice, wended her way joyfully over rough tracks and slippery slate paths, singing to her horse. She was with the men and women she loved better than any. She loved Canis, born to be lord of all Britain, as all the warrior maids loved him. He stood above all other men, although he was not as tender a man as Hywel. Cerdwa, the greatest and most beautiful of all the warrior maids, had said that Canis would never die. In the camps of the Britons during the campaign of Queen Boadicea, Cerdwa would stand with her violet eyes full of laughter, mocking other warrior maids for their attachment to certain men.

" Oh, lovesick dolts, these are only men, and are nothing. Canis is a god. Did I not see him break the back of Bilbo the Roman scourger, and Bilbo taller than a Druids' temple and wider than an oak? Men cannot destroy Canis, nor even the gods. He will live for ever."

Feneda had been there, had seen her and heard her.

She loved Lydia because Lydia was as brave as Cerdwa, and even more beautiful. She loved Cea because who could not love the brown-eyed, imperious daughter of their proud and fiery Queen? And she also loved Hywel, the Trinovante captain. Was he not the happiest of warriors, now that he no longer languished for Lydia? He was caring and affectionate over paths loose with shale or slate. And he made such whimsical jests about the evil smell of her bandages.

" Is it the scent of a new flower you wear today, Feneda?"

" Aye, a flower unknown before. Is it not seductive, Hywel?"

At this kind of response, he could not resist kissing her. It turned Feneda rosy. He must surely care very much for her to kiss her so often when her bandaged arm exuded such a pungent odour. She would beg Grud to remove it tonight. Her wound no longer throbbed, and was only a little painful. Indeed, there was no pain at all whenever Hywel kissed her. She wondered if he would wed her. He had not yet said he would. So when he would have kissed her again, as they slowly climbed into the heart of the mountains, she said, " Hywel, is a maid for kissing at each turn in the way?"

" A maid is for kissing, wedding and bedding," said Hywel.

" I have heard," said Feneda, looking at distant blue ridges, " that it is not unusual for a maid to be asked first."

" Goose," laughed Hywel, " have I not just asked you?"

" Hywel, you said—oh, Hywel!"

They climbed on, the eight of them, the escort of warriors following. Cloud was again sitting above ridges and peaks, and the day was coolly autumnal. But the exertions of the ascent warmed them. The only sounds were their own. The clatter of horse, the slither of shale and the murmur of voices, all turned into echoes that vibrated, hung and receded. And when they finally reached the broad way, and stood to observe the great wide valley, there was wonder in the eyes of Caleda and Bergotix, delight in the eyes of Feneda and Hywel. The score of escorting warriors arrived, their mounts throwing up their heads, and each man and each horse knew that what lay ahead was a limitless tract of land over which they could gallop, and that there was room to breed healthy fourlegs for trading with the lowland nations. That land, walled by the sloping, ridged heights, surely meant they had reached a place where they could live in peacc.

But even as they drank it in, there was the noise of quick-moving men dropping from stone coverts, from the slopes on their right. In moments, they were surrounded. There were three score of them, men in long kirtles, with cloaks that were folded and wound around shoulders and chests. They were almost as hairy as Agra and his friends. They were not tall men, but they were sinewy and agile, and each man showed a daub of red dye on his forehead. Their weapons were various and many, their small round wooden shields studded with metal. Some carried swords that had once belonged to Romans. Eyes glintingly curious and intense stared at Canis and those with him. One or two looked as if they wanted to grin at the presence of horses. Mountains were for goats and sheep, not horses.

No one spoke. The warriors of Canis braced themselves, and Lydia felt the heavy sinking of her heart. From the circle of Deceangi, one man stepped foward. His thick shaggy hair was of deep gold, streaked bizarrely with grey; and his light brown eyes seemed full of tiny gold flecks. His beard was golden, his mouth red. He spoke in a dialect they did not understand. When he received no answer, only an inquisitive look from Canis, he spoke again.

" Alas," said Canis, " if you do not know our tongue, you may wag your own all day and still make no sense to us. We are an ignorant people."

" Ah, in their ignorance do you speak for them?" asked the golden man in their own dialect.

" At times," said Canis. Dilwys woke up and gurgled at his back.

" Why are you here, lowland man and carrier of babes?"

" To find where we may live in peace," said Canis, " and if we have not mistaken your friendly faces, we have found it here."

"We are here." The golden Deceangi man waved his hand, carelessly embracing here, there and everywhere. "We are not looking for company."

Lydia shivered, and Cea's apprehension was sharpened by the pain of sick disappointment. These were men of the mountains, men who knew every ridge and peak hereabouts, every advantage and every pitfall; and they no doubt used their knowledge to harry and destroy all intruders not to their liking. Bergotix thought, oh my life, they show ugly and villainous through their hair. But then he remembered his father had always said fear a man for what he is, not for what he looks like.

"We will not sit on your backs," said Canis, "but will dwell by ourselves. We are a simple people, and seek only to be free of Romans."

The golden man's eyes seemed full of silent chuckles.

"Ah, Romans frighten you?" he said cheerfully.

"Rather we are inclined to fall over them," said Canis, like a truly simple man, "for they are always in our way. Therefore, it is better for us to live here where we will only be in each other's way."

"Lowland man," said the golden man, while the rest of the Deceangi looked on in a way Caleda did not like, "you cannot live here except by our leave."

"We do not need a great deal of room," said Canis, "for as you see, we number only a few, with one babe."

Lydia and Grud knew what had inspired that bluff. It was what that old grey man had said. Those below did not go up, those above did not go down. If these men were the robbers of the Deceangi chief called Urwin App Erryn, Canis wanted to know if they were aware of all the warriors and people toiling slowly upwards from below. They could not be seen. There were too many twists and turns, too many bold physical variations. And although Lydia strained her ears, she could hear no sounds.

The response of the man was simply to say, "I see what I see." The strange golden-brown eyes passed from Canis to

Lydia, boldly scanning her. Lydia suddenly felt icy cold, as if her garments had been stripped from her and she stood naked in the keen air. There was menace in the silence of the mountain men around them; but in the covetous eyes of this one man there was, for Lydia, far greater menace. "There is more room here for a few people than in all the rest of Britain," the man went on, "but none for you, lowlander, unless we make a bargain." His hand came up to stretch the lobe of his ear. "You will find it a bargain governed by the generosity of my tender heart, since we might kill you all here and now, take what we want and leave your flesh to the wolves."

They had not been attacked below by Carriog, thought Canis, because Carriog knew how many they were. This man did not know. His hunting grounds were here, and in the west and north. East and south took him downwards, into the pastures of Carriog.

"What bargain is this?" Canis asked the question mildly, observing that although the man was dealing with him, his eyes were on Lydia.

"I will bargain for the woman," said the golden-haired man, nodding at Lydia. "Give her to me, and as my name is Urwin App Erryn and the gods my redemption, you may have this land here for your own. Go, travel a thousand leagues in any direction from here, and you will not find a bargain half as favourable. All this land and all your lives, just for one woman. I am a generous fool, but that is how I always bargain for what I will have. And I will have the woman. That one." And again he nodded at Lydia.

Ice froze her. She could not wrest her eyes from the hypnotic compulsion of the golden-brown. She waited for Canis to coldly deny the man. But Canis did not. He seemed, indeed, as if he considered the offer a tempting one.

"As you say," he said eventually, "it has the makings of a favourable bargain. Also, since we are strangers who do not belong here, and since—as you have said—you might kill us and take this woman without further quibble, no one could say you are not as generous as you suggested. However, our ways are not perhaps your ways. And in a matter of this kind, our way would be to ask the woman if she herself agreed to the bargain."

Urwin App Erryn showed his big teeth in a brilliant smile. The moist red fullness of his mouth made Lydia shudder.

"Here," he said, "it is our ways that prevail. It is not our way, when discussing a bargain, to refer any part of it to a woman. It is not what a woman is for. She is for what is decided for her. What woman knows her own mind? To help you reach your decision, lowlander, remember that I will have her, aye or no. I would prefer she came peacefully, however, and not have her scream and kick."

"Peacefully will be better for all," said Canis, "so if you and your men will withdraw twenty paces, we will discuss it with her, then speak with you again."

"Harken, carrier of babes," said Urwin App Erryn, "I will have her regardless, but out of nicety will withdraw as you wish. Let none of your men draw weapons, for if they do you will all die, the woman excepted."

He gestured to his men and withdrew with them, but without yielding the advantage of encirclement. Cea was in horror and fury.

"You cannot," she whispered fiercely to Canis, "I would rather risk conflict with them. And see, they know that if we do fight, they are likely to lose half their number."

Cea's willingness to risk all on her behalf brought hot tears to Lydia's eyes.

"We cannot risk you, Cea," said Canis, "nor will we. But you are right. They would rather intimidate us than fight us."

"Lord," said a warrior, "mount your horse and let Princess Cea, Caleda and Ludicca mount theirs too. We will help you break through them, and we will hold them off while you escape through that valley. You cannot bargain with Ludicca as the prize."

"Truly, you cannot," said Bergotix. "And these Deceangi are a stringy lot, for all their whiskers."

393

" He will not," said Caleda in her calm way.

" We will stand or fall together," said Hywel.

" We will stand, we will not fall," said Feneda.

" Stand? Fall? What are you about?" Grud was querulous. " Canis has said our Princess cannot be risked. There will be no fighting, only thinking."

Even so, the warriors spat on their hands, though they did not draw any weapons. Lydia felt numbness creeping over her, a numbness born of horror that Canis should give even a moment's thought to the suggested bargain.

" Our way is not their way," he said, " and what App Erryn wants he cannot have, unless Lydia herself finds him too agreeable to resist."

Lydia, deathly pale, was near to swooning.

" You would wish me to consider him?" she whispered. " Oh, you cannot even ask me to. You cannot! "

" He will not," said Caleda again.

" Lydia," said Canis, " do you think we would sell you to the Deceangi, even if it were a thousand times more favourable? Never. And is the land theirs to give? And would they give it to us? Aye, perhaps they would, but they would return in the night to kill us, and take it back from us. Now, did not the old man say yesterday that the Deceangi tribes will not stand together except against Romans? And that they eat each other? App Erryn has three score men against us now, and might find another three score. But what others will help him in a fight to win a woman for himself alone?"

" But he has said he will kill us now, and take Lydia regardless," said Feneda.

" I will die here with you," breathed Lydia.

" He will not want that," said Canis, " he is too hot for you. We cannot risk losing our Princess, he will not risk losing you. He will still bargain. For today at least. Let us see." He called Urwin App Erryn, who came forward with a smile on his face.

" Will I take her now?" he asked brazenly.

" Not now," said Canis, " for she asks the favour of a day to condition herself to leaving us. This is the way of any of our

394

women, when asked to leave those she has known and loved. Therefore, if you must have her, App Erryn, come and take her at this time tomorrow."

Lydia stifled a choking cry. App Erryn fingered his beard. He mused. He pursed his lips. He glanced at the score of hardy-looking warriors. He considered again the dark, lustrous beauty of the green-eyed Lydia, and he sighed.

" So," he said, " at this time tomorrow, then, I will come and take her. Do not think to slip away in the night, lowlander, for it will serve no purpose except to deliver her to one Carriog. He will not treat her as lovingly as I will. Further, when we come tomorrow we will take ten of these tasty fourlegs, for though we do not ride them, they make satisfying provender. Also, to ensure your good faith, give us two of your people here. One man and one woman. We will take them with us, and bring them back tomorrow, unharmed in every way—if you are here to receive them."

" Neither that, nor the ten horse, were part of the bargain," said Canis.

" I make the bargain, you are only here to agree," said App Erryn.

" We will go with them, Bergotix and I," said Caleda.

" I did not say so," said Bergotix, " but I will go, and take Hywel with me."

" I have already said, we will take one man and one woman," insisted App Erryn.

" Bergotix and I will go," said Caleda.

" It will be Hywel and me," said Feneda.

" Let Caleda and Bergotix go," said Canis, and his smile for Caleda was such that her very bones melted.

And so Caleda and Bergotix, the Brigantes, went with Urwin App Erryn and his mountain men as hostages. The Deceangi took them and disappeared with them, vanishing along the winding, upward tracks.

" It will be different tomorrow," said Canis, " so let us see now as much as we can of what this valley holds for us."

" Monster! " gasped Lydia and ran to cast herself down in

the turf which greenly carpeted the approach to the valley. She was heartbroken and inconsolable. Because of Cea, he could not comfort her as he might otherwise have done; he could only tell her she had no cause either to weep or worry. Lydia put her hands over her ears, making herself deaf to everything but the noisy anguish of her heart.

It was a long time before the first of the main host appeared, and it was dark when at last all three thousand warriors and people were disposed in fair comfort over the immediate area of the sheltered valley. They were full of buzzing and murmuring at the wonder of their new home. There was hard endeavour in front of them, much tiring work to be done, before their great encampment of dwellings could be constructed. But Canis had already selected the site, in the highest part of the valley. In the centre of the encampment would rise the royal house, which like the palace of Queen Boadicea would contain many apartments, and house men and women worthy of holding important posts or high office. Men such as Andudo, veteran campaigner, and Grud. And women such as Caleda, born for gracious service.

For the moment, however, all were content to wrap themselves up and sleep. All except warriors detailed to watch. And Lydia. As twilight faded, and the mountain ridges grew massively dark, Canis found her tearfully miserable.

" Lydia, you are in foolishness," he said.

" Go from me," wept Lydia, " I hate you, contempt you. You have put me in shame and torment. Go from me."

" This is worse than foolishness."

" Oh, that you could give any thought to selling me! It is unendurable! "

" Did I not say we would not? "

" What was that except artful words? Oh, monster, you told him to come and take me tomorrow."

" You have twisted my ears over this, but I am in more concern for Caleda and Bergotix than you."

At such cruelty, her cry was strangled. She knew him so

well—what he would do to protect Cea, to safeguard the house of Boadicea. If he had to strike an unspeakable bargain, he would.

"Go," she gasped, "go, and leave me to die."

"I cannot," said Canis, "for I made a promise to Julian. Lydia, everyone but you understood why we treated App Erryn in the way we did, and why we persuaded him to give us a day's grace."

"Aye, you treated with him," she cried, "and told him to return tomorrow, and I know why. It is because you would do anything for Cea and her people. Even to selling me, if that is the only way you can have this land!"

She could hardly believe her ears when she heard him laugh.

"I might get much for your beauty," he said, "I should get little for your intelligence."

"Oh!"

"Lydia, never have I known you so foolish. App Erryn will not take you, nor would I let any man. He will be back tomorrow with as many men as he can muster, but not as many as he will find he needs. Our concern must be for Caleda and Bergotix. If he is confident and knows nothing of how many of us are here, he will bring them with him. If he does not bring them, then we must outfox him in some way—for we will not give you to him, or sell you to him." He stooped and brought her up to face him. The darkness was kind to her red eyes. "But we had to bargain with him. He had three score men, we had less than half that number. I think we would have made a harder fight of it than he expected, but we could not risk it. Sometimes, Lydia, it is better to talk than fight. Bravery is always more expensive than words."

"Oh," she sighed, "I have been foolish. But when you gave so much thought to App Erryn, and so little to your poor Lydia—"

"Poor Lydia?" His face was dark. "I will endure anything in you except misery and self-pity."

She was so blindingly hurt by this that compulsively she struck back.

"Sell me, then! Give me to App Erryn! Destroy me utterly, you are cruel enough to. Aye, I remember when we first met how you gave me only brutality. You are only a barbarian, after all, a barbarian—" Her voice died on a gasp, and a tremor shook her. Aghast, she would have bitten her own tongue to take back what she had said. But could not. It had been spoken. She had called him barbarian, as she had so often in the days when she thought she hated him. She lifted stricken eyes to his, and waited for him to crush her and discard her. But he was not angry, nor was he cold. He was silently laughing at her.

"There speaks my true Lydia," he said, his hand lightly caressing her shoulders, "there speaks my sweet but true Roman. So say on, Lydia, what else am I that is not to your liking? It is good for any man to know his shortcomings, especially one who is in so much conceit of his virtues."

Now he was mocking her; but with such good humour that —reckless of who might have seen her—she flung herself into his arms.

"Canis, forgive me—I did not mean what I said, I did not!"

"But I prefer your fiery spirit to your woeful misery," he said. He laughed again, pressed her close for a moment, gave her brief bliss with his embrace, and then left her. She heard his voice calling softly back to her. "Do not forget to look beautiful when App Erryn comes for you tomorrow."

* * *

When the Deceangi arrived the following morning, there were a hundred of them. They brought Caleda and Bergotix with them, at which Canis allowed himself a faint smile.

As to Urwin App Erryn, for all his bold confidence his eyes widened to see the number of people there. He soon, however, perceived they were mostly women, children and

398

old men. Of warriors, there were only those he had seen yesterday. Leading his men, he came down into the valley; and Canis received him. Caleda and Bergotix walked with Deceangi men around them. The two Brigantes showed no signs of ill-treatment, only a pleasure at being back again. They had been the objects of curiosity among their captors at first, and then been ignored. So much so that they had been forced to remind the Deceangi that Brigantes, like all other people, sustained themselves on food. It had been given to them. They had spent the night in a mountain cave; and though it was not the last word in comfort, they thought it better not to complain. There was no telling how these fierce mountain people reacted to complaints from hostages who were also intruders.

" Here are your two people, returned to you as promised," said App Erryn to Canis, " and here are you with women and all sorts who were curiously invisible yesterday."

" Did Carriog not send you word that our women and our all sorts were on their way up?" asked Canis innocently.

" He is not a communicative man. No matter," said Urwin App Erryn airily. He had the air of a man who, in his own territory, could not be denied taking what he wanted. " Where is the green-eyed woman, and where are the ten beasts?"

" The woman is here," said Canis. He called, and Lydia came forward from a group of women, whose curiosity matched that of the silent Deceangi. The bold bright eyes of App Erryn glistened to see her. The morning was golden, with mist over the valley, and Lydia had a shining lustre to her hair and richness to her honeyed beauty. The Deceangi chieftain drew a long, sighing breath. Hers was a perfection of face and form which few women possessed. He smiled as he saw the tremor on her mouth. App Erryn was an unashamed voluptuary, more especially when the woman was as beautiful as this one.

Although his strange eyes, covetously roving, made her flesh creep, there was not in Lydia the fear of yesterday. She saw he had brought more men with him today; but as Canis had said, they would not be enough.

"When the horse are here," said App Erryn, "it will be a bargain completed."

"They will be here," said Canis, "and then, as I said yesterday, you may take them and the woman."

He whistled. The clear notes winged until they were swallowed, it seemed, by the misty haze the autumn sun drew up from the lush greenness. The air was soft. It would be cold later, when the sun had bedded beneath the ridges.

From afar came faint sounds, like piping echoes of the whistle. Then there was silence.

"Ten horse, where are the ten horse?" asked App Erryn and began to tug on his beard. He did not like the silence. Or the lack of any signs of hospitality which should accompany the conclusion of an agreeable transaction.

"Where, for a mountain man, are your ears?" said Canis.

App Erryn listened. The air began to vibrate. He stared down the hazy valley. Far off muted thunder rolled, the echoes floating back from the soaring hills of green. The ground trembled, and as the sounds of thunder increased, he saw the horse. There were more than ten. There were hundreds. They came out of the haze, the Iceni and Trino-vante warriors riding them in a massed gallop. They raised no cries of war, they came on waves of drumming hoofbeats, the enduring survivors of Bodicea's mighty host. The Deceangi men held their breath to see the moving forest of fourlegs topped by the glitter of a thousand spears. The Deceangi had seen Roman cavalry ride, they had not seen the Iceni and the Trinovantes.

App Erryn rolled saliva round his mouth and spat. He could see them, he could not count them. The pounding noise of the gallop outraged his ears, the earth shook beneath his feet, and it seemed that even the escalating ridges and slopes receded before the mighty onslaught of a thousand horse. When they were so close that App Erryn could see the rolling eyes and tossing manes, and when it seemed they would thunder over him and his men, they wheeled, swerved, and turned from massed formation into a streaming column that became endless. Endless it was, in that it encircled App Erryn and his men. Then a thousand horse reared, plunged and stood.

App Erryn showed his big white teeth between full red lips.

"So," he said, "you bring me more than I asked for, lowland man."

"Even more than that," said Canis.

For then came the wild warrior maids, all that were left of those who had followed Queen Boadicea, all whom Canis had drawn to the banner of Princess Cea, and these less than three hundred. A wanton law unto themselves, except that they had a great respect for Canis, who thought nothing of tossing an unruly one into a bush, they came out of the golden, hazy mist like joyful Amazons. With flying hair of black or tawny, brown or red, their legs and thighs supple and naked, they too rode galloping fourlegs. And where the warrior men had come only in thunder, the warrior maids came in thunder and song. Even above the noise of their gallop, the Deceangi heard their singing cries. Lydia felt their ecstasy, their surrender to the joy of movement, and her blood leapt. She was of them, for them, with them. And Feneda led them, using only one arm, her wounded limb slung. She brought them in a heady, infectious charge and the mountains flung back the sounds of their gallop and their song. The circle of warrior men opened to let them through and Feneda took them in a wheeling swerve inside the perimeter of men. They rode high astride their woollen-clad saddles, laughing to see the hairy Deceangi with red dye on their foreheads, and calling, "Oh, mountainous ones, we will shave you and eat you!"

It was then that Canis said to App Erryn, "Here are all the horse, friend. You may select the ten you want, take them from their riders and use them as provender. And you may take the woman you want. If you will."

And App Erryn knew that he could not take either the horse or the woman without fighting a thousand and more warriors.

"This is a sorry finish to our agreement," he said, "and no true son of an honourable father would act in such bad faith as this."

"It is a question of ways," said Canis. "Yesterday we were outdone by your ways. Today you are outdone by ours."

App Erryn's laughter was bitter. His desire for the dark-haired woman was greater now that he could not have her. However, what obtained one day need not obtain on another.

"I am cheated," he said, "and you cannot deny it."

"Bring us goats," said Canis, "and you will find the gold we give you will compensate you."

App Erryn reflected and then said, "If you have as much gold as that, we will bring you all the goats you need."

"For all the goats we need, we will give you six gold Brigante crowns."

"Six?" App Erryn's eyes gleamed.

"Four," said Canis blandly.

"Five."

"Five, then."

"So be it," said App Erryn. "I relinquish the woman and the horse. I will have my men bring the goats. I am a generous fool, so much so that I will even return to you the man and woman we took with us."

It was the best face he could put on his bitter disappointment. Canis smiled. The Deceangi chief thought it a hard, uncompromising smile in view of the outcome.

"Go your way, App Erryn," said Canis, "and as you go, put from your mind any further thought concerning this woman. She is not for you."

App Erryn shrugged. He could bide his time. He turned to go, then turned back.

"Who are you, breaker of agreements and spokesman for the simple?" he asked.

It was Princess Cea who answered him.

"We are Iceni and Trinovantes, and not so simple," she said. "We have fought and defeated Romans, and will fight and defeat all others who seek to destroy us. And he whose name you wish to know is Canis the Wolfhead—of whom all Britain has heard by now, except those who are deaf."

App Erryn regarded Canis with calculated indifference. He was not, in his own territory, a man to yield lightly his reputation to another's.

"Have I heard of you? I cannot remember. Perhaps Romans spoke of you, but I do not listen to Romans. No matter, you are here now. One day perhaps we will go against Romans together."

"If our ways coincide," said Canis, "perhaps we will."

App Erryn turned his eyes on Lydia. They were like the eyes of a cat. She sensed that his frustration had in no way weakened his desire. He would try again one day. She shivered a little. He ran his hand over his beard. He said, "Are you disappointed that I am not able to take you with me today?"

She looked at Canis. He smiled. It gave her back her spirit.

"Oh, I am in woe," she said.

"Ah," said App Erryn, "then when I have been paid for the goats, I will use the gold to buy you according to custom. That way I can take you with me and turn your woes into joy."

"Your customs," observed Canis, "are not our customs."

App Erryn laughed, but departed without saying why he laughed. His men followed him silently, except that some of them noisily spat. The people of Cea watched them go.

Hywel and Feneda were the first to dismount, to hurry to Caleda and Bergotix, and welcome them back. It was much later when Canis sought out the two Brigantes. He found Caleda with a child's tunic over her knees, patching it as best she could with strands of wool and a wooden needle. Bergotix was elsewhere, working with other men on the construction of crude shelters to provide temporary comfort, until stronger dwellings could be erected. It was something the men could do for the women, other than fighting.

Caleda rose from her work, the slightest flush on her handsome face. Canis gave her the courtesy of his hand. He often made her feel she was far more than she was. He did so now

403

with his courtesy and with his words, as he praised the part she and Bergotix had played with the Deceangi. Her flush deepened, because of his words and his smile.

In her unassuming way, she said, " We could not do else, lord, Bergotix and I."

" Could you not? Caleda, from your country Brigantia we brought horse, chariots, flour and gold—and in these things we were favoured. We also brought you and Bergotix. In this we were enriched. I am greatly in your debt, Caleda."

Caleda felt her facade of tranquillity slipping. His effect on her was always disturbing.

" You have given Bergotix freedom and new life, lord. And he is more than happy, more than grateful."

" It is easier for a man to search out a new life, Caleda. Are you yourself in any content?"

Though the flush came again, she did not turn her eyes from his.

" I am in constant wonder at myself," she said, " and sometimes I am in quite foolish content."

" Foolish?"

Behind him, the mountains soared; but he did not seem any less commanding than when he had stepped into her humble dwelling in Brigantia.

" It is when you speak with me," she said, pink beneath her smooth tan. " It is immodest as well as foolish. I am even more absurd than Bergotix, who is the sweetest husband— despite the fact that the weapons you have given him now make as much clatter as his tongue. Lord, are you sure you are not a prince or a king?"

" As sure as I am that in you, Caleda, Brigantia lost a woman who would have made a far handsomer princess than Venturia."

A thought struck Caleda, and she bubbled with warm laughter.

" But, lord, the Deceangi said that Bergotix and I were barbarians! "

People nearby turned their heads. Caleda, noted more for

her gracious serenity than her noisy mirth, was laughing loudly; and Canis, the grim scourge of Paullinus himself, was laughing just as loudly.

A woman smiled. They all smiled. They all began to laugh.

It was something to let the mountain gods know they were a cheerful people.

16

The new kingdom of the house of Boadicea was born. The great valley claimed by Cea and her people stretched and wound for leagues. It was intersected by the lake and the gorge into which surplus waters tumbled and roared. Mountain streams fed the lake. With men who understood the flow of waters, Canis explored the course of the streams and the lower depths of the valley, wishing to find out if there were any signs that pointed to flooding during winter rains. They found none. All courses led to the lake.

So they began the formidable task of raising earthworks, and building their fortified encampment. The people laughed and sang at their work, toiling from daybreak to dusk in the face of oncoming winter. They built temporary dwellings that would house them and keep them dry until the encampment came into being. In the construction of these they used timber from their forest that spread upwards on the southern side of the valley. And they used horse to pull the loads. The horse, with the grazing so lush, did not seem to mind. The finer craftsmen began to fashion the wooden spindles the women needed to spin their yarn, while foraging warriors laid claim to sheep they found straying.

The Deceangi brought the promised goats, in return for the promised gold; and at last Cea and her people had milk, a boon to women with infants. App Erryn himself came with his men, ostensibly to collect payment in person—but more obviously, thought Canis, to see what was afoot, and to take stock of Lydia again. The golden-haired man thought little of people who toiled as the Iceni and Trinovantes did, saying no true men of the mountains were hewers of wood and diggers of soil. But he did not mention Lydia or offer to buy her with the gold Canis gave him for the goats. He took the money and went away in peace.

However, each time sheep were taken several Deceangi would turn up to argue quarrelsomely about it. Each argument was settled by Canis handing over more gold, for the women clamoured at all times for wool.

If the Deceangi watched them, the Iceni and Trinovantes made no secret of the fact that they watched the Deceangi. They mounted vigilant patrols, day and night. They suspected that if they did not, the Deceangi would sweep down on them to snatch horse, kill men and take women. Canis suggested to Andudo that it would be as well to discover what would happen if they tempted the mountain men. Andudo thought it would show them whether App Erryn intended to be an indulgent neighbour or an acquisitive one. In the event of the latter, said Canis, the Iceni and Trinovantes must convince the Deceangi chieftain that it was not worth his while.

So for five days and nights the camp was without its usual watchful eyes, or so it appeared. It looked as if the people from the eastern lowlands had come to regard themselves as secure. So on the sixth night, the Deceangi slipped down from the heights as silently as mountain bats. But no sooner had they reached the perimeter of the night-shrouded camp, than a blackbird whistled. For App Erryn and his men, hard and fierce warriors though they were, their excursion became a desperate affray, as they found themselves fighting not for the booty but their lives. For the Iceni and Trinovantes, the most merciless and accomplished warriors in all Britain at this time, it was an opportunity to warn the Deceangi off for good. If the mountain men could see like wolves in the dark, the men who had lived in dark forests could see even better. With a hundred slippery and hungry men, App Erryn had meant to snatch what he could as quickly as he could, perhaps even Lydia. But Canis and Andudo were not to be caught out as obviously as that. Less than thirty of the Deceangi escaped; and App Erryn, not without courage and guile, also wriggled free. But it was a bloody and salutary lesson, and the women

407

of the men who were slain called down the curses of the dark ones on their chieftain's head, and spat in his face.

It left Cea and her people in peace. It made Lydia worry less. She was healthy, happy. She had Dilwys, and Dilwys was growing into a beautiful child. Feola, her nurse, brought her to her mother several times a day, so that Lydia could laugh at a new dimple or fatter gurgle. It enraptured her that Canis was the father of so lovely a daughter. She saw him each day, most often with Cea, but sometimes not. This was her life. She thought of no other. And she looked only for signs that she was his love. A glance, a word, a gesture, anything.

He had not wed Cea. That was because he would not wed one woman as long as he was in love with another. When the great encampment was finished—and towards the end of winter they were raising the vast earthworks—she would have her own stone and timber house. Canis would then do what he could not do now, spend hours with her at night.

The winter was cold, the mountains blue and white with ice and snow; but there was so much work to do. Yet they were all so hardy that few complained, although the old ones grumbled so that they should not go unnoticed. And when spring came with its burst of new life, a number of marriages took place—including that between Hywel and Feneda, and that between Andudo and his warm-hearted widow of Durvulavum. Her two children he took for his own, as consolation for losing Cyella. Feneda, fearless warrior maid, was as misty-eyed and shy a bride as any ordinary maid. And Hywel proved so teasing a bridegroom, as well as so virile, that Feneda was pink at the onset of each night, and even pinker at dawn.

Lydia was in some envy. She was also in some hope. For Canis had still not wed Cea. In the end, it would be as Diana contrived it, he would wed only his faithful Lydia. She shut her ears and her mind to that which people began to buzz about. They did not know what she knew. And she knew that Canis could not, would not.

She was with Grud when Caleda came to her one day. She

was more often than not with the mystic, acquiring more knowledge of medicine from him, and attending the sick with him. Caleda drew her aside, and though not given to procrastination, she spoke at length on matters which Lydia thought so unusually trivial that she began to suspect the Brigante woman had something on her mind which she was reluctant to impart.

"Caleda, what is amiss? It is not like you to go round and round."

"Mistress—"

"Caleda, do not call me mistress."

"I wish you would not be so humble," said Caleda.

"I wish you would not be, either. Are we not friends?"

Caleda felt compassion for the Roman woman, whose beauty had not brought her what she most desired. Caleda did not know how to soften the blow.

"I only came to talk to you," she said. "There is not a great deal happening, although I have just remembered that the elders have this moment proclaimed that Princess Cea is to wed Canis in seven days."

Lydia looked as if she had not heard. Her eyes were blank, uncomprehending. Then she swallowed and said as if each word hurt her throat, "What is this you say, Caleda?"

"It is true, Lydia," said Caleda gently.

Lydia paled. She swayed. Caleda put out her hand. Lydia stiffened. In pain, she whispered, "Caleda, I thought us friends—but friends do not come with news like this."

"Princess Cea is his destiny, is she not? That is what I have heard. But you are his understanding. There is sweetness in that—"

"Oh, Caleda!" Lydia was stricken. "That is not sweetness, that is not even true. How can it be when he is to wed Cea?" She saw the compassion Caleda had for her. It broke her pride; and she turned and ran, seeking a place where she could hide her mortally wounded being from every curious eye.

For the rest of the day she lay in torment. She could not collect herself, she could not think coherently, for her mind was in as much pain as her heart. She could not go near Cea or Canis, could not bear to look on those who had put her in such anguish.

When night came she could not sleep. She could only toss and turn, feverish with the torment.

It could not be, it could not.

Diana would never countenance his rejection of her.

She was his love, Cea was only the daughter of Boadicea.

How shall I endure?

How shall I ever sleep, knowing she is in his arms?

How could he be unfaithful to the mother of his child?

And so it went on—all night, and all day and every night. And when she saw Canis, she could only look at him with all her pain clear in her eyes, so that he might know how he was destroying her. Yet all he said was, "Lydia, it cannot be otherwise." She shuddered, the paleness of haunted night upon her, her eyes encircled by dark rings, and she said in a hissing whisper, "I did not think that when a man loved a woman he would kill her by merely saying 'It cannot be otherwise.'"

She was too blinded by anguish to see the pain in his own eyes; she could only turn from him and run from him, as she ran from others. Those who knew her well, realised the depths of her despair; but they did not force their pity on her. They knew, as Canis did, that it could not be otherwise. Lydia alone could help herself at this moment. Grud went about muttering fiercely, and did not hesitate to say to Canis, "You knew the inevitability of all this, and so should not have done to Lydia what you did do."

"You are an old goat," said Canis sourly.

It was not like him to be short-tempered.

Lydia did not go near him again, neither to beg him, nor reproach him. She spent the days remote from most and aloof with others. Her only constant companion was her torment.

It was different with Cea. The Princess was in warm happiness. Even as a young girl of ten, she had known that no other husband would do for her but Canis. While Lydia lived in

410

despair, Cea lived in delicious anticipation. Each day, the elders came to instruct her in the rites of the ancient ceremony as it concerned princesses, and on the seventh day maids came to beautify her and adorn her for the long ritual. The elders were satisfied that although relics attaching to the ceremony of a royal marriage had disappeared for ever when the Romans sacked Venta Icenorum, copies of those relics would suffice.

It was a day of spectacle for the people, joy for Cea and torture for Lydia. In the numbed vacuum of her mind, Lydia had cherished the hope that she was living only in a dream. But when the ceremony began, and Diana did not cause the mountains to disintegrate and destroy the world with fiery ash, Lydia realised she had to endure the unendurable. She did not know how she found the strength to stand and watch. Every moment racked and seared her.

Through eyes dry and burning, she looked at Cea. The Princess was radiant and beautiful. She was clad in new-woven raiment that covered her from neck to feet, and her auburn head was garlanded with crowns of spring flowers. Her brown eyes were suffused and emotional. She stood within the ritual circle of seven white-robed maids. Canis stood apart, ten paces from the circle. He wore his tunic and his studded belt, his plain cloak fastened by a single bronze clip. Lydia's burning eyes saw him only as her unfaithful love. He did not see her. She thought him strangely introspective. His eyes seemed to reflect dark clouds, although the day was bright with spring, the mountains green-clad. And Lydia knew he was not thinking of Cea, but of her proud, tempestuous mother, his dead Queen, who to him was undying. He loved Cea only because she had been born of Boadicea; and because of this, for Lydia his rejection was the more cruel. But this was his way—to follow the course he had set himself no matter what hurt he gave to others. He was dedicated to the restoration of the house of Boadicea, to making it strong again, and to this end would not draw back from condemning his faithful Lydia to years of anguish. How many Romans had died because of his hard, pitiless dedication? They could not be counted. And now he would slay another Roman, one who had an inextinguishable love for him. Now he would slay his Lydia, for from this day, although she would walk and talk, sleep and wake, she would be dead.

Three thousand people encircled the timber dais erected for the ceremony, and as they watched they sighed with emotion. It was not possible for Celts to be stiff of lip or unblinking of eye on such an occasion. Only Lydia was apart from the sensitive joy of the moment. The holiest of the elders poured forth the ceremonial words, until Lydia thought the ritual would have no end. Each incantation made her want to cry out in bitter protest. Feneda was close to her, watching her; and suffered for her, as she saw the pain in the stricken green eyes. Feneda sighed, for she was so happy herself. Lydia had to accept that Canis must do what he had to.

Lydia found it all so unbearable. The mountain peaks, even when mantled by winter ice, could not be as cold as her heart. The circle of white-robed maids, the figures of Cea and Canis, and the intoning priests, all served to engulf her in freezing despair. And the ceremony itself was an affront to great Diana, who had given Canis to her. It was unwise for a woman to affront the goddess, it was even unwiser for a man. No goddess was quicker to revenge herself on a man than Diana. She would destroy Canis for rejecting his loving Lydia and taking Cea to wife.

Wife. At last the unbreakable knot was ritually tied. Oh, how cold, how icy the bright day was. Unable to feel any of the joy shared by three thousand others, Lydia stood in lonely, inconsolable suffering as the ceremony was completed by the breaking of the circle of maids. The names of Cea and Canis were singing on every lip, as the Princess came forward to pledge herself to her husband and he to her. This they did by closely embracing. It signified they were one and indivisible, and that there was neither room nor wish for any to come between them. Then they drew apart, and took each other's hands.

"Now you are my dearest husband," breathed Cea.

"And you my cherished wife," he said in response. He kissed her amid the din of jubilation, and the kiss was like heady wine to Cea. He was hers now, bound to her by solemn rites, and surely bound even more by love. He touched her colourful robes and said, "You are beautiful, Cea. How came you by magnificence as well?"

"By the skill and ingenuity of the women," she said. "Oh, it is a happy day for me. Is it for you?"

"For both of us," he said, and kissed her again, smiling as the warrior maids sang to him and the warrior men acclaimed Cea.

She said, "There are so many people, we must go down to receive all their good wishes."

They descended and were immediately crowded and teased, though Andudo and Hywel kept Cea's robes from being crushed. Grud was there, and in his own mysterious way he was able to show one eye benign for Cea and the other darkly warning for Canis. Feola, nurse to Dilwys, paid glad homage. Bergotix was jovial, Caleda composed, saying to Canis in her quiet way, "Lord, I wish you joy of this day."

Lydia approached, in compulsive intensification of her torment. She pressed numb lips to Cea's cheek, but said nothing. For Canis she had only a look of bitterness. Then she went, thrusting her way through the press of laughing people, until at last she was able to give wings to her escape. She ran and ran, but not to her small dwelling. She went on, out into the wide valley, which already showed great areas of tilled earth.

It was Grud who eventually found her in the grey twilight, lying within the edge of the forest, broken, desolate and weeping.

"I have brought you food," he said, "so come, sweet mistress, eat. What is any day but one more step towards a friendlier tomorrow?"

"Oh, Grud, I cannot eat, I will never eat again. Grud, how may I endure such pain, how may any woman?"

"Any woman may not, but you will," said Grud, folding

his bow legs to sit beside her huddled form. "For as Queen Boadicea was brave enough to endure even greater torment than yours, so are you brave enough to endure this."

She wept afresh, tearing at the grass with distracted hands, thinking only of Cea and Canis, and of Cea in his arms. Where was the release from such torture, how could she live through the night, knowing that Cea possessed him, knowing that he more than any man knew how to pleasure a woman? (Had Feneda told her that Hywel had an unequalled talent for this, Lydia would merely have thought Feneda intoxicated by the state of being newly wed.)

It was Cea alone who from now on would experience bliss. She, Lydia, had been cast aside. For her there was only pain.

"Do not bring me food, Grud," she wept, "bring me only poison. Give me your physician's gift of sweet oblivion. I will take it gladly and die gladly."

"The food is here," said Grud matter-of-factly, "and also warm coverings, for I know you intend to lie out here all this night, so that dampness and cold may add enjoyably to your misery. I know nothing which gives a miserable woman more satisfaction than new misery. I have brought myself some coverings also, since it is not right for you to be alone as you drown yourself in tears."

"It is of no consequence," she groaned between shivering teeth, "for if I survive this night, I will kill myself tomorrow. Aye, I will wait until he comes warm from her arms, and then in front of his eyes I will take his own dagger and plunge it into my heart. In this way he will suffer for his cruel, selfish responsibility in the matter of my death."

"As you do this," said Grud, his round eyes innocently surveying the gloom that was now cloaking the world in darkness, "do not forget to uncover yourself, so that he may see the beauty he is responsible for destroying."

Her weeping was suddenly checked. There was the tiniest gasp, and the pain of remembering Canis tearing her blood-stained tunic and shift to uncover her in the moonlit wood. So Grud had been awake too at that moment. But she would not concede anything, and only said, "I could not be so shameless, even in my greatest hurt."

"Aye, the fair form of a beautiful woman is sacred," said Grud, "and not to be uncovered in any way, except perhaps to bring to the woman that which she most covets."

"Sometimes," said Lydia coldly, keeping her face from him, "your tongue is as hateful as his. So go your way and do not trouble about me."

"I am here, mistress, and will remain here. I will let you do nothing that does not do justice to your sweetness and bravery."

She was silent for a while. Then a dry, shuddering sob shook her, and she said, "Grud, I will love him no more, I will reject him and tear him from my heart. I will not even look on him again. I will take another man."

"That is more commendable than misery and tears," said Grud approvingly, "and though Hywel is now wed to Feneda, there is Yantes, a fine and proud warrior. Or there is Brunel or Yonwyn—"

"Be quiet," she stormed, beating the ground, "I do not want any of them. I want him—oh, Grud, he is the father of my child and has wed Cea. I knew him to be cruel, but not as cruel as this."

"Also," said Grud to the gathering darkness, "you knew him to be promised to Cea. You knew him to be indivisible from the house of Boadicea. This is his destiny, and he cannot escape it. Princess Cea must have a child, and by Canis. No other sire will do. It was the wish, the command of the Queen herself. All this you knew."

The torment raged more bitterly then.

"Grud, do not speak of that, I cannot bear it, I cannot bear all it means. If she gives him a child, a son, it will bind her to him like clinging vine. Aye," she went on miserably, "because of this, my mind is firm in its resolution, Grud. Tomorrow I will kill myself. But first, because of his cruelty, I will kill him. As he lies dying, he will see me turn the dagger on myself. This I will do, I will strike swiftly and fiercely."

415

"Ah," said Grud pleasantly, "your spirit is returning, your blood running quick and hot again. Already you are better. So come, mistress, eat."

He pushed the food towards her, where she still lay face down. She lifted her head, gave an outraged cry and dashed the platter away.

It was as Grud knew it would be. She lay there throughout the night, scarcely moving, the darkness shrouding her. He put the warm coverings about her, and sat looking at the night. She slept, but very fitfully, and each time she awoke from anguished dreams she sighed and moaned. Grud did not sleep at all, but it did not bother him. He was one whose young-old eyes could stay as open as his philosophical mind. He did not know how old or how young he was, only that once he had been a youth of forest lands and had served Callupus the Wolf, Iceni chieftain and father to Canis. He had seen Canis grow from child to boy, from boy to man, had seen him become a scholar and warrior, but how old or how young he himself was he did not know. He only knew that the mysteries of life were no mysteries, merely complexities and paradoxes brought about by the whims of women and the foolishness of men.

To Lydia it was the longest night the world had known. And even when dawn at last broke, it only meant she had exchanged anguished dreams for stark realities. There was to be no sweetness, no relief, only the pain of being unloved and rejected. She had thought she might mercifully die during such a night, and it was bitter to discover she was still alive.

Grud was there when the light became bright. He had gone at dawn, and returned now with food. She was cold, and so she ate it; but with her face averted. However, she said, " Oh, Grud, if only all men were as tender and loyal as you."

" I am nothing, sweet mistress," said Grud.

*　　*　　*

Lydia abjured Canis. She put a cold, unyielding fortress around her heart, and took herself from his sight. With Dilwys she went away each day to the forest, accompanied by Andudo, a natural woodsman. There was always a great deal of timber required for the building of so many things, and much had to be felled and set aside for seasoning. Andudo had charge of those who worked each day on hewing, stripping and shaping. In abjuring Canis, it was necessary for Lydia to be as far from him as she could, and so she helped with the forest work. She deserted Grud, whose close and skilful assistant she had become. Grud was frequently in contact with Canis, and she could not effectively abjure the latter if she shared this contact. So she said to Grud, " I have decided to do different work, to go with Andudo each morning and help in the forest."

" Ah," said Grud, scratching his thigh.

" I do not wish any argument from you. I shall go early every day, and take Dilwys with me."

" Ah," said Grud.

" Do not mumble or dispute it with me. I have made up my mind."

" There is the question of Feola," muttered Grud, " who has been a faithful nurse to Dilwys and has looked to her each day while you—"

" Dilwys has been Feola's concern for too long. Now she is my concern alone. As to other matters, should the Deceangi chieftain, Urwin App Erryn, offer to buy me with gold, as he said he would, tell Canis that if I am to be sold, then Dilwys must be sold with me."

" Ah," said Grud, looking for nothing to look at.

" Though a discarded woman is of little worth, her child is priceless. So Canis must see that justice is done to Dilwys, and a fair price agreed."

" Ah," said Grud.

" Do not argue," said Lydia coldly.

Those who worked in the forest were cheerfully industrious. Andudo was in his element as he selected and marked the most suitable trees for felling; and he toiled amain with his helpers at the laborious business of hewing them down. They bit into the stout wood with iron axes and crude chisels, and chips flew for hours before each giant crashed. But it was a man's work and satisfying. Lydia worked with some warrior maids, the maids full of song as they stripped and branched the fallen trees. Dilwys was not the easiest of responsibilities, she was in her second year and wanted to crawl and wander. Lydia put her on a long tether attached to a tree, away from the dangers of toppling timber and swinging axes. The child had a light wooden cradle, in which Lydia put her to sleep; but Dilwys did not take kindly to too much sleep, and nor was she altogether happy at the constraint of her tether. But on the whole she was a contented child, and gurgled when the warrior maids sang to her.

Lydia worked feverishly. It provided an antidote to her mental misery. She was horrified, however, at what the work did to her hands. But since her purpose was inflexible and since she was unloved, what did the state of her hands matter? Effectively she kept herself remote from Canis. If he came to the forest, as he sometimes did, she snatched up Dilwys and hid from him. At dusk each evening, she returned to her tiny hut; and when night came she lay down in tiredness to seek the relief of sleep. But sleep was always fitful, her unhappiness ever present, and no night was any less bearable than the preceding one. However, for the space of seven feverish days Canis did not see her, neither did Cea.

Cea was in bliss, giving herself ardently to Canis, loving him in all moods; and whether he was unmercifully teasing her or fully pleasuring her, it was all one to her. Her greatest longing was to give him a son.

She said to him one night, " Canis, because you bind me to you so strongly in love, surely I will conceive a strong son for you."

" Will I ask for sons, when the house of Boadicea has been notable for its beautiful daughters?"

" But, Canis, do you not want a son, a princeling?"

418

" Whatever you may conceive, son or daughter, either will be dear to me."

But Cea was determined to have a son. Lydia had given him a daughter. She would give him a son. She made offerings to the Great Father. No woman, not even one destined to be crowned Queen, would be too proud to call on the Great Father's help in such a matter. Canis, who thought little of gods, did not think any of them could determine the issue any better than Cea and himself, but did not say so. His indulgence of all the whims and desires of the Princess followed the pattern of years. His regard for her was tender and unalterable. She was Boadicea's only surviving issue, and when by a word or look, or by a little touch of haughtiness, she reminded him of his incomparable Queen, he could deny her nothing.

Cea thought him more than indulgent. His attentiveness delighted her. Sometimes he was unusually quiet. She thought this showed him to be aware of the solemn responsibility of his union with her. The joy was something else.

She wondered what had happened to Lydia. Grud mumbled that Lydia now worked in the forest with Andudo. Cea ventured to say that of all people Lydia was the last, surely, to enjoy wrestling with primitive wood. Canis said nothing.

Caleda came looking for him one day. He thought her as graceful as ever, despite the pioneering hardships. She would not wear the short tunic affected by so many maids and women, being modestly disposed to hide her legs inside a robe.

" Lord," she said, " this is a whimsical way of life for me. I am not, by your command, to stir cooking pots. And as the palace of the Princess is not yet built, I cannot take up my post as a robe attendant. What work am I to do?"

" I have seen you at all kinds of work, Caleda."

" In time, I may be more restricted," she said. " I am with child."

His smile was such to make her glad she had not stayed in Brigantia.

" Caleda," he said, " does this mean that Bergotix has at

419

last found there is more between husband and wife than argument?"

"It means," she said, her coppery hair shining in the clear light, "that the child is as much your responsibility as his. For if you had not come to our hearth in Brigantia, I would not have had any children. Also," she went on, with her eyes on the distant peaks, "although the child was conceived as I lay with Bergotix, yet at the time I was thinking of you. Will App Erryn come again to venture his fortune with Lydia, do you think?"

His eyes danced a little at this.

"Caleda, I have never remarked your passion for argument, which Bergotix insists you have. I have, however, noticed your way with words. Now, am I to know whether you come to me worried about what work you shall do, or what circumstances truly obtained at your child's conception, or what App Erryn has in mind concerning Lydia? Which of these am I to resolve for you?"

Caleda put on a face of serene innocence.

"Lord, I merely thought you would be pleased to know I am with child."

"As I am."

"Where is Lydia?" she asked then, and he knew her innocence for what it was.

"I am neither her kinsman nor her guardian, neither her husband nor her watchdog," he said, and she shrank a little at his harshness, for he had never before spoken in such a voice to her.

As bravely as she could, she said, "But when a woman gives up everything she has to follow a man—he is all these things to her and more."

"All women," said Canis grimly, "have a way of giving up everything one day, and a way of claiming it all back on another."

"I have displeased you," she faltered, and turned to go.

"You are not at fault, Caleda, you are only in an excess of concern for one you love. I am in an excess of irritation."

420

His mood was uncompromising when he took to horse the next day and rode down the valley.

At noon Lydia brought Dilwys free of her tether and into the open. Cloudy was the sky and fresh the day. It had rained overnight and looked as if the afternoon would also be wet. But it was fine at the moment, and Lydia found the air sweet after the humidity of the crowded, virgin woodlands. Also, it was time for food, and for Dilwys to toddle and tumble as she would. She broke up the food, and fed it into the pink, hungry mouth. Dilwys took it happily, eyeing her mother in a way which Lydia could only construe as the gratitude of an infant in healthy need. Did she have blue eyes or grey? Not grey, not that colour, for his eyes were grey. She had rejected him, so Dilwys must not have his eyes, it was enough that she had hair of shining chestnut, for Canis had hair that was deep brown and tinted with copper. Oh, Dilwys, you must be only of me, not of him. You are all I have.

Dilwys gurgled and dribbled. Lydia surveyed the mountains. They did not get less formidable, or less beautiful. How stonily blue, how starkly cold they could look on days as cloudy as this; yet the sense of security they gave was constant. Absorbed, she gazed at the distant ridges, but could not detach herself from the aching desolation that lay so heavily on her.

In her abstraction, she heard nothing until behind her there suddenly spoke the voice of her world.

"Aye, that way lies Rome. Do you yearn for it so much?"

She froze. For a moment she was icily rigid. Then heat attacked her and turned her faint. He was there, at her back, he had come as silently as a fox. The band of rejection she had put around her heart snapped, as if it had never been; and at once she knew she could never put him out of her life, as she had known all along. But she would not show it, she would not; and when the fire died down, she would be ice and snow and as unforgiving as he was pitiless.

She took a deep breath.

"Who speaks of Rome?" She simulated indifference. "Is

421

it you, Andudo? Come, then, sit beside me and pet Dilwys, and I will tell you of Rome. I will also tell you of the men of Rome, and of other men—"

Iron hands took her, brought her upright, whirled her about—and Lydia found herself eye to eye with her enduring Briton. His bitter contempt terrified her. Anger she could have fought with her own anger, anger would have given her some joy, for it was an emotion of deep feeling—but to see such contempt ran the blood clean from her heart.

" So," he said chillingly, " you think in your sullen sulks to remove yourself from those who love you. So you may, if this is what you wish. But you are not the sole dispenser of what is needful in the life of a child. Dilwys is mine. Take her up and bring her to Feola, who lives within my sight and has been loving nurse to her. When you have brought her, then you may go and sulk where you will, for as long as you will. But not with Dilwys. She is to grow up with laughter about her, which is what we owe to children. She is not to be saddled with peevishness. Bring her."

Never, since the days when he and she had been bitter enemies, had he given her such cruelty. He had no love for her, none at all. He hated her. Her world reeled, broke and shattered. All she had left was her pride, and it was this alone which stiffened her distraught, suffering being. She sought to break free, to tear herself from the iron hands on her shoulders, but could not.

" Bring her? To you? Never," she panted, " never! She is mine and only mine! "

" Beat your breast, tear your hair, do as you will," he said coldly, "but she is mine also. Take her up, and bring her to Feola." He released her, and so unexpectedly that she staggered.

" Never," she panted again, flinging back her hair, " never. I keep her with me, wherever I am, wherever I go. Aye, and for her comfort I will not disclose to her that her father is an uncivilised barbarian."

The flame that leapt to his eyes pierced her. Then he was

like cold stone, his contempt a chiselled permanency. He strode to Dilwys, he lifted her. Dilwys laughed in delight. She knew who her father was, barbarian or no, and already had her pink hands around his heart. He cradled her and walked away with her. Lydia cried out and ran in panic after him. She beat at his back, his shoulders, but he paid her no more attention than if she had been a feeble and unlovely child. He remounted his horse, Dilwys within the circle of his left arm and wetting his tunic with her excited dribble. He began to ride back the way he had come. He heard Lydia cry out in broken despair. His mouth tightened, he went on, he checked, then turned and rode back to her. He handed Dilwys down to her. Lydia's eyes were streaming.

"Aye," he said, "she is yours, then, for you bore her bravely. But she is mine also, and I will not be denied sight of her. Bring her to me an hour each day. That is little enough to ask. But to spare you any sight of me, do as I have said and give her each time to Feola. Feola will bring her to me."

Lydia, hugging the wriggling frustrated child to her, sank weepingly to her knees.

"She is all I have to comfort me in my suffering," she wept, her pride broken.

"Is it writ in your book," said Canis harshly, "that suffering is for you alone?"

She flung up her head to cry out in protest; but he was gone, riding away with a cold deliberation that was far worse than if he had gone in fury.

Torment at its most unbearable returned to her. Her heart was a hammer of pain in her breast, her body racked. Oh, if only he would ride back to her. She would go on her knees and beg his understanding.

All day she ached for him, for the sound of his voice, for anything that would ease her. But he was bound in marriage to Cea, and she, Lydia, was less to him than any woman here. No other woman here would name him barbarian. What had he meant when he said that suffering was not for her alone?

He had Cea, he had the affection of all his warrior maids, and did not know what real suffering was. Each night, he and Cea—

Oh, Diana, put these thoughts from me, for truly these give me greater torment than any other.

Sweet goddess, fend for me, contrive for me, bring him back to me, restore his love for me.

Only that, only his love, I will not ask for anything more, I swear.

She took Dilwys to Feola the next day, but hastened away in case he appeared; for she could not trust her emotions in the presence of others. If he did appear and spoke only one kind word to her, she would weep an ocean of tears.

Cea saw her, and hurried after her.

"Lydia, oh pray you, not so fast. Am I not to speak with you these days?"

Lydia had to stop. A little way off, the great earthworks of the encampment swarmed with busy workers, but she was dully unresponsive to all it meant. Cea caught up with her. She will flaunt her every joy in my face, thought Lydia, she will look at me and her eyes will tell me that she has everything and I have nothing.

But Cea was gentle and quite without artifice or unkindness —which were, in any case, foreign to her nature. Her own heart was at ease, her suspicions forgotten, and her jealousy as if it had never been.

"Why, Lydia," she said, "we have not seen you for so many days and have missed you. Have you new friends?"

"I help with lighter work in the forest," said Lydia, looking anywhere but into the eyes of the one who had everything, "and Andudo is there. I also have Dilwys."

"But, Lydia," said Cea gently, "there is Feneda, who has so much affection for you, and is hurt at not seeing you. And there are others who ask why you do not come to their fires in the evenings."

"It is only that I am tired in the evenings," said Lydia.

She was tired, thought Cea, there were rings around her eyes.

"Lydia, sometimes circumstances have prevented us being as close as we might. But I know what you have done for us, and I truly love you for it. I will not let you desert us for ever."

"You have always been kind to me," said Lydia in a suppressed voice, "but I have lately been thinking that perhaps I will return to Rome."

Cea winced and said, "Lydia, you could not." But Lydia, only too conscious of why Cea was so obviously happy, turned hurriedly away and fled. Cea was astonished to see that she actually ran. Even in her most suspicious moments, Cea had never realised the full extent of Lydia's passion for Canis.

Lydia made her way to the head of the valley. She began to pass warriors patrolling the area of approach.

"Mistress Ludicca," said one, "I am not sure I am to let you go on from here."

"Canis has said I might climb to that point," said Lydia, the lie an uncaring recklessness as she vaguely indicated stony slopes and winding tracks.

"Do not go beyond our sight," said the warrior. He thought her beautiful, as did all the warriors, and there were few who would not have risked their lives for her, Roman or no. And today there was a strange, haunting quality about her looks, her green eyes darkly huge in her pale face. "My lady, are you well?"

Well? Could he not see that she was dying?

"I am well enough, and will not be long," she said, and he watched her in curiosity as she began to climb the winding ascent. She wore her cloak, her tanned limbs hidden, and she went like a woman walking in her sleep. She was not objective in the direction she took. It did not matter where she went. She wished only to escape the valley, and hide her new wounds. She went where her feet led her. She climbed wanderingly. The tracks were treacherous in parts with loose shale. She was aware in time that there was a drop on one side that was sheer and dizzy. She wondered what it would be like to spread her arms and leap, to fly into space and to fall endlessly until

425

blackness engulfed her and the pain of heart tormented her no more.

Dreamless would be eternal sleep.

She might have asked Diana to take her, to lift her and cast her into the void; but felt with new despair that even Diana had turned her face from her.

She climbed on. She came to a slippery path which widened, and suddenly there was a great black hole in the wall of the mountain. She stood before it, but quite incuriously, her mind clouded and her body strangely light. A voice called, the voice of an old woman.

"Do not stand there, Roman, but enter. The wolves were here in the night, but have long since gone. So enter."

Lydia went slowly into the cave. She could not see, it was so dark. Then the glowing red of a fire came to her eyes, and by its light she saw smoke-blackened walls, a stony floor and a crone of a woman who sat to draw warmth to her old bones.

"So, you have come at last, Lydia of Rome. Many a weary turn of the sun and the moon I have waited. Sit you."

"Who are you to have knowledge of me?" asked Lydia. But she sat as the old one commanded, on a boulder, many of which littered the cave.

"I am of little consequence," said the old woman. She was wrapped in a dirty woollen cloak; she was white of hair, and her face bore a million wrinkles. "But I know you well enough. In you is the reflection of an Iceni queen. In the long ago when the bright gods warred with the dark ones, the Iceni were born of mountains and so have returned to them. Their destiny is yours also, and is writ in the stars and here also." She pointed to the fire, and a flame leapt as if the skinny yellow finger had drawn it from the red heart.

"I have no destiny but death," said Lydia.

The old woman chuckled. It was like the rustle of dry, withered leaves stirred by the wind.

"How now, glum looks, what mood and what nonsense is this? Did the gods of light bid me wait here for one with

426

misery on her face and gloom on her tongue?" The finger stabbed at Lydia. "Who are you to define destiny, to decide it? That is the province of the gods alone—and no man or woman, not even Canis the Briton or Lydia the Roman, may decide their own. Yours has been fashioned by Diana, though she is too haughty and sensitive a goddess for my liking, and sometimes deals irrationally instead of reasonably with a favoured one."

"I have no destiny but death," repeated Lydia.

"Words cannot cheat the gods," said the old woman, "especially the words of women, who are profligate in their use of them, and waste a thousand for every one of sense. If you are unafraid of age, look into my eyes and I will give you the truth concerning yourself." Lydia looked, feeling herself impelled by a strange compulsion. Eyes mirroring the ghosts of uncountable years drew her own. The fire leapt, and the eyes that were yellow orbs encircled by red rims became flame-yellow and then golden. And the golden hues became fiery russet, like the world at sunset. "Think you," said the ancient voice, "that when you were a girl child in Rome, and were destined even then to be here this day, that the gods had only death awaiting you? Death is not destiny, but the purest and most incorruptible lot of us all. Woman of sorrow, where is your spirit, where is your faith?"

"Ancient mother, I have lost both," whispered Lydia, "for he has cast me aside and taken another."

"What of that?" The eyes glowed. "Have you not said again and again that it would content you merely to stand in his shadow?"

"I am a woman, and cannot be bound today by what I have said in the past."

"Then you are bound only by your mood of the moment, which is the way of the weak, not the strong. Where is your courage—aye, even your pride—that you wallow in gloom like a child? You were born to wilfulness, but not to peevishness. You were born to become a Princess of Britain. Aye, though you name the gods differently in Rome, they are all the same

427

and speak with the same voice. See, there is your life and there your destiny, Ludicca of the Iceni!" Again the finger stabbed, this time towards the heart of the fire, and again the flames leapt. Lydia turned her eyes on the fiery embers; and there in the leaping yellow and red, she saw her world as it had been and as it was.

Clear in the fire was mighty Rome, built on the Seven Hills; and in a garden high on one hill, she saw a child who was herself at almost ten years of age. There was discontent on her face. A man appeared, a tall man, a Briton, with shadows softening his features as he looked at the girl child. And her discontent became a yearning. He came into the flames and out of them, and left her only with her yearning.

Rome receded before pictures of tribal Britain. She saw a straight road, a speeding chariot, and in the chariot she rode with her brother Julian. She saw herself, a capricious and spoiled maid of nineteen. She struck at the straining, galloping pair with spiteful whip, her cruelty a reflection of her discontent at unfulfilled life. Into the flames came the tall Briton again, and she saw her own eyes, as green as the lush wildness of Britain, staring at him, growing brilliant for him. But he mocked her, tormented her—and frenziedly, sobbingly, she struck at him.

The flames leapt, destroying the picture and giving birth to another. There was a great courtyard and a tall, graceful woman bound to a stake, her robe and shift ripped to expose her naked back. The woman had wondrously bright hair—and though her face was hidden, Lydia knew her.

Boadicea—oh, Boadicea. Not that—take it from my sight. Old woman, mystic eyes of the gods, let me not see this. But she did see. Again there was a whip, a whip of pitiless knots, wielded by a vast and fleshy scourger, and the proud naked back was savaged until the blood ran thick and red. The flames hissed in outrage and burned the image to produce another. Lydia herself was there, spiteful and jeering, and also the scourged Queen.

And Lydia spat at her.

A sobbing cry so disturbed the black depths of the cave that even the red-eyed spiders retreated.

Lydia, disembodied, was unaware of her own cry. Only her tortured eyes were alive, as the fiery canvas painted her torments, her desires, her hate and her love. Always there were Britons and Romans; but Rome itself grew dim, and Britain clearer. The images were constantly of herself and Canis and Boadicea the Queen, he either cruel or mocking or indefinably remote, Boadicea either wholly unfathomable or hauntingly majestic. Vaguely in the background, there sometimes appeared another woman, soft and shadowed, whom Lydia knew was Cea.

The fire dimmed only to leap into its brightest flame, and within that flame was the face of Boadicea. The hair was a crown of radiance, the magical blue eyes soft, the wide sweet mouth curved.

" Lydia, Lydia, do you not know you are of me? Am I not in your eyes? Oh, foolish one to be in such contempt of yourself. Love is not to possess but to give. To weep is to lose all. To be strong is to gain the world. See me and know that I am your strength, your spirit, your destiny."

The flames died, the fire returned to a warm glow. But Lydia's eyes continued to burn.

" I am confused, ancient mother. What is my destiny?"

" Was it not there for you to see? Were you not led in all things to Britain and to Boadicea? Are you not as indivisible from her as Canis? Who is left among the people of Britain who can emulate such a great Queen? None. What other queens are there who will not be forgotten as soon as they are dead? None. The gods of light, therefore, cannot let the spirit of Boadicea die and the land perish. Her spirit must pass to one within whom it will exist as proudly and fiercely as it did within her—for is it not written that the spirit of Boadicea will armour the indestructibility of Canis for a thousand years?"

" Which one is this, which?" whispered Lydia.

The dry rustling chuckle issued again, and the bony finger stabbed again.

"Who gave up mighty Rome to follow Canis, the greatest of all Britons? Lydia the Roman. Who took up the shining axe of Cerdwa, beloved of the forest gods, and smote the most evil Roman of them all? Lydia. Who will armour Canis with the undying spirit of his Queen? No, not Princess Cea. For though she is regal, she is too gentle, and is only the mirror in which Canis sees his Queen. Lydia alone may be to Canis his great need and understanding, for in Lydia alone dwells that which was once of Boadicea herself."

"How can this be?" breathed Lydia. "How can it be?"

"Ask this of the gods, not of me." The old woman stirred the fire with a stick. The stick glowed, burst into flame, and she cast it into the depths of the cave. There was a hiss and a scurry as it fell. "Foolish are the ways of men, capricious the ways of women, but beyond all mortal comprehension are the ways of the gods, for have they not invested in a Roman woman the spirit of Britain's proudest Queen? Go to your destiny, Lydia—which is not death, but Canis, who of all men was the only one to equate his Queen. Take him. He is yours."

The red-rimmed eyes withdrew, the million wrinkles faded. The fire spurted, failed and smoked, and the smoke hid the crone. Lydia rose in bewilderment. In bewilderment, she went from the cave, and the sudden light blinded her. She stood, she closed her eyes. She opened them, and with her mind confused she began to descend the sloping track. She was unaware of the blue sky scattering light cloud, of the sharpness of suntipped ridges, and of eyes that shone greedily to see her. And when Urwin App Erryn emerged from a recess to confront her, she almost thought him no more than another image projected by the flames. But when he smiled, boldly and sensuously, she knew he was pitiless reality.

"It was only a matter of waiting for a more fortuitous day," he said.

She screamed as he took her and flung her into the arms of two other men. They bound her, gagged her and carried her upwards. Horror shrieked at her, and her mind fought the roaring redness of hysteria. Here was her true destiny—App Erryn,

430

rapacious defilement, and death by her own hand after defilement. The horror overwhelmed her, and she rushed into limpness, unconsciousness.

In the cave the ancient crone chuckled.

"Now at last will the dark ones mark you for their own, Urwin App Erryn. For you have laid hands on the favoured of the bright ones."

Lydia did not know how far they had carried her before her mind returned to life again. She heard the voice of App Erryn, though she did not understand the dialect he used. She was set on her feet, her bonds untied and the foul gag taken from her mouth. When she would have cried out App Erryn smote her lips with the back of his hand.

"Woman," he said, "you are for giving pleasure, not for making loud noises. Let me hear so much as a whisper and we will roll back your tongue over a stone and make you painfully mute."

They pushed her and thrust her, hastening her upwards. She saw vast spaces, and the gigantic wall of a mountain born of the earth to live in the sky. The Deceangi were in fine spirits, highly satisfied with their prize, the ease with which they had taken her, and the fury it would put Canis in. It was time that cheating lowlander had a setback.

"Did you go to old Cronna to ask where you might find me?" It was App Erryn's rich voice, full of good humour and sounding as if his tongue was lovingly caressing each word. She did not answer. Despite the sun, despite her cloak, a new one, she was cold with the coldness of death. She was dying on her feet, stumbling as they roughly urged her onwards. She looked despairingly this way and that, seeking a place and an opportunity to break from them and hurl herself into space. Oh, Dilwys—Canis—I am lost, lost.

One man preceded her, one man walked by her side, and App Erryn was behind her. The man by her side was ever ready to touch her. Each time she stumbled, he took hold of her, his hand lingered and her flesh crawled. Once fierce anger came to displace her despair, and she turned on him with such spitting fury that momentarily he was discomfited. Then he laughed, and said something to App Erryn. And behind her App Erryn said amiably, " My kinsman Chaligwyn is losing patience with you, you trip over every stone like a hobbled she-goat." His hand touched her back and pushed her on. He was in a hurry to get her beyond the long reach of Canis, and in even more of a hurry to dispossess her of all that she wore. He believed in indulging his eye before committing his flesh.

Every step of the difficult way they hastened her. And she knew that when they finally disappeared with her, she would be lost forever to her adopted people, and that even Paullinus could not make her more inaccessible to Canis and his Britons than App Erryn. His domain in these regions would defy deliverance by the strongest force. Huge chasms deep with blueness opened up amid ever-changing contours, but what was any chasm if not the welcoming emptiness of death? Again she stumbled, again the man by her side was only too ready to encircle her waist with hand and arm. His blood leapt at her vibrant softness—and he was, after all, kinsman to App Erryn. Kinsmen did favours and received concessions. Tempted to discover more of the shapeliness of this woman, he pulled her round to face him. In his grinning hairiness, the dye on his forehead an ugly splotch, he was all that was repellent to Lydia. Oh, that she had called Canis barbarian, and he with his strong clean body and his worldly grey eyes. There was sickness upon her as she felt the Deceangi man's arm tighten around her; and in her mind was a wild, despairing cry for Canis.

Out shot the long arm of App Erryn to part his kinsman from the woman, who was his alone until he tired of her. But even as his hand gripped Chaligwyn's shoulder, a hiss disturbed the air and a sharp-pointed javelin buried itself in his kinsman's back. Lydia saw the fierce eyes open wide in shock. The arm dropped from her waist; and with a look of surprise and dismay on his face, Chaligwyn crumpled, fell forward and rolled over. He kicked and writhed in a vain attempt to reject misfortune.

The shaft of the javelin snapped from the embedded point, Chaligwyn choked and his blood gushed.

Swift as mountain wolves turning to bay the hunter, App Erryn and his comrade spun round. There below them on the winding ledge of the slope was Canis, the light of the westering sun gilding his figure. Lydia's eyes suffused with misty green joy; and her heart, which had known so much pain, drowned in a sea of ecstasy. The softest of moans broke from her. She lost him as hot tears blinded her. Was he there? Or was he but an extension of so much unreality, a figment conjured up out of despair? No, he was there. And his face was carved in brown stone, his grey eyes cold and chilling as they surveyed App Erryn. And the Deceangi chieftain, who had challenged death many times and not lost yet, drew a slow breath. Canis spoke, his resonant voice as chilling as his look.

" Did I not say, friend, that she was not for you?"

App Erryn, who had indeed heard of Canis, but had not been disposed to let what he heard discourage him from taking what he wanted, laughed. A man intimidated by a threat went miserably to his gods.

"As you see, lowlander, you were mistaken," he said. " I have her. You were also mistaken in making such a bloody hole in Chaligwyn's back, for he was my closest kinsman."

Lydia was rooted, but her blood was pulsing, surging. She was radiantly alive again. Her hammering heart poured joy into every vein. It was no dream, no conjured image. Her love had come for her. He would let no man take her. Tears blinded her again, she shook them away. She saw his hand move, and he drew from his belt the bright, deadly axe of Cerdwa. And the singing voice of Cerdwa was in her ears and sighing like a murmurous, musical echo in the space around her.

" None could stand against Canis and Cerdwa, none."

And Lydia knew that App Erryn was to die. But there was the other man. She would have flown to Canis to stand by his side, to aid him, but App Erryn caught her by the arm and flung her back. She fell sprawling, and might have slithered over the abyss had she not clawed and held on to stone with des-

433

perate, straining fingers. The other man thrust out a foot to prod her and warn her. A sword glittered in his hand.

The cold eyes of Canis were colder.

" Come," he said softly to App Erryn, " one or both of you, and Cerdwa will kiss you to death as sweetly as either of you could wish."

App Erryn's full red mouth parted to show his teeth. He drew his sword, he eyed the axe. What was a clumsy axe against a sword of stabbing light, wielded by no less a warrior than himself? Yet it was true he had heard of Canis.

Canis advanced upwards.

" Step cautiously, Iceni," said App Erryn, golden-bright and talking his man into indecision, or so he thought, " for we have a way of killing a man that is all our own. It makes him glad when the mountain wolves arrive to speed his dying."

" You will make fat food for them," said Canis, looking at no one but App Erryn.

" Blabberer," laughed App Erryn and kissed his sword. The other man spat on his.

Lydia's joy retreated, beset by fear. There was so little room for Canis to fight them both, the endless drop was so close. And App Erryn was measuring him, whilst beside him the other man was tensed to spring.

Oh, Diana, save him for me, save him even for Cea, but save him.

Canis, however, did not wait for the intercession of a goddess renowned for her tardiness in aiding men. Looking into the face of App Erryn he knew when the man was ready to come at him. Cerdwa spoke, and the axe flew. Like a flash of hurtling light it took App Erryn full in the face. It smashed flesh and bone and eyes. App Erryn reeled and crashed. He lay senseless and dying. Almost before he hit the ground Canis pounced and retrieved the axe. The surviving man leapt back, shrieked a curse, spat hugely at Canis, then turned and fled, leaping and springing upwards. Canis went after him, passing Lydia in his rushing pursuit. He stopped, picked up a weighty piece of shale and flung it as he had flung the axe. It smashed on the sloping stone wall close to the head of the fleeing mountain man. He turned, shrieked another curse, then leapt upwards again in reckless retreat.

Canis let him go. He would not come back. Lydia, numb and breathless, watched in joy as Canis returned. But he scarcely gave her a glance. He lifted the body of Chaligwyn, carried it to the edge and sent it down into space. He bent over App Erryn, who was faintly gurgling in his own blood. He had not long to live. Canis sent him over the edge. It was what App Erryn would have wished.

Lydia still lay sprawled. Sulla the centurion had taken her because he was a sadistic man. Paullinus had taken her because he was a vengeful one. And App Erryn had taken her out of lust. Canis had delivered her from all three. She was not unloved. Not even though he had wed Cea. She waited for him to speak to her, to lift her up. But he stood where the track overlooked the emptiness, as if in sombre reflection of two men who had lived vigorously and were now dead and invisible. How grim he looked. Why did he not come and give her his hand?

She called to him.

" Canis, I am sorely bruised."

He turned.

" How so? By reason of his loving embrace, or by reason of your wilful indiscretion?" His voice had the bite she dreaded. Her heart, a moment ago so joyful, shrank within her. What had she done?

" He threw me brutally. Canis, I am hurt."

" He is dead now. That is a satisfactory return for a bruise."

" But see—oh, Canis, see your Lydia." She was desperate for his compassion, his attention, his touch. As he came towards her, she opened her cloak to reveal her sun-browned legs. She drew up her kilted tunic and showed him the smoothness of her naked thighs. There was the semblance of what might have been a faint blue bruise on her right thigh, but that was all. Canis looked down at her, and without compassion. He bent,

435

he reached, took her by the arms and pulled her to her feet.

"Lydia," he said, "will you show me every wound you do not take? Will you uncover yourself each time you wish me to humour you? I thought you a woman, with beauty, pride and intelligence. But instead you are a foolish child, who in complete lack of all sense, placed herself in the arms of App Erryn."

Lydia stared at him, horrified that after all she had endured he could be so hard.

"Canis, do not speak like this, do not look at me so. Oh, I swear I did not mean to play tricks. I only wished tenderness from you. And you are hurting me, hurting more than my flesh—"

"Where has gone my true Lydia?" His voice was softer now, and she recognised the mockery she knew so well.

"Let me go!" She wrenched free. She would not be treated like this, for hers was not the blame. She had not been faithless, she had not cleaved to another as he had. "Oh, you are monstrous to malign me as you do!" she cried. "I have been in anguish, but kept it to myself. And yet you came to me without either pity or understanding, and said I was in sulks when I was only in pain. Oh, you are grim and hateful, and I will not be treated so, I will not! I will return to Rome!"

His grey eyes searched her. She stood up to him.

"To Rome, you say?" Usually so self-controlled, he gave way for once to anger. "Then tomorrow I will give you horse, warm clothing and an escort of ten warriors to take you back to Calleva Atrebatum."

That final cruelty, after so much else, crushed her. The blood drained from her face to leave her deathly pale. The ground fell away from her as she sagged and crumpled. He caught her, lifted her, and she hung in his arms like one lifeless, her long black hair like a dark tumbling curtain.

He was bitter with himself as he looked down at her still face.

"Lydia, you knew it could not be other than it was between Cea and me," he said, "but to speak of returning to Rome is

436

wilful folly. What can I do with you. Or myself?" He kissed her unknowing lips. " Wake up, foolish Roman."

He glanced up as he heard sounds. They were coming, those he had been waiting for. Andudo and Hywel appeared over a crest. Behind them followed warriors, including Bergotix and Feneda.

Earlier that day Cea had advised Canis that she liked neither the way Lydia looked nor the way she had spoke. Canis said, " It is a hard time for her, Cea, for now she is finally parted from Rome, and there are few people who do not have some love for their birthplace."

" She spoke of returning to Rome."

Canis did not answer that. But when a warrior came to say that Lydia had left the valley half an hour ago and not returned, he reacted grimly and swiftly. He went after her at once, delaying only to tell Hywel to follow with a dozen warriors who were speedy climbers. Feneda demanded to be among them, swearing she would kill App Erryn if he was the cause of Lydia's disappearance.

" Then follow on," said Canis briefly.

" Bring her back, lord," said Feneda, " she is brave and beautiful, and has lived this week with a broken heart, as you know."

" I am not in a position to mend her heart, only to see to her welfare," he said, and gave her a look that might have quelled the temper of a less fearless maid.

He went ahead, moved by an urgency compounded of anger and worry. He climbed swiftly and reached a point close to a cave. Here she could have gone one of two ways. One path led upwards. Another was an alternative route back to the valley. It was long and winding and brought one down to a spot far from the head of the valley. Had she taken that and then continued on to her work in the forest? No, it was late afternoon and the forest was far from here. She had finished her work to bring Dilwys to Feola. Even so, in her mood of the moment she could be wandering and brooding along that winding path. To have continued upwards would have been indiscreet beyond anything. The hard surface of the tracks left no signs, no marks. His anger grew, his worry mounted.

Suddenly the cave spoke with an old woman's voice.

" So you are here too, Canis the Briton. But I have no words for you. You know your destiny. It is to find Boadicea again. As to Lydia of Rome, App Erryn has her. Find her, and you will look into the eyes of your Queen."

" Old chatterbox, I have looked into her eyes and seen green turn to blue. And that reflects the image not of any queen, but a senseless child. The eyes of all children are blue, especially children who will not grow up."

A chuckle followed his rushing departure. He climbed at a pace that was reckless in any man who had not been born in the mountains, but his urgency lent him agility. Such was his anger and fear for Lydia that had he come upon her and found her in no danger, he would have shaken her until her bones rattled. He did not know what he was to do with his temperamental Roman love. She must know that Cea had first claim, first consideration. She must also be aware that despite his feelings for her and his affection for Cea, his one love was his dead but undying Queen. He could not love any other woman.

If the old hag who lived in that cave was right, if App Erryn did have Lydia, then App Erryn would be given no chance to take her again. Cerdwa's axe would slice his head off.

He found her in the end, and App Erryn also. He had done to App Erryn what he had known he must do, what old Cronna had known he would do. And he had kept Lydia from throwing herself into his arms. He owed Cea that much at least. It was not a tender way of treating a beautiful woman; but she had been indescribably foolish, and he had been more than angry. She must live in fierce pride, not woeful sulks.

Andudo and Hywel hurried up, Bergotix and Feneda close on their heels. Bergotix, for all his limp, kept up with everyone. He found that having one leg just a little shorter than the other gave a man an unexpected advantage over sloping tracks

438

and shelving ledges. Feneda, seeing Lydia limp in the arms of Canis, suppressed a cry.

" Is she lifeless?" she called. " Say she is not, say so."

" She is only a little bruised, Feneda," said Canis, with a slightly rueful smile. " And perhaps a little mortified as well. She will recover in a moment."

" Where are those who took so sweet a woman?" asked Bergotix. He had never known such a life as this. It was all that a man could wish for. There was little softness about it; but what did softness do for any people, except make them unequal to life? Also, Caleda was happy and much less prone to twist his words around his teeth. Although she did not want to be a warrior woman, Canis had promised to teach her to throw a spear. And she with child. She said the exercise would be good for a woman in her condition. Truly, thought Bergotix, a wife was for indulging but not comprehending.

Feneda saw the blood on the ground.

" There were three," said Canis, observing the colour returning to Lydia's face, " including App Erryn. One survived and ran. Not App Erryn."

" You could not have done less for Lydia," said Feneda.

All the warriors were there now. Lydia's eyes opened. She stared vacantly, found herself in the arms of Canis and coloured up. Her mouth quivered, and he set her on her feet. She swayed; Feneda gave Canis a fierce look, and put her arm around Lydia.

" Come, Ludicca," she said, " we will take care of you. Andudo will carry you. He is gruffer than most, but tenderer than others. Oh, we are glad to have you safe again."

" Tomorrow," said Canis, " by her own wish she will return to Rome."

Lydia gave a soft moan. Feneda did not think too kindly of Canis. Neither did Lydia.

" Never," said Feneda passionately, " she belongs to us. You may let her go, lord, but we will not."

" I will tie her to a tree, that will hold her," said Andudo.

439

"And I will untie her," said Hywel. "That is no way to hold any woman."

"It will only be as Lydia wishes," said Canis, as the mountain peaks began to glow in the evening sun.

"Monster!" cried Lydia woundedly. "Monster!"

"Let us go back," said Canis. "For truly I am beset by a woman and her inconsistency. Are there any women who can say that what they want one moment is what they want the next?"

"And are there any men who can say they are not responsible for that?" said Feneda with spirit. "Ludicca is not to return to Rome, she is not."

"Where will we find another like her?" asked a warrior. "Canis, lord, you must prevail on her."

Lydia shook off her mortal hurt. So, he would let her return to Rome. He would not let App Erryn have her, but he did not mind what Caesar might do to her. However, she would not return, never. She lifted her chin, she stood straight and proud and upright. She flung back her hair.

"I am my own mistress," she said, "and will go nowhere except by my own free choice. Nor will I have any man say I must do this or must do that. I scorn such arrogance. Aye, Feneda, let us go back. And let us leave a certain incontestably arrogant man to follow on. Perhaps on the way he will—in his great infallibility, which sets him above such ordinary mortals as us—fall and break his neck."

And she and Feneda began the journey back, escorted by the cheerful warriors. Andudo, left with Canis, saw that Canis was smiling.

"What did she say to so amuse you?" he asked.

"She is in good heart again, Andudo," said Canis, which answered Andudo's question, but not to Andudo's understanding.

Feneda, who knew why Lydia had been so unhappy, said to her as they went on their way, "Ludicca, despite so much, you surely will not leave us? Surely you will not go back to Rome? Say you will not. Rome would not love you as we do."

"Rome?" said Lydia, her mind on Canis and how she might win him back. "Rome? What is Rome to me? Here is my home, my land, and here are all my friends. Feneda, look back. Does he follow? If so, does he look grim?"

Feneda looked back. The vista was a panoramic glory, bathed in the light of the descending sun, the sun of the season of new life.

"He follows with Andudo. He does not look grim. He is smiling."

"Smiling?" Lydia's voice was an angry hiss. "Oh, the cold, bloodless fiend, the most unspeakable fiend that ever was! He bruised me and reviled me, and he smiles! Oh, Feneda, how can a man break a woman's heart, deliver her from App Erryn, speak in anger to her—and then smile? Oh, I will, then, I will go, I will return to Rome!"

"Ludicca, you must not. You cannot."

The sun was golden red, and in a while the mountains would open to receive it. There was fire over every peak, and glowing colour investing every space. The air was cooler by the minute, and Lydia drew her cloak tighter around her suffering body. Oh, what had she done that had made him so angry? He had come for her, as he had more than once before, and she had seen his face as he looked at App Erryn. In it she had read certain death for App Erryn, and also the conviction that he would let no man take her from him. To her, that meant his love for her was enduring, despite Cea. But he had not been at all loving, he had been cruel. What had she done?

Her deep breathing hurt her throat as with Feneda she made her way down loose, treacherous paths. They must reach the valley before the sun disappeared and twilight made the going more difficult. They must not be caught by darkness. She shivered. Her escape had been such a near thing. Only because the Deceangi had been burdened with her had Canis been able to catch them up. Why, when he had obviously been so fiercely determined to find her, had he been so unkind to her?

She would not be treated like that, she would not. She would stand against him, fight him and even go tooth and nail

441

against him. She would use her tongue as woundingly as he used his. Anything would be better than running away from him, not seeing him. She would provoke him, win him back by giving him taunt for taunt, cruelty for cruelty. Aye, she would. She would not let him crush her, no, never. She would revile him each time he mocked her, she would name him barbarian—

Oh, no!

But she would fight him, she would.

She went swiftly downwards, her body hot now, her eyes glowing. Her pride and spirit were strong again. She caught her foot on a stone. Feneda flung out a hand to catch her arm, and Lydia turned her head to excuse her clumsiness. Feneda caught her breath. Oh, how beautiful was Lydia the Roman. Her dark, flowing hair caressed by the golden-red sky, her face vivid with life and her eyes—they were green, they were always green, sometimes brilliant, sometimes soft, but green— but not green—

" Ludicca, your eyes—it is the light. Ludicca, I thought your eyes green, but they are bluer than blue."

" No, they are green, Feneda. I have seen them in morning waters. Feneda, does he still follow, does he still smile?"

" I cannot see him," said Feneda, glancing back. " Perhaps, as you said, he has fallen and broken his neck."

Lydia froze, then swung wildly round to take Feneda by the wrist, and the warrior maid winced at the grip put upon her.

" Feneda, no, I never said so! Oh, if I did and Diana heard me—he has mocked her so often—if she heard me and—"

" Ludicca, can you believe Canis would fall and break his neck, and Andudo still come whistling?"

There was Andudo at the rear of the warriors, and he was softly whistling. The warriors passed Lydia and Feneda, telling them not to stand with their mouths open. Lydia's eyes strained to see why Canis was not with Andudo. Oh, how radiant was the sky, how fiery the mountains and how breathless her heart amid this world of glowing ridges and great sloping carpets of grass. Where was he?

442

He came into view, behind everyone else. Her heart breathed again.

"Feneda, go on. I will wait for him."

Feneda, understanding, went on by herself to catch up with Hywel. Andudo, passing Lydia, said to her, "You have put him in better humour than he was."

She waited. It was hard to control her emotions. He loomed up, outlined by the glowing colour. Such was the effect of perspective that he seemed taller than the distant peaks. Oh, she thought, he must be sweet to me, he must.

"Is it Rome you stand and dream of, Lydia?" he asked.

Bitterness welled, and fury trembled in its wake.

"I scorn you, contempt you," she said fiercely.

His laughter was a deep murmur. Oh, the fiends, he was hot from Hades itself. Even Pluto could not stomach him, and had cast him from the infernal regions. But no, he was not hot, he was cold, unfeelingly cold.

"Lydia," he said gently, "is life so miserable?"

She turned to rush from him, but his arm swept around her and drew her close against him. At the unexpectedness of the gesture and contact, her body ran with the heat of confusion. Her resolve to fight melted; and with her face hidden in his shoulder, she tumbled into passionate agitated exposition of cause and effect.

"Oh, Canis, it is not life that is miserable, it is myself—and it is you who have made me so. What have I done? I have only loved you. That is all I am guilty of. But I am to be punished for it as if I had committed a far worse crime. Is it not enough to make any woman unhappy? But I will not have you speak to me as if my unhappiness is also a crime. I will not be treated in such an unfair way, I will not. Nor will I return to Rome." She lifted her head as she spiritedly returned to defiance. "I will stay, and I will not have my moods commanded by you. If I wish to sulk, I will. If I wish to scream, I will. I will stand and give you taunt for taunt, cruelty for cruelty—oh!"

Oh, indeed. He was laughing. By all the fiends of darkness, he was laughing. Incensed, she tore herself free and struck at

443

him. He caught her flying hand. He took it, turned it palm upwards, and pressed a warm and gentle kiss on it. Lydia drew a breath of sweetest pain. Canis looked into her eyes. Suffused, they luminously reflected the radiant sky.

" This is my true Lydia, my most wilful and fearless one. Give me taunt for taunt, then, and cruelty for cruelty, and even call me barbarian—"

" Oh, no! " She brought his hand emotionally to her breast.

" Aye, even that," he said, " as long as you do not sulk your way back to Rome. Be in beauty and pride, for that is when you are most endearing to me."

" Oh, Canis! " She flung her arms around him, pressing her warm body to his. " Never will I go. I will endure that Cea is your wife, I will, but only tell me you have love for me, only tell me."

" I will tell you," he said sombrely, " that as Cea belongs to all that which governs my endeavours, so do you belong to my heart—and have done since a day when the wind caressed your hair and the sun danced in your eyes. It is without reason, the consequence of one moment on a day no different to other days, but even so it could not unbind me from Cea. This I thought you understood. I did not expect a woman such as you to be so—"

" To be so woeful? " She clung to him like a drowning woman. " But I thought myself unwanted and unloved, and to have you heedless of my pain was unbearable."

" So you chose the pleasure of existing in misery. That is the way of some women, it is not the way for you. I will not have you in tantrums and sulks, but in pride and spirit."

The flushed sky was crimsoning and Lydia's eyes were lambent with the flame of the sinking sun.

" I am a woman," she breathed, " and must have my tantrums. But what are these, what are any moods and emotions, when set against all we have had, all we have shared, all we have known? What is life to me but the joy of being with you, of loving you? I will stand forever to say you are my life and my reason. And here I will lie where the mountain is green,

444

and give you the sweetest proof of my love." She moved, sinking down on a grassy slope, taking his hands to pull him down with her. The mountain peaks caught fire, and down below on the lower slopes they heard the softly-murmurous song of their warriors. " I am Lydia, and I am as much a part of your great Queen as Cea is, and more than Cea is. And though your destiny binds you in many ways to her, only through me will you find Boadicca. I am here, Canis, and oh, my life and my heart, give me joy as I will give it to you. The sun has not yet gone, and our moment together now will be the most fleeting but the most precious in all the years of the world. Be dear to me, my lord, be dear to me."

His eyes searched her as she lay there.

The gods reached out.

She was Lydia of Rome, but not of Rome. Her beauty was invested with a radiance that was of incandescent sky and fiery mountain peaks, her tumbled hair a dark glossy cloud, her face tender with love, her eyes misty with the indefinable emotions of life itself. And Canis was held by wonder and dreams, for through the mist the eyes of Lydia that were green were not green but the haunting, mystic blue of Boadicea, his Queen.

He spoke and his voice was the whisper of the world at night.

" Now there is magic in you, for now in you is the image of the Queen, who is my one love, my single love, my only love."

Her tears were drawn from the heart of Diana herself as she drew him down to her.

Take him. He is yours.

The sound that echoed and hung so softly but clearly above the endless gulfs was the cry of a woman.

* * *

At the gate of a villa in Calleva Atrebatum, Julian Osirus stood with his fair Iceni wife, Cyella. She leaned with her

445

head on his shoulder as they gazed in wordless wonder at the brilliance put forth by the sun. It was dying in a blaze of glory in the western sky. Cyella's heart was strangely squeezed.

Where were they? She could hear their song, see the wind in their hair, the sun on the face of Canis, the laughter in the eyes of Cea, and the love in the eyes of Lydia.

She said a little huskily, "Where are they now, Julian, where?"

"Since no Romans have sent or received word of them, Cyella," he said, "then assuredly they are within their mountains. And if the gods have grace as well as meaning, they dwell at last in peace."

"And Lydia, our dearest sister?"

"She is at the end of searching and the beginning of life. She belongs now to Canis and the people of Queen Boadicea. But she will send us word. We will hear of them again, for Lydia will endure and so will they all."

* * *

Two Roman soldiers rode hard over country that had once seen the marching, singing hosts of Boadicea. They galloped close to a mighty forest, making fast pace to the distant road in an endeavour not to be caught by nightfall. They had come from Lindum. Not far from a great oak that stood as a solitary sentinel before the forest, one horse pitched by reason of a deep rut. The soldier sprang clear; his comrade pulled up and rode back to him. He dismounted, and the two of them anxiously examined the fallen animal, which to their relief, shook its head and climbed back onto its four legs. They were about to remount, when the dying sun broke clear of thin cloud to cast a strange red light over the oak and the ground around it.

It was here, over two years ago and in the last light of a tragic, blood-red sun, that Canis and Grud had buried Boadicea the Queen. And in an adjoining grave, lay Cerdwa the forest maid.

446

The effect of the sudden glowing light was eerie. It held the Romans mute for a moment. Then to their ears came a rustling, as if a wind was disturbing the forest, though they felt not the lightest breath of it themselves. This was followed by a stirring of grass, by the whisper of song, by the faint sound of far-off chariot wheels and the hoofbeats of a thousand horse and a thousand more. And the sounds lifted to the roof of the forest, and the singing grew to a paean of fifty thousand voices in the sky.

The Romans froze.

And the singing host gave voice to the joyful, melodious cry of a name.

" Boadicea! Boadicea! "

Then there was only stillness and silence, except that as they unfroze there came from the ground close to the oak the softest echo of a woman's enraptured cry.

They mounted in cold terror, galloping their frightened animals in frenzied flight to the distant road.

*   *   *

There is a place above the feet of the mountains, a place that was once a great valley, but is now a vast lake of deep, shimmering water. And the bed of the lake, known only to men long ago, is said to be covered with tumbled, fallen stone. Some say it is the stone of the Druids, because it is shaped stone and because in Roman and pre-Roman times it was the Druids who made much use of shaped stone for their places of worship.

But some who have drawn their conclusions from the mists of time will tell you that if all the stone were lifted from the lake, and each great piece fitted to its neighbour, there would rise the four mighty walls of the royal house of Boadicea, which was built on a fortified encampment in the valley by the Iceni and Trinovantes for Princess Cea, daughter of Boadicea.

What happened when it was built, and how Canis, the

447

greatest warrior of his time, further endured and contrived, is part of the saga of Boadicea's people. As is the life of Lydia, for all that she was born in Rome and was devoted to Diana, a Roman goddess of neurotic complexities.

In any event, Lydia was indivisible from the undying spirit of Queen Boadicea. As was Canis.